The Blackest Bird

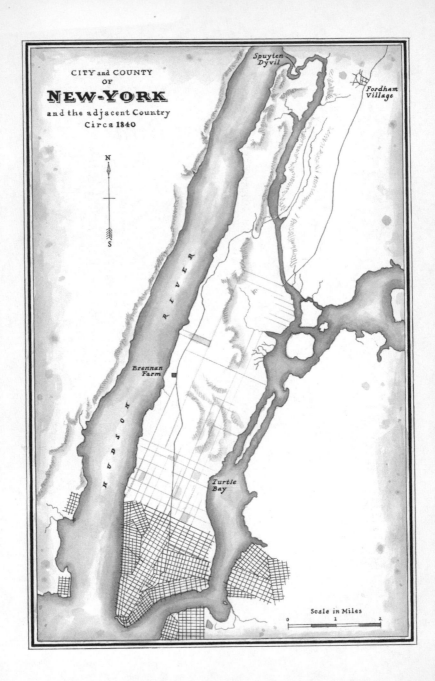

CITY and COUNTY
OF
NEW-YORK
and the adjacent Country
Circa 1840

N

S

Spuyten
Dyvil

Fordham
Village

R I V E R

Brennan
Farm

H U D S O N

Turtle
Bay

Scale in Miles

0   1   2

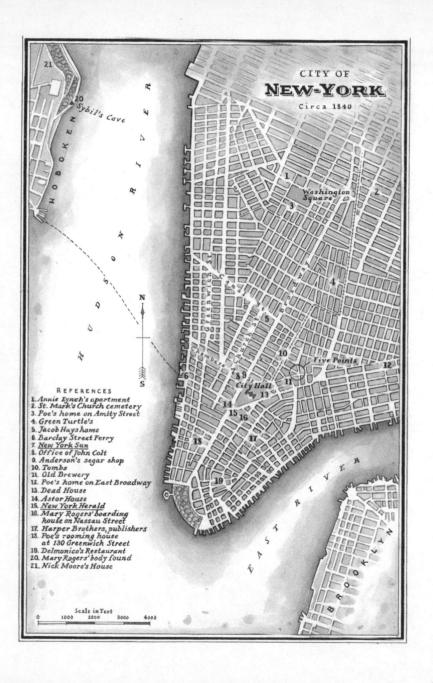

CITY OF
NEW-YORK
Circa 1840

HUDSON RIVER

HOBOKEN RIVER

EAST RIVER

BROOKLYN

Washington Square

Five Points

City Hall

Broadway

Canal Street

Church Street

Chambers Street

N
S

REFERENCES
1. Annie Lynch's apartment
2. St. Mark's Church cemetery
3. Poe's home on Amity Street
4. Green Turtle's
5. Jacob Hays home
6. Barclay Street Ferry
7. New York Sun
8. Office of John Colt
9. Anderson's segar shop
10. Tombs
11. Old Brewery
12. Poe's home on East Broadway
13. Dead House
14. Astor House
15. New York Herald
16. Mary Rogers' boarding house on Nassau Street
17. Harper Brothers, publishers
18. Poe's rooming house at 130 Greenwich Street
19. Delmonico's Restaurant
20. Mary Rogers' body found
21. Nick Moore's House

Sybil's Cave

Scale in Feet
0   1000   2000   3000   4000

Also by Joel Rose

New York Sawed in Half

Kill Kill Faster Faster

Kill the Poor

The Blackest Bird

A Novel of Murder in Nineteenth-Century New York

Joel Rose

W. W. Norton & Company   New York   London

For information about permission to reproduce selections from
this book, write to Permissions, W. W. Norton & Company, Inc.,
500 Fifth Avenue, New York, NY 10110.

Manufacturing by RR Donnelley, Harrisonburg
Book design by Amanda Morrison
Production manager: Andrew Marasia
Cartography by David Cain

Library of Congress Cataloging-in-Publication Data

Rose, Joel.
Blackest bird : a novel of murder in nineteenth-century New York / Joel Rose. — 1st ed.
p. cm.
ISBN-13: 978-0-393-06231-1
ISBN-10: 0-393-06231-7
1. Hays, Jacob, 1772–1850—Fiction. 2. Rogers, Mary, 1820–1841—Fiction.
3. Murder—New York (State)—New York—History—19th century—Fiction.
4. New York (N.Y.)—History—1775–1865—Fiction. I. Title.
PS3568.07634B55 2007
813'.54—dc22
2006031703

ISBN 978-0-393-33061-8 pbk.

W. W. Norton & Company, Inc.
500 Fifth Avenue, New York, N.Y. 10110

W.W. Norton & Company Ltd.
Castle House, 75/76 Wells Street, London W1T 3QT

1 2 3 4 5 6 7 8 9 0

The Blackest Bird

Who drinks the deepest?—here's to him!

—Edgar Allan Poe

1

July 26, 1841,
Midnight

Make no mistake, the task at hand affects him deeply. He is not entirely cold-blooded after all.

Still he proceeds, tearing long strips from the hem of her dress, tying the white lengths around her waist and neck, fashioning a crude makeshift handle by which to carry her.

As he works he cannot bring himself to look her straight in the face, can hardly bring himself to look at her at all.

The wooded path is clear, although overgrown to each side with grabbing brambles and dense vegetation.

Not far off, the river laps, its briny tang strong in his nostrils.

Across the expanse of water, he can just make out the lights of the city gleaming through the rising mist.

Somewhere in the current, he thinks he hears the dip of oars.

Overhead, there is no moon visible, but many stars, bright through the high canopy of trees.

The deed is done.

A feeling of sadness and longing comes over him that is not akin to pain, but resembles sorrow only.

He wrestles with the dead weight of her, leaving the body by the riverside while he scours the bank looking for stones and rocks of a size large enough to weigh her down.

His thoughts go to her. *What have I done?*

"Oh, Mary," he murmurs to himself, may even have spoken her name out loud. "Oh, Mary."

2

Old Hays

His name is Jacob Hays. But in the popular penny prints, the *New York Evening Herald,* the *Sun,* the *Tribune,* the *Mercury,* throughout the city, high constable of the metropolis, he has come to be known as Old Hays.

Sixty-nine years of age, he has stood his post for nearly forty years, having first been appointed head of the force in 1802 by Mayor Livingston.

As a young man of the Watch, Jacob Hays had made his reputation at the bull-baiting ring atop Bayard's Mount, where he garnered renown for wading into the midst of throngs of warring, drunken brawlers. Equipped solely with his long ash constable's staff, he would proceed from one to another, knocking the hat off the most vituperative, then, when said individual went to retrieve his aggrieved topper, sending him flying with a swift kick to the rump, effectively rendering his participation harmless. In this way, proceeding from cove to sport to magsman and back again, he had put an end to many a free-for-all, many a melee.

Old Hays is known for being an exemplary and honest man, one of moral and religious character. His keen, deep-set brown eyes lend intelligence to a stolid face, mahogany complexion, and beetle brow. The rigid set of jaw and mouth, the large ears alive with tufts of coarse hair resembling nothing less than stiff gray antennae, these afford him an air of calculated study, the demeanor of one all-seeing.

A steadfast, inflexible, inexorably truculent type, considered a terror to all evildoers, Old Hays believes he can distinguish the criminal physiognomy from the physiognomy of the honest man. He has made a lifetime study of the science, exploring fully the face—or countenance—as index to character. Neither man nor woman passed him on the street he did not study, categorize, remember. He was the constabulary's first shadow, what had recently come to be called in the city "detective."

Among numerous other crime techniques, he is given credit for being the first to tail a suspect, in addition to development of the strong-arm tactic of interrogation best known as the third degree.

He had come on board the force as a youth in the lowliest of roles, when the Watch boasted no formal organization, comprised almost exclusively of a small corps of roundsmen and an equally small phalanx of "leatherheads," glorified night watchmen, their sobriquet derived from their only uniform, a leather fireman's helmet favored by the men, front brim cut away, and shellacked until the leather was hard as iron.

Earlier that Tuesday morning, having just sat down to his newly accustomed cup of coffee, what he called "Javanese," prepared, at her insistence, by his daughter, Mary Olga, in the Hays family longtime residence, a modest red brick home on Lispenard Street, Old Hays had received an urgent message, delivered by the Negro sextant of the Scotch Presbyterian church on Grand Street, the same Scots church where his family had worshipped for many years, his wife before she died, his sons before they died, where he and his daughter still worshipped. The note, signed by the reverend doctor himself, urged Old Hays' immediate presence, saying that overnight, thieves had stolen the copper sheathing directly off the church steeple and somehow gotten away with it, pleading for him to appear in person with utmost dispatch, which he had done, although to no avail. The copper was long gone, and a more thorough investigation of the metal yards and smithies would have to be undertaken and carried out by someone younger and more spry than he.

The reverend doctor made point to mention the youth bands, saying they had been seen around the church of late. He especially named Tommy Coleman and his gang of Forty Little Thieves, who had a clubhouse around the corner and up the block from the church on Prince Street, and Hays did promise he would ferret the laddie out and have a word with him. With not much more discussion, he then called to his longtime driver, Balboa, an elderly Negro dressed elegantly in bottle green waistcoat and yellow cravat, waiting for him at the kerb.

With Balboa's hand up he climbed back into his carriage, a closed black barouche, and within minutes was standing in his office at the Tombs, in front of the barred window, in a slip of noonday sunlight.

Sergeant McArdel of the Night Watch, having entered the small room from the corridor, now stood in the doorway behind him, clearing his throat.

"What is it, Sergeant?" Hays inquired, turning to his ham-faced, ginger-headed aide.

"A gentleman has been here to see you, sir," McArdel said.

Thirty-nine years old, Sergeant McArdel was seventeen on the force, but only three years full-time. Before that he had worked days as a hod carrier, chiefly in the Third Ward, around Columbia College. Such employment as the sergeant's, outside the force, was not an exception, nor was it singular. Most of the Watch held outside work in order to supplement their meager salary (officially, eighty-seven cents a shift) afforded them by the city's Common Council and Board of Aldermen.

"If I may say so, sir," McArdel added, "the man was in a general state of alarm."

The prison, in whose bowels Hays maintained his office, had been built three years previous, in 1838, replacing the old Bridewell. Properly titled the Manhattan House of Detention for Men, or, in some circles, the Hall of Justice, the somber building, built on pilings and constructed from gray Weehawken stone block at the intersection of Elm, Centre, Anthony, and Leonard streets, on the western shore of the old freshwater Collect, a large pond, once the primary source of all New York City drinking water, was, from the day of its initial groundbreaking and ever after, popularly known as "the Tombs."

The high constable's office was located on death row, off the large Bummers' Cell, where a continual string of drunks, rowdies, and bingo boys were paraded daily, to be held until such time when they might sober up, pay their fine (typically $2.50), and be on their way.

The day was unseasonably hot, even for the deep New York summer of late July, the humidity cloistering and oppressive, particularly for a man of the high constable's age. The combination of weather and miasma rising from the poorly filled-in swamp below the prison was taking its toll on his constitution. He swabbed at his forehead with a large handkerchief as he swatted away from his yellow oak desk one of the prison's many cats, tolerated to keep the jail's rodent population somewhat at bay, his attention momentarily taken by a deep voice lecturing at stentorian volume to those incarcerated in the Bummers' Cell. The topic: the devil Intemperance.

"My apologies, sir," Sergeant McArdel continued, "but he, the gentleman in question, gave his name as Mr. Arthur Crommelin, was here this morning. It seems a young woman with whom he has some history has turned up missing, and his concern, and evidently that of others who know her, including her own mother, is mounting. This gent, therefore, come in to have a word with you, but you not being here, he's had a word with me, sir."

"Just so," said Hays. "Who is she?"

"This Crommelin gave her name as Mary Rogers, sir."

Hays' eyes narrowed. "Mary Rogers?"

"Is her name familiar, sir?"

"It is."

"Do you know her, sir?"

"If it is the same Mary Cecilia Rogers of Pitt Street who was once employed at the segar shop of Mr. John Anderson on the Broadway near the Publishers' Row, it seems to me she went missing once before about three years ago. Did your gentleman mention such an occurrence?"

"He did not, sir."

"If I recall kerrectly, her mother came in at that time, too, also in a state of general alarm. She claimed the girl had left a suicide note, but Miss Rogers turned up, not more than a week later, saying she had been visiting with an aunt in Brooklyn, and knew nothing of her mother's concern. I suspected at the time she was somewhere else."

"Where would that have been, sir?"

"With her paramour."

"I would not be surprised if it were a similar occurrence now, sir," McArdel nodded.

"Nor would I," said the high constable as he turned from the iron-barred window and the yard beyond. "Nor would I."

3

Murder

Two days passed as usual for one in the position of high constable. With stultifying summer heat stifling the metropolis, crime boiled out of the dank Five Points, bubbled from the polluted colored enclaves along Minetta Creek, spewed along the moist docks of the fetid and unwholesome waterfront.

On Rose Street a sallow-faced barrowman was murdered by a cutthroat for his wheeled cart, four puncheons of rhum disappeared off the wharf at James Slip, three autumn morts were discovered strolling uneasily east on the Fourteenth Street, fully swathed beneath their dresses in bolts of watered silk, pilfered not five minutes before from the Endicott dry goods emporium. A young doctor from the City Hospital, accused by a medical colleague of buying the bodies of a diseased mother and child out of the bowels of that rank harborer of human distress, the Old Brewery, was found dissecting his victims' corpses in a basement operating theater on Hester Street. Three toughs affiliated with the Charlton Street gang, out for a night of pirating, drowned in the Hudson River (here called, as it often was, the North River) when their stolen dory was struck and capsized by an oceanbound three-masted bark.

So FOR OLD HAYS went the inimitable current of the city, the daily and nightly course of the constabulary, leading him to that Thursday morning, some minutes before ten, when a nervous young man in a plexus of high agitation, giving his name as Daniel Payne, his profession corkcutter, appeared at the Tombs' gate and asked for High Constable Jacob Hays.

"I am the fiancé of Mary Cecilia Rogers," the sallow-faced cull, escorted in by Sergeant McArdel, announced to Hays in a voice thin and much tinged by anxiety.

Until that moment the high constable had barely given second thought to Mary Rogers and her newest disappearance, having judged the girl to be enjoying another assignation with another beau.

As soon as the corkcutter introduced himself, however, Hays knew he had been mistaken.

"I am informed my rival, Mr. Arthur Crommelin, has visited here yesterday to inform you of certain circumstances surrounding my intended, and probably to implicate me," Payne continued. "No matter. She has been found." He did not look at Hays, but at the floor. A tremor passed through his body, and his words caught in his throat. "I fear she is d-dead," he stammered.

A cold hand crept up from the high constable's bowels to seize his intestines. "Dead?" he demanded. "How so, sir?"

"Mr. Crommelin is a onetime lodger at the Rogerses' rooming house, where I myself am a lodger. Before my arrival, he was Miss Rogers' intended, although I have now supplanted him. Yesterday, after coming here, Mr. Crommelin took it upon himself to launch a search for her. He went to Hoboken after having received news in a grog shop on Dey Street of a young woman fitting Mary's description having been seen on the ferry. Once in New Jersey, he stumbled on a crowd surrounding a body by the riverbank near the Sybil Cave, and it proved to be she for whom he was looking."

He began to sob her name, "Mary."

"She had drowned?" Hays asked, studying the man as he choked and murmured.

"Something more, I fear."

"More?"

"Mr. Crommelin attests she has been murdered."

Old Hays looked upon the corkcutter intently. "And Mr. Crommelin is quite sure he is not mistaken, that Miss Rogers was not merely the victim of a terrible accident, a tragic drowning?"

"No, no," Payne said almost indignantly. "Crommelin said murder. He admitted the water had taken a terrible toll on her face and body, and at first, he said, he had not been confident it was even her, but now he is sure. He returned at first light this morning, delayed, he said, due to his late testimony in front of the coroner's inquest. He carried with him several bits of ribbon, a swatch of fabric cut from Mary's dress, flowers plucked from her hat, a garter, and the bottom hem from her pantalette—all given him, he said, by the coroner, Dr. Cook, in order to show to Mrs. Rogers in hope of ascertaining positive identification of her daughter. Additionally, he said he took it upon himself to take a lock of Mary's hair and one of her shoes, which he thought telling because of her unusually small feet.

"All have been identified by Mrs. R. as Mary's." Payne began again to sob. "It is undoubtedly her, sir."

4

Between Two Tides

Early that afternoon, having boarded the ferry at the Barclay Street pier, Old Hays crossed the Hudson River to arrive within an hour's time at the office of the Hudson County coroner, Dr. Richard Cook.

Dr. Cook, a tall, lean man, took a seat and indicated one for Hays. He intertwined his long, bony fingers in a sort of steeple in front of him as he settled down to the business at hand.

He told Hays that on the previous evening he had testified in front of the Hoboken Board of Inquiry to the following effect:

The body in question was that of Mary Cecilia Rogers, aged twenty-one years, resident of 126 Nassau Street, New York City, New York. Miss Rogers was victim of murder by person or persons unknown.

"The remains were found by two fishermen," Dr. Cook said, referring to his notes, "Jimmy Boulard and Henry Mallin, over on the steam ferry from Manhattan for a day's outing."

About noon, while heading north on the footpath from the Elysian Fields, the pair had spotted what they took as a bundle of rags bobbing in the river a few hundred feet from shore. They waded out to get a better look, upon which they realized what they were seeing was a bloated and hideously disfigured corpse, floating in the shallows, half in the water, half out. Following this discovery, they ran back to the Elysian dock, where they commandeered a skiff and rowed out to the spot where the body remained adrift, caught between two tides.

"She had been killed most brutally," Dr. Cook told Hays, "the crime committed without question by more than one person. It is my feeling that this young woman was most likely attacked by a gang of wretched blackguards. In all probability, soon after being set upon, she fainted, and before she was able to recover, her murderers had tightly tied not only restraints around her wrists, but also a piece of fine lace trimming around her neck. This lace alone would have prevented her from breathing again."

"Was there any foam, as might be the case with the drowned?"

"I observed no foam. About the throat were bruises and impressions of fingers. In evidence was an ecchymose mark, about the size and shape of a man's thumb on the right side of the neck, near the jugular vein, and two or three more marks on the left side resembling the shape of a man's fingers. The arms were bent over on the chest and rigid, so tight and stiff I had to use force to straighten them. The right hand was clenched; the left partially open. It appeared as if the wrists had been tied together. On both the left and right wrists were circular excoriations, apparently the effect of ropes. The hands had probably been tied while the body was violated, and untied before being discarded. All indications are she had been bound, gagged, throttled, and then raped before being thrown in the water."

"Is there any sign that she had been drugged beforehand?" Hays asked.

"There were none. The face was suffused with dark blood, some of which issued from the mouth. Her flesh and features were swollen. The veins highly distended."

"I knew her," Hays sighed deeply. "I buy tobacco at the store in which she once worked. She was a vibrant young woman."

Cook glanced up from his notes. "You would never know it now," he said. "A crime of this nature, it is all very disturbing. It makes you wonder the state in which we live in our society." The coroner shook his head in sadness before proceeding. "Her dress was much torn in several places and otherwise disordered. From the outer dress a long slip, say a foot wide, had been torn upward, extending from the bottom of the frock hem to the waist, but not wholly torn off. Instead, it was wound around her waist a few times and secured by a slipknot. Not a lady's knot, mind you, but a sort of buntline hitch secured in the back, reminiscent of that tied by a sailor."

"A sailor?" Hays muttered. "To what effect do you surmise this arrangement, Doctor?"

"As far as I can tell, the knotted strips formed a sort of handle, used to transport the body."

"Then she was not killed by the riverbank?"

"No, she was not."

"I see," said Hays. "Do we know where she was killed?"

"Not as of yet. There was considerable excoriation upon the top of her back and along both shoulder bones, and excoriation also at the base of the back, near the hips. In my estimation, these were produced by the victim struggling to get free while being held down to effect her violation. This act was without doubt carried out while she was laid down upon some hard surface: a hardboard floor, the bottom of a boat, or somewhere similar."

"But not, for example, on a bed?"

"Absolutely not."

Cook returned to his notes once more. He squinted at his own cramped handwriting for some seconds before returning his attention to Hays. "Her dress, immediately beneath the frock and between the upper petticoat, was made of fine muslin. One piece, about eighteen inches in width, was torn clean from the garment. This piece was used to cover her mouth, again utilizing a sailor's hard knot at the back part of the neck; I suspect this was done to smother her cries and that the gag was in all likelihood held tightly in place over her mouth by one of her ravishers. Again, the flesh of the neck in this general area was much swollen. I must say the piece of fine lace trimming of which I before spoke very nearly escaped my attention. I found this length so tightly, so severely tied about the neck as to be virtually hidden from sight; it was completely buried in the flesh, again fastened by a sailor's hard knot, which lay just under the left ear. Around it her flesh was much distended. I only came upon it by observing a deep crease encircling her neck. Passing my hand behind her ear, I accidentally felt, rather than saw, the small knot, which I supposed to have been the trimming of her collar, so deeply buried as to have been initially obscured from view."

"From such description, would this arrangement alone not have sufficed to produce death?"

"It would have exactly. I would calculate she had been sexually attacked several times before expiring. Perhaps by as many as three men."

"And previous to that?" Hays asked.

Dr. Cook hesitated almost imperceptibly. "I found her to have been a person of kerrect habits and chaste character," he said.

A sudden sharp pain shot from the high constable's right knee to his buttock, very nearly making him squirm. His physician, Dr. John Francis, had informed him he suffered from poor circulation and chronic arthritic dysfunction of the leg joints, particularly the knee, ankle, and hip, among other varied ailments associated with advancing years. Sitting or standing in one position for any prolonged length of time often resulted in excruciating discomfort for the high constable, although it was not in Jacob Hays' constitution to complain. "Where is the body now?" he asked. "I'd like to view her."

Dr. Cook frowned. "Because of the heat, I have found it necessary to inter her in a temporary grave. I'm afraid the state of her was untenable."

"Yet you are convinced this is Mary Rogers? There is no question? Despite the profound decomposition of her features, you are sure?"

"I am sure. All circumstances point to it, and she has been positively identified."

"By the law clerk and ex-suitor Crommelin?"

"Yes, by Mr. Crommelin. He and his friend came upon the body while I was making my preliminary examination."

"His friend?"

"A gentleman giving his name as Archibald Padley, also an ex-lodger, also a law clerk."

"What exactly did these two gentlemen do and say?"

"A curious crowd had gathered. They pushed through the throng for a closer look. At some point, Mr. Crommelin voiced alarm to my colleague, Gilbert Merritt, the Hudson County justice of the peace, that he feared he and his friend knew the identity of the corpse. After closer scrutiny, however, the companion backed off from his statement. He claimed, given the state of the facial features, he could not be sure. But this Crommelin knelt and took the arm of the corpse in his own hands, and carefully pushed up the fabric of her dress sleeve, proceeding to minutely study the hair on the forearm beneath, seemingly its quality and quantity. Following some moments of his examination in this manner, tears welled in his eyes. 'I know her,' he stated. 'With certainty I know her! This is Mary Cecilia Rogers, and I am fearful this blow will kill her mother.'"

"Her mother?"

"Yes."

"Those were his exact words?"

"Yes, that is what he said."

"And you took his identification as fact."

"I might have preferred a blood relative, the mother called in to question, for example, but frankly, the condition of the body was appalling, especially for such a relatively short time in the water. In this heat, her dissolution was of such rapid and profound nature, I feared to subject the mother, who I understood to be quite old and infirm, to any more anguish, or compromise the body any further, unless evidence be lost before being corroborated by another."

"The New York coroner, for example?"

Dr. Cook smiled sheepishly and shrugged. His blue eyes sparkled. "If you will."

"So you are hopeful to see the City of New York taking over this investigation, Dr. Cook?"

"My superiors are reluctant to take jurisdiction. After all, the victim is a resident of your metropolis, High Constable, not New Jersey. True, the poor girl's body washed up here, but this outrage, you cannot possibly argue, very likely took place within the confines of your fair city, not ours. So in the end, I have to agree. Who, sir, better able to see this criminal atrocity to its logical end than a man of your remarkable skills and acumen?"

❦ 5 ❦

The City Brain

Because Old Hays had a daughter of his own, the last surviving of his children, the other four, all sons, having succumbed during the feral yellow fever epidemic of 1822, all within the short span of a sweltering, humid August weekend, the death of the segar girl Mary Rogers took on for him added significance. His cherished youngest, also a Mary, in her case Mary Olga, although called by family and friends exclusively Olga, was not that many years older than Mary Cecilia Rogers herself, and therefore the death of the segar girl evoked for him a special poignancy. Sarah, his wife of forty-eight years, had fallen ill from arrhythmia of the heart only January last. She had just made dinner, had taken her place at the table, when she lost consciousness and hit the floor, facefirst. She woke almost immediately, but as her eyes blackened, her organs began to fail, and within three days his most beloved was forever gone. Since then, understandably, his daughter had assumed a role something more than precious to her father.

Hays did not usually make habit of having his emotions become involved in his cases. He knew even if he had acted when first he had heard of this newest disappearance of the segar girl, there was surely nothing that could have been done. She was already dead.

Still, burrowing guilt had taken hold of him.

From the time of her first disappearance, Hays knew Mary Cecilia Rogers to be in her twenty-first year, having been born in Connecticut in 1820. Her mother, Phebe Mather Rogers, had married into the family of the sour Puritans Increase and Cotton Mather. But Phebe's first husband, Ezra Mather, had died of an infection at thirty-seven, leaving her with two children, a boy and a girl. She remarried, this time to a descendant of another well-known Connecticut family, religious zealot and Quaker James Rogers, founder of the troublesome and dissenting Rogerene sect. Mary was born when Phebe Rogers was forty-two years old, the only child of that union. Hays recalled there had been some spurious talk that Mary was not Phebe's child at all, but her granddaughter, the out-of-wedlock child of Phebe's daughter, also called Phebe.

In 1835, when Mary was fifteen, James Rogers had been killed in a Long Island Sound steamboat explosion, leaving mother and daughter in a state of economic travail.

During the financial panic of 1837 they had moved to New York City, where they hoped there would be chance for better circumstance. At first they had lived at 116 Liberty Street at the home of John Anderson, a young shopkeeper and family friend of Phebe Rogers' first husband, Ezra Mather.

Anderson was proprietor of a segar shop on lower Broadway, at number 319, opposite City Hall Park. Up until that time the shop had been the meeting place of a disappointingly craven lot of loafers, gamblers, and blacklegs, most drifting over from a nearby establishment of poor reputation which Hays knew all too well, called "Headquarters."

At seventeen, Mary was unquestionably a great beauty, and Anderson was very much aware that such a fresh young lady as she would attract the respectable and influential male clientele he so craved to transform his establishment. He offered her a job, and after conferring with her mother, Mary accepted.

To all accounts, with Mary's presence behind the counter, Mr.

Anderson's expectations were met, and his segar shop, purveyor of "Anderson's Solace Tobacco and Snuff," located just a few short blocks from the busy and influential Publishers' Row and Printing House Square, soon became the meeting place for all sorts of important newspaper and publishing types, including many writers and editors.

At the time of that first disappearance, Hays had been told by her aunt, Mrs. Downey, and her cousin, Mrs. Hayes (no relation to the high constable, the names spelled differently), how Mary loved and thrived on the attention paid her, and she reportedly talked often in a gush about the varying men who frequented the shop.

Her beauty was only part of her charm, these female relatives said. Mary was vibrant, outgoing, comely, and graceful. Admittedly, she was somewhat given to wildness. Occasionally she had been known to slip out from the family residence on Liberty Street for secret assignations and rendezvous. With whom, she never divulged.

As previously stated, the first mystery surrounding Mary occurred three years before this present tragic disappearance, almost a year after the start of her employ at Anderson's. At that time, Mr. Anderson and the rest of her admirers at the segar shop were thrown into a sudden state of high tizzy when she unaccountably disappeared. Her mother turned, in a mood of grand and helpless flux, to the newspapers and the wealth of varied publishers and reporters, all of whom knew and admired her daughter. Mrs. Rogers tearfully admitted that she had found a suicide note on her bureau and had become understandably panic-stricken.

Stories appeared in the *Evening Tribune* as well as the *Journal of Commerce*, the *Sun*, the *Mercury*, *Atlas*, and *Commercial Intelligence*. The depictions, tinged with melodrama and despondency, expressed dread that Mary may very well have destroyed herself, explaining how she had for some months been paid particular attention by a suitor (unnamed) who frequented her employer's tobacconist's shop.

It was related that this gentleman had since ceased his attentions and left the city. As portrayed in the *Tribune:* "vanishing like the smoke of one of that gentleman's segars in thin air."

When questioned by Hays at the time, Anderson alleged that this difficult affair (for her) had so taken its toll on the impressionable young lady as to produce the circumstances of mind which the press accounts described.

During the course of his investigation Hays had asked Anderson several times who the mysterious gentleman may have been. Anderson contended he did not know. He mentioned several names upon whom he might speculate, among them the American men of letters Fenimore Cooper and Washington Irving, the acerbic southern critic Edgar Poe, at the time a resident of New York, and the laureate poet Fitz-Greene Halleck. Even the name of the swashbuckling frog Alexis de Tocqueville, author of *Democracy in America,* and the eminent British scribbler Charles Dickens came up, the latter a snuff-seeker, and as such, a frequent guest in the shop while on his last American book tour; all customers, all purportedly infatuated by Mary.

Again at that time, in support of what Mrs. Rogers had reported in the press in regard to her daughter taking her own life, Anderson, upon reflection, told how when last she left his establishment, he feared Mary might have taken with her a shilling from the till with the intention of purchasing poison.

With the fertilizer of this revelation, now even further speculation blossomed in the public prints and among the many gossips of the hub, only to soon wilt when Mary reappeared some weeks later, none the worse for wear, speaking innocently of a visit to a relative in Brooklyn.

During her absence much curiosity had been engendered, but when she returned and learned how John Anderson had spoken quite liberally to the broadsheets about her personal affairs, particularly in regard to men, Mary stormed from his establishment in a fit of pique, never to return.

Anderson expressed sadness to see Mary go. She had months earlier left his home on Liberty Street for her cousin Mrs. Hayes' home on Pitt, made uncomfortable, her mother revealed, by the man's over-solicitation and unwelcome attentions.

Additionally, there was some belated speculation, especially in the sixpenny *Commercial Advertiser,* to the effect that Mary's disappearance might have been concocted by Anderson (with cooperation from Mary) as a way to attract business to his segar and tobacco enterprise.

Now this.

IN THE TOMBS' COURTYARD, Balboa awaits the high constable, standing in front of the barouche, feeding the dappled carriage horse a stubby carrot, at the same time engaged in easy conversation with another Negro, a man employed as prison sweep.

Stepping into sunlight, Hays signals his driver that he is needed. "Yes, suh, Mr. High," Balboa says, breaking off his conversation, and without a further word he opens the carriage door.

Hays climbs in and takes his accustomed seat facing forward in the back, supported by a brocaded East Indian pillow. The prison gates open and the carriage exits onto Elm Street, to make a sharp left.

Nassau Street began one block from the southeastern edge of City Hall Park, a winding street just beyond Park Row, home to the city's publishing and newspaper industries, what is known as "the City Brain."

Some twenty-six newspapers and magazines maintained offices on Nassau Street. The Rogerses' boardinghouse stood at number 126, between Beekman and Ann streets, a flat-roofed three-story red brick building, nondescript among a block of similar structures.

After using the large brass knocker, introducing himself to she who answered, and asking for the Widow Rogers, Hays was ushered into the home by the colored maid.

The front door of the boardinghouse opened onto the parlor floor. Two matronly women and a sullen girl of about fourteen were gathered in the dark-draperied room, surrounding a seated old woman, dressed in black, Hays immediately recognized from his previous audience with her three years before. The high constable took the grieving mother's

cold hand in his. Her lap was covered by a pink and black wool crocheted coverlet despite the warmth and humidity of the day. Hays
peered into the mother's bleary, reddened eyes, noting her blank stare.

"Mrs. Rogers," he said gently, "do you remember me? I am Jacob
Hays of the constabulary."

She said nothing, and the expression on her face, faraway and otherwise distracted, did not change. It was as if, standing in front of her,
holding her frail hand in his, he had made no impression of being
there on her whatsoever. At one point her glance did seem to wander
in his direction, but she did not focus.

Those attending her as she sat stiff and wan in the parlor were her
aforementioned colored servant, one Dorothea Brandywine, now
standing off to the far side behind her, the two matronly women, and
a girl, also mentioned, introduced as a cousin to Mary, a resident
worker in the house; the two older women, one Mary's cousin, Mrs.
Hayes, and the other her aunt, Mrs. Downey of Jane Street.

Hays inquired of Mary's cousin, Mrs. Hayes, if it was not her home
on Pitt Street where Mary had been living and from which she had
vanished from sight three years previously. Mrs. Hayes said that it
was, the high constable noting she was pleased he remembered.

Mrs. Hayes explained that shortly after that incident Mary and her
mother, financed by funds supplied by Mary's half brother, a seaman,
had rented this residence from one Peter Aymar.

They eked out a small living running the boardinghouse here.
Mary's mother was able to do little, feebleness and bone fatigue having set in, so it had fallen on Mary to take charge of the daily chores
and administration. Mrs. Downey said that of late, there had been an
air, nearing desperation, surrounding Mary, but when pressed, she
could not speak of what disturbed her.

Hays returned his attention to the grieving mother. If she had been
listening to the course of his conversation with Mrs. Hayes, she gave
no indication. In deference to her years, her loss, and the devastation
such tragedy had obviously wrought upon her person, he chose not to
press her personally with any undue questions at this time.

Instead, he requested of Mrs. Downey if a list of all boarders over the last year might be prepared for him, any tradesmen who frequented the house, and any visitors.

With that Hays bid his leave. He once more took Mrs. Rogers' frail hand in his thick fingers and told her he was sorry for her loss. He said that he hoped God would give her strength, and then left.

Once outside, against the hubbub and racket of the district's afternoon traffic, the daily standard commerce and hurried foot transit on Nassau Street, Balboa had already helped his superior up into the police carriage in front of the boardinghouse when a tall, thin-faced gentleman in a great rush made his appearance from the rear of the building.

"High Constable, a word with you, please!" he shouted, running at great speed to catch up.

Balboa reined the horse at once.

Hays glanced at this individual, a florid man in a gray suit, with matching vest, white cravat, and well-combed and oiled hair. This gentleman's flinty gray eyes met the high constable's steady gaze momentarily before breaking off.

"Pardon me, sir," the thin man said, stepping close to the carriage and speaking through the open window. "I am Arthur Crommelin, perhaps you have heard of me." His breath came heavily from the exertion of having run to catch the carriage. "It is most urgent, High Constable, that you are made aware of certain elements involved in this case," he continued, his intake of air now regulated. "Last night, following the medical examiner's inquest, much to my annoyance, I was forced to lay over at the Jersey City Hotel due to a delay in my testimony in front of the coroner. I returned as soon as I was able early this morning on the first ferry across the Hudson. High Constable, excuse me, but I must express my feelings," stated Crommelin. "There is something amiss, sir."

"Amiss beyond murder, you mean, Mr. Crommelin?" said Hays, studying the man. "Because, indeed, sir, murder itself strikes me most assuredly amiss enough."

Crommelin blinked. "Without question, of course. A most unfortunate choice of words on my part. But what I mean, sir, last night,
while I was delayed, my friend and companion Mr. Padley returned to
the city after giving his coroner's testimony in Hoboken. He told me
that he entered the Rogerses' home with a certain intent neither to
render harm nor fear unto the widow or intrude on the grief that
would surely descend upon her as soon as she was informed of the
horror that had befallen her poor, wronged daughter. But upon deliv-
ering the terrible news, sir, it was Mr. Daniel Payne at her side, and
although, according to Mr. Padley, she, the elderly and bereaved
mother, took in air in great sucking gulps to steady her breath and
seemed shocked with the most certain knowledge of her child's death
by murder, Mr. Padley has confided in me that Mr. Payne was
strangely calm, as if the fact of his intended's death was already a
foregone conclusion, if you see what I mean. As if he knew; had foreknowledge, sir."

"Foreknowledge?"

"Exactly, High Constable."

"Meaning?"

"Meaning, sir," Crommelin cried, "in deference to you, it seems suspicious, sir, that Mr. Payne's reaction—the man who was lover and
betrothed to the deceased—would not show a forewhisker of emotional reaction, if you see what I'm getting at, and when last night Mr.
Padley came right out and in no uncertain terms suggested to Mr.
Payne he cross the river to attend the coroner's inquest and perform
the duty of a gentleman, he declined. All this strikes me as strange,
High Constable Hays."

"Strange. And suspicious?"

"And suspicious, too, sir," Crommelin admitted. "Most certainly."

Hays ended the conversation, hoping his distaste for this gentleman was not evident. "Just so," he said—what might have been taken
by a certain kind of inferior mind as agreement.

❧ 6 ❧

In the Lair
of the Green Turtle

D ue to the fact that Mary Rogers' body was found in New Jersey,
by law the high constable was required to procure the approval
of the mayor's office before embarking on a full investigation.

Mayor Robert Morris had taken ill with gout, however, and
to Hays' irritation, the acting mayor, Elijah Purdy, an effete, ineffectual man not much to the high constable's liking, refused to be
forthcoming.

"The morass and implication," declared Purdy, "the potential for
disaster, are more than needs to be undertaken on the behest of our
city at this time. If this poor young woman was indeed murdered in
New Jersey, High Constable, as indicated by her body washing up on
their side of the North River, it follows it is then New Jersey's responsibility to pursue inquiry, not ours."

"I think their local authorities might refute that conclusion," Hays
responded without trace of a smile.

"What, might I be so bold to ask, would those in authority in
Hoboken desire to happen?" asked the acting mayor.

"Coroner Cook and Justice Merritt both would be happy to see the
constabulary here in New York take charge. Although they acknowl-

edge the tragedy of the murder, both feel strongly that the crime falls neither under their general auspice nor within their expertise, and that they, therefore, would be better served, as would the victim, if they were not made responsible for its solution. They assert the crime of murder has been carried out on one of our citizens within the confines of our own city limits. Their contention is the body of Miss Rogers has only by chance and current found its way to their shore, perhaps even after being dumped on our side of the river."

"And what do you think, High Constable?"

"I see their point. Dr. Cook and Justice Merritt are both respectable men. Both feel we are better suited to proceed with such an investigation. I do not disagree. My single concern is to see justice done for this unfortunate young woman."

"As is mine. But the fact is, High Constable, dead bodies found floating in the waters surrounding Manhattan Island must not be so uncommon. I can only say, occupy yourself elsewhere, High Constable. Have the good grace to allow Jersey to take care of herself."

Hays reminded himself so went the swagger and sway of this fair city. The hidden subterfuge of power, its whim and whimsy, never failed to infuriate him, no matter who was stuffing the ballot boxes. Having dismissed Balboa, Hays angrily strode up the Broadway to the clip of his constable's staff, muttering to himself.

His daughter Olga awaited him in the kitchen of their home. Dinner was kept warm in the coal oven. His favorite, a flat beef roast, called *brust deckle*, purchased from a Hebrew butcher at his small stall in the Centre Market. (This particular cut of meat from the underside of the cow, which Olga had prepared with root vegetables and tomato gravy, tended to be very tough, marbled as it is with fat and lean between the bone and main muscle of the animal. If cooked slowly at low temperature, however, the strong connective tissue will turn into a kind of gelatin that dissolves back into the meat and breaks down very slowly and flavorfully. It was her father's favorite. Her mother used to make it for him once a week, and Olga thought it nothing less than her duty to continue the practice.)

Hays kissed his daughter's warm cheek. "Good evening, Miss Hays," he said.

"By the look of you, Papa, you've had a hard day," she remarked.

He told her about Mary Rogers, his frustration. He confessed, "A young girl alone in the city, it is what gives me pause with you, my daughter."

She smiled. "With me, Papa, you have nothing to worry about."

While her mother was alive Olga worked six days a week in Brooklyn, teaching English at the Female Academy. Since then she had quit her job to stay home and look after her father and the house, only taking occasional print and copyediting jobs as they came along from the Harper Brothers, Publishers.

"I worry about you, too, Papa," Olga chided her father. "An old man alone in the city . . ."

She told him, if he did not mind, she would attend later that night with her friend Annie Lynch, a colleague and friend from the Female Academy, a lecture at the New York University.

"Edgar Poe, the poet and critic, is scheduled to lay his tomahawk into Longfellow and Halleck," she told him. "I admit to being captivated!"

THE NEXT MORNING, via Balboa, Hays sent a card to Dr. Cook in Jersey City with his request for the coroner to leave the body of Mary Rogers where it lay in its interment for the time being. Because of Acting Mayor Purdy's restrictions on his investigation attributed to jurisdictional objections, the high constable wrote, there was little he could do presently, but problems of this nature had their way of working themselves out.

Have patience, Old Hays urged.

Meanwhile, at 11 a.m., the high constable undertook to pay a visit to Forty Little Thieves gang leader Tommy Coleman, the youthful irreverent that the reverend doctor of the Scots church had mentioned as being a possible suspect in the pilfering of the copper sheathing off the church's steeple.

From the Tombs, the high constable made his way north across Canal to Prince Street, where, underneath the arch between Sullivan and Thompson streets, lay headquarters to Coleman's gang in a bucket of blood operated by a giant colored woman, known in her district and beyond as "the Green Turtle," owing to the fact she resembled nothing less than a huge reptile of the order Testudine, family Verde.

The dirty and dingy double doors descending into the Turtle's lair stood open to the street, although half hidden below ground level. Upon entering, Hays took pause for his eyes to adjust somewhat to the darkness, before continuing cautiously down the narrow fifty-foot subterranean passageway, painted dead black. At the passage end he found the front room dim and half full, but immediately the occupants, seeing who had entered, chose to abandon the premises, scurrying for the door, faces averted or half covered by caps. After some moments, with no further acknowledgment of his presence, the high constable took opportunity to pound his constable's staff hard against the much-trudged and splintered floor in order to attract attention. With the sharp resounding of the staff, the smattering of filthy sawdust on the black boards jumped.

When still no response came, he turned from the bar, a tattered and dented sheet of metal, hammered to planks extended between two empty hoop-staved tar barrels, and took a seat at a nearby three-legged table in order to wait more comfortably. He made subtle show of continuing the light tapping of his long ash baton on the fetid floor.

Behind him there now came the rustle of movement. He turned as the Green Turtle, her skin as deeply shaded as the color of a ripe plum, entered the groggery through a curtain in the rear. She was a massive woman, weighing, Hays would guess, something in excess of three hundred and fifty pounds, outfitted with two huge Colt five-shot Paterson pistols stuck in a wide leather waistband buckled around her ample middle. Pressed against the small of her back but very nearly concealed by layers of flesh, he observed, she carried two bone-handled daggers.

She hesitated momentarily before strolling heavily behind the bar, where she stood, without saying a word, ham-sized arms akimbo, her gaze measured and glaring. In this manner she assessed Hays through bloodshot eyes from underneath a tiny black hat adorned with droopy black feathers, her black hair beneath in severe rolls.

"Madam?" He signaled her.

Taking no heed, she began polishing the sheet metal in front of her with a vigor that led Hays to imagine she applied herself thusly lest the hidden microbiology residing thereon rise up and infect her or her valued customers. Hays very nearly smiled to himself. What would have been the audacity? Could the bar top have been the copper absconded from the steeple? He rose and approached to stand directly in front of her. At closer scrutiny, he took the alloy for zinc. So not pilfered from the church, but likely from somewhere else.

Making one last swipe with her polishing cloth, she finished what she was doing as he watched, the surface in front of her now duly damp and disinfected to her satisfaction.

Again without a word, she poured a large portion of rhum from a cracked blue flagon into a chipped yellow ceramic bowl. Sloshing the drink, she pushed the yellow vessel unceremoniously in front of him.

"I need to have a word with Tommy Coleman," Hays said to her, not touching the poteen.

"You don't say."

"You know who I am, madam?"

"Truefully, I don't care who you are," she said. "I don't care your business. But I know who you are, Mistuh Ol' Hays."

He pushed the bowl of swill away from him. "I repeat myself, madam. Tommy Coleman. I am after him."

She said, "A bit of the devil might do you some good, Mr. High." Then, thinking better, she picked up the cracked bowl he had rejected and drank deeply of the elixir she had poured out for him. "Mr. High," she commended, "here's to your health and the Lord our God looking out for you and your kind." She glanced at the back curtain. "You'll find him through there."

The curtain in front of Hays trembled ever so gently in some secret draft. He reached the heavy drapery, pushed it aside, and moved through it into a back room not so different from the front: several ordinary battered wood tables, dusty floor, dirty sawdust, two filthy windows, one half open, painted black. Three young men stood, one sat, inside the curtain, lounging. Hays knew them all for who they were. Standing: the bugger Tweeter Toohey, an adroit pickpocket despite him having one withered arm, and one withered leg; Pugsy O'Pugh, known to be no nocky-boy him, Tommy's second-in-command; and Boffo the Skinned Knuckle, a squat boy built like an outhouse, the gang's strong-arm captain.

And seated: Tommy Coleman himself, slouched against the wall, feet up, underneath a portrait of George Washington, at a much-knife-scarred table, the smirk on his youthful face bearing witness to his youthful bravado.

Hays rewarded each young gangster the benefit of his studied glance before descending on Tommy, looming over him.

None of the boys looked away.

"Mr. High," Tommy pronounced.

"Master Coleman."

"Are you in search of me?"

"I am."

"You don't find me venturing north past Canal Street to do my business, and no leatherhead, not even no high constable, better dare come here to my den if he values his life and the life of his family." Tommy spoke soberly; Hays hoped more for the impress of his cohorts than for him.

"Is that so?" said Hays.

"I make no idle threat, suh," Tommy persisted.

"No?"

"No."

"Do you know why I am here, Tommy?"

"Should I?"

"You were reported outside the Scots church."

The big grin reappeared. "Church?" Tommy shook his head at the other boys. "Not likely."

The curtain stirred. A beautiful barefoot girl in the familiar calico dress of a hot corn girl, no older than Tommy, seventeen or eighteen maybe, carrying a cedar bucket suspended from around her neck, entered. A two-year-old in similar garb trailed her. Seeing Hays, the hot corn girl abruptly halted and shrank back against the wall.

The little girl murmured, "Mama."

Hays studied mother and daughter, noticed something of Tommy in the tot. His auburn-colored hair. His freckled nose. He turned back to Tommy. "The copper sheathing off the steeple is gone."

Again Tommy shook his head. He grinned, showing prominent white teeth outlined by dull brown. "I do'nah do metal," he shrugged. "Them native gangs, the Butcher Boys, the True-Blue Americans, they are more likely participants."

"Not you?"

"Not me. Not mine."

The little girl murmured, "Da."

Tommy turned and scooped his daughter off the floor. When he returned his gaze to Hays, the high constable asked, "What about the Hudson shoreline at Weehawken, Tommy? Have you and your tribe done outrage there?"

7

News of Murder Breaks
in the Public Prints

Not much of the murder of Mary Rogers appeared in the newsprints in those first days following the discovery of her body. Only a small mention on July 29 was made of the crime in the *Commercial Advertiser:*

BODY FOUND FLOATING IN NORTH RIVER

but beyond that nothing.

It wasn't until the morning of August 1, 1841, that news broke in James Gordon Bennett's *Herald*.

MURDER!

cried the headline.

BODY OF SEGAR STORE GIRL FOUND

"The first look we had of her was most ghastly," began the account. "So much violence had been done to her, her features were scarcely visible."

When we saw her, she was laying on the bank, on her back, with a rope tied around her, and a large stone attached to it, flung in the water. Her face and forehead so butchered that she had been turned into a mummy.

On her head she wore a bonnet—light gloves on her hands, with the long watery fingers peering out—her dress was torn in various portions—her shoes were on her feet—and altogether she presented the most horrible spectacle that the eye could see.

And so it was, the body of Mary Cecilia Rogers, the Beautiful Segar Girl. It almost made our heart sick, and we hurried from the scene, while a rude youth was raising her leg, which hung in the water, and making unfeeling remarks on her dress.

Bennett demanded nothing less than immediate and full-scale action leading to an arrest.

A CALL TO ALL CITIZENS!

A murder of such atrocious character must be taken from the realm of mere police report so that especial attention will be paid, and our young women protected.

After reading this, Hays remained silent for some seconds before wondering of his daughter, "Do you feel like you need protection, Olga?"

"I feel so sorry for her, Papa," she admitted. They were in the kitchen together. "I am beginning to fear in this city all young women—all women—need protection."

If anything, his daughter was too much like himself. When he first told her of Mary's murder, her first concern had been for how much she, the victim, must have suffered.

"Has Balboa arrived yet?" Hays asked her.

"No, Papa, not here yet."

"Then do me the good service, Olga. Run to the news hut and buy the gamut of newsprints."

"All?"

"The *Commercial Advertiser,* the *Mercury,* the *Times,* Greeley's *Trib,* the *Sentinel,* the *Sun.* Whatever you can lay hands on. Whatever the boys are hawking."

"Certainly, Papa. But I don't think the *Tribune* will be in yet. It's an afternoon paper."

"No matter. Whatever is available. Take some coins from my pocket purse."

The newspaper shed, two blocks northwest from their home on Lispenard, stood at the corner of Church and Canal. She returned less than fifteen minutes later carrying eleven papers.

The high constable by this time was fully dressed for the day's demands, and waiting for her. "Do you mind, dear, would you thumb through these with me and see if there is any further mention?"

She undertook the eleven sheets with him, although nothing more was to be found. The only mention proved the one in the *Herald.*

"Mark me on this," Hays told her, putting down the large magnifying glass that more and more enabled him to discern the newspapers' small typesets, "the other prints will be on the topic soon enough."

It was at this point that Balboa arrived. Olga pressed upon him a cup of coffee, for which he thanked her, and drank, unsweetened, straight down.

As Hays predicted, by late afternoon, making quick note of increased *Herald* sales, the other public prints, in rapid succession, took up the crime.

All were full of the death of the segar store girl, many in extra editions with enriched, lurid detail. Particularly, the *Sun* now advanced Mary had been abducted, raped, and strangled in a display of hideous violence performed by diabolical, unrepentant gangsters. Mentioned as possible culprits were several papist Irish groups including the Dead Rabbits, Kerryonians, Roach Guards, and Plug Uglies.

Rather than the Irish, the native gangs, the Bowery Butcher Boys and their brethren, were implicated in the *Mercury:* "no matter how loudly the latter group of rapscallions might deny their culpability in like cases of murder and rape."

Other suspects, these mentioned in the *Evening Journal,* were the Chichesters, Five Pointers, and the Charlton Street Gang, river pirates by profession, and known to own a rowboat.

"Three hundred and fifty thousand souls live in this city," opined Walter Whitman, a young reporter recently come to the *Brooklyn Eagle* from the *Argus.* "And of these some thirty thousand we might humbly deem as ruffians. Ergo, we as citizens should never knowingly negate the possibility of their participation in crimes of this horrid and sordid nature."

Speculation of all sorts raged for ten days.

The *Commercial Advertiser* now alleged it was not Mary's body at all that had been discovered, but the body of some other unfortunate creature. The real Mary, the *Advertiser* conjectured, was hidden, out of public view. For whatever reason, remained unexplained.

Thrice during this period High Constable Hays sought out Acting Mayor Elijah Purdy, still sitting stead for unwell Mayor Morris, in vain attempts to elicit the acting mayor's approval in order to commence his investigation.

But Purdy declined the first time and the second, and on the third attempt refused to even meet with High Constable Hays.

Throughout the city, citizens continued to thrill to the story. Newspaper sales soared to previously unrecorded heights. A young woman who had experienced both the freedom and perils of the city, ending up the way Mary Rogers had, enthralled and frightened all. Many young women refused to leave their homes alone on any errand for fear they would be the next victim.

Hays' thoughts deferred to the murder and Mary Rogers at the expense of all other constabulary concerns, frustrating his days, which then ended with sleepless nights wherein he found himself worrying about his own daughter. Without the endorsement of the mayor's office, however, the high constable remained powerless.

In the *Herald* of August 9, Bennett reiterated the charge that it had been gangsters who killed Mary Rogers. But this time he pointed his rather bent finger at a band of Negroes.

That evening the *Evening Signal* published an account claiming a witness who swore to having seen Mary Rogers on the Sunday morning of her disappearance in Theatre Alley with a gentleman with whom she seemed quite intimate.

Next morning over breakfast Olga pointed out to Hays an additional report in the *New York Mercury* wherein Mary was said to have been spotted later that same Sunday after the incident in Theatre Alley at the foot of the Barkley Street pier, boarding the Hoboken ferry with a "dark-complexioned man."

Eyewitnesses reportedly thought him a naval or army officer. For some reason again remaining unexplained, the *Mercury* charged, this military gentleman later choked Mary to death.

At that point, having little firsthand knowledge, Olga, rather, calling his attention to various leads and information after reading of the events related in the prints, the high constable took it upon himself to steam-ferry to Hoboken to have further word with Dr. Cook.

As in his own city, in Jersey's Hudson County no investigation of any consequence had yet to begin, limited, like the high constable, by the recalcitrance of local authorities.

Hays asked the medical examiner if there was any merit to the *New York Mercury*'s assertion that Mary had been murdered not by a gang, but by an individual.

Dr. Cook coughed, said there might be that possibility, the body arranged in such manner to mislead investigators, but he would have to reexamine the remains to ascertain for sure. "This will not happen at present, however, High Constable," Dr. Cook said. "As you well know, my superiors are locked in a game of wills with your superiors. Both hang on the other, awaiting the other's lead, and as result nothing is done."

In the rising tide of old age, Hays was finding his patience wearing thinner and thinner. "You said Mary was chaste at the time of her death, Doctor. Do you stick to that assertion?"

Cook blinked. "Again I would have to reexamine the remains."

"Why would you allege this if it was not true?" Hays asked.

Dr. Cook looked away. "To save the young lady's reputation," he admitted softly.

"I see." This much Hays understood. "May she have been with baby?" he asked gently.

"There was no indication of any such thing."

"But you examined her fully on this point?"

"I did, and found that there was not the slightest trace of pregnancy."

"You are sure of that?" Hays pressed on.

"Yes, I am sure."

Studying Dr. Cook, Hays felt strongly otherwise.

FINALLY, TWO DAYS LATER, on Wednesday, August 11, more than a week and a half after the first news had reached the public, Hays received word in his Tombs office that a group of well-known and influential citizens, all of whom had known Mary Rogers from standing her position behind the counter at Anderson's, were to meet at 29 Ann Street, at the home of townsman James Stoneall, to form a Committee of Safety, and to offer monetary reward sufficient to elicit from the public information leading to the arrest once and for all of the murderer or murderers.

At 7 p.m. Mr. Stoneall called the meeting to order in his parlor and introduced ex-mayor Philip Hone to address those gathered.

Hone, a very tall, slender man, bowed before beginning. "The youth and beauty of the victim," he said solemnly. "The idea that such a young and beautiful girl could be seduced and murdered within hailing distance of this our great metropolis. Each, the former and latter, having quickly conspired to produce intense excitement in the minds of we, the city's most prestigious populace!"

In conclusion of this thought, the ex-mayor exclaimed: "We must do something! *We must.*"

He turned to Hays and addressed him directly. "High Constable Hays, sir, our unfortunate, our innocent, our sweet Mary has clearly and unfairly, to her, fallen victim to the brutal lust of some of the gang of banditti that walk unscathed and violate the laws with impunity in this moral and religious city. I presume, as of yet, no discoveries have been made, and so I must implore you, we all do, you must persevere and you must be successful."

Taking his cue, Hays answered he would like nothing more, but he first need have mandate to begin. "Acting Mayor Purdy, unfortunately, prevents my investigation," Hays told them all.

Something will be done about that, it was sworn in response.

To the good, but notwithstanding, to stimulate immediate action, while the mayor's office was dually dealt with and made right, $300 was pledged for reward on the spot.

This sum offered quickly grew to $748, eventually to reach the grand total of $1,073, including public money pledged from Albany by Governor Seward. The biggest individual contributors ($50 each) proved to be Bennett, the newspaper publisher, and Anderson, the segar shop owner.

It was hoped a premium of such proportion would assure a swift solution to the crime, but it did not. With several of the public prints, including the *Herald* and *Mercury,* demanding culmination to the horror, not to mention the fact that High Constable Hays had made plain his frustration with Acting Mayor Purdy, a citizens' group representing the Committee for Safety, was sent straightaway to his office to demand immediate attention.

Unable to resist such pressure, Purdy sent a card for Hays' appearance, and upon arriving at City Hall, the high constable received direct orders, matter-of-factly delivered, to travel with all speed to Hoboken, and once there to disinter the corpse of Mary Cecilia Rogers from her temporary crypt and bring her back home to New York, whereupon he would commence his investigation to all of his skill and ability, to hopefully solve the crime with utmost alacrity.

Hays accepted the change in charge with accustomed grace. He dispatched Sergeant McArdel, who quickly secured a police rowboat and six oarsmen. On board with Hays was Acting Mayor Purdy (exclusively at his own insistence) and the New York medical examiner, Dr. Archibald Archer.

Dr. Cook and Hudson County justice of the peace Gilbert Merritt awaited Hays and the New York contingent at the Hoboken Bull's Head Ferry dock. From there they proceeded to the location where Mary's body had been sepulchred three feet deep in a double-lined lead coffin. The heavy tomb was unearthed and then transported by flatbed wagon back to the rowboat, propelled across river, not without considerable effort (a terrific thunderstorm erupted, with howling winds and driving rain), to be deposited on scrubbed pine boards at the Dead House behind City Hall.

Phebe Rogers was sent for from her home to make final determining identification. The old lady staggered into the cavernous Dead House, supported under either arm by the two ex-roomers, Arthur Crommelin and Archibald Padley, but, despite Acting Mayor Purdy's insistence, was unable to bring herself to gaze upon the body. Decomposition had already taken place to such an extent that no trace of the once-beautiful girl could be recognized in the black and swollen features, and Hays reiterated to the acting mayor for the third time his conviction that it was unwise to insist the old woman perform this hellacious duty.

Instead, through an anguished veil of tears, the grieving mother, with Hays at her side, eventually identified her daughter's body by articles of clothing stripped from the corpse.

That evening when Hays returned home from the Tombs, Olga already had dinner laid out on the table. She also had a newspaper tucked underneath her arm. "Annie Lynch brought this to my attention," she explained, referring to her dear friend from the Brooklyn Female Academy. "It is an admonishing tract from the *New York Advocate of Moral Reform*. Papa, the editors have taken this opportunity to voice their moral repugnance with the state of affairs in our society," she snorted. "Mightn't I read you what they opine?"

"Most assuredly, my dear, if you don't mind me having a seat first." At this late hour, after a day such as this, it was comfort he sought.

She began:

> "One word to the young ladies who may read this, from a voice from the grave, speaking to you in tones of warning and entreaty,
>
> Had Mary Cecilia Rogers loved the house of God, had she reverenced the Sabbath, had she refused to associate with unprincipled and profligate men, how different might her fate have been!"

8

The Investigation
Begins in Earnest

Later that night, having returned to his office at the Tombs, High Constable Jacob Hays officially registered the death of Mary Cecilia Rogers as murder, whereupon New York coroner Dr. Archibald Archer confirmed in the Dead House the results of the autopsy performed by Hoboken medical examiner Cook, with the exception of listing cause of death as "DROWNED," whereas Coroner Cook had it listed as "STRANGULATION."

Hays fumed. Over the years, the more he had grown to depend on them in his investigations, the more skeptical he had grown of doctors, their acuity and theory. He had asked this specific question of Dr. Cook: Had Mary Rogers been drowned? To which said medical man had responded unequivocally that she had *not* been drowned, citing the absence of frothy blood in her mouth as proof.

"Dr. Archer," Hays now pressed the New York man, "according to your colleague Dr. Cook, Mary Cecilia Rogers was dead before she went into the water. How say you to this?"

Archer relented without a fight. He said it might indeed be so. "Consider Dr. Cook kerrect," he said. To which Hays knew he could rely on neither of these men, but would have to pick and choose what was valuable and what would prove less than gospel.

In spite of the hour, Hays trekked back across Chambers Street and up Centre to his office to consider the facts he had at hand. Once seated in his hard chair, two or three of the prison's ubiquitous mousers began to gather about him with their annoying mewing and pestering.

Hays was no pussyite. He made no bones about that. He could not stand the felines. Yet, perversely, the prison cats seemed to take particular delight in him. Hays took that as testament to their misconceived character.

He considered the possibilities of the crime as they presented themselves to him:

1. Mary Rogers died at the hands of a gang of ruffians.
2. Mary Rogers died at the hands of a beau, or ex-beau, in the murderer's misplaced estimation, somehow wronged by her.
3. Mary Rogers died at the hands of a stranger: until the day of her death, someone she did not know.
4. Mary Rogers died by her own hand. (Unlikely, considering the manner in which she was found trussed.)
5. Mary Rogers had not died. She was in hiding, and the body was not the body of Mary at all, but of another, as yet unidentified.

The first possibility struck him as the strongest. Mary's death was related to some band of local riffraff. Both coroners seemed to corroborate the facts. Mary Rogers' body had been violated by several men, perhaps as many as three, perhaps more. On any given summer Sunday afternoon numbers of hooligans were about, rowing over from Manhattan or taking the steam ferry.

Once again Hays went over the facts. On the Sunday, the last day Mrs. Rogers was to see her daughter alive, Mary left the Nassau Street address at 10 a.m. Church was out, and at that hour many people were on the street. She was a beautiful young woman, well known from her employ at Anderson's. Hays judged tens if not hundreds of people must know her by sight.

Someone must have noticed her.

He called Sergeant McArdel into his office and ordered him to dispatch a constable each to the *Evening Signal* and *New York Mercury* to wrest the names of those individuals mentioned in the newsprints' columns who claimed to have observed Mary.

As a result, an umbrella maker from Rose Street was questioned who said he had seen a girl who may have been Mary shortly after ten that Sunday morning in Theatre Alley, a short lane off Ann Street, leading to the stage door of the Park Theatre. There, he said, the girl ran into the arms of a waiting gentleman, greeting him as one might a lover, and then repairing with him up the alley in a northerly direction to an ultimate destination, the witness swore, he knew not where, nor, when pressed, could hope to know.

An accounts clerk at the New York Bank, out for an early Sunday morning promenade, was also ferreted out and detained. He said he saw Mary, or a girl meeting Mary's description, on Barclay Street. She was heading in the direction, he remembered, of the Hoboken ferry, whose station was at the extreme west end of that street.

Additionally, a contingent from the Day Watch dispatched to canvass the ferry quay found a young man who concurred with earlier testimony, saying he, too, saw Mary, or, again, a girl who looked like Mary, boarding the ferry with a "dark-complexioned man." Other passengers vouched similarly, attesting they remembered the fellow. Two among them, daily riders, agreed he may have been a military man, a naval or army officer.

On Old Hays' orders a force was sent across the river to Hoboken, tramping the bank south to Jersey City and north to Weehawken.

A German woman, Mrs. Frederika Kallenbarack Loss, proprietress of Nick Moore's House, an inn near to where the body had been found, reported the presence that Sunday of a group of some fifteen ruffians who had rowed over from the city in two small boats, and had proceeded to cause havoc all afternoon long. Mrs. Loss also revealed that same afternoon a young woman of Mary's description had patronized her establishment.

Word was immediately sent to Hays of Mrs. Loss's recollection. Balboa drove the high constable to the ferry wharf, and he was on the next boat over, standing the journey at the rail, gazing north at the wide scope and magnificence of the Hudson. Upon landing at Hoboken, Hays was immediately taken by stage north to the Nick Moore House.

Hays found Mrs. Loss to be an immigrant woman, although not a recent immigrant, he thought, from the traces of her accent. She was decidedly big-boned and strong-featured, her hair a yellow color, streaked by almost imperceptible strands of gray and pulled back in a loose bun. Her eyes were unsettling and icily blue.

Mrs. Loss recounted to Hays (smiling almost coquettishly) the fateful day of what was presumed to be Mary's murder:

A girl had come into the inn on the arm of a gentleman. Once more agreeing with other witnesses, the man was again described as dark-complexioned.

"Could he have been a navy man?" Hays asked.

She was not sure. She did not think so.

"An army man?"

Again, she was not sure. "He might very well have had a military bearing," she conceded, "but he remains unfortunately dim in my mind."

But what Mrs. Loss did recall was that "the child" seemed "a very nice girl" with fine manners and airs. She ordered a glass of lemonade and bowed smartly upon taking her leave.

Mrs. Loss remembered her particularly because she had on a dress similar to one that had belonged to Mrs. Loss's sister-in-law, recently deceased. Looking back, Mrs. Loss now presumed this girl to have been Mary Rogers.

There was more.

Later that night, Mrs. Loss told Hays, she recalled having heard screams. At first she thought it to be her middle son, Ossian, whom she had sent to drive a bull to a neighboring farm. Fearing he had been gored, she took to the road, following the track all the way to the neighbor's barn. There she found her boy none the worse for wear, and thinking nothing more about the screams, so many people having come across the river and enjoyed themselves that day due to the heat wave, she took him firmly by the arm and returned to the roadhouse.

During Hays' interview with Mrs. Loss, Adam Wall, the local stagecoach driver who had picked Hays up at the wharf and brought him to the inn, came into the roadhouse for some warranted refreshment, the day being as hot as it was, ninety-three degrees.

Overhearing the conversation, Mr. Wall intruded, eagerly offering that he had viewed the corpse of the dead girl the Wednesday of her discovery on the riverbank. He told Hays he had recognized her straightaway as a young woman he had picked up at the Bull's Head Ferry and brought to Mrs. Loss's roadhouse only a few days before, on Sunday. He remembered upon dropping her off that there had indeed been packs of hoodlums roaming the woods and enclaves that afternoon particularly. He especially remembered one gang who had invaded the little mud shanty next to Mrs. Loss's, seized all the cakes, and ate them, refusing to pay anything and threatening anyone who dared interfere.

According to Mr. Wall, the gang remained about the shoreline until dark, when they departed in a hurry by rowboat, but not before dragging the daughter of a family, over for a day's outing, out of their boat and having their way with her despite the protestations of her father.

Mr. Wall told Hays he had not personally witnessed the abduction of the daughter, but this is what he had heard, although from whom he could not remember. Hays, noting the slow manner in which Mr. Wall's eyes rose to meet Mrs. Loss's eyes, immediately knew the source of this tidbit of gossip to be her.

9

In a Clearing

A week later, in the tepid middle days of September, word reached Hays that Mrs. Loss had come forward to Bennett at the *Herald* with a remarkable revelation.

Her two younger sons, she recounted, Oscar and Ossian, aged nine and twelve respectively (Charlie was the eldest at fifteen), had been playing in the woods near her home, north of the old Weehawken ferry dock. In a clearing they had come across a variety of discarded clothes, gloves, handkerchief, and parasol, the lot of it inhabited by crawling bugs of the type that fester in wet discarded articles.

These found articles themselves were much mildewed and moldy, trampled down, she said, in a thicket near a cove in the woods. The parasol and handkerchief had the initials *MCR* embroidered on them, leaving no doubt to whom they belonged.

Hays traveled immediately to Mrs. Loss. The clothing, the parasol, the gloves, alleging to be Mary Rogers', were all laid out in the downstairs bar at Nick Moore's House.

"Why, my good woman, were these articles not left in place?" Hays demanded upon viewing them exhibited in this manner.

Mrs. Loss shrank back from his anger, and said in her defense she was fearful someone not connected to the case would find them and remove them.

"Not likely, considering they have remained undisturbed and unnoticed for such a period, and only now have been found," Hays fumed, gauging the woman and her intent. Was it stupidity or slyness? "Madam, the placement of the articles in the clearing might have given me clues to how the murder was committed," he explained slowly.

Mrs. Loss apologized profusely. "I did not realize the severity of my action, and the actions of my boys. I can only hope and pray our thoughtlessness will not impede your investigation further, High Constable. If it would be any help at all, I would not mind in the least to help you reconstruct their placement," she offered.

The purported scene of the crime proved to be a curious, if convenient, alcove in the woods. The area was furnished with three large rocks, one of which formed a sort of seat, while a second formed a makeshift backrest, and the third a footrest or ottoman. The clearing was heavily surrounded by dense brush.

As Mrs. Loss said, every last article had been collected and removed by her and her boys. Not a shred left. Hays had only Mrs. Loss's word for where they had been found and under what circumstances ("Here was discovered a strip of torn dress, thrice impaled on a single thorn"). The area was much trampled upon, attesting to what might have been sign of a colossal life-and-death struggle. There were indications leading from the clearing to the river that something of weight had been dragged.

The following day, September 17, 1841, a steel-point etching appeared on the front page of the *New York Herald* depicting the Nick Moore House, its clapboard siding, the wooden stairs and rail going up, the single dormer in the center of the shingled roof.

Beneath, in large bold type, was printed the legend:

THE LAST PLACE ON EARTH
WHERE MARY ROGERS WAS SEEN ALIVE

Opposite, also on the front page, a poem inscribed "To Mary," credited to the city's laureate poet and signed "Fitz-Greene Halleck," took residence in the lefthand column.

> *Mary had been noticed at some public places*
> *   (The Battery and Broadway)*
> *For hers was one of those glorious faces,*
> *   That when you gaze upon them, never fail,*
> *To bid you look again; There was a beam,*
> *A lustre in her eye, that oft would seem*
>
> *A little like effrontery; and yet*
> *   The lady meant no harm; her only aim*
> *Was to be admired by all she met,*
> *   And the free homage of the heart to claim;*
> *And if she showed too plainly this intention,*
> *Others have done the same—'twas not of her*
> *   invention.*
>
> *But where is Mary? She has long been thrown*
> *Where cheeks and rose wither—in the shade.*
> *   And although, as I once before have said,*
> *I love a pretty face to adoration,*
> *Yet, still, I must preserve my reputation.*

❧ 10 ❧

What Colt Did

Inside the same day's edition of the *Herald* featuring the Nick Moore House etching and the Fitz-Greene Halleck ode of tribute to Mary Rogers, the family of a Transport Street printer, Samuel Adams, posted a desperate notice:

MISSING FROM HIS PREMISES

Beloved husband, father . . .

A cash reward was offered for any information leading to the return of this vanished man.

A week passed with no word on the whereabouts of the gentleman in question, whereupon Old Hays received a card at his office in the Tombs that a body had been found sepulchred in a crate in the hold of a packet steamer lying at the foot of Maiden Lane.

With McArdel in tow, Hays proceeded to the waterfront. There indeed, aboard ship, from below, there came the most fearful smell.

"We 'ave been delayed a week on our way to New Orleans," the captain told the high constable. "When this morning come this 'orrible stench from the 'old, I tole me mate, break cargo, and that is what 'e done."

With his handkerchief clasped over his nose, Hays descended to view the remains of he who would later be identified as the printer Adams, without clothes, wrapped in canvas and stuffed, knee to chin, into a wooden box.

"Do you know how the crate got here?" Hays asked.

Both captain and mate said they did not. "Delivered by a cartman, it was, but who might 'ave employed 'im or who that feller was, I du'know."

That evening Hays had McArdel advertise in several of the penny papers for any individual who might have brought a box to the ship.

The next day, the sought-after cartman, his interest drawn to the advertisement and solidified by the money offered as a reward by the family, came forward. He told of carrying a wooden crate, leaking a dark liquid that may have been blood, from the corner of Chambers Street and Broadway to the east side docks at Maiden Lane.

Hays asked could he recognize that person who had employed him.

"He wasn't just your everyday kind of fellow," he said. "No, not him. He was a high bloke, he was, with plenty of lucre."

"How much did he pay you?" asked Hays.

"Gave me a five-dollar gold piece, he did."

"Did that not alert you, sir?"

"Alert me to what?"

A granite building stood at the corner of Chambers and Broadway where the cartman indicated he had made his pickup. Hays walked the length of sidewalk, and by the public pump discovered a discoloration of the cobbles that may have been bloodstains.

He sent McArdel into a number of nearby buildings until he returned with a professional bookkeeper by the name of Wheeler. Mr. Wheeler told the high constable a week before he had been sitting in his office with a young lad who was a pupil of his. It was between three and four o'clock, he said, when a very agitated gentleman rushed in from the street and up the stairs. Soon, the bookkeeper said, he heard the sounds of an argument, the cry "You lie!" followed by the sounds of a struggle, what might have been swordplay.

"Swordplay?"

"That is what it sounded like, sir. I remember looking up from my work and saying to my pupil, 'Did you hear that? What was it?'"

The bookkeeper continued, "My room is next to another engaged in a similar field. He keeps accounts, although he instructs in the art of ornamental penmanship as well."

"What might this gentleman's name be?" asked Hays.

"John Colt. After hearing such noise and such fright, everything suddenly had gone silent. Stealthily I crept to Mr. Colt's door, from where I was sure the commotion emanated, and peered through the keyhole, displacing the cover, which was down, with the handle of my pen."

"What did you see?"

"A man I assumed to be Mr. Colt with his back to the door, stooping over something and quietly raising it. There was no noise. All was still and quiet as the charnel house."

Old Hays had heard enough.

"Do you know if Mr. Colt is in his office at this moment?"

"I cannot say. I think he is."

The man who answered Hays' knock was tall and lean, handsome of his style, well haberdashed, not a mollycoddle exactly, but a fuss-budget, what surely might have been taken by a cartman, or anyone of a certain predisposition, as a high bloke.

"Mr. Colt?" Hays inquired.

"Mr. High Constable," the man answered.

It would not be quite accurate to say John Colt looked cool to Hays, but he did not appear exactly flummoxed either.

"You recognize me, sir?"

"I imagine there are few in this city, High Constable, who would not."

"Just so," Hays said. "Sir, I am here under the most regrettable of circumstances. Are you of the acquaintance of a printer by the name of Samuel Adams?"

Colt's expression barely changed, but, as perceived by Hays, change it did. "I am not," the suspect said.

"You are certain? A gentleman by the name of Samuel Adams?"

"I am certain, sir. I do not know this individual."

"I see. And you are not the one to have sent a crate packed with the body of a man, *this man,* this gentleman whom you do not know, Mr. Samuel Adams, to New Orleans?"

Colt stepped back, smiling in what Hays saw as a disturbing, most unsettling manner.

Still, he denied all.

Hays tipped his bowler to him, bid him good afternoon, and returned to the street. He ordered McArdel to post a man outside the building with instructions to follow Colt wherever he might go.

McArdel himself was to proceed immediately to Adams' home and place of business to see if there might be any record, or anyone with knowledge, perhaps his wife, of a previous connection between these two gentlemen, Mr. Adams and Mr. Colt.

HIGH CONSTABLE HAYS was a well-known figure. Many criminals were stopped in their tracks when they heard uttered the warning, "Beware, Old Hays is after you." Before dawn the following morning, the high constable, with Sergeant McArdel accompanying him in accustomed role of strong arm, came for Mr. John C. Colt at his home on Washington Square. After awakening the suspect, Hays requested that he accompany him to the Dead House, where, unbeknownst to him, the body of Samuel Adams was lying under a sheet.

The atmosphere in the Dead House justifiably brought a chill to Colt. In the cold and cavernous room, Hays reposed questions to him, and again the suspect assiduously denied the murder of the printer Adams, denied even knowing him.

Bearing him no heed, Old Hays persisted with his questioning. He was accustomed to initiating his interrogation with a warning: "Good citizens will tell the truth."

He would intone this statement just so, cracking his staff in accompaniment on the hard floor for additional effect.

Adams' body remained covered, and the room in the Dead House was dark and sinister.

Hays suddenly swept the sheet off the corpse. "Look upon this body!" he ordered Colt. At the same time, he carefully shone the beam of his lantern on the remains. "Behold the cold and clammy body of your victim, Mr. Colt! Have you ever seen this man before?"

Colt jerked back, terrified, and cried out in horror, but Hays, unrelenting, shoved him forward and pressed his head down until the suspect was forced to stare into the clouded eyes of the dead man.

"Murderer!" cried Hays. "Confess! Now, have you ever seen this man before?"

Colt broke into sobs. "Yes, Mr. Hays, as God is my witness, he is Samuel Adams and I have murdered him."

A WARRANT was subsequently sworn and acted upon in the name of John C. Colt, and a confession to the following effect written by the alleged perpetrator.

"On the morning of Friday, September 17, 1841," Colt began, "my publisher, Mr. Samuel Adams, called at my home on the north side of Washington Square, telling my manservant, Dillback, he had something most urgent to discuss with me. At the time, according to Dillback, he was told most politely I was still asleep.

"Mr. Adams asked if I could not be awakened," Colt continued. "Dillback, who is an Englishman and beyond scrutiny, replied that I could not.

"Mr. Adams then requested paper and pen, sat down at the hall writing desk, and wrote a short note to me. He requested if I might not be given it as soon as I awakened. Then he bid good day and left."

———

AGED TWENTY-SIX, John Colt was scion to the Colt armament business, the youngest of three brothers; his eldest brother being Samuel, the patriarch of the family and inventor of the Colt Paterson repeating revolver.

Young John, however, was not part of his brother's firearm business. He aspired instead to the literary life and to literary fame.

His course?

Whatever means necessary, according to some detractors, including Olga Hays, who knew him vaguely as a hanger-on at Harper Brothers, and so informed her father.

Artistic considerations were said to be of little concern to young John. His first published work was a treatise on decorative handwriting. His second, a discussion of accounts.

But this new book was different. "A collection of poetry," Colt happily explained to anyone who would listen.

For the pleasure of seeing his latest typeset, Colt had made financial arrangement with Mr. Adams in order for him to print the thin volume. And, indeed, the purpose of Mr. Adams' visit that morning of the crime pertained to that very agreement, and certain accounts still outstanding for Adams' printing and publishing services rendered.

Of only slightly less consideration to the money owed apparently was the quality and craft of Mr. Colt's work. Evidently, in printer Adams' estimation, the author's poetical dabbling contained no meritable quality, and no craft. In no uncertain terms, Adams questioned the mettle of the poet, the honesty, integrity, and frankly, when a poem showed promise, the very authorship. Word had reached Adams that the best poems signed "Colt" were actually penned by the critic and poet Edgar Poe, commissioned for pennies from the rightful author owing to that man's purported financial difficulties. Adams had apparently lent ear to rumors of scandal. He had heard Poe might even now be revoking his arrangement, decrying Colt for plagiarizing his work, and planning an exposé in the public prints.

Colt rose daily at midday. His coffee and an Anderson aromatic segar in light green wrapper were brought to him in bed each noon along with that morning's newspapers and a single red rose in a glass vase.

Adams' note, sealed in an envelope smudged with black, inky fingerprints, was tucked under the linen napkin. Looking at it, Colt first took a sip of coffee before slitting the envelope.

He read the note and jumped up, spilling both coffee and vase.

Crying for Dillback, the manservant, he demanded his horse and carriage be readied immediately. He dressed and ran from his home into the street even as his mistress, Caroline Henshaw, tried to calm him.

His carriage pulled up, but apparently Colt now had second thoughts.

"Mayhem may very well have been at play on my mind," he admitted in writing, "because I now declined to enter the vehicle. Instead, I dismissed coach and driver and headed east on foot from my home, skirting Washington Square before cutting south on the Broadway, with every intention of confronting Mr. Adams at his printing house offices on Nassau Street. Halfway downtown, however, I thought better of it, and again altered my plans."

Colt maintained a second-floor office and studio at the corner of Chambers Street and Broadway. He now repaired there, and was sitting at his desk when, some hours later, Adams burst in, very much flushed with excitement and the exertion of running up the stairs. The irksome printer rushed across the room and waved his bill for services directly in Colt's face.

Colt said he pushed him away, demanding, "What is the meaning of this?"

Adams shouted he wanted his money. He then plunged into what Colt called a spew of "gossipy gibberish," slanders he had apparently heard from certain well-oiled lips, such as that Edgar Poe was the rightful author of more than a few of the poems included in Colt's prospective book, and not he, Colt. A lawsuit had been threatened, and Adams shouted he wanted no part of it.

Colt admitted in writing the charge made him somewhat nervous, knowing the temperament of Poe. Yet he claimed all the verses were his, that if anything, Poe was an admirer, and that all charges were ridiculous, the result of petty jealousies.

"Pay me or I'll expose you!" Adams threatened. He drew out an example of work considered suspect, slammed it hard on the desk, and shoved it across to Colt. Colt lowered his eyes in order to read. The bit of doggerel had appeared unsigned in an 1841 volume of the *Police Gazette*, but Colt claimed authorship.

In this Christian age,
'Tis strange, you'll engage
When everyone's doing high crimes to assuage,
That the direst offenses continue to rage;

That fibbing and fobbing
And thieving and robbing,
The foulest maltreating,
And forging and lifting,
And wickedly shifting
The goods that belong to another away,
Are the dark misdemeanors of every day.

And then too, the scrapes of seductions and rapes,
And the foulest of crimes in the foulest of shapes.

Colt claimed he was nothing less than abashed.

"Have you lost your mind, man?" he swore he cried at Adams. "This is mine by all that lives and breathes. I wrote it."

"I think not!" Adams countered, according to Colt. "And even if it is yours, I tell you I want my money! What you call your work is nothing more than the tragic waste of an innocent tree of the forest!"

Colt said he chose to remain calm in the face of this humiliation.

With no gentlemanly course save to stand up straight, take the high road, as it were, and protest no more, he said he deemed to defend oneself against such slur unseemly.

Still Adams refused to back down or apologize in any shape, manner, or form, the printer finally stating without further equivocation, reiterating, that he would not, under any circumstances, print the work he had previously contracted, referring to it now with utter deprecation as "work of this genre and quality."

"What genre and quality is that, sir?" Colt, by his own admission, raged.

"Nebulous genre. Lewd, melodramatic, exceedingly poor quality," shot back Adams. "Does that encapsulate it for you, sir?"

Colt said he reluctantly resigned himself to Adams' disparaging and mocking onslaught. He claimed again to having attempted reason with Adams, assuring this man that some of the foremost literary talents of the day admired his work. He again mentioned Poe specifically, saying, even as they spoke, the poet and critic was petitioning the Reverend Rufus Griswold, literary editor of *Graham's Lady's and Gentleman's Magazine*, for his inclusion in his forthcoming definitive tome, *The Poets and Poetry of America*.

Adams, Colt said, laughed in his face.

"From here one thing led to another in rapid succession," he further admitted, as angry sentiments, including the phrase "You lie!" were exchanged.

Before he knew it, Colt further submitted, words finally came to blows. With no further provocation or warning, Adams was suddenly on him, the printer in an irrational state.

In his own defense, Colt said, once physically drawn into the melee, he did not believe he could properly protect himself. He quickly came to realize he was at serious disadvantage and without proper weapon. He emphasized that day he was not carrying one of his brother's revolvers, nor did he keep one in his offices. Moreover, he wrote in his confession, his weaponless state lent credence to the fact that he had not sought, nor anticipated, trouble of any kind when he left his home earlier that afternoon.

Nevertheless, Colt conceded that after several slight blows were exchanged, he was finally provoked, and forced to take initiative. He went directly onto the "offensive" after having been on the "defensive" for what he recalled as an unspecified length of time.

With no other choice, he now struck Adams violently with his closed fist. The men grappled with each other, and Colt was eventually shoved against the wall, his side pressed painfully into the sharp table corner.

There was a curious two-headed tool, half hammer, half ax, on the tabletop, what, he said, is called a broad hatchet. Why it was on his desk, or even in his office, Colt said he knew not and could not remember. Still, he admitted that he immediately seized hold of this instrument and instantly struck Adams several blows to the skull with its sharp edge.

Even after these, Adams continued to struggle. The wounded man grabbed a flowing silk kerchief, a type of ascot or stock, Colt wore around his neck, and began to twist. As it became tighter, Colt admitted, he went into a veritable frenzy. Fearing for his own life, he now struck repeatedly a cascade in and about Adams' cranium with the tool, following these with several additional solid blows.

Adams finally stopped struggling but Colt could not stop himself, taken up now with an admitted hysteria. He continued the barrage until a knock on the door caused him to gain hold of himself.

"Hello?"

"Yes, Mr. Colt? You are wanted down on the receiving platform."

When he heard the knock on the door and his name called, Colt confessed, he was instantly startled, then taken aback, suddenly coming to his true senses in regard to the magnitude of his deed. He stole to the door, fully conscious of turning the key so as to lock it.

He sat for a few moments, sick from what he had done and hoping no one had heard the noise of the fearful beating, sitting quietly, waiting whatever his fate may be.

"There was vast amounts of blood on the floor," he recalled.

Afraid it would begin seeping down into the apothecary store below, he said, he swabbed the floor thoroughly with a towel he found hanging on a doorknob and wrung out the blood into a bucket of water that stood in the room.

"The pail was, I should think, at that time about one-third full of water, and the blood filled at least another third surely," he wrote in his confession.

About this time a second knock fell on the door, to which Colt chose to pay no attention.

"Wondering what was best to do, I remained until dusk on a seat near the window in the office," he remembered, "gazing on the body, forlorn, a silent space of time, I admit, with horrid reflection."

❧ 11 ❧

Aftermath to Murder

The idea for the Colt revolving handgun came to John Colt's brother, Samuel Colt, while the latter sailed on board a transoceanic liner to England. Traveling in the company of middle-born brother James, second of the three Colt brothers, Sam, the eldest, had positioned himself on the bridge, where he became entranced with the spinning of the ship's spoked wheel. He spent the rest of the voyage carving a wooden prototype of a gun barrel capable of a similar spinning action. Upon docking at Leeds, the brothers booked immediate return passage, steaming directly back across the Atlantic to New York and their fortune.

According to John's written confession, later published in its entirety in a supplement edition of Bennett's *Herald*, on the night of the Samuel Adams murder, his brother was booked at the City Hotel on Chatham Street near the southern edge of City Hall Park, but when he stole out of his Chambers Street office and hurried south across the park to see him, Sam was engaged in negotiations in the hotel's reading room with two gentlemen, one a Brit, the other a Russian, and only a few words passed between the brothers.

"I sat patiently," John wrote, "trying to wedge a word in edgewise in an attempt to communicate my dire peril to my sibling, but to no avail. Serious money was being discussed and the terms were complicated. My brother has never gotten along well with the British, and the Russians are a total enigma to him," John explained.

"Exasperated by my brother's indifference, I finally stood, made a noise in my throat, and exited the hotel, scarcely noticed. I then retired to nearby City Hall Park, where I walked a bit. A turn I enjoyed wholehearted, serving to clear my head, heart, and lungs. My thoughts, I confess, kept coming back to the horrors of the excitement that had only recently transpired, the possible trial, the public censure, the false and foul reports that would inevitably be raised.

"I knew full well there would be those who would wish to take advantage of the nature of my situation, making the deed appear worse than it really was for the sake of a paltry pittance.

"I knew I must somehow disengage myself from all circumstance. After wandering in the park for more than an hour, I settled on a course of action and returned to my room.

"A crate stood in the offices, and I succeeded in stuffing Adams inside, being careful to wrap the body in canvas in order to absorb the excessive amounts of blood which was still leaking. The head, knees, and feet were still a little out, but by reaching down to the bottom of the box and pulling the body a little towards me, I readily managed to push the head and feet inside. The knees still projected somewhat, and I had to stand on them to get them down.

"With this task accomplished, I then fit the cover to the box and nailed it shut using the same hammer/hatchet tool with which I had dealt Adams the death blow. A poetic conceit, I concede, not lost on me.

"I then removed all clothing from the corpse to prevent identification, because my plans now included shipping the body south to New Orleans in a steamer. I therefore took the bloodied clothes, shredded them, and took them to the backyard privy, where I threw them in, together with Mr. Adams' keys, wallet, money, pencil case, and all other incidentals.

"Thereupon I returned to my room, cleaned up the last of the blood, took the water pail, carried it downstairs, and threw its murky contents in the street, following with several pails of fresh water from the pump opposite the outer door of the building in order to wash away the reddish brown stains.

"After rinsing the pail, I then carried it back upstairs, returning it clean and two-thirds full of water to the room, opened the shutters as usual, drew a chair to the door, and leaned the back against the inside of the door underneath the knob as I closed it. I then locked the door with the key and went at once to the Washington Bath House on Pearl Street near Broadway.

"On my way, quite by coincidence, I met, of all people, Edgar Poe, in the city from Philadelphia on what he said was business.

"The man is an acquaintance," Colt wrote, "but somewhat more than that. He was peering into a tea shop window on Ann Street. I invited him to accompany me to the bathhouse as my guest.

"As we walked, I did my utmost to maintain my calm and hide my trepidation in light of what had only recently transpired, but eventually I did mention to my friend the claim of Adams that rumor was on the wind that he, Poe, had written the poems signed with my name, and the work, not to mention both of us, would soon be under public scrutiny.

"To his credit, Mr. Poe dismissed such notion as ridiculous. He instead offered me his best wishes for good luck for the book's appearance. He mentioned to me a new poem of his own, at this point a mere sketch, but for which he seemed to have great hope."

COLT WENT ON in his *Herald* confessional to claim Poe purportedly admitted the idea for the verse came directly from a line in Dickens' *Barnaby Rudge*, one extolling an owl, Colt thought, which Poe had conjectured to him he might very well transform into a black bird, perhaps a crow, or raven.

Colt admitted he could not quite remember, and had not read Dickens' book.

Once at the baths, Colt wrote, the two men fell back and spent the rest of the evening discussing the murder of Mary Rogers. Colt alleged they both knew this young woman from Anderson's and shared remorse for her fate. According to Colt, Poe confessed to him that news of Mary's death had distressed him greatly, more so than he might have thought.

At this point, Poe turned to him, confiding in a craving for opium. He asked if Colt knew of any person from whom such potion might be procured. Colt, invested in being immensely well-regarded among his fellows for his late night gallivants through the city's darkest corners, what was known as "elephant hunting," readily mentioned a retreat he knew, a place known as the Green Turtle's, beneath the arch on Prince Street, warning Poe that the proprietress, a woman of enormous girth, was exceedingly dangerous.

Afterwards, the men bid good night and Colt went home. He reported he lived with his mistress, as he described her: his lady love, Miss Caroline Henshaw.

Upon his entrance into the bedchamber, Miss Henshaw awoke to ask where had he been. He said he told her he had been with a writer friend from Philadelphia, although he did not mention Poe's name specifically.

Colt confessed he dared not tell Miss Henshaw what had transpired earlier in the day, and pretended instead to be inspired from his meeting with the unnamed poet. He retired to his desk to write, although he said he was not able to compose a word. Eventually she became quiet and slept, her breath regulating, and only then did he follow suit, slipping into bed and, after a long period staring sightlessly into the dark, eventually falling asleep as well.

The next morning, having thought better of his predicament, he hired a burly man to carry the crate containing the body of Adams downstairs from the printing office. Refusing Colt's assistance, the rough, powerful man hefted the makeshift coffin onto his back, muscling it down the stairs and into the street. Colt said he then paid the brute some twelve cents for his efforts and went off to Broadway, where he located a cartman, who would in fact be his undoing. When reward was offered for any knowledge of the whereabouts of Adams, this was the lout who came forward to tell the authorities how he had taken a suspicious oblong box from Colt's granite building to a packet bound for New Orleans lying in the East River at the foot of Maiden Lane.

The boat had yet to sail, so the wooden crate was dug out from the hold, and sure enough, opening it, the captain and his mate found the printer, stinking, dead, stiff with rigor mortis, and in the most uncomfortable-appearing position.

❧ 12 ❧

Death of the Corkcutter
Daniel Payne

The killing of Samuel Adams by John Colt succeeded, finally, in driving the murder of Mary Rogers off the front page.

BODY FOUND IN BOX

There was no question of Colt's guilt. Here was his confession in full, printed word for word in the *Herald.*

The rest of the penny papers were left to scramble, taking up mere points of law, exemplified by cogitation in that weekend's *Tattler:*

PREMEDITATED MURDER OR SELF DEFENSE?

The answer presumably to this curious legal conundrum would dictate whether "Homicide Colt," as the headline writers had come to call him, would live or die.

And so with this debate ongoing, public opinion found itself thusly consumed, until three weeks later, the sixth day of October, when all reverted once more to Mary Rogers.

On that afternoon Mary's betrothed, the forlorn corkcutter Daniel

Payne, haggard and worn, appeared at Mrs. Loss's roadside inn, the Nick Moore House.

As reported by Bennett on the front page of the *New York Herald:*

> Mr. Payne stood in the establishment and inquired of Mrs. Loss the exact location of the spot where Miss Rogers had met her death.
>
> The unhappy man then sat down and commenced to drink a number of brandies before stumbling out.

Two days later Payne was discovered, an apparent suicide, on what was believed to be the exact spot of Mary Rogers' murder, in the same small clearing where Mrs. Loss's two sons, Oscar and Ossian, had found the scattered articles of her person, leading many to speculate, even conclude, that the corkcutter was guilty of his intended's murder.

> Others besides Mrs. Loss had seen Mr. Payne drinking and wandering about the general area.
>
> Mr. Samuel Whitney, a patron of the Phoenix Hotel, told how Mr. Payne had appeared at the hotel bar late the night following Mrs. Loss's encounter with him at the Nick Moore House.
>
> "He looked red and a little intoxicated," Mr. Whitney said. "And he seemed weak and could hardly stand up."
>
> During the course of the evening, Mr. Whitney further reported, Mr. Payne spoke to him in the following manner:
>
> "Suppose you know me? Well, I'm the man who was to have been married to Mary Rogers."
>
> Mr. Whitney said Mr. Payne then mumbled, "I'm a man of a good deal of trouble."

An empty and shattered bottle of laudanum from the Deluc Chemist on Nassau Street, only steps from the Rogerses' home, was found near the body. The Hoboken police were quickly notified of the death and forwarded immediate word to High Constable Hays in New York City.

A storm rose up early that evening. Hays, with Acting Mayor Purdy, who again insisted on inviting himself to accompany the high constable and Sergeant McArdel of the Night Watch, rode over in a small boat through the squall to investigate.

Upon their arrival, wet and chilled, the high constable was handed a note found by Dr. Cook in the dead man's pocket. It was addressed:

TO THE WORLD

"Here I am on the spot," Payne had written in a clear if not strong hand. "God forgive me for my misfortune in my misspent time."

"He has died as the result of congestion of the brain, brought about by irregular living, exposure, and aberration of the mind," Dr. Cook responded to questions posed to him by High Constable Hays pertaining to the exact cause of death.

Hearing this, the acting mayor let out an unsettling, self-satisfied yelp, proclaiming to one and all, with the death by his own hand of the corkcutter Daniel Payne, the mystery of the murder of Mary Rogers was solved, the murderer unmasked, the puzzle complete.

"Obviously, the young man had been rebuffed by the segar girl," Purdy lorded. "My friends, it is the only explanation that need be drawn," he continued with his pontification. "Mr. Payne, in what can singularly be called a fury of rejection, commenced then to throttle her, and abuse her in a violent, intimate manner. He then proceeded to murder her on the spot of the very clearing where he himself has now died by his own hand. Warranted by every observation, here lies our culprit."

Hays paid silent attention to this smugly delivered conclusion, fixing first the invidious acting mayor, then Coroner Cook, with his famous steady, cold gaze before declaring:

"Not so, gentlemen. I have made life study of the police science of physiognomy. Daniel Payne was not one to escape my scrutiny. He is not our man."

One Year Later

OCTOBER 1842

🌟 13 🌟

His Is the Rampant Temerity

It is a cold and rainy day on the streets of Philadelphia. Overhead, the slate gray of the sky is uniform, one somber shade. He has made plans with hope, as if hope might make a difference. His is the sudden uplift, the abrupt downward spiral. He blames magnetic fields gone haywire, celestial powers askew, the powers that be looking down on him askance, as he is convinced they have always done.

Sissy is dying. His wife is dying. She ruptured a blood vessel while singing. Since then his life has been one of constant despair. God help him, in his mind he has taken leave of her forever, and has undergone all of the agonies of her death.

He shoves his hands deep in the pockets of his greatcoat, the same greatcoat he wore as a cadet during his stint at West Point, but now, twelve years later, the garment so much worse for wear, a miserable reminder, one of so many, of his failure.

Muddie has done yeoman's work. She has patched the heavy garment a dozen times: where the wool has worn thin, where the moths have lain in wait, where the insects have laid their eggs and watched them hatch. It is these hatchlings, the moths' loathsome larval offspring, that have had their fill, leaving behind a dozen holes.

No matter, he reassures himself, moth holes are inevitable, even in the best of broadlooms.

But to be truthful, all those patches and darns are telling. Everything is telling on this man. He does not disguise well.

Yet he deems himself genius.

But if he is a genius, why is he not recognized? Why is he so poor, so destitute, he must beg to eat? Why does society reject him?

A man of his vast talents?

His name is Edgar Allan Poe, although he loathes the Allan part, and eschews it. He prefers to be known simply as Edgar Poe. Or Edgar A. Poe. Or E. A. Poe. Or Eddie Poe. Or even E.A.P., as in his first published work.

His darling little wife, his Sissy, his Virginia, calls him "Brother," or "Buddy." Sissy's mother, Muddie, his aunt Maria Clemm (he and Sissy are first cousins), calls him Eddie or "dearest Eddie." His stepfather, the despised John Allan, the Allan of Edgar *Allan* Poe, called him Ned.

He has no recollection of what his real father, the disappeared actor David Poe (Muddie's brother), called him.

To his dead mother, Eliza Poe, née Arnold, "the Little Actress," "America's Sweetheart," famous for her stage role as Little Pickle in *The Spoiled Child,* he seems to remember he was "darling."

He tells himself it is his lack of tenacity. His rampant temerity. His passion. His emotion. The unrest in his bosom. The burrowing fear.

Stop!

He disgusts himself. His indulgence with self-pity is reprehensible. What has he done to deserve this fate? He must stop this. He must. After all, everything could change. A letter has arrived. He has an offer. Some much-needed funds.

He has been invited by the family of John C. Colt, a vague acquaintance, to travel to New York City to write a final portrait of their young penitent, sitting in his jail cell, awaiting death. The letter signed by family patriarch Colonel Samuel Colt himself.

John Colt, "Handsome John," "Homicide Colt," "Colt the Homicide," christened in the public prints "failed poet," "doomed poet," "*poète maudit*," held in the Tombs, the New York House of Detention, for the murder of his publisher, Samuel Adams.

Poe could not help but smile to himself. He would have liked to do the same: Murder his publishers! Kill Billy Burton. Eviscerate James Harper.

Mr. Poe lives with his family, his women, in Quakerdom, in the City of Brotherly Love, in a small, neat, but only partially completed house on the rural edge of the city sprawl, on a quiet ordinary street named for a tree and a scourge: Locust.

His aunt Muddie, his cousin Sissy, the only ones left who love him.

Sissy, married to him when she had just turned thirteen; he twenty-six, twice her age.

Sissy so sick now, he has very nearly abandoned all hope. Yet with each accession of the disorder that plagues her, he loves her more dearly. He feels all the agonies of her death even as he watches her cling to her life with ever more desperation.

He admits to being constitutionally sensitive, nervous to a very unusual degree.

He rids himself of this thought. Here is opportunity to redeem himself, opportunity afforded by Colonel Colt and his family on behalf of the unfortunate John.

He kisses Muddie and Sissy goodbye. They kiss him back, say, "God's speed, dearest Eddie." He leaves the meager house in the middle of the day, a dark and brooding figure beneath a dark and brooding sky. He fingers the few coins remaining in his pants pocket, hopes there are enough for the rail ticket, the ferry across the river Styx.

The good Colonel Colt has forwarded him ten dollars as an advance against the completion of the word portrait of his brother John. He has given the lion's share of the funds to Muddie for food and medicine for Sissy.

He has discovered an elixir he calls "Jew beer." A strange Hebrew fellow down the road makes it in his barn. It is the only medicament Poe has found that causes Sissy improvement.

Darling Virginia, what she does for him! So infirm, her health so fragile, although she remained plump and round-faced, her voice so sweet still when she rises to sing his favorite song, "Come, Rest in This Bosom."

For all the world he looks beaten, even before he starts on his journey. He fingers his one joy. With him in their canvas case, now stuffed in his greatcoat pocket, he carries his augments, his talismans: his steel pen, the nib worn perfectly through use to the slant of his hand, his pocket notebook, his precious ink in its heavy corked ceramic pot.

With his instruction Sissy concocted the brew. She is so proud to help him with his work. The tint, a careful mixture of red and black, heavy to the red, a single drop of black added, two, three, so the black dye drifts in the red, transforms the crimson into the color of blood.

The pocket notebook, buff pages cut meticulously by her, perfectly folded, bound with leather thong, the smooth paper protected by a buttery-soft black-dyed goatskin-leather cover.

He buoys himself. He tells himself once more the idea to go to New York is a good one. After all, Gotham is the literary capital of America, and E.A.P. no small American literary figure.

Adding *t* to Poe, he reminds himself, makes *poet*.

Truth be told, in Philadelphia nothing has met his expectation. Nothing has been satisfactory. How many tales has he published? Sixty? How many poems? Reviews? Yet he has nothing. For how many weeks must his family be forced to eat bread and molasses and nothing more? How many times can he expect his dearest Muddie to show staunch face at the Christian mission seeking charity?

For a year he was employed as editor of *Burton's Gentleman's Magazine,* but some of those stints with drinking had poisoned the minds of detractors and ended his job, although he assured friends that temperance was not an issue, that intemperance was as far removed from his habits as day from night.

The true issue, if you want to know, was the feral stupidity of the publisher Billy Burton.

Bilious Billy, he called him.

Bilious Billy of the title page.

Bilious Billy the buffoon!

Once the man had been a successful comic actor. He had come from England with great success and fanfare. That was before he had incredibly taken on the mistaken mantle of publisher and—even more laughable—writer!

What made the fool think himself capable of such pretense?

Haggard!

Billy Burton—this man—had the audacity to warn him, to warn *Poe*—Poe the Poet—that he must tone down his reviews, to rid himself of his ill feelings toward his brother authors.

No matter. Monetary need rewards its own humiliation.

"The troubles of the world have given a morbid tone to your feelings," Burton had lectured Poe upon his firing. "It is your duty to discourage such outpour. Take some exercise, man! Rouse your energies. Care!"

The ignorance of him! The arrogance!

Upon reviewing his recently published "Murders in the Rue Morgue," the *Philadelphia Inquirer* had proclaimed: "This tale proves Mr. Poe a man of genius."

Mere puffery, you might say. But his peers, the people who know, his fellow literati, respect him. Fear him.

Fear his mind. Fear his tongue. Fear his wit. Fear his pen.

How many times had Poe explained to Burton that he worked from a mental necessity to satisfy his task and his love of art? Fame forms no motive for him. "What can I care for the judgment of a multitude, every individual of which I despise?" he insisted. "A man of large purse has usually a very little soul which he keeps in it."

On that note Poe bolted from the editorial offices of the *Gentleman's Magazine*, leaving his ex-boss Bilious Billy staring after him, his beady little eyes swallowed by his fleshy face.

Poe's desire is to answer to no one but himself. To sit as his own arbiter. To his thinking, to coin one's brain into silver, at the nod of a master, is the hardest task on earth. He loathes to work for another imbecile again. He will tell you the greatest number of those who hold high place in our poetical literature are absolute ninnies. Nincompoops. Name your names: Longfellow, Cooper, Irving, Halleck, Bryant. Bloated reputations, derivative aesthetics, undeserving practitioners.

The laudation of the unworthy is to the worthy the most bitter of all wrongs, Poe would tell you. Yet no man living loved the praise of others better than he. So he trods the smoothly cobbled streets of Philadelphia on his way to Central Station, to some opportunity, to the unknown. Head down, keeping his eyes upon the ground, studying the herringbone of cobblestones, the stereotomy of the streets. Benjamin Franklin once said the Philadelphian could always be told from the New Yorker. New York was so crudely cobbled the poor Gothamite found himself listing merely from habit while walking fair Quaker-dom's smooth stones.

Poe himself was fairly listing at that very moment, with each step the momentary shreds of optimism and resolve falling away from him, him fairly falling, falling into that strange beaten posture of his, as if fate has had her final say and there is nothing more to be done.

During the remainder of a dull, dark, and soundless day, he goes on, his West Point greatcoat pulled close. Philadelphia so quiet that day, as every day, striking him as Sunday.

The wind is shifting. Above him the cloud cover is shredding. As he walks the sky splits apart, revealing slivers of bright blue and streaks of glistening yellow sunshine. He straightens hopefully to his full height. The crack of blue sky and warming golden rays no more than a mere wink and nod for him, him rejecting any signs of any good in the cosmos, as transient as a glint of gold in the ether.

He coughs.

He removes a frayed clean handkerchief from his pocket and presses it to his lips. God save her. God, please, save his innocent little wifey.

❦ 14 ❦

Somewhere Deep
in the Distance Stereotomy

Somewhere deep in the distance, far away, yet perhaps surprisingly near, as the train slowly chugs forward out of Central Station, Philadelphia, picks up speed, and rumbles out of the city, bound for points north-northeast and New York, six hours away, the poet hears bells. His eyes widen with their knell.

He had miscalculated. As he stood in the vast lobby, inexorably alone, at the ticket booth, a sodden man in round steel-rimmed glasses staring out at him from behind the cage, he realized he had not sufficient funds for fare to Hoboken and still enough coin to cross the Hudson on the ferry.

He begged the clerk for consideration, received none, had been forced to settle for a ticket to the penultimate station along the line instead, as far as his money would carry him, holding in abeyance his last few pennies, just enough for ferry fare. He would make his way somehow from railroad junction to boat quay, even if he had to walk. He was a good walker. He had walked before.

The train, steaming over the flatlands, past Camden, past Trenton, is dark in the afternoon with the day's ill weather. Night is descending. As it grows darker still, the cast of oil lamps behind sconces festooned on hardwood paneling causes eerie shadows to play.

His notebook is open. All around in the dim light his fellow passengers pore over the penny papers, the popular magazines. Women knit, crochet. He waits for the music of the muse to seize his hand, his ear, his heart, to drive him down, down into his seat, with his pen, the paper, the pot of blood-colored ink laid out in front of him, and to lead him, rescue him from those death bells clanging. What tale of terror their turbulence tells!

The brain, that organic jelly that resides inside the skull at its core, this is his difficult organ. His head is oversized. Outsized. It is literally a great thing. A massive entity unto itself. It resides on a slender stalk, a slender neck upon a slender body. The head a great weight. If only the stem and root were stronger. He falls into a deep slumber.

Sometime later, confused and disoriented, he is awakened by the booming voice of the conductor, a bewhiskered man in pressed blue serge, announcing the station stop, "Paterson!" and without thinking he scrambles to his feet and abruptly gets off from the coach.

He stands on the platform and peers into the darkness as the train steams away, leaving him with dense unrest and the clattering din of iron wheels.

Standing in the cold and damp, breaking away from the long empty tracks, he surveys the road. He looks for what? A dray operator or teamster who will be good enough to carry him to the Colt gun factory.

This, he suddenly realizes, is the reason he has come awake in this desolate town. Here lies Colt's Paterson factory, the manufacturing plant of the Patent Arms Manufacturing Company, holder of Colt's patent, maker of the Colt Paterson revolver. If Samuel Colt is on premises, if he will listen to reason, perhaps, just perhaps, he might increase Poe's rate of remuneration for the word portrait of his brother.

As if in a sign that all is right, a wagon turns onto the street some one hundred yards away.

Poe starts. Signals.

The driver, a gaunt man in black, head like a skull, stares at him as he nears, reins in, says nothing at first, just staring, and finally says, "Going up the Old Gun Mill," his voice a deep resonance. "If you're getting in, get in. Don't have all day," showing teeth like tombstones.

Poe throws up his satchel. Dust rises and falls. He climbs up, takes his place next to the man. He says, "Thank you, thank you. You are very kind," in his soft Virginia accent, looks back over his shoulder at the empty flatbed, save now his cracked leather bag, the patina of dust settled back down.

The wagon lurches forward.

For a good long while the two ride in silence, their eyes fixed in front of them on the four roan horses' undulating haunches, the steam rising from the old animals' faded strawberry flanks.

"Picking up a load a them there revolving guns," the driver eventually says. "Bring 'em down Bayonne. Then back up the block cutter to Weehawken. Pick up a load of cobblestone."

Poe brightens. "Weehawken? Would you object, sir, if I were to ride with you as far?"

"Don't mind if you don't."

Colt's gun works occupied a group of buildings, an old silk mill, on the bank of the Passaic River at the intersection of Van Houten and Mill streets.

To Poe the factory seems surprisingly quiet, but then again it was late in the day, after 7 p.m. Poe enters the general reception area, where he is met by a clerk. He requests Colonel Colt and is asked his name. Poe gives it. A few moments later the clerk returns and leads him upstairs to a large office overlooking the river. Several pistols and muskets adorn the wall.

Colt is on his feet. "Mr. Poe? My pleasure. Have we met, sir?" He is a big man with abundant facial hair and shaggy muttonchops, holding a big segar, although it is not burning. His eyes, deep-set, are somewhat crooked in their twin sockets. Poe has the curious if uneasy sense that Colt is making use of these gleaming twin orbs in some undescribed, aggressive pursuit. To peer inside him?

"No," Poe says, "we have not met. But you know who I am?"

"But of course. My brother holds you in such high regard. Anything I can do for you, Poe. Anything. You are on your way to see John right now, is that it? I know he has been expecting you."

"Yes, I am. Sir, this is embarrassing, forgive me," he says. "I understand we have made an agreement, and I am very grateful for it, and, I assure you, it is not my habit not to abide by the agreements that I make, but in this case, is there any way you can see in your heart, Mr. Colt, to improve my contract? Monetarily, I mean. You see my wife is ill, and right now I am to be paid fifty dollars for my work, which I emphasize is a fair price, but fifty more would make life that much more easy for me at present given my circumstances. I am sure you see."

Colt laughs. The mention of money has drawn his attention. "My dear Poe," he booms. "Money is the bane of us all, is it not? Our scourge. Never enough. Never." He laughs, good-naturedly, a bass crescendo. "You do know, sir, that I am in bankruptcy?"

Poe's eyes widen, turn down. "No, I did not know."

"If it was a gun you were after, a fine repeating revolver, nothing would be easier. I'm sorry to say money is another story. I thought I would have a fat contract with the army, but it has all gone to hell."

He shakes his large head sadly.

"I'm on the verge of going under here, Poe. To be frank, your timing could not be worse. What with John at the hangman's door, and my munitions business what it is. I've been blowing things up since I was a boy, Poe. You've probably been writing them down just as long. How does that strike you for irony? Look here, Poe, this is the complete outfit."

On his desk he opens a cloth-lined wooden case. Inside, the blue-finished gun is held in place with small wire loops. He removes it. In script is marked on the barrel: "The Patent Arms M'g Co. Paterson, N.J. Colt's Patent," and on the cylinder "Colt." The only adornment Poe can see is an engraving around the cylinder. "We offer two choices of etching," Colt explains. "The first is of a centaur with two revolvers in hand, killing two horsemen, as you see here. The other depicts the scene of a stagecoach holdup. When you buy the gun, you get a complete case outfit. Here a combined bullet and powder flask. It loads five measured charges of powder and five bullets simultaneously. In addition there is a magazine-capping device that holds fifty percussion caps that feed singularly, one at a time. Also included is a bullet mold, a brass cleaning rod, and this tool that combines several uses, including screwdriver, hammer, and rammer. All of that plus an extra cylinder to be carried ready-loaded, thus giving ten shots without reloading."

"Ingenious."

"I can't give them away. You, sir, won't even take one."

"I have no one to shoot."

"Come, come, come, there must be someone," Colt booms.

"I would need to think about it." Poe smiles weakly.

"The Texas Rangers in their quest against the Mexicans have been my best customer, but the United States Army in Florida have declined. A man can shoot fifty shots in ten minutes with this weapon, Poe. Fifty! But I cannot make money."

As he left the offices Poe could still hear the reverberation of Colonel Colt's big voice as if it were an echo, even though the only echo to be noted was in Poe's head. *Fifty,* he could hear Samuel Colt saying. *Fifty. Fifty shots in ten minutes. But I cannot make money. Fifty dollars? My brother, you say?*

"I was only hoping for something more," Poe had pleaded. "Given my straits. Perhaps not fifty. But even ten will do."

"Ten?" Colt again shook his craggy head. "You can't be serious."

In the end he settles for three dollars.

Poe hurries back down to the loading platform. The drayman's wagon is now fully loaded with oblong boxes, the words "Colt's Repeating Carbines, Property of the Patent Arms Manufacturing Company, Paterson, New Jersey" stenciled across the slats.

Poe climbs aboard and they are on their way.

Again, for a time, nothing is said. As they clatter over the cobbled city streets of Paterson, a one-sided but animated discussion of inner-city travel and paving bricks develops. Poe speaks of stones made smooth for stereotomy, his personal aversion to round cobbles.

The drayman's response is to Poe surprisingly negligible, and there follows another period of silence where both men refrain from talk, only the renewed clop, clop, clop of horses' hooves and the rattle of metal-treaded wheels.

"I am a poet," Poe tells him after some distance, aware of the gauntness of the man. "My name is Poe. Perhaps you've heard of me?"

The driver grunts, shakes his head. "Never."

"I am well known in some circles."

The driver, who Poe decides may or may not be a revenant, spits a stream of black tobacco juice. "Not mine." He snaps the reins. His horses break into a trot for a few steps, then resume their lugubrious pace.

"I only mention it because you said Weehawken and my latest story is inspired by an event that took place there, in Weehawken."

The driver casts eyes upon him but says nothing.

"Have you never heard of Mary Rogers?" Poe continues. "The beautiful segar store girl found floating in the Hudson River shallows a year ago last summer. I have written about her, a story set in Paris, but the parallels to the crime in New York are prescient. The authorities think it is a gang, but I point my finger at an acquaintance. The same man—"

"If you don't mind me asking," the drayman interrupts, "what have you to do with it?"

"Nothing. Nothing at all," Poe retreats. "I knew her. I knew Mary. Something is telling me to stand on the spot where she died."

The gaunt man turns his black eyes again on Poe. Poe holds the gaze, intrigued, as if looking into another world through the glistening orbs. Their beady coal beam seems to bore into the poet, save there is not a pittance of expression on his cadaver-like face. The driver turns back now to the motion of the horses' huge hindquarters.

To Poe's imagination he is indeed Death's drayman.

The teamster flicks the reins again, and the long leather traces crack across the equines' broad backs with negligible result.

Again nothing is said for some half mile, the driver unreadable, ruminating. Finally he spits out another black stream, the bile of hell.

"If I were you, Mr. Poo," he says, once more through those tombstone teeth, the devil's leer, "I'd be letting the dead rest."

❦ 15 ❧

The Sunday Sermon

High Constable Jacob Hays sits beside his daughter Olga, having assumed their accustomed spots in the church pew. The Sabbath sermon is under way, and the reverend doctor, a robust man of impressive girth, is having his say. Hays looks up to study the prelate's curiously small but bright eyes gazing paternally down on his congregation.

"Women," the man of God shouts over the gathered heads, knowing his voice to be a magnificent instrument, "what shall we do with them? They must learn their place. Our young women, these women we care for and love, I ask you, do we dare let them find their own way in this harsh and unforgiving world? Do we dare let them have their heads? Look no further lest we forget her, poor Mary Cecilia Rogers. How far did this aggrieved maiden stray from the Lord? Who among us is prepared to answer the question? To endure the consequence? No, we must come to the fore. We, with the help of the Lord, must be their guide."

After the service the pastor stands just outside the open double church doors on the topmost step, greeting his parishioners as they exit and descend.

Hays shakes the man's warm, puffy hand. "Well said," the high constable compliments, with a wink to his daughter and only, perhaps, the slightest touch of detectable mischief.

"Do you think so?" The tiny, luminous eyes of the reverend doctor sparkle with pleasure.

"I think so," rejoins Hays.

Olga takes her father's arm and they descend the church steps together, the reverend doctor having failed to even register Olga's mixed look of scorn and pity.

Old Hays smiles at her. "Don't think I'll be permitting you out again," he teases somberly. "You'll not have another job outside the home on my watch."

"Oh, Papa," she laughs gaily. She has always very much enjoyed her father's sense of humor, rare as it sometimes was.

"It's a different age, I'll give the reverend doctor credit for recognizing that much. But somehow I don't think him standing up there lecturing, 'Don't do this!' and 'Don't do that!' is going to put an end to it."

"No, I think not," she agrees.

"Still, it's the fashion of the time, just as the reverend doctor says."

"Yes, it is."

"Or beginning to be such."

"All you have to do is look at me, your own daughter, if you have any doubt, Mr. Jacob Hays."

He couldn't or wouldn't argue.

"Shall we walk?" he offers instead. "It's a beautiful day, and I prefer a lively jaunt to the sedentary carriage right now."

"We certainly can walk, Papa. I prefer the physical exertion myself."

"High Constable?"

Old Hays knew the voice, the tone, and what it meant, too well. "Yes?"

"Sir?" The man waits. It is Sergeant McArdel, standing with Hays' driver, Balboa. Balboa is outfitted in his Sunday best, forest green pantaloons, yellow shirt, yellow stock. Both men, McArdel and Balboa, were at attention.

As dictated by local ordinance, chains were set up at either end of streets fronting churches to keep away traffic and keep down the din during Sunday services. The Scotch Presbyterian Church on Mott Street was no exception.

The black police barouche was parked at the kerb just outside the chain link.

McArdel tipped his hat at Olga. "Morning, missy," he says.

"Morning, Sergeant," Olga answers.

"Sir?" McArdel turns. "I need your ear."

"Then have it," Hays grumbles, taking a step to the side and saying, "Excuse us, dear," to his daughter.

With that the sergeant joins him and they walk off a little distance. "My apologies, sir, but there's been a rather grisly discovery behind Cow Bay this morning."

"Where?"

"In the rear alley that leads from the tenement."

"What kind of discovery?"

"Three bodies, including a little girl."

Hays glances over at his daughter. She is taken in rather heated conversation with the reverend doctor. Balboa is holding the carriage horse, Old Joe, by the rein.

"Do we know who they are?"

"We certainly do, sir. The Butcher Boy Ruby Pearl is one of them."

"And the others?"

"The wife and child of Tommy Coleman, sir."

✺ 16 ✺

A Man Condemned

John Colt, in his cell on the Tombs' death row, his face thickly lathered by his manservant, Dillback, reclines in a fine leather patent chair of his brother's invention.

Outside, in the prison courtyard, carpenters construct the gallows, what they call the "picture frame." The basic structure is already complete, the carpenters preparing to test the progress of their work.

John does his very best to ignore the commotion without.

Sam Colt has designed the reclining chair for his youngest brother's comfort during this, his final confinement. The Colonel has sent the chair over, along with John's writing desk, his personal library, and custom-made green velvet curtains to give the cell some semblance of warmth and privacy. Lovely fresh flowers stand in a crystal vase on the table.

Eventually John's annoyance peaks. Dillback is poised over him with a razor. John abruptly pushes him away, leaps to his feet, and hurries to the high iron-barred window.

Standing on his cot in order to be able to see, he peers out, sees the gallows, the workmen in caps and coveralls. He watches as the carpenters attach a heavy sandbag to the thick rope dangling from the crossarm. A counterweight, tethered at the opposite end, comes running down, jerking the sandbag aloft.

A single image occupies John's head. He pictures himself in the prison courtyard, alone, underneath the gibbet. He sees himself fitted with the hemp necklace, sees his neck jerked sharply at the end of the rope.

He remembers the words of Samuel Johnson, author of the *Dictionary of the English Language,* subject of the Boswell biography. "The prospect of being hanged," wrote Johnson, "focuses a man's mind wonderfully."

Young John stares out glassy-eyed for some time before Dillback takes him by the arm and leads him back, firmly insisting the lad down into his chair for the resumption of his toilet.

Colt sits but refuses to recline. Head in hands, his eyes closed, a horrible chill runs through him. His jaw quivers. He hugs himself.

The manservant gently pushes him into a more workable position, refreshes the shaving soap with horn-handled, boar-bristled brush, and begins again to meticulously scrape whiskers from chin, cheek, jowl.

❧ 17 ❧

The Bridge of Sighs

The door from the Hall of Justice opens and Tommy Coleman is led in. As young as he is, the accused is already as hardened a cove as there is in local environs. He is aware as all eyes turn on him. He heeds not a single soul.

Following his arrest, his hearing has just ended. Across the Bridge of Sighs he comes, escorted by two prison guards, one of whom tap-tap-taps his keys like castanets against the iron handrails.

The Tombs is arranged in four tiers with catwalks skirting each. Each catwalk is connected to the next by stairs, a bridge spanning the two sides of each gallery. On each bridge a guard sits idly reading or dozing. On the ground floor an iron Franklin stove sits idly, ready to heat the whole; diffuse light filters down from a skylight above the fourth tier.

Next to the cold stove, High Constable Jacob Hays sits. As he is led to his cell, Tommy Coleman, the unrepentant youth, feels Hays' eyes boring in on him. He chooses not to meet them, staring down at his feet instead.

He is escorted to a cell on the first tier. A key is fitted to the lock by a harelipped keeper, and the door, reminiscent of that fronting a furnace, replete with small grated window, swings open.

"Step inside, hardbody," the jailer says, removing the boy's leg irons and wrist shackles before prodding him inside. "That's a good young feller."

The door clangs shut, the lock reengaged. The keeper smirks and is gone. His flat footfalls slap the granite cobblestones of the cell block.

It is late October yet warm, Indian summer. Still the prison floors are chilled and damp. Tommy gives his cell the once-over. Stone floor, stone walls, iron-barred window and door. A wooden slops bucket in the corner reeks of human waste. He knows all too well, from the experience of his brother Edward before him, that this is death row, and no rabbit-sucker was meant to leave this place alive.

He has made peace with his fate. If asked, he would not have said he was innocent. He would have said he was guilty.

But he considers murder too strong a word for what he has done.

What he has done, Tommy Coleman, is kill, and if he had to do it all over, he would have killed again, just the same.

❦ 18 ❦

The Tombs

The Tombs is an unholy place. One drafty corridor links to another drafty corridor. One drafty cell abuts another drafty cell. The stink and unhealth of the swamp rises from beneath the foundation. The mortar is mildewed from moisture, foul from mold.

In the spring of 1842, the author Charles Dickens, on tour of the United States for a book he was writing, *American Notes for General Circulation,* requested specifically to visit the prison.

As High Constable Jacob Hays watched from his desk, the great man, the most popular writer in America despite him being an Englishman, was escorted through the Tombs' corridors, at one point inquiring of his guide, a jailer named Trencher, "Pray, my good man, from where does the name Tombs derive?"

"Well, it's the cant name," came the reply from the blue-suited keeper, meaning the argot used by beggars and thieves.

"I know it is," Hays heard the novelist snap, obviously impatient with those he perceived as simpletons. "But why?"

"S-some suicides happened here, when it was first built," the beleaguered guard ventured. "I-I expect it come about from that."

Hays rose from his desk then and came over to where the author stood.

"Forgive me, sir, for the interruption, but this is not from where the sobriquet comes. If you will, the House of Detention became known as the Tombs because a number of years ago the whole of this city was taken over with an Egyptology phenomenon."

With Trencher looking on gratefully, Hays introduced himself and went on with his account.

A writer from Hoboken, he explained, H. L. Stevens, had set out for Arabia, returning with a manuscript entitled *Stevens' Travels,* which became a sensation for the publishing house owned by Mr. George Palmer Putnam. The author made drawings to accompany his text, and one of these depicted an ancient mausoleum deep in the desert. The idea of this romantic crypt whetted the public's collective imagination, the city fathers deciding in a moment of inspiration that the newly planned prison must be a replica of this Saharan vault.

THE FIRST MAN ever executed in the Tombs had been none other than Tommy Coleman's brother, Edward Coleman. Hays saw him hanged in the prison courtyard on the morning of January 12, 1839, shortly after the building's completion; his offense, the murder of his wife, a hot corn girl.

Hot corn girls walked the streets, selling their wares out of cedarwood buckets hanging by a strap from around their necks. Barefoot, known for their striking beauty, dressed in calico dresses and plaid shawls, these young ladies and girls came out of the poorest neighborhoods, especially the Five Points, their song familiar in one version or another to every city dweller:

Corn! Hot corn!
Get your nice sweet hot corn!

Here's your lily white hot sweet corn!
Your lily white hot corn!
Your nice hot sweet corn!

Smoking hot!
Smoking hot!
Smoking hot jist from the pot . . .

Sports, picturing themselves blades, trailed the hot corn girls on their routes, vying for their attention, entranced by their cry. Competition among the girls was intense—as it was among their admirers. More than one pitched battle erupted over the favors of a hot corn girl, more than one deadly duel.

Edward Coleman pursued, and eventually conquered, a girl so fetching, so beautiful, that she had come to be known above all others as "the Pretty Hot Corn Girl."

Years earlier the city gnostics had undertaken to fill in the old freshwater Collect. Employing poor labor and public works, the brilliant ideapots ventured to have the surrounding hills shoveled down west of the pond near Broadway. After draining off the water, they planned to use the earth and bedrock from this excavation as a base foundation.

In addition a large open sewer was dug. Originating at Pearl Street, it ran through Centre Street to Canal and then followed an original streambed to the Hudson River on the west side. It was hoped this sewer would effectively keep dry the newly drained surrounding property, and thus appreciably add to the stock of usable acreage.

Local politicians congratulated themselves and anointed the project a success as multitudes of the rich clamored to build houses on the landfill, and for a time, everything was quite lovely. Hays had one single roundsman seeing to the security of the entire neighborhood, and at the southern end Paradise Square, on a balmy summer evening, was just that—*paradise*.

But then disaster struck. The underground springs that had once fed the Collect proved to be improperly capped, and the landfill had been mixed in large part with common garbage. The lovely new homes began to sink into the soft ground, springing doors and windows, and cracking façades. Water seeped into foundations and filled basements. Noxious vapors and fetid odors began to rise from below, cholera and yellow fever seeping upward.

All at once the rich moved out and the poor moved in, mostly penniless Irish immigrants of the lowest class and freed Negroes. The neighborhood came to be known as the Five Points, renowned as the worst slum in the world, according to what Dickens was saying, surpassing even London's fabled Seven Dials for its misery.

Tommy Coleman's brother, Edward Coleman, pictured himself a fierce, rough cove. His was the Forty Thieves, one of the first truly large criminal gangs to roam and terrorize New York's streets. Under his clever leadership, the gang established themselves in and around Rosanna Peers' greengrocery on Anthony Street, behind the Tombs, in the heart of the Five Points slum.

Outside Mrs. Peers' grocery, on racks and in bins, were displayed piles of decaying vegetables. These were touched by no one, especially the tomatoes, which were regarded as poison.

Inside, in the back room, congregated Coleman's ruffians: thugs, thieves, holdup artists, soaplocks, pickpockets, political sluggers, and no-gooders; one and all, at an instant, armed and ready to follow their leader's command, to rise and roam, primed to terrorize the local streets, especially after indulging in the fiery liquor served up by Mrs. Peers at a price unequaled by the nearby, more established drinking emporiums, saloons, groggeries, and assorted buckets of blood.

To give him his due, vicious and intense, Edward Coleman's acknowledged talent was indeed to lead and organize this hoary crew of cutthroats. In a city chockablock with rapscallions and street toughs, his was the first gang with designated leadership and disciplined members. In a weak moment, Old Hays might even have admitted to guarded admiration for the man's skills. After all, under Coleman's tutelage, his gang's membership in general substantiated over time a more honorable lot than the average jaded politico or two-shilling heeler walking the city's ward streets.

But as pretty as the Pretty Hot Corn Girl was, marriage to a man the likes of Tommy's brother proved to be too great a hurdle for her to overcome. Three weeks after the ceremony at Our Lady of Contrition, in a fit of alcohol-fueled rage, Edward Coleman murdered his wife, and for this senseless act was sentenced to pay the big price.

Eager not only to witness the dramatic end of the Forty Thieves gangleader, but also to view the new Tombs penal facility for the first time, so many city dignitaries and men-about-town came out to attend the event, it took the condemned man more than twenty minutes to shake all the hands extended him by well-wishers.

Finally, he took his place beneath the gibbet and the hemp necklace was looped around his neck, the counterweight poised in position.

Outside the prison walls hordes of his base underlings, including his adoring fourteen-year-old brother Tommy, not admitted due to warden's orders for fear of disruption or worse (jailbreak), cheered and shouted his name.

At a signal the weight dropped, the scientific intent being that the condemned would be jerked by the neck into the air, what had come to be known as "the jerk to Jesus," there to dangle unto death.

But on this morning, in front of Old Hays' eyes, the rope snapped with a frightening twang.

Loud voices rose from the crowd, "Will of God! Will of God!" as Edward Coleman, smiling broadly, stood stock-still, unfazed. The frayed rope still looped about his neck, he winked at Hays.

Vocal supporters gruffly began to shout, "The Almighty has intervened!" demanding that he be spared.

Refusing to hear anything of it, Monmouth Hart, warden of the Tombs and one of the most ardent admirers and customers of the murdered Pretty Hot Corn Girl, interceded, and with Hays standing at the gibbet edge watching, calmly instructed the hangman to restring the murderer and try again.

This time all went as planned to hip-hip-hoorays and loud hoorahs from the solid citizenry in attendance, Edward Coleman's body swinging from the crossbeam in front of Old Hays for a full fifteen minutes before Coroner Archer came forth and gave the sign for it to be cut down.

❧ 19 ❧

The Sister of the
Pretty Hot Corn Girl

When Tommy Coleman married the Sister of the Pretty Hot
Corn Girl, over a thousand members of the Five Points gangs
attended the wedding, and there was much shouting and loud
singing among these roughs, toughs, and bruisers of her anthem in
chorus with the laughing, drunken Irish hordes tramping through
the streets.

TOMMY COLEMAN had run into his future wife, the sister of his dead
brother's murdered wife, one night after not seeing her since his
brother's hanging. She came in off the street into Murderers' Mansion, One-Lung Charlie Mudd's bucket of blood on Little Water
Street.

The last time Tommy had seen her she was being escorted through
the Tombs' front gate by sheriff's deputies to stand near the gibbet,
close enough to touch the naked wood. She had come to Tommy's
brother's hanging for one reason, and one reason only: she wanted to
see the man who had murdered her sister pay the big price and swing
for what he had done.

That night everybody in the Mansion knew her, knew who she was, what had happened, her and her family's torment. The girls from the neighborhood admired her for her strength and wherewithal, and bravery, the way she wore her air of tragedy, and she was so pretty, just like her sister, they longed to be like her; and the men, in awe of her beauty, felt the stirrings of wanton lust if nothing else.

She was known by sight on the street and whispered about. Not only because she was the sister of the city's most famous hot corn girl, but also because she stood squarely on her own two feet, and had aligned herself with none other than Ruby Pearl, the rough-and-tumble leader of the Bowery Butcher Boys, and she, it was gossiped, if not said out loud (certainly not to her face), was in way over her head.

Not only because she was Irish Catholic and Ruby Pearl Protestant, him a prideful, east-of-Bowery, native true-blue American, her a potato-eating Irish lass from "the P'ernts," but also because she was only sixteen and he a hardened eleven years her senior, and Protestants didn't come a-social-calling in that neighborhood from where she was from, especially right there in the heart of the Fourth Ward, and old Ruby Pearl, he could be a very bad fellow, if not the worst. Very rowdy he was, and tough on women of all ages, save maybe his own mother.

When she sashayed into Charlie Mudd's and Tommy glanced up, he had been cavorting there with his boyos, Tweeter Toohey, Pugsy O'Pugh, Boffo the Skinned Knuckle, and the rest of their lot. Her face flushed, full of rage, her dressed in gingham, her hot corn bucket slung over her shoulder like a weapon, her breath coming fast, he saw her, her excitement and anger transmitted to every patron imbibing in the Mansion, everyone laughing and singing and carrying on, and Tommy knew right there and then in his heart of hearts, this bleak mort was destined to be his bleak mort, none other.

Tommy Coleman did not deceive himself. He had no self-delusions what he was getting into. He had heard the talk. He knew to whom she belonged, and what her feelings had to be toward him personal, given her deceased sister and his executed brother. There had never been love lost between them, even when things were going good with their respective siblings. He didn't give a flying fig. He knew what he wanted, what he had to have. He knew no matter what had preceded, anything was possible in America.

So he sat there, biding his time at the knife-scarred table, having patience, waiting for something fateful to happen, biting his lip to blood as she stormed around Charlie Mudd's emporium so angered and full of herself, beautiful and barefoot, the strap of her cedar bucket crossing her bosom.

There was a commotion and into the Mansion stalked Ruby Pearl himself, surveying the drunks for her. What she'd been waiting for, judging from the look on her face. She marched across the room, stood in front of him, rage sparking off her, and you better believe every citizen in One-Lung Mudd's Mansion knew old Ruby, big as he was, strong as an ox, tough as a sheep shank, was in trouble.

Ruby Pearl was not known for an abundance of brains so he might not have known he was in dire straits yet, leastways that was the only way Tommy could ken it. Which, you have to figure, is why Butcher Pearl said so casually to her in front of all these citizens, "Why you make me follow you in here, you damn mort? Why you coming in here? Why you ain't out working still?"

"Am I in?" she shot back without fear. She had that God-given ability, young as she was, that enables a woman to put an edge in her voice that sets a man off.

Ought to have made Ruby Pearl be more aware, but not knowing the whims and subtleties of the female gender, having worked the whole of his life in slaughterhouses and market butcher stalls, Ruby Pearl only heard what he thought—affront and disrespect—and he hauled off to strike her.

Tommy was on his feet, crossing the sawdusted floor fast, coming to her defense.

Except the Sister of the Pretty Hot Corn Girl didn't need (or

want) any strong-arm protection offered up by the likes of Tommy
Coleman.

She despised Tommy Coleman.

She caught Ruby Pearl's big arm in midair, before he could strike
her, and she just sneered up at him like he was nothing, lower than a
worm, a mesomorph, holding him fiercely, digging her fingers into the
flesh and muscle and tendon in the seam of his thick wrist, the electric
ganglionic nerve, smelling on him the overpowering smell of dead
animals, her crazy smile, if you can call it that, a smile, God, could you
believe it? In his cell Tommy grinned to himself as he remembered
how beautiful she was!

Tommy was left to standing and staring. There was nothing for
him to do, just look on and grin, Ruby Pearl dispatched just like that.
Everything taken care of by this beautiful girl, neat as a pin.

Nevertheless, Tommy felt like he needed to make his presence
known, and then he was of a mind to have a word with old Ruby.
After all, he, Tommy, had got up and crossed the room this far, might
as well go all the way.

Butcher Boy Ruby Pearl, wobbled from beer and oysters, toughest
of the tough, roughest of the rough, whirled, rubbing his wrist where
his bleak mort had pinched him, or whatever she'd done, and turned
on Tommy, now focused in on this nemesis, glaring at him as a man
glares at another when it is understood between them that their manhood is at stake.

Ruby Pearl knew Tommy Coleman, knew him all too well, knew
how crazed and dangerous he was; loathed him. Loathed Tommy as
Tommy loathed him.

"Pearl," Tommy spoke.

"Step back, Coleman," Ruby countered, "before I punch your park-
ing railing through your face."

"Don't you know that's no way to treat a lady, boyo?"

"I ain't no b'hoyo of yours. Don't call me no b'hoyo, b'hoyo! I'm
Ruby Pearl, Bowery Butcher B'hoy. Mr. Pearl to the likes of you,

Coleman." And advancing on the Sister of the Pretty Hot Corn Girl, he growled mightily, "Go back to the street, you. Make money, and leave me to deal with the likes of this nickey. I don't want you to see what I'm gonna do to him."

"Mr. Ruby Pearl, you don't belong down here in this part of the city," Tommy Coleman said. "This ain't your neighborhood, this ain't your ward. I think you better go home, back to your Bowery ways. Before you can't, boyo."

"Meaning what?" Ruby Pearl was not a man to step down lightly. "I'm here to see my mort. On her invitation. This is a free nation if you know it or not, you little Irish runty pig."

Ruby was over six feet two inches tall and weighed more than two hundred and twenty pounds, with the torso of a side of beef. He grew up on the street. But sometimes the biggest and the strongest, the slyest and the most adept, cannot win. Looking around him, Ruby knew when he was put down and could not persevere. Even against a straw-weight lad a foot inferior, a hundred pounds lighter than he.

Tommy's gang, Tweeter, Pugsy, Boffo, a dozen others, their hands on their slungshots and daggers, surrounded him.

"You'll get yours, Coleman," Ruby growled, looking from one to the other. "I'll be back one day to dispatch you to hell, or I'll meet you on the streets and grind you into the paving stones then. You know that, don't you, wee one, when you don't got your life preservers around."

"I'm not scared, mate," Tommy told him.

"Neither am I," retorted he.

All in attendance at Mudd's Mansion that night, every single one, pressed forward one step to witness what was to transpire.

"One last thing, Mr. Pearl. From now on, stay away," Tommy warned, spitting on the floor between Ruby's feet for punctuation. "This here mort is not your mort no more."

"Oh! Oh! Oh!" Pearl said. "Now you're telling me stay away from what's mine."

"I don't like no man who hits no woman."

"No? Well, it ain't no secret I don't like you, Tommy b'hoyo. And I don't much like no Irish pig runt rat telling me what to do."

"Stay away, Ruby. Stay away if you don't want to be took out."

RUBY PEARL SWORE up and down the Bowery that vengeance would be his. He enlisted the other local native gangs to join his throng of Butcher Boys: the True-Blue Americans, the American Guard, every last stick and straw of the rest of the Bowery russers, making threat to march on Tommy Coleman's wedding, the festivities of which were to be held in Paradise Square, and fillet Tommy on the spot in front of his new bride, making her a widow.

Armed guards, all emanating out of Eire, and all over six feet tall, were volunteered, primarily out of the ranks of the Plug Uglies and Kerryonians, to protect the nuptial celebration. These giants, in their reinforced stovepipe hats and hobnailed boots, were located strategically on the Five Points side streets and alleys and around the wrought iron fence that surrounded the square, as added deterrent, per Tommy's orders, a rusted but workable cannon placed on Cross Street facing east.

But all was quiet and the wedding went off without incident.

Still, a small, festively wrapped box came, delivered by a toothless old woman in a yellow head rag. In it was the carcass of a dead white piglet, and a note that read: IT'S NOT OVER YET, with no signature, no nothing, but Tommy Coleman needed no signature to know the low style of a Bowery Butcher Boy.

❦ 20 ❦

The Dark Deeds
of Ruby Pearl

After Tommy Coleman married the sister of his late brother's late wife, as it turned out, some citizens of the metropolis were not exactly in his corner. The doomed romance of his brother and his new wife's beloved sister hung over many. Her parents were desperate for fear that the terrible scenario would be played out again, and before the marriage, in their most intimate moments, even she, the Sister of the Pretty Hot Corn Girl, said to him that she was repelled at the same time as attracted.

Now people were saying that she was even prettier than her sister, prettier than the Pretty Hot Corn Girl. Her head could be turned. She was not above that.

Many gossips said Ruby Pearl had put out the word right after the romance began: Any Bowery Boy or True-Blue American found buying an ear of corn from the Sister of the Pretty Hot Corn Girl would find himself answering to the Butcher Boys.

After Tommy had won the hand of his future intended, it proved more than a victory for him, it was a statement, because not only had he vanquished his rival, Ruby Pearl, domo of the hated Bowery Butcher Boys, but also (maybe even more importantly) it was wider acknowledgment to all that a brash, clever rogue the likes of Tommy Coleman might live a life of leisure off the steaming ears sold out of that cedar bucket.

No one ever mistook Tommy Coleman for a gentleman. After marrying her he had no qualms about partaking in his new wife's success, evidently having desired the Sister of the Pretty Hot Corn Girl, whether he knew it or not, not only for love, not to mention what a bleak mort like her represented in his ward, but also for the lucre she'd bring in.

But not surprisingly, with all the warnings and dire onus, the gay blades, the biggest contributors to her business, stayed away in droves, and the Sister of the Pretty Hot Corn Girl found her income shrinking.

Like his brother before him, Tommy Coleman was not good in taking disappointment, especially disappointment of the economic kind. Scarcely eight weeks into the marriage, when she came home with less than five shillings, Tommy became volatile. Day after day, her income had failed to measure up to his expectations. By now, at the end of two months, he was able to endure no more. She had been making sixteen, eighteen dollars a week, now she made only five. Since they were married she handed all her money over to her new husband, but Tommy did not like only five shillings, and they were squabbling, shades all over again of her murdered sister and his hanged brother.

"Can't you make money on your own?" the Sister of the Pretty Hot Corn Girl shouted back at him following Tommy's rage and rampage against her. "Give me a break? Why don't you use your gang? Do you always need to depend on me?"

"You're right," Tommy admitted reluctantly. "I have the boyos and they'll make plenty of conscript for me when I give the say-so."

"So there you have it," the Sister of the Pretty Hot Corn Girl said gaily to her husband, and kissed him.

"The only catch is, they're not you. It speaks well of a bloke to be supported by his woman."

"I'm going to give up peddling corn on the street for a while,

Tommy," she said. "I'm pregnant," truly heartfelt, touching even him who was not so touchable. "I'm tired. Maybe I need to rest before the baby comes."

"Okay," Tommy relented as the notion of an heir intrigued him. "But just until the baby finishes suckling. We got a good thing going here. I'd hate to see you spoil it."

Tommy had wanted a son, but he swore, his eyes misting, that the newborn Daughter of the Sister of the Pretty Hot Corn Girl was the most beautiful baby in the Five Points, and maybe on the face of the earth.

"The spitting image of her mother!" he boasted.

For a number of months Tommy did not mind that his wife was not on the street plying her trade, raking in the money. His Forty Little Thieves were doing well for themselves, lying in wait, jacking drunks, stealing purses, smacking heads, leaving their victims naked and unconscious on the sidewalk for the roundsmen to discover and— if luck was with the mark—wake.

But then one crisp day there came a problem.

Two skull-bashers, older boyos left over from the reign of his brother, Crags Mahoney and Greedy Armond, who had run in the days with the original Forty Thieves, were strolling by the waterside, near the seawall at Castle Garden, when they came upon a newly arrived German immigrant. The man had twelve cents in his pocket. They clubbed him and tossed him in the river, where he promptly drowned, while Crags and Armond repaired back to the Green Turtle's to divvy up their plunder.

First they asked for a drink. The Turtle took a hose and squirted some swill down each of their gullets. Then Greedy Armond, living up to his name, announced that because he'd tossed the fat German into the river he deserved seven cents of the twelve.

"No!" Crags Mahoney retorted. It was he who had struck the blow that put the man out. If anyone deserved seven cents, it was him. Common sense said if the man weren't jacked out, Crags argued,

Greedy Armond never would have been able to lift him up to propel him over the seawall in the first place.

Such a statement infuriated Greedy Armond. With deep conviction he took hold of Crags' nose in his teeth. Lest his nose be bit off, Crags pulled a knife and slid it between Greedy Armond's ribs. Unfortunately for Crags, the knife between the ribs barely slowed Greedy Armond, although he did let go of Crags' poor nose, but sorry to say, the alcohol-swollen fleshy bulb of it was still clenched in the vise of Armond's brown teeth.

For the next half hour the two of them rolled around the barroom floor, looking for advantage. Eventually Greedy Armond got hold of the knife and thrust it in Crags' throat.

Crags collapsed on the floor, weak from loss of blood. Seeing him helpless there, Greedy Armond promptly stomped him to death with his heavy hobnailed boots.

Tommy Coleman and all the Forty Little Thieves present that evening at the Green Turtle's, of which there were many, stood in abject silence.

After that Greedy Armond made good his escape, leaving poor Crags lying dead on the floor with his head caved in.

The timing of these two rogues couldn't have been worse. Only a few weeks before, the body of Mary Rogers had been discovered floating in the Hudson, and from Jersey came word that Fourth Ward gangsters might have been at work in the woods nearby.

For rowdies it was not a good time to call attention to oneself.

When it was learned that Five Points gangs were prime suspects, Sergeant McArdel of the Night Watch with five leatherheads came around the neighborhood to Rosanna Peers' greengrocery and One-Lung Charlie Mudd's Murderers' Mansion, asking for alibis. Old Hays came poking around the Green Turtle's again, for the second time questioning Tommy.

No one could ever connect any of the Forty Little Thieves strong enough to the killing of Mary Rogers to make indictment. Still,

Tommy's income took a dramatic plunge, seriously wounded by his gang's persecution, the inevitable result of such social and political heat.

Tommy flatly told his wife it was time for her to hit the city byways again. Always thinking and considering, he had his own ideas for her to improve sales from what they had been at their best. Not only would she walk the streets of the Broadway by City Hall Park peddling her wares, but their little daughter, the beautiful blue-eyed two-year-old Daughter of the Sister of the Pretty Hot Corn Girl, dressed identically to her mother, carrying her own little cedar bucket, would also toddle the streets. Their sweet voices in tandem a sweet song of jingling coins:

> *Corn! Hot corn!*
> *Git your lily white hot corn!*

> *All ye that's got money,*
> *Poor we that's got none,*
> *Come buy our lily white hot corn*
> *And let poor us'n git home!*

What realistically might the expected income from such a setup be? The righteous man dare not hope, confabulated an ecstatic Tommy, but even a conservative soul might in these hard times speculate twenty a week minimum.

So here was the motive, later to be underscored by a staunch prosecuting attorney in the Essex Street police court, and eventually pondered by a jury of Tommy's peers, because less than a month after they had returned to the city's best thoroughfares to peddle their golden wares, the Sister of the Pretty Hot Corn Girl, like her doomed sister before her, and even more tragically, her beautiful darling, the little innocent Daughter of the Sister of the Pretty Hot Corn Girl, were found in the back of Cow Bay, lying in the mud, beaten to death.

Nearby was discovered the body of the thick-necked, redheaded native American butcher Ruby Pearl.

At Tommy's trial (Tommy would never forgive High Constable Jacob Hays for confronting him with the bodies of his brutally murdered wife and daughter in the Dead House), the wily prosecutor alleged that Pearl had once again become paramour to the comely Sister of the Pretty Hot Corn Girl. That Tommy had discovered their reentanglement, finding them in the back of the loathsome Cow Bay alley spooning and kissing there, and that he had grown vicious mad, lost all control, and had made short shrift of them both, and then, as afterthought, laid waste as well to his young daughter, the Daughter of the Sister of the Pretty Hot Corn Girl, learning or suspecting or having fallen prey to either poison notion or malicious rumor that the Daughter of the Sister of the Pretty Hot Corn girl was not the fruit of his loins at all, but the child of Pearl.

Tommy denied all this in court.

"Lies!" his defending lawyer, young Hummel of Centre Street, pronounced in his high-pitched Bavarian immigrant's mutilation of the English language. "Scurrilous lies!"

Tommy testified in his own defense. "Now this is what happened that fateful night. Nothing more, nothing less. My wife and daughter was out working, but they was late and I grew worried. I went out looking for 'em and come acrost that native rat, Ruby Pearl, in the back of Cow Bay alley, my wife dead at his feet, my daughter tossed off in the corner, like a rag waiting for the picker."

Tommy's eyes gleamed in what purported to be memory. He went on with his blithe recollection: "The redheaded bastard was standing over them he was, they no longer of this eart'. I challenged him. I said, 'Whatsamatta, boyo? Why you do this?' He says, I swear, 'Whaddya care? I did it. What you gonna do about it?' Right there and then I took him out, and mark me if I don't feel good about it."

Now, ignoring his lawyer, rising to face Ruby's supporters, who were in attendance that afternoon at the proceedings, challenging, shouting, "You hear me you low-life butcher apprentices!" Tommy's gaze flitting back across the curiosity seekers, to the box, swiveling back to catch the black-robed judge, looking him square in the eye, the jury, "Now which one among you would not do the same?"

But unfortunately for Tommy, his twelve peers did not buy his story. With High Constable Jacob Hays looking steadily on from the gallery, he was condemned to be hanged, and remanded to the Tombs to meet his fate forthwith.

🌸 21 🌸

During His Time
in the Tombs

D uring his time in the Tombs, John Colt never suffered. Rarely
did he seem rattled, bothered, or unsure.

The Colt family never dreamt John would be found guilty of the
capital act of homicide, much less condemned. When he finally went
to trial in the winter of 1842, they hoped for a verdict of self-defense
or, at worst, manslaughter. Justice in the city had traditionally been
available to the wealthiest for a price. It was John's misfortune, however, to have committed what his lawyers called "this lamentable act"
in the midst of a reform movement.

Following the murder of Mary Rogers, citizens of exaggerated
morality and heightened conscience began to find their way to elevated positions of opinion and power in the public discourse. With
the death of Mary Rogers still unsolved and the more recent crime
against Samuel Adams, these reformers pitted themselves in opposi-
tion to those corrupt agents of the law who readily made themselves
available, according to the reformers, to be bought off by wealth, privilege, power, and/or sex, in the form of sin and evil.

Certain editors, particularly Horace Greeley at the *Daily Tribune*,
railed his fellow citizens to take a stance, to fight the good fight

against the evils of corruption, indiscriminate power, and entitled class.

Greeley, although against capital punishment (and the eating of animals), saw himself on an evangelical mission on behalf of virtue and decorum, and had publicly dedicated his print to the moral, social, and political well-being of the people.

At the rival *Herald*, James Gordon Bennett scoffed at what he termed "this posturing."

"Greeley is nothing more than a galvanized New England squash," Bennett charged.

Bennett's most important single journalistic precept was that a newspaper publisher should make a great deal of money. Before the trial, he unearthed and printed gleefully all kinds of purported dirt in regard to John Colt, including that he had been a Mississippi knife fighter, a gambler, and had once even seduced away the comely quadroon mistress of a riverboat captain, only to abandon the harlot after he had had his fill with her.

But sensing a change in the wind—and never failing to recognize an opportunity to sell a great many more newspapers—just before the trial was to begin, Bennett seamlessly changed direction, to take sides with the sainted souls.

HOW AS A SOCIETY CAN WE ALLOW A MAN LIKE JOHN COLT TO ENDURE?

wondered he in the *Herald*, utilizing its boldest black ink.

Seeing their chance and seizing it, even more self-appointed do-gooders, men of God, temperance kings, and self-styled preachers, now quickly enlisted in the crusade, making their own demands for equal rights and proper justice for all under the law, rich and poor alike.

John Colt became the symbol of whom these demagogues demanded example needed to be made. Not only had Colt murdered the tradesman Samuel Adams, but it was also now endlessly written in the public prints how he was living in sin and taking advantage of the innocent young woman Caroline Henshaw.

Still worse, the unmarried Miss Henshaw, it was now publicly revealed, was with child.

Bennett, with his knack for indignant superiority, led the community in calling for John Colt's blood in retribution for his moral denigration.

To fight back, the Colt family hired a team of lawyers to represent John's case at his trial in the Essex Street police court. Leader of the bank of three attorneys was Colt family cousin Dudley Selden, a former representative to the Democratic Congress in Washington. Second-in-command was John Morrill, earlier that year the successful defender of the "female physician" Ann Lohman, known better by her nom d'abortion, Madame Restell. Last but not least was transplanted activist New York attorney Robert Emmet, son of the fiery Irish rebel Thomas Emmet.

The three law hounds were rumored to have been retained with a onetime payment of two thousand dollars, and promised an additional eight thousand dollars in stock in Samuel Colt's new arms manufacturing company.

There was never a question that Colt had killed. He had admitted so graphically after his arrest in his very public confession published by Bennett in the *Herald*. But his legal team's allegation was that his response to Adams' aggression was one of self-defense, that he had been insulted, then attacked, and it was only when he was himself being choked and in danger of losing his life that he picked up the lethal instrument off his desk, in order to protect himself, and unfortunately, what the two-headed tool was was half hammer, half hatchet, and the result turned morbid before he even knew what it was he was doing.

Judge William Kent presided at the trial that promised much sensationalism. As conjectured in the public prints, controversy centered on the point of law was Colt's act murder or manslaughter?

Gossip on the street swirled about the feasibility of an insanity plea for the accused. Middle Colt brother James Colt fed a story to Bennett that insanity ran in the Colt family. He cited the case of their sister, confessing she had poisoned herself to death.

John himself, James contended, had several times become insane.

The trial began pretty much by rote. John was attracting so much vitriol and bad publicity his team of three defenders tried to have the press banned from the courtroom.

To no avail.

Judge Kent ruled that it would indeed have been strange in the vast and vibrant city of New York if such a murder had not precipitated such shock and outrage.

"But I have no doubt," declared he from the bench, "that this court will remain uninfluenced by contamination from without."

A number of witnesses were called to attest to the character of Samuel Adams, including his clergyman, who most earnestly told a parable to the court about how one Sunday the murdered printer was moved to tears by his sermon.

There was no talk of insanity.

Instead, Selden, Morrill, and Emmet followed a course for self-defense. Samuel Adams was a hothead, they alleged. If John Colt had been bent on murder, he would certainly have carried with him that day one of his brother's pistols, several of which he owned.

The prosecution made curious response. "How do we know Samuel Adams was not in fact killed by a pistol ball to the skull?" they questioned. "The doctors who examined the corpse may have been wrong in regard to the murder weapon."

This unusual foray by the prosecution at first mystified the defense.

Needing to parry the tactic, Selden called his cousin Samuel Colt to the stand. Colonel Colt approached, carrying two of his revolvers. The first was a large blue Paterson, the second a smaller pocket model.

A thick book, it appeared to be a leather-bound and embossed copy of *Barnaby Rudge,* was set up at several paces and Colonel Colt asked to shoot at the volume so that it might be ascertained what kind of holes the pistol balls would make.

He fired the larger gun. The noise of its discharge caused much shock in the gallery. But the bullet penetrated only nine pages, although dimpling twenty-four more. The second round, from the pocket pistol, made very little impression at all on the same book.

In the gallery, James Gordon Bennett jumped to his feet and stormed from the courtroom.

WHAT KIND OF DEMONSTRATION IS THIS?

he cried in a hysterical extra edition that hit the streets within hours that very afternoon. "What did this little bit of theater prove, if anything?"

The families of all three attorneys are heavy investors in Samuel Colt's armament business, and this sham performance is nothing more than a weak attempt at publicity for Mr. Colt's foundering business.

Not so, denied the defense, although not refuting they were being paid for their efforts, at least in part, with stock certificates in the Colt company.

Back and forth went the arguments in front of Judge Kent until a resolution was finally decided upon. Although the defense vigorously objected to this proposed solution as well, the judge ruled the body of Samuel Adams must be exhumed. The corpse should then be decapitated, and the head alone brought to court in order to fit the hatchet blade to the fatal wounds, once and for all making certain if the curious two-headed tool was indeed the murder weapon.

"However painful it might be," Judge Kent charged over the howled objections of Morrill and Emmet, "justice must be served, and the head produced."

The next day the coroner, Dr. Archer, sat calmly in court with the murder victim's head in his lap until he was called to the witness stand. On request, amidst barely restrained pandemonium, he held the severed head high and exhibited to the jury that the hatchet blade fitted the wounds perfectly, proving it was indeed the offending weapon.

John hid his eyes during this exhibition, but his fate was sealed. Throughout the course of the trial he had remained unrepentant and stoic. In his summation to the jury, the prosecutor, James Whiting, charged this was emblematic of his cold-bloodedness. In addition, Whiting made caustic reference to Colt's immoral relation with Caroline Henshaw, the fact that they were unmarried and expecting a child in little more than a month's time, a fact he knew would weigh heavily on the jurors' minds.

"God forbid I should say anything against her," spoke Whiting in his summation. "She is about to become a mother, and if there is anyone who would pray for this man, it is she."

The prosecutor here fixed John Colt with an unveiled eye. "She approached his bed, he threw her from him. She knew she was not his wife, and she dared not press it. But do not blame her, do not blame this slight girl, blame the one whose heart is such that he could seduce her, and keep her in abjection. Had she been his wife, he could have poured his sorrows in her ear; she would have clung by him; she would have gone with him to his prison; she would have accompanied him even to the gallows. But he chose not to marry her. Let this be a warning to women: Let them learn not to put their earthly and eternal happiness in the keeping of such a man as this."

Afterwards, Judge Kent delivered his final instructions to the jury. He told the twelve that since John Colt had already confessed to killing Samuel Adams, the task they had at hand was only to decide if he was guilty of manslaughter or guilty of cold-blooded murder.

"John Colt's gay air," he said, "his careless air, his coolness, the firm manner in which he walks the precipice, this must be judged exclusively to determine if it is sufficient to bring him in guilty of murder."

After ten hours of deliberation, the jury returned their verdict at four o'clock on a Sunday morning, the second week of February 1842.

The decision: John C. Colt, guilty of murder.

Even after the devastating conviction the Colt family did not lose heart. They appealed. Paraded in were hordes of prominent sycophants and accomplished citizens, called upon by the family to lend voice in support of the terrible circumstance. Publisher G. P. Putnam, two of the four Harper brothers, James Fenimore Cooper, who had only recently published to great acclaim *The Last of the Mohicans,* former actor and lyricist John Howard Payne (no relation to Mary Rogers' once betrothed, Daniel Payne, the suicide), the eminent Washington Irving, city poet laureate Fitz-Greene Halleck, and *Knickerbocker Magazine* editor Lewis Gaylord Clark, to name but a few.

Even the eminent Charles Dickens was enlisted from overseas to write a letter in support, which he did forthwith, anointing the murder "The Tragedy."

Eventually Governor William Seward himself traveled down from Albany to the Tombs to personally visit with the condemned and the Colt family, positioning himself within the green velvet shrouds of John's death row cell, speaking in whispers with the three Colts, Samuel, James, and John.

But in the end, after the state supreme court denied the final appeal, the governor could only apologize, wishing God's speed to the youngest of "the formidable Colt brothers," as he called them, because even by him, His Excellency Governor William Henry Seward of the great Empire State of New York, regrettably, nothing more could be done. The court's sentence of death was to be enacted at 5 p.m. on November 18, 1842.

🐚 22 🐚

The Ponce

While Tommy Coleman watched from his cell, the harelipped keeper keys the entry door, permitting a colored waiter, wheeling a silver cart, to pass into the corridor. The waiter stops in front of John Colt's cell and calls through the curtain, "Suh, your luncheon is arrived," waiting dutifully to be acknowledged and summoned inside, Colt having just returned from his period of exercise in the yard.

The guard lifts a couple of the silver covers, gives the food underneath the once-over.

He winks at Tommy. "Smells good enough to eat," he grunts, and laughs, pleased with his wit.

A man, hefty, cross-eyed, with bushy auburn muttonchops, materializes in front of Colt's cell.

"My time," he announces to nobody in particular, then shouts, "Dillback, you going to let me in?"

"Not now," Colt's manservant replies from within. "Find it in yourself, sir, to return after lunch."

"After lunch?"

"After Mr. Colt eats."

For a brief moment, the hefty, cross-eyed man stands silent. But then he shrugs and backs off to Tommy Coleman's cell.

"Won't you be having your meals sent in from Delmonico's eating emporium, Master Coleman?" he quips, a hard gleam in his crossed eyes.

"What makes you think I give a fig what a ponce does?"

"Let me introduce myself, young man. I'm Bennett, editor of the *Herald*. Besides making specialty of the crime story, I pride myself on a keen nose for human interest. So said, do you, Tommy Coleman, have anything to say for yourself, humanwise?"

Tommy spits on the floor through the bars. The sputum splatters Bennett's black leather shoes.

"Just tell your fellow citizens how it feels, Tommy," Bennett persists, unfazed by the expectorant. "Don't hold back, laddie."

"Hold back what?"

"Killed your wife, killed your daughter, didn't we?"

Tommy merely glowers, does not answer.

Bennett has his notebook out. He steps forward. "Who represents you?"

"Represents me?"

"Your black box. Your lawyer."

"What do you care?"

"Don't be so downhearted," Bennett scolds. "You can't give up now. Seduce me; get me interested in your case, Tommy, the reading public. I may very well come to your defense, tell your story for you. If there's something in it for me. My news rag, that is."

"What could be in it for you?"

"Sales. Circulation. Think about it, man."

"Think about what?"

"I'm telling you. Your story."

"My story?"

"How you were taken up by society, taken advantage of, a poor Irish 'yout'' from 'the P'ernts.' Ordinarily, no one gives a damn about a rapscallion like you. I don't have to tell you that, young man. But I wield the power to change everything. That's what they mean by power of the press. And that's what's meant by human interest. In human interest is the power to change the world." He glances over at Colt. "It's the great equalizer. More powerful than Sam Colt's revolver. Everything can change."

Tommy looks across the corridor at Colt too. "How?"

"I'm telling you. Don't you listen? The power of the press. How many times do I have to say it? The written word. You can only imagine. Do you read?"

Tommy is distracted. In Colt's cell, Dillback is helping his master into a burnt umber lounging jacket and deerskin slippers.

"Listen, man, you've got to excuse me, I have an appointment to interview Mr. Colt there. Ah, the condemned, what sadness he brings. Over there he sits to his meal. It's his time now."

"They say I murdered my wife," Tommy halfway ventures, somehow nervous at the prospect of being abandoned. "I ask you, why would I murder my wife?"

Tommy sees Bennett is distracted himself now. "Yes, isn't that the way of it?"

"You want me to confess?"

"Not right now, young man. Later."

Bennett recrosses to Colt's cell, but as he does, Colt's servant draws the curtain closed in Bennett's face, announcing luncheon served, and Master John not to be disturbed.

Throughout the day and every day, with the fateful date of execution so quickly approaching, long lines of journalists and gazetteers have waited their turn for audience with the condemned.

Bennett turns back slowly from John Colt's cell to stand once again in front of Tommy Coleman, shrugs, and says, "So, did you do the deed of which you are accused, Tommy-b'hoyo?"

Meanwhile, cross corridor, behind the privacy of the curtain, Tommy can hear the Negro waiter proffering entrée to Colt.

Tommy's voice rises, indignant, in response to Bennett's question. "No, I didn't do what I am accused. I loved my wife, I tell ya."

In each cell, on each tier, heads turn, strain to hear, strain to see.

"They say I murdered my poor little daughter." Tommy's voice, resounding down the cell block, assumes a higher timbre as he continues. "Why would I murder my poor little daughter? I loved her. I'll tell you who I did murder, if you want to know. I murdered the native blackheart who did murder my wife and child. That butcher Ruby Pearl. When I came upon them he was standing over their poor dead bodies with a bloody cudgel. What was I suppose to do? I struck him down! By God, you're right about that. I struck him down. I smote the bastard where he stood, and for that I'm not afraid to die. Let them take me out!"

"Silence!" the voice of Old Hays cuts through the corridor. "Remember, we practice the silence system here."

Tommy looks from Bennett, to Hays, standing in his office door, constable's staff in hand, to Colt's cell.

Bennett glances over to see if the condemned has finished with his luncheon. He apparently has not. The curtains remain drawn. Once more Bennett ambles over, stands outside the cell, calls Colt's name.

"I'm afraid you'll have to wait a moment more, sir." Dillback sticks his pale face through the curtain. "Master John is just having his aperitif."

"Aperitif, that's good." Bennett smiles cordially at the manservant, does not insist.

Tommy watches as Bennett returns again to his cell.

"Tsk! Tsk! Tsk!" Bennett sidles close to the bars, peers through where Tommy stands on his cot looking out the small raised barred window at the courtyard, at the scaffold reflecting in the thin, cool sunlight. Bennett speaks through the bars in a soft voice. "Don't despair, Tommy. I'm here to help. Lend voice to your anguish. It's my duty as a man of the press, a newspaperman of conscience. I'm an editor on public duty. All my reporting is dedicated to serving the legitimate interests of the people. My readers are entitled to know every last fact and conjecture connected with your case, and only I can provide them."

Without turning to look at him, Tommy makes a noise that isn't particularly pleasant or even human.

Across the way, the curtains are finally thrown open. Bennett turns. Master Colt and his servant's eyes rise in unison, meeting Bennett's before looking away.

"Don't worry, Tommy," Bennett says, peering back cross-eyed into his cell. "I won't let you escape God's green earth without your due. There's no justice in the world," he adds, speaking loud enough for all on the row to hear without strain, "and that's the truth."

Old Hays takes two or three steps down the corridor, cracks his staff on the stones, catches Bennett's eye before turning back to his office.

Bennett speaks more quietly now, more discreetly. "Men like you, Tommy," he says, "you make your own justice."

"I expect nothing from nobody, and get it," Tommy answers.

"Remarkable how we just accept our lot in life, eh? I take my hat off to you, Tommy. I really do. You're the real hero. And here's the headline: Yours is the true saga of the underclass! Admirable! Admirable! The gangs of New York, the bleak morts. I am going to make a note of it right here in my notebook for future reference."

Tommy watches the pinch-faced fellow's lead scratch paper.

"Wish we had more time this go-round, Thomas," Bennett speaks cheerfully. "I really truly do," looking behind him at Colt. "But like I said, it's Master John's time which has come. You'll get your chance, eh? We all do. Remind me, when's your exact date?"

"I don't know. Not till next month, I think."

"Next month? Dear dark December. So soon. How time flies." Bennett laughs unpleasantly. "Still, plenty of time left for us to do our work. No?" He squints his turned eyes.

Excusing himself, Bennett steps once more to Colt's cell.

This time the curtains part fully, opening into the inner sanctum and remaining open for audience. The view Tommy has through this barred portal is, to his mind, as if attending Bowery theater, Colt's cell the illuminated stage.

Tommy imagines himself the audience, captive witness to all that transpires in front of him. He watches Bennett flash his broadest smile as the ponce rises to greet him. Bennett offers his hand, says something that passes for pleasantry.

Sadly for Tommy, because the drama is just beginning, his interest kindling, nearly as soon as Bennett departs, another scribbler takes his place in front of his cell, making demand for Tommy's attention, another in the long line of eager scribes awaiting their turn at Colt's cell, to have a last word with him before he passes to that better place.

This one is lean, very young, not much older than Tommy himself, with cropped beard and clever, clear eyes. He situates himself—to Tommy's annoyance—directly in his line of sight, says his name is "Whitman, Walter," used to write for the *Argus,* but now employed by the *Brooklyn Eagle*.

"Hoopla! Huzzah!" Tommy is not impressed.

"You interest me," this Whitman says, ignoring the mockery. "You're Tommy Coleman, aren't you, brother to Edward Coleman?"

Tommy grunts. He does not particularly care for the looks of this Jack Sprat, and would have been perfectly content to be left alone so he could get back to his watching the bit of performance drama unfolding in front of him across the way.

Colt and Bennett are busy spitting and cussing. Colt is having none of Bennett and won't answer his questions, which he blasts as impertinent.

"The newspapers!" Colt cries. "You are the true mischief-breeders. You are the unprincipled and remorseless murderers!"

"The man's a reptile," Whitman says.

Tommy looks at him. "Who?"

"Citizen Bennett. He makes his path with slime wherever he goes. He is a midnight ghoul, preying on rottenness and everything repulsive."

"Is that so?"

Tommy turns back, watches as Bennett, grabbing for his notebook, leaves in a fury. His final words to John C. Colt under his breath, unintelligible, decried in venom.

23

Armagnac

Later that evening, after his master's bath, Dillback draws the green velvet curtains back and helps his handsome charge into formal dinner wear.

Shortly, Mr. Colt's meal arrives on a silver cart, the same black man from Delmonico's pushing it, a white napkin draped over his arm. Silver serving dishes cradle sliced steak, cream of tartar dressing, and asparagus hollandaise.

While Colt eats, the door opens leading down from the Bridge of Sighs. Footsteps approach. Tombs warden Monmouth Hart hurries onto the cell block, head down, a packet of newspapers neatly folded under his arm.

He drops one on Old Hays' desk, continues on to stop in front of Colt's cell.

"I don't know your offense, but whatever you did to this gent, you got his dander up. This was sent over a few minutes ago from the *Herald* offices with a special note it be delivered directly to you, Mr. James Gordon Bennett's signature. Wants you to have first gander straight off the press. Story about you it is."

"I don't want to see it."

"Can't say that I blame you. Not particularly a flattering portrait. I'll leave it just the same."

The warden pushes the newspaper through the bars, where Dillback stoops to pick it up off the cold, damp floor.

In his cell Tommy Coleman is napping, the soft, steady hum of his peaceful snoring audible.

Colt is back with his dinner. He picks up the public print from where Dillback has left it on his dinner tray, cannot help it, peruses the headline, set in glaring 48-point type.

WHAT'S GOING ON HERE?

it asks, the byline beneath Bennett's.

> Let us take a stroll through Murderers' Row in the Tombs and glance in on Homicide Colt.
>
> Alas, Master John's not at home just now. He's departed his cell, performing his daily exercise, a stint about the yard.
>
> Finally he appears, booted and gloved. He may have his seal-skin coat on, or he may appear in a light autumn affair of exquisite cut and softest tint. In his hand is a gold-headed switch, which he carelessly twirls during his promenade.
>
> Upon his return he changes shoes, now he wears his feet encased in delicately worked slippers and his body swathed in an elegant dressing gown, faced with cherry silk. Certainly his prison garb is not of the common taupe and black variety.
>
> Lunch for Mr. Colt is not usual prison fare either, it is something other than bread and water. No, lunch is quail on toast, game pâté, roasted reed bird, fowl, vegetables, coffee and cognac, and, of course, following, might come a visit from the beautiful Miss Caroline Henshaw, his mistress, in whose wake he may retire to his patent extension chair, of his brother's invention, lolling there, puffing an aromatic Havana, pondering the indignities of Life.

Colt throws down the paper in disgust. The nerve of him! He knew Bennett could not be trusted. The man is shunned by all society. He shouts for the manservant Dillback, pushing away what is left of his dinner in a fury, his appetite gone. Following which angry exertion he sits quietly in the gloom.

All is silent, all is still. His mind is so beheated, so besotted with rage, it is not functioning clearly. Everything seems a fog.

In the courtyard a horse whinnies. The hammering on the gallows has begun anew despite the late hour and lengthening shadows. A priest is standing staring at the carpenters in the waning vestiges of oil light.

"They don't want no screwups like the way they did my brother."

The voice startles. Tommy Coleman speaks to John Colt as they both peer into the half-light. "They already had enough screwups. That's what's on the damn warden's mind."

"Silence! How many times do you have to be told?"

"Nobody gets out of life alive, boyo. You, me, nobody."

Colt can't help himself, he shudders. He carefully gets down from his perch on his cot, where he could peer out the high barred window, collapses into his reclining chair, and closes his eyes.

This has been a strenuous day for him. For most of the afternoon he has been either talking to newspaper hacks, eating, drinking, or smoking. Now, with the diffuse light of the lamps shining in the high window of his cell, he is feeling the fatigue.

He packs his pipe with Anderson cut tobacco and calls for his servant, loudly requesting reading material.

Dillback responds almost at once.

"The latest effort of Mr. Poe," the manservant announces. "I thought you might like it, sir. A second tale of ratiocination, following the magnificent 'Murders in the Rue Morgue.' And I know how much you admired that. This one you may find of even greater interest, sir. It's the Mary Rogers case, thinly disguised."

Colt sits up. "You can't be serious?"

"I am."

"Mary Rogers!" He scratches his face, coughs. "He mentioned he thought to work on something of the kind, but I gleaned it just a lark. What has he to say?"

"He claims he will unmask the killer. This is but the first installment of three."

"Let me see it! Where is the man anyway? Wasn't he supposed to be here already?"

"Mr. Poe is late. As you well know, Mr. Poe is often late, and cannot be trusted, among other things, to be on time. Especially if he's on one of his sprees."

Colt stared down at the magazine: *Snowden's Ladies' Companion.* He thumbs to the story, "The Mystery of Marie Rogêt," and reads and rereads nonstop for some forty-five minutes, all the while puffing away on his pipe in great fury, impervious to all interruption, until, quite late, a man is led down the corridor and admitted to his cell.

He is a rather elegantly attired gentleman, dark mustache, with a full expanse of forehead, but his apparel threadbare and darned, his overcoat a veritable Joseph robe of discreet reweavings and patches. He is slightly stooped in physique, not standing to his full height, as if life has taken its toll, pressing its heavy weight down on his narrow shoulders.

"Mr. Colt . . ." The man has a southern accent, quite charming in its way.

"Poe! How nice to see you again! How nice of you to come!"

"I told you before, sir, I would not, for the life of me, pass up the opportunity," Poe is saying. "I remain intrigued. To be beckoned, sir, by one in such distress, under such duress."

"Distress? Duress?" Colt laughs with pleasure. "You speak poetry, monsieur." He grins sharply. "You know, that's not how it is, sir, we are friends. Need I remind you, for men like us, as we both know, all is puzzle, all is enigma. I am a writer *comme vous.* Still I take pride that I am a fatalist. I hope full well that I can take anything the cosmos offers. After all, what is my death to me, but my life? You flatter me, Poe. You flatter," and Colt once more laughs at himself richly.

A bottle of spirits appears in the hands of the manservant, and a foil of powder, laudanum, from the fob pocket of Colt's smoking jacket.

Colt shows the foil, taking the bottle, holding it out for Poe to admire, a last word, "Armagnac," hanging in the still air across the expanse of cell block.

24

Anderson's Segar Shop

He knew not how or where he spent the night, but upon the light of day Edgar Poe awoke in a muddy alley below the Five Points, his tongue swollen, his body stiff and debilitated, a filthy wad of laudanum-soaked cotton wool hanging out of his ear.

Eventually he struggled to his feet, his soiled clothes wet and cold. He managed to stumble to the street, where he encountered two urchins, who, when asked the name of that alley in which he had been lying, replied, "Paradise."

By late afternoon he had found his way somehow to stand next to a statue of the eminent explorer and writer Sir Walter Raleigh, patron saint of the tobacco trade, outside John Anderson's segar shop on Broadway, the very shop where Mary Rogers had once worked.

Despite the cruel autumn weather, as darkness came on and the lamps were well lighted, the throng rushing past Anderson's door increased behind him on the sidewalks, two dense and continuous tides of population, one flowing uptown, one down.

Poe stood, his nose pressed to the glass, his bright eyes peering wistfully through the square panes at the display of twist and plug tobacco, his features obscured, a dark shadow cast across his face from the gas lamp.

At that moment, a carriage with the golden initials of John Jacob Astor on the crest pulled up opposite him at the kerb, and the city's laureate poet, Fitz-Greene Halleck, who worked as Astor's personal secretary, descended to the sidewalk and approached the shop.

Halleck stopped dead in his tracks, momentarily taken aback by the apparition looming in front of him, for that is what Poe looked, despairing and desolate, hovering in front of the shop: a ghost, a spectre.

"Great heavens, Poe!" Halleck exclaimed. "Is this you?"

Poe's eyes rolled wildly beneath his knit brows. He smiled ruefully, squinting at Halleck through red-rimmed orbs, much bloodshot and unfocused, and nodded that it was indeed he.

" 'Come to the bridal chamber, Death!' " intoned Poe in trembling voice. " 'Come to the mother's, when she feels for the first time her first-born's breath!' "

Halleck stood markedly unnerved, chilled by his own words directed back at him by this strange presence.

"Are you making light of me, Poe?" demanded Halleck. For it was from a verse Halleck himself had penned in regard to the murdered Mary Rogers from which Poe quoted.

Going into a spasm of coughing, Poe fished a filthy handkerchief from his trouser pocket and wiped his mouth. His chin fell upon his breast. "I have had a difficult time of it this night past," he mumbled. "And all this day I have walked several miles through the cold and rain, and, seeing a light here, thought that perhaps Mr. Anderson would let me warm up somewhat."

"Why of course, Poe. I'm sure. Come with me."

Holding tight to the suffering fellow's elbow, Halleck helped Poe inside.

"Here is the stove behind the tea boxes, almost red hot. Take off your coat and dry it by the warmth. What will you have, some of this port? You know Mr. Anderson surely. Mr. Anderson! A glass for Mr. Poe."

Poe looked helplessly to Anderson, standing openmouthed behind his display cabinet. "A feeling for which I have no name has taken possession of my soul, sir," Poe explained. "I know not what to do. Please excuse me."

Anderson jumped forward. "Poe! Heaven above, I didn't recognize you. What state you're in, man! Sit down. Sit down."

Poe allowed himself to be led by Halleck and Anderson to a bent-wood chair near the stove. The stove was one of the Franklin design, made of cast iron and set on half-inch-thick masonry tiles. The stove was positioned near the rear of the shop, behind the handsome oak and glass display cases, surrounded by a number of chairs and a rough table, with plenty of room for a group of talkative men to gather. Halleck and Anderson managed to sit Poe down where it was warm and he could dry himself and his clothes.

"That's all right, Poe. That's all right," Anderson said. Poe settled uneasily, Anderson doing his best to prop him up. "Here, some of this port will warm your inner humours," the proprietor said, patting Poe's back.

An uncontrolled shiver ran through Poe's body.

The wine, provided by Anderson for the pleasure of his customers, shimmered red as blood in a decanter of cut crystal. He poured out a goblet for Poe, another for Halleck, and one for himself, and the three bent their elbows in homage to the old port.

Poe drank his wine very quickly, without lip or smack, and as the warmth spread, he was simultaneously flushed with the dual feeling of both thankfulness and resentment for the attention and camaraderie the other men paid him.

Keeping a guarded lowness of tone, Halleck made attempt at soothing the dispirited wretch, inquiring of his writing, the progression of his editorial career in Philadelphia, the state of his wife's health, what had brought him to New York.

Poe responded monosyllabically.

"Are you hungry?" Anderson asked. "Here are some crackers, and here is some English pineapple cheese to go with them." He cut slices from a great orange wedge and laid the crackers out on a platter in front of the poet.

Poe gobbled a half dozen in rapid course. His mouth still full, he took a gulp of the sweet wine, before beginning quietly to again mumble lines of verse, more to himself than the others. His voice, tremulous and unsteady at first, became increasingly rich and melodious, indeed assuming the attributes of an actor commanding the stage. The port had taken hold, and his tone was now a more civil one, his charming accent bespeaking America's southern reaches, soft, and less marred by the difficulties of drink, drugs, and the harrowing night previous.

And so he went on in the singsong that so transfixed his listeners:

"The loveliness of loving well.
When falsehood was a ten-fold crime
I held no doubt—I knew no fear
Of peril in my wild career.

Uncheck'd by sarcasm.
Uncheck'd by scorn.
So plighted in my early youth
What was there left me now? despair—
A kingdom for a broken—heart."

Upon completion, Poe looked sheepishly toward Halleck.

Halleck nodded, moving his great head but an inch, down and up.

The front door opened. The effete editor and poet Lewis Gaylord Clark of the *Knickerbocker* entered, quietly took off his coat, and sat by the fire, silently mouthing his hellos so as not to disturb.

"You've committed my poem to memory!" Halleck was saying. "My God, Poe, why? My concern with the why and wherefore of your memorization of this, my homage to the memory of our Mary, one and all, prevents me from being more obstreperous. I didn't know you to suddenly be so taken up by my poesy."

"I commit to memory much I judge of worth."

"Is that so? I'm much touched and honored," Halleck smiled. "And surprised. How things have changed. As I remember last time I fell under your scrutiny, sir, you condemned me. Your appraisal of my poems after the reissuing of 'Alnwick Castle' was to deem them 'unintelligible and banal,' if my recollection is kerrect."

"We all make our mistakes, Halleck," Poe winked grotesquely, "and we all in our turn have been driven to preserve our reputations and write of our Mary, too. Isn't that right, Clark?"

Poe glanced at the newly arrived gentleman while downing another long draught from his port glass, which Anderson had seen fit to refill.

Poe returned his gaze to his benefactor. "Would it alarm you, Halleck, if I were to state that I am not, in fact, so impressed with your work? Does it not strike you odd, old fellow, especially now with our friend Clark joining us in the room, how many of we writers who frequent this welcoming shop of Anderson's have seen fit to write of our dear departed Mary?" He glanced at Clark contemptuously. "Some better than others, sir."

A poem of Clark's in tribute to she whom he called "the Beautiful Segar Girl," had appeared on the third interior page of the *Commercial Advertiser* a few weeks after the discovery of the murdered girl's body.

Poe had condemned Clark many times over while editor at Billy Burton's. Nevertheless, without further send-up, and without allowing Clark time to react, Poe now began to recite his turgid homage:

> *"She moved amid the bland perfume*
> *That breathes of heaven's balmiest isle;*
> *Her eyes had starlight's azure gloom*
> *And a glimpse of heaven—her smile!*

> *Who that has loitered up Broadway*
> *But marked her mid the evening light*
> *(Encircled by the young and gay)*
> *With the face that said her soul was right!"*

Here, the shop's proprietor, Anderson, was seen to wipe a tear from his eye. "She was just so," he blurted. "I truly never met a girl with soul so right and beautiful as Mary. You have put it perfectly, Clark."

The others remained silent. It was well mentioned among the gossips that Anderson had been very much in love with Mary. In some circles there had even been talk that he was in some way implicated in her demise. "My Mary! My poor Mary!" he now cried, looking around, unable to contain himself as tears welled. "I miss her so. You know I cannot even bring myself to hire another in her place."

At that moment, saving the man further embarrassment from this sentimental outpouring, four noisy and animated gentleman entered the shop, caught up in their own personal conversation in regard to a business transaction just completed; they were all four well known to the lot: the Harper brothers—James, John, Fletcher, and Joseph—from the printing and publishing house of the same name.

These gentlemen were much aflutter, having just secured the deeds to a number of buildings that would extend their firm from Cliff Street down John as far as Pearl, making theirs the largest publisher in the land and the largest employer in the city.

James Harper, the eldest brother, with his eye unapologetically on the mayoralty, was an acquaintance of the troubled Poe, if not much of an admirer. He greeted him sourly, going over to the stove where the poet was convalescing to engage him in conversation, asking what he was doing in New York.

Poe answered quietly he was in the city to see John Colt.

Joseph Harper, the youngest brother, much full of himself and also not much a fanatic of Poe or his reputation, snorted. "Word is the Colt family has engaged you for some quick-form portrait of gallant John in hopes of saving his pitiable self from the gallows. Is there any truth to that talk?"

Poe looked at him through half-closed eyes. "There are some secrets, sir, which do not permit themselves to be told," he said.

"Quite so. Quite so," James Harper interrupted. "But set the record straight, Poe. This is the story in circulation. You look all to hell, Poe. Tell us, what has befallen you now?"

All of the Harper brothers had by now poured themselves ample tumblers of port and retired to the segar case.

"Now and then," Poe said, looking back from Joseph Harper to James, "the conscience of man takes up a burden so heavy in horror that it can be thrown down only into the grave. Thus, the essence of all crime is divulged. Alas! . . . We all believe what we will, eh, Mr. Harper?"

"I've seen the first installment of your 'Marie Rogêt' story in *Snowden's*," interrupted Halleck, looking over from the segar case, where he had risen to choose a rhum-soaked crook. "To a man, we all stand in admiration of your work, Poe. You've brought back the wondrous Dupin from the 'Rue Morgue' murders. Bravo!"

"There is certain talk that you will unmask the murderer of Mary Rogers in your final chapters," Joseph Harper said. "Is it true, Poe?"

Anderson almost dropped the decanter. "The murderer unmasked!" he exclaimed. "Who?"

All grew very quiet as they awaited Poe's answer. The Rogers murderer still remained very much unknown, High Constable Hays and the Watch concentrating as their chief suspects first on any number of gangs of ruffians, then on a long list of spurned lovers, all to little gain.

Poe pursed his lips. "My enterprise is in three installments," he pronounced, his dramatic intonation precise, although considerably fueled by port and the undivided attention of the gathered. "With the third, gentlemen, all shall be known."

James Harper, in his surliness, would not let it sit, would not allow Poe his moment, even if drunk. "What will be known, Poe? Go on! What have you to tell us, sir? Do you have knowledge, something to which none of the rest of us is privy?"

Poe stared at Harper.

"How might you have come to that, sir? Perhaps you have discovered that Mary was in love with another. Some cad. A monster." Harper persisted. "Perhaps you have discovered who the monster is.

Surely she was in love with someone, or do you think she was still only enamored by you, sir?"

Poe blanched, but before he had a chance to answer or even digest what had been said, the door flew open and a howl of wind and pelt of driven rain permeated the sealed environment. A troika of newsmen, bundled against the weather, Greeley of the *Trib,* Bennett from the *Herald,* and the dandy Whitman of the *Eagle,* bustled inside, brushing beads of moisture from their oilcloth coats.

Poe looked up as the three made their immediate way toward the warmth.

"Gentlemen," Bennett croaked, reaching for the port, "we bring astonishing tidings in the Mary Rogers case. Are you aware, my friends, Mrs. Frederika Loss, the innkeeper over at the Elysian Fields, was shot late last night. We three have just come from across the river. Even as we speak she lies on her deathbed, talking of nothing else save Mary, and her own place in the poor girl's death."

"What you say?" Anderson was nearly beside himself.

"Shot, quite by accident in the knee, by one of her sons," Greeley told him, "but the life is running out of her."

He had taken off his coat and hung it on a hook, and was lighting a small black segar. "The middle boy, Ossian, one of the two who found the collection of clothes and possessions near the Sybil Cave. In her final delirium Mrs. Loss is saying that the ghost of Mary Rogers is hovering over her bed and urging her to tell the truth."

Poe stared at him through dark, bloodshot, rapidly blinking eyes.

"And what truth is it that Mrs. Loss would like us to believe on her deathbed?" inquired James Harper, glancing purposefully at Poe.

"That the girl was at her inn in the company of a young physician who undertook to procure for her a premature delivery," said Whitman. "According to Mrs. Loss and her ravings, Mary Cecilia Rogers died during the execution of the act."

The color drained out of Poe's face as he half rose from his chair. "Lord help her," he murmured.

He groped behind him for his seat and fell back heavily into it. Suddenly he was quite sober.

"Are you all right, Poe?" Halleck reached for him.

Poe barely heard.

He left the confines of the little shop, so rich in aroma and warmth, stumbling forward, sick, sick to his heart.

❦ 25 ❦

The Night Soil Cart

It has stopped raining. In the cool night air, Poe staggers, catches himself.

His senses have left him. Voices merge in his ears in one dreamy indeterminate hum.

He moves slowly, deliberately, continues north from Anderson's on Broadway, past Leonard.

It is another city here, on this broad stretch of the Broadway. Here is where the fancy prance. Every night they can be seen, the privileged citizenry of the great metropolis in continuous tide of population, taking their evening stroll, their noses in the air, top-hatted gentlemen, coats and pantaloons of black and brown, the architects and attorneys, the bankers and mercantilists, the stockjobbers and businessmen, men of leisure, and men actively engaged in affairs of their own. Even at late hours, by the time the lamps are well lit, they tarry beneath the cherry trees that line the promenade.

The rays of the gas lamps, feeble at first in their struggle with the dying day, have at length gained their ascendancy, throwing their fitful and garish luster over astonishingly lovely ladies in crimson silk dresses, black satin hats, green velvet ribbons, demure peach-colored veils. It seems to Poe every eye falls on him. But it is his narcissism.

He despises them. Hates them, one and all. He hates what he perceives as their disdain. Hates them for what they have. Hates them for what he has not. But above all else Poe hates himself.

Mary Rogers died during an abortion.

That is what they said.

Oh, Mary, have you died so?

On Canal Street he stumbles on the kerb. He rights himself, heading left toward the riverfront, where he hopes to find a cheap rooming house, a place to rest his heavy head for the night. From where he does not know a five-dollar gold piece has miraculously appeared in the pocket of his greatcoat. He does not remember asking Halleck for a shilling.

Had he asked him? He might have. The moment escapes him.

A night soil cart clatters on the cobblestones in front of him. The smell of the cart, the odor of human waste and open sewer, the great piles of horse offal and ashes, waist high, lining the sidewalks. He hears an oysterman shouting, offering his ware. A coal truck rumbles and rattles by. Pigs root in the gutter. They are the city's scavengers. A sow with one ear, an ugly brute, with scanty brown back like the lid of an old horsehair trunk, spotted with unwholesome black blotches, watches Poe over her peaked snout.

Mary. Mary. Mary.

Poe nearly stumbles into a man in a camlet coat carrying a lantern in one hand, a large staff in the other.

Poe mumbles, excuses himself, glares at the curious-looking fellow.

The man has stopped. He is studying Poe from beneath his bowler hat. He is an older gent, no longer spry on his feet, if the large staff he is carrying is any indication. Poe glares back at him through drooping eyes. There is something familiar about this fellow, his dwarfish legs, his large upper torso, his passive, intelligent face. Strange tufts of hair, near antennae, grow from his large ears. But who is he? Poe cannot remember. Cannot place him.

He staggers on, searching for his bed. "Mary," he murmurs. "My darling Mary." A thought suddenly entering his fevered brain: *What sweet rest must lie in the grave!*

❧ 26 ❧

Snowden's Ladies' Companion

Coming in off the prison yard that dark and dreary night, pausing only momentarily to look in at the Bummers' Cell, the high constable returns to his desk.

Outside, the night is moonless, unseasonably cold and penetrating, especially for this early in November, the iced wind ripping off the North River and through the body with no regard for a constable's camlet coat. The harsh weather is taking its toll on Old Hays.

At his desk, by the stoked coal stove, it is warm.

After shedding his outerwear, his constable's lantern, and staff, the high constable rubs his legs, then marches away in the direction of John Colt's cell, his clipped footfalls echoing off the floor stone.

The man on the street, his countenance, has stayed upon him.

Behind the grate, Colt's curtain is drawn. Hays calls, "John Colt?"

Dillback, the manservant, parts the green velvet. "Sir? Can I be of help?"

"I need a word with your ward."

"Mr. Colt is not available."

"He will make himself available to me," Hays tells him evenly.

"I'll see, sir."

The Englisher disappears. Hays can hear low voices before Dillback returns.

"If you will, sir, the good gentleman will be with you shortly. He is just dressing."

The curtains reclose, only to reopen a few seconds later to their fullest.

Colt is wearing the dressing jacket mentioned by Bennett in his *Herald* diatribe.

Hays admires the cherry red color of the facing. He runs seasoned eye over Colt. He deigns the man's complexion too smooth, his mustache too clipped, the trimmed muttonchops too refined, the nose too aquiline. There is no noticeable surface defect, no ridge, no bump, no crook. Everything is too perfect. The facial epidermis, to Hays' observation, does not bespeak confinement. John Colt's skin is not enough callow, but shines with a peculiar polished veneer of high gloss. Even the eyes are hooded, the cornea glazed. The detective cannot see in. All of which tells Hays this is a malefactor, one who takes himself and his malfeasance above society.

"The gentleman who visited you yesterday, the late night arrival?"

"Poe?"

"Poe? Is that his name?"

"It is." Colt's eyes narrow. "Why do you ask?"

"His appearance interests me. His military greatcoat. Does he always wear it?"

"He attended West Point at one time. He claims to keep the coat as reminder. He is Poe the editor and poet. A critic of outstanding reputation as well. Edgar Allan Poe? Come, High Constable, you must know of him."

"I know of him. 'The Murders in the Rue Morgue.' Quite remarkable." Hays smiles. "I was much taken by that fellow Dupin and the workings of his mind."

Colt smiles back. "I would think you would. The character is a shadow after all, modeled on a figure not unlike yourself no doubt.

You should have introduced yourself to Mr. Poe when he was here. Shame on you, High Constable Hays. It would have pleased him greatly to have his talents recognized. It is what we all who toil by the pen live for. To be recognized by our readers. You and he, in my estimation, would get along quite well. He is a gentleman, a man of fine character, although of late he has fallen on harder times, and it has caused some aberration in his personality."

"I'm sorry to hear that."

"He comes to add editorial eye to the work I have been committing to paper here."

"Spending your last days with your pen, are you, Mr. Colt?"

"That is what I do. I am a writer. The pen is my sword." Colt's eyes gleam.

"Indeed it is. Live by it, die by it. It is exactly what led you here, if I'm not mistaken, your writing, your sword, as it were."

Colt hesitates. "In a sense," he says.

Old Hays studies Colt coolly.

"I remind you, High Constable," Colt says, "the path down to hell is a facile one, but acting on the fierce moodiness of one's temper need not qualify as capital offense."

"The court of oyer and terminer saw it differently, sir, wouldn't you say?"

"Now that you mention it, yes, they did."

"So you are adept at writing, but Mr. Poe is more so. Is that how it is?"

"Perhaps. Yes, I would say so."

"Has he ever been in trouble with the law?"

Another slow smile bends up the corners of Colt's mouth. "Why would you ask that?"

"Something about the man. I just now ran into him on the street. His physiognomy is of some remark."

As Hays watches, Colt's countenance takes on a certain resolute shrewdness.

"It is interesting you say that," Colt ventures. "The man writes of horror and murder, foul deeds in foul places. Scarcely a tale passes off his pen that lacks a character being pecked at or bit, gnawed at or chewed. As a matter of fact, I have only right now read a new story of his based on the atrocity of the Mary Rogers murder case."

"Mary Rogers?" Hays is interested. "What has he to do with Mary Rogers?"

"More than you might think. I know Mr. Poe and Miss Rogers to have been quite close at one point." Colt turns, retreats a few feet back into his cell, where Hays can see him face his bookcase. He scans for a few seconds before finding what he is looking for. He plucks from the shelf a slim yellow magazine, the name *Snowden's Ladies' Companion* printed in brown ink on the cover.

With a grim expression set on his lean, handsome face, he returns to the front of the cell and hands the journal through the bars to the eminent detective.

"I refer you, sir," Homicide Colt says plaintively, "to page 13."

❧ 27 ❧

Murders
in the Rue Morgue

The name of the story is "The Mystery of Marie Rogêt." The high constable starts his reading of Poe's obeisance to the Mary Rogers murder at his desk, but the light in the Tombs' cell block is dim, and his rheumy eyes dimmer, even with magnifying spectacles and hand lens.

As far as Old Hays can make out, the story begins with Poe theorizing, something about an ideal series of events which runs parallel with a real series of events. His reference, cited as an epigraph, is quoted ostensibly from Novalis, the German, whoever Novalis may have been.

Two hours later the high constable is rudely awakened by one of the jailhouse cats jabbing a raptor claw into the fleshy end of his nose. He growls, swats the beast away, struggles unsteadily to his feet, immensely unhappy, and instead of continuing his reading there in the dark and chilly Tombs, decides to bring the magazine home with him for his daughter to read to him.

How life reverses itself!

How many times when she was a little girl did he rush home from the Bridewell to read to Olga before bed a chapter of her favorite, the novel *Charlotte Temple*?

And now here he is, in need of her to do the same for him. What humbling rewards fatherhood brings!

WHEN OLD HAYS, fatigued to the marrow of his bones, pushes slowly and heavily through the ground-floor door leading into the family kitchen, despite the late hour, he finds Olga still at the kitchen table awaiting him.

She looks up. Behind her, on the stove, the black iron kettle is on the fire, the water boiling. In the half-light of the kitchen, the gas lamps flickering, Olga's face, his precious daughter's face—as he gazes upon her—is the face of a handsome, alert woman with a strong inner light, not his silent fear, not some dry spinster, not an aging woman without hope of ever finding—what?—a suitable husband.

"Papa." She brightens with first sight of him.

He kisses her cheek, apologizes for the hour at which he has come home.

She waves off his apology. Balboa delivered earlier that evening her father's message that he would be late, and not to wait dinner for him. She was neither worried nor concerned, she assures him.

He sits heavily.

"I'm making hot water and lemon. Would you like some?"

"Are you feeling all right?"

"Of course I am."

He associates the concoction with illness and illness only. Jacob Hays could have his arm cut off with a dull saw and not blink, but when someone in his family takes ill, he becomes very nearly apoplectic. The only time he ever felt faint in his entire lifetime was when Olga at the age of nine badly cut her knee in the backyard with an ax. The only time he felt powerless was when he watched his four sons die in front of him, all in three days, all during the yellow fever epidemic of 1822, when he watched his wife succumb to congestion of the heart, how many years was it now?, only two, could it have been so recent, yet so long ago?

He mumbles something.

"What?"

"Would you like some?"

"Yes. Yes, I would."

He watches his daughter as she busies herself quartering a hard, dry Florida lemon. She manages a few drops of juice squeezed from one pale wedge, then another, into a flowered cup, drops in the stiff, pale rind, and fills the ochre and maroon cups with hot water.

Hays coughs, and she turns to him as she sets the cups and saucers on the black enameled wooden tray. The tray is hand-painted, depicting a sparkling waterfall in the Kaatskills. With a glance toward her father, Olga carries the tray from the stove to the table.

Hays bends, rummages through a battered leather satchel. "Olga, I need to ask a favor from you. John Colt has given me this copy of *Snowden's* magazine. It features a story of Edgar Poe, just published. Colt tells me Mr. Poe claims he has unraveled the Mary Rogers case once and for all."

Olga, now seated, picks up the magazine off the table.

"Are you aware of any of this?" Hays asks.

"As a matter of fact, I have heard something, Papa. When I went to pick up manuscripts at Harper's, there was some talk. But I've not read Poe's tale yet. It is certainly on my list. Especially now."

"My dear, can you fill me in a little on Mr. Poe? Certainly you have mentioned his name, and certainly we have read stories and poems of his together, but remind me, who is he exactly?"

"I don't know him personally, Papa. I know only of him. I have seen him at readings and lectures, and have encountered him once or twice at the offices of the Harper Brothers, although we have never spoken and there seems to have been a falling-out between him and James Harper. He is without question very ambitious. His parents are said to have been actors, and he has some of that highly dramatic air, the air of the stage. His life is one apparently tinged with tragic failure and unrequited genius. He has written many striking romantic poems addressed to vulnerable, doomed women."

He tells her about the hausfrau Frederika Loss dying in Hoboken from a bullet accidentally fired by her son, her raving of Mary dying during an abortion.

"Seeing this gentleman earlier this evening, taking gauge of his countenance, his demeanor, I have one of my trepidations," he says.

"Trepidations? Meaning what?"

"That Mr. Poe might be involved in something untoward."

"You mean involved with Mary Rogers beyond his endeavor in his written tale, I presume."

"As you say."

"How so, Papa?" she further inquires. He observes the glint in her eyes. "As lover or abortionist?" she persists.

"If Mary Rogers had merely died during an abortion, my fury would be one thing, Olga. But her body, brutalized as it was afterwards, makes my fury something else."

"Perhaps the individual who committed such atrocity acted in need to hide the deed of the premature delivery, and in some perverse manner save the poor girl's honor."

The keenness of his daughter's mind continually startles Hays, and pleases him. "It is possible," he says. "From the little I know of Mr. Poe, from the tone and aspect of the stories he chooses to tell, to his most distinctive physiognomy, all my experience tells me this is a troubled man, Olga. How that trouble manifests itself is my sworn duty as high constable of the city of New York to discover. Mary Rogers' honor or not."

"I shall not argue with you that Mr. Poe seems troubled," Olga concedes. "As I say, I don't know him personally, but my own instincts, everything I see and hear of him, tells of a man at sea. But that does not make him a man capable of committing such crime upon this poor girl. I reserve my judgment. I certainly know his work, Papa. Last

May, as you might remember, I went to the New York University with Lynchie to hear him lecture and recite."

"And how did you find him?"

"I thought him transfixing."

"And this new work?" Hays asks, studying his daughter. "What do you know of it?"

"He calls it a sequel to his story 'The Murders in the Rue Morgue.' You remember that tale, Papa? I thought it wonderful, although I think it annoyed you at the time. It is the one set in Paris with an orangutan ape as murderer. It struck me as quite amusing in its own perverse way, with witnesses mistaking the monkey's harsh chatter for a foreign language."

Hays looks harshly on her. "Murder is never amusing, my dear."

"I don't mean to say that it is, Papa. The story appeared about a year ago."

"Shortly after Mary Rogers' murder, you mean?"

His eyes are steady upon her. She blinks before continuing.

"If you recall, I read the story to you in the sitting room downstairs. It involves a man, in fact, not unlike yourself, Papa, a detective, who, although not an officer of the law, works closely with the Parisian gendarmerie to unravel mysteries too puzzling for the limited skills and imagination of the police. As for the story's author—Mr. Poe—he is feared for his tomahawk, if not well respected or well liked among his peers. Personally, I know I look forward to articles and criticism bearing his name."

"You say he is feared. Feared by whom?"

"He is prone to wield his criticism with a savage hand. The literati justly watch him with wide-open eyes."

Hays removes his handkerchief and wipes away some discharge from his eyes. "As an author, he appears consumed by murder and detection, dear," he says.

Olga shrugs. "In these—what he is more and more calling his tales of ratiocination—ratiocination being the act of deducing consequence from premise, Papa—he fixates on the detective process, the proposition arrived at by logical and methodical reasoning, leading to the deciphering of crime."

She pours more hot water into her father's cup, sits down next to him at the kitchen table. The clock in the hall strikes 2 a.m.

" 'Rue Morgue,' " she murmurs in satisfying memory. "If nothing else, Mr. Poe is master of the strange and vague pleasures of the written word." She picks up her own brimming cup and carries it carefully to her lips. "The part I liked best, of course, Papa," she says, almost gushing with delight, "was the beast—the orangutan."

Old Hays removes *Snowden's* from his satchel, squares the magazine on the table with large, blunt fingers. "With this tale, according to John Colt, Mr. Poe is claiming to uncover the murderer of Mary Rogers, accomplishing what the constabulary have been unable to do. As I say, I have had a careful look at this man, Olga. His demeanor, his air. His physiognomy is striking. He is self-absorbed and long-suffering. In the end, taking all in collusion, I do not trust him."

Her eyes grow wide. "Trust him for what?"

"John Colt has made allegement that Mr. Edgar Poe and Miss Mary Rogers were once very much emotionally embroidered. In my investigation there was always vague talk of a lover, a gentleman that much older than she, someone I was never able to identify. Because here is only the first installment, with second and third installments to follow, one in each of the next two months, we shall apparently have to wait for Mr. Poe's revelation. Until then I think I would be remiss in my duty if I did not closely examine the text thus far to ascertain exactly what it is your Mr. Poe knows. And if his miraculous fictional tale does reveal some theory or bit of information gleaned from the fact of real life to which I myself am not yet privy, I shall want to know how this savage genius of yours with his cruel tomahawk has gained knowledge of what he speaks."

She almost grins. "Papa," she says, patting her father's age-spotted hand, "he is not *my* Mr. Poe, savage or otherwise. Papa, I'll gladly read his story tonight, under the covers where he is surely meant to be read, and we can talk about it in the morning. Meanwhile, why don't you take yourself upstairs and get some rest. Papa, you look so tired."

He nods, kisses her cheek, wishes her good night, and, head down, tired feet plodding forward, Old Hays, high constable of the city of New York, makes his way toward the stairs, his bed, and the much-needed sleep to which his daughter refers.

28

The Mystery of Marie Rogêt
Part One and Part Two
but Not Yet Part Three

Why she had never married, Olga Hays could not have said. There had been a gentleman, a scrivener, in her life some years before, but then she had experienced a change of heart. After that there had been no men, and after her mother's death she had devoted herself to her father, although she would never have said she had sacrificed herself in any way for him. Nor would she ever confess it unsettled and frightened her to see him getting old, as if it reflected on her.

As her father had told her, it was the Mary Rogers case barely disguised. Olga read the first section from the November *Snowden's* in its entirety that night by lamplight at the kitchen table, and then reread it and took notes in her bed, although not under the covers, but sitting up against the feather pillows. It was not one of Poe's horrors or grotesques, a dark and perverse story that lent itself to such delights as being frightened out of your wits while devouring the text nonstop by candlelight in bed.

No, "The Mystery of Marie Rogêt" was unlike the author's "The Masque of the Red Death" or "The Pit and the Pendulum." And although the narrative featured the same character, the investigator Dupin from "The Murders in the Rue Morgue," it was not of that masterful level.

The next morning, with as little sleep as she had, Olga rose early and put the fire on, but before preparing breakfast, she went out to the offices of *Snowden's* on Dutch Alley, to beg from a printer's imp with whom she had some acquaintance the latest issue of the *Ladies' Companion,* the December, with the second installment.

She then returned home, steeped her tea, sat at the kitchen table, and read the second installment before her father awoke, making notations both on paper and in the margins as she went along.

What Poe had done, his tactic as it were, had been to take the real-life murder of Mary Rogers and transfer the crime to Paris. He renamed Mary "Marie," slightly changed her age, the dates of the crime, and her place of business, substituting a Parisian *parfumerie* for John Anderson's New York segar emporium.

The body of the work began with the author discussing coincidence, what he called the "Calculus of Probabilities," highlighting specifically the extraordinary details of an atrocity against a young woman in Paris which he contended with little opacity would serve to mirror in the minds of all readers the murder of Mary Cecilia Rogers in New York City.

In the story, Marie is the daughter of the widow Estelle Rogêt. Her father is dead, as Olga knew was Mary Rogers' own father. Madame Rogêt runs a Parisian pension, a small hotel, assisted by her daughter.

Poe wrote that when Marie reached the age of twenty-two years, her beauty attracted the attentions of a Monsieur Le Blanc (the character meant to stand in for John Anderson) who ran a perfume shop in the basement of the Palais Royal. She went to work there, and thanks to her, the business became a sensation. But after a year of employ, suddenly all Marie's admirers, who were myriad, were thrown into a state of confusion when she inexplicably disappeared.

At the time, Poe continues, Madame Rogêt was terrified that the worst had befallen her child. The Parisian public prints had taken up the story, and the police were called in. But just as the investigation was to begin full pitch, the missing Marie unaccountably reappeared in good health, saying she had spent the week of her disappearance with a relative in the country.

What followed then, Poe relates, was much gossip, and Marie, not able to withstand the snide innuendo, left the *parfumerie* and the employ of Monsieur Le Blanc, retiring to run her mother's pension on the Rue Pavée Saint-André.

Five months later Madame Rogêt is once more thrown into a fit of anxiety, as are her daughter's friends and admirers. Marie has again disappeared. After three days, nothing is heard from her, but on the fourth, her body is found floating in the Seine.

"The atrocity of the murder," Poe writes, "the youth and beauty of the victim, and, above all, her previous notoriety, conspired to produce intense excitement in the minds of the sensitive Parisians."

Olga puts down her pen. Her father, in his dressing gown, his feet bare to the cold floor, stands in the kitchen doorway, staring bleary-eyed at her.

"Olga, is there any Javanese?"

She stands immediately. "Yes, Papa, certainly."

"And some dry toast? That's all I think I can bear right now."

"Of course."

"What time is it?"

She still has the kettle on and is reaching for the bread knife. "Are you feeling all right? It is almost noon."

Hays looks at her. The whites of his eyes are alarmingly red, the hanging folds of skin beneath an amalgam of blue and black, almost bruised. "Certainly, I feel fine." He glances at the kitchen table, to her notes and the two issues of open *Snowden's*. "So, have you gotten to it?"

"Yes, I have read it," she says. She had a thin slice of bread, the way her father liked it, on the toasting rack in the oven.

"And?"

"I went out this morning and begged a printer's imp I know at *Snowden's* the second issue. What Mr. Poe has done is impressive, Papa, but perhaps not his best work."

"I do not need literary criticism, Olga," he snaps. "I need to know the content. Is it possible that this man knows something I do not?"

"Most of it seems to be taken from the public prints, almost directly."

"So the answer is no?"

"I cannot be certain yet, Papa."

She can see clearly Poe's construct. The chevalier C. Auguste Dupin is with certainty modeled after her father. "The Chevalier's remarkable analytical ability was so highly touted by the local Parisian constabulary," Poe writes in "Marie Rogêt," "that they gave him credit for intuition," an observation gleaned almost word for word from a profile of her father published in the *Police Gazette*.

"The story is related by an unnamed narrator," she explains to him, "the same who narrated the story of 'The Murders in the Rue Morgue.' This fictional individual does all the chevalier's legwork while the chevalier remains in his comfortable Parisian apartments. The narrator visits all the newspaper offices in Paris ferreting out every word published having to do with the crime. Dupin then reconstructs the timeline and all movement using this press and the vast and varied published accounts. Mr. Poe, I suspect, has done the very same thing, Papa, used the New York prints, mainly, it seems, along with the weekly compendium the *Brother Jonathan* to cobble the story together. He basically admits as much within the context of the story."

Hays nods. "Go on."

She sets down her father's coffee and burnt toast in front of him.

"On Sunday morning, June 22, in a year Mr. Poe chooses not to name, at nine a.m., the grisette Marie Rogêt leaves her mother's residence. She says goodbye to no one but Monsieur Jacques St. Eustache—the character representing Mr. Daniel Payne—and to him, and to him only, does she remark that her intentions are to visit her aunt on the Rue des Drômes, two miles away, and not far from the banks of the Seine River. Arrangements had ostensibly been made by St. Eustache to meet Marie later that evening to escort her home, but heavy rains fall in the afternoon, and assuming she would stay with her aunt that evening as she has in previous similar instances, he does not feel it necessary to keep his promise. Later that evening, however, when apprised of Marie's failure to return home, Madame Rogêt, who is described by the author as an infirm old lady, seventy years of age, is heard to express, as I know did Mary's own mother, to the effect she feared she would never again see her daughter alive.

"The next day, when still Marie has not made appearance, St. Eustache sets out, only to ascertain she never arrived at the Rue des Drômes. A tardy search is instigated at several other points in the city, but with no result. It is not until the fourth day that a Monsieur Beauvais—Mr. Alfred Crommelin—making inquiries for Marie on the shore of the Seine, is informed that the corpse of a young girl has been found floating in the waters. After some hesitation Beauvais identifies the corpse as that of the missing perfumery girl.

"Following several days' passage without a mention in the press, one of the local weekly papers takes up the theme of the murder, kindling an outpouring of public emotion. As a result, several individuals are quickly arrested on suspicion. There is no evidence, however, and they are released.

"The family's colored maid then comes forward. She testifies she overheard Madame Rogêt and Marie in furious discussion, Madame unflinching in desire for her daughter to break off her prospective marriage to St. Eustache, which, according to the maid's account, in the end Marie concedes to do.

"St. Eustache is now detained by the French authorities, and at first gives an unintelligible account of his whereabouts during the Sunday on which Marie left home. Under further scrutiny by the local gendarmes, however, a more thorough affidavit is submitted, and every hour of St. Eustache's whereabouts adequately accounted for.

"Mr. Poe's tale continues to do nothing more than follow fully the course of known events, Papa. As in your investigation, in the end both the characters representative of Mr. Payne and Mr. Crommelin will be fully exonerated by the Parisian gendarmerie. As time progresses and all remains fallow, a thousand contradictory rumors are circulated through Paris, and the city's journalists busy themselves with specious speculations.

"Dupin contends because there was no person whatever who came forward who saw Marie after she left her mother's door, there is no evidence that Marie Rogêt, in fact, was in the land of the living after nine o'clock on that Sunday. Therefore, there is no proof that, up to that hour, she was alive."

Olga refers to her notes, then directly to the text. "'On Wednesday noon,'" she reads, "'at twelve, a female body was discovered afloat on the shore of the Barrière du Roule. This was, even if we presume that Marie was thrown into the river within three hours after she left her mother's house, only three days from the time she left her home— three days to an hour. But it is folly to suppose that the murder, if murder was committed on her body, could have been consummated soon enough to have enabled her murderers to throw the body into the river before midnight. Those that are guilty of such horrid crimes choose darkness rather than light. Thus we see that if the body found in the river was that of Marie Rogêt, she could only have been in the water two and a half days, or three at the outside. All experience has shown that drowned bodies or bodies thrown into the water immediately after death by violence, require from six to ten days for sufficient decomposition to take place to bring them to the top of the water.'" Olga looks up. "Is all this true, Papa?"

"He belabors his point, Olga. Go on, please."

"Parts of the story are excruciating, but it is presumably science the author is after, Papa. Or some semblance of it. Mr. Poe would most certainly have us believe the scientific method is the key to detection."

"I would argue instinct in intimate collusion with science and logic might better serve the shadow, but who am I to disagree with Mr. Poe and the advance of his sophisticated methodology?"

"Stop, Papa. The theory that engenders the most notice is an idea that Marie was not dead at all, but still lived, and that the corpse found in the Seine was not hers, but that of another. In the story Mr. Poe conspires to have the newspaper *L'Etoile*, correlating to the *New York Star*, allege it could not have been Marie in the Seine, but the body of another, making reference to the apparent apathy of the Rogêt family toward the corpse, surmising this apathy inconsistent with the supposition that these relatives believed the corpse to be hers. According to the print, the most telling point is that no one from the family bothered to go across the river to view the body. 'For an item of news like this,' Poe quotes *L'Etoile*, 'it strikes us as very coolly received.'

"Dupin takes exception. To him, this is not the case. He defends Madame Rogêt. He makes excuses for her, saying she was exceedingly feeble, and was so agitated by the circumstances of her daughter's death she could not possibly attend to any duty. St. Eustache, rather than receiving the news coolly, according to Poe, was so distracted with grief Beauvais had to prevail upon friends and relatives to attend him lest he commit harm upon himself.

"But for his supposed compassion," Olga continues, "Monsieur Beauvais now becomes the prime suspect."

She returns to read from a marked excerpt from the magazine text. "'Monsieur Beauvais appears to have the whole matter locked up in his head. A single step cannot be taken without Beauvais. For some reason, this individual determined that nobody should have anything to do with the proceedings but himself. He seems to have been very much averse to permitting the relatives to see the body.'

"Emphasis is added to this suspicion, Papa, after the character based on Archibald Padley comes forward to say a few days prior to Marie's disappearance that he had observed a rose in Beauvais's keyhole, and the name 'Marie' inscribed on the slate outside his door."

"All this has been thoroughly investigated, Olga. Arthur Crommelin did receive a rose from Mary Rogers. Her name was inscribed on his chalkboard in her hand. There is nothing new here," he grumbles.

"Indeed, as you say, Papa, in the story, as in real life, all these men and admirers of Marie are eventually exonerated, and so, despite all else, the generally held opinion falls back on a gang of desperadoes, that they had seized Marie, borne her across the river, maltreated her, and then murdered her.

"After still further analysis of the facts, however, a newspaper Poe here christens *Le Commerciel*—obviously, the *Journal of Commerce*—weighs in, concluding that because a piece of one of Marie's petticoats had been torn from her dress and tied under her chin and around the back of her head, evidently in order to prevent screams, the murder could not have been committed by such a gang of common ruffians. Mr. Poe reasons these fellows too much revere their pocket handkerchiefs, so this act must have been carried out by fellows who had no pocket handkerchiefs. The correlation being, that if rogues such as these had had pocket handkerchiefs, they would have used them. The reasoning, therefore, the deed was not carried out by ruffians of the common sort.

"Logic does hold its wonder," allows Hays, straight-faced.

Olga glances up but chooses to ignore her father's flippancy. She goes on. "Soon follows the discovery in a thicket in the Paris *bois* that parallels the discovery by Mrs. Loss's sons. She is here called Madame Deluc. *Deluc*, as you well know, Papa, being the name of the chemist on Nassau Street where Daniel Payne procured his laudanum."

"I am impressed by your diligence, Olga."

"Thank you, Papa. I'll take that as a compliment. To go on: Further included here is a description of the alleged scene of the crime, including the stone throne, the display of petticoat, and silk scarf. Poe's narrator describes the scene thusly: 'The earth was trampled, the bushes broken, and there was every evidence of a struggle. The ground around bore indication of some heavy burden, as if a body had been dragged from this hidden spot down to the riverside.' The narrator here refers to a public print, *Le Soleil*—in our language, the *Sun*—and their breathless declaration: 'There can be no doubt that the spot of the appalling outrage has been discovered!'

"Madame Deluc is immediately deposed. She is said to remember the Sunday in question. A young girl arrived at her inn in the company of a dark-complexioned man. She claims she particularly noticed her because the dress she wore matched perfectly the dress of one of her relatives, recently deceased. Also the girl wore a noticeable scarf, which Madame Deluc admired, and therefore remembered. According to the madam's testimony, the couple stayed for a short time, then left, taking the road which soon led into thick woods.

"Shortly after, a boisterous gang of miscreants made their appearance. Madame Deluc alleges they ate and drank at her establishment, then left without paying, upon their departure following the same route as the young girl and man. According to her, the rowdies returned to the inn at dusk before once more recrossing the river, this time in great haste.

"Having never left his apartment, but based on all these newspaper accounts, Dupin concludes Marie's murder is an ordinary crime, although a particularly atrocious one. There is nothing, he claims, outré about it. Because it is so ordinary, he charges, the solution to the mystery was hoped by the local police, therefore, to be easy. Yet their conclusion, it follows, should have been the opposite. The solution is difficult, Dupin offers, dictated by the crime's very ordinariness."

"I'll give him in this he may be kerrect," admits Hays.

"In this story, Papa, unlike that of the masterful 'Rue Morgue,' author Poe, as I see it, makes use of his fictional detective as mere prop, in transparent groping, I suspect, in order to have we readers marvel at the uncanny power of his own marvelous deductive insight and logic. Mr. Poe writes those covering the mystery for the newspapers and public prints have made it their business to picture a mode for the crime. Many modes even. And, in turn, a motive for the criminal, many motives. According to Mr. Poe, each of these modes and motives holds at least some possibility to afford solution to the mystery, and within their number then, he contends, must lie by necessity the actual and inevitable solution."

"What is he saying? Within the realm of all possible must lie the inevitable?" Hays almost laughs.

"I shall neither argue nor object," says Olga. "Mr. Poe is sometimes prone to cite the obvious, Papa. But lest we forget, he reminds us the sole objective of our newsprints is to create sensation rather than to further the cause of truth, all in the seminal interest of selling more newspapers. Dupin sets himself the task, therefore, to dismember every point made in the press, emphasizing, however, that it is not with the prints that he has issue, but with the truth. He insists on proceeding methodically through the entire scope of the investigation, stating he will discard the interior points of this tragedy to concentrate his attention upon its outskirts. Not the least usual error in investigation such as this, he charges, is the limiting of inquiry to the immediate, with total disregard of the collateral or circumstantial event. As example, he alleges it is the malpractice of the courts to confine evidence and discussion to the bounds of apparent relevancy. The larger part of truth, he charges, arises from the seemingly irrelevant. The criminologist must calculate upon the unforeseen. A comprehensive survey of the public prints, says Dupin, will afford us some minute points, which shall establish a direction for his inquiry. His goal is to point his finger at the shortcomings of the police, the limitations of their inquiry, ultimately resulting in their inevitable failure.

"He affords himself a week to conduct such study. At the conclusion of that period he comes back to his friend and confidant, the narrator, and places a series of newspaper extracts in front of him. The first, from the *Evening Paper*, ostensibly focuses on the disappearance of Marie.

"Although earlier in the story Poe wrote it was merely three months before that Marie had first disappeared, he now states it was actually two or three years since a disturbance very similar to the present was caused by her disappearance from the *parfumerie* of Monsieur Le Blanc in the Palais Royal. It appears an oversight on the author's part. The crux of the account is that at the end of a week after her first disappearance, Marie reappeared at her customary *comptoir* as well as ever, with the exception of a slight paleness not altogether usual. Given this previous absence, therefore, we of a rational and ordered mind should assume that the present absence is a freak of the same nature, and that, at the expiration of another week, or perhaps a month, Marie will be among us again.

"The second extract is marked from *Le Mercurie*. Again the referral is to Marie's previous disappearance. Here, however, it is now unequivocally stated as well known that during the week of that first absence from Le Blanc's *parfumerie*, Marie was all the time in the company of a man much noted for his debaucheries. *Le Mercurie* claims to have the name of the Lothario, but, for reasons of their own, forbears to make this information public."

"Does Mr. Poe ever see fit to name this individual?"

Olga shakes her head. "No, he never does. Not yet at any rate."

"Do you feel he knows who it is?"

"I cannot say. Let me go on, Papa, please. The third extract is from the *Morning Paper*, in which the author calls attention to an outrage of the most atrocious character perpetrated near Paris the day of Marie's disappearance. A gentleman with his wife and their daughter, engaged about dusk the services of six young men who were idly rowing a boat to and from near the banks of the Seine. The family was conveyed across river by this crew, where they left the vessel. The daughter, however, soon realized she had forgotten her parasol. She returned for it, was seized by the gang, carried out into the stream, gagged, brutally treated, and finally taken to the shore at a point not far from where she had originally entered the boat with her parents. The villains escaped, but the police are said to be upon their trail, and the article asserts some of them will soon be taken. Concurrent to this outrage,

Poe writes, the *Evening Paper* received anonymous written communication to the effect that Marie at the same time, or nearly the same time, was the victim of a band of blackguards."

"What is the point, Olga?"

"It is interesting you voice the question, Papa, because Poe's narrator asks the same of Dupin. 'What is the point?' Dupin insists it is mere folly to say that there is no supposable connection between Marie's first and second disappearance. 'Let us admit,' he writes, 'the first elopement to have resulted in a quarrel between Marie and her lover, eventually leading to her return home, even if at first she was planning to never return home again, but run off with him forever. We are now prepared to view a second elopement as indicating a renewal of Marie's unnamed lover's advances, rather than as the result of a new proposal by a new individual. In other words, we are prepared to regard this second disappearance as a making up of the first *amour,* rather than as the commencement of a new one.'"

"So Poe wants us to believe one man was involved in Mary Rogers' life, then and now, the instigator of her first disappearance, and the instigator of the second as well?"

"Dupin supposes this lover may have been interrupted in his first villainy by some unnamed necessity of departure, so he has seized the first moment of his return to renew the base designs not yet altogether accomplished. He concedes it is possible to say in the first instance there was no elopement as imagined. But what if there was subterfuge at the base of not only the first but also the second? According to the chevalier, we may imagine Marie on the occasion of the second instance thinking thusly: 'I am to meet a certain person for the purpose of elopement. It is necessary that there be no chance of interruption—there must be sufficient time given us to elude pursuit—I will give it to be understood that I shall visit and spend the day with my aunt. I will tell St. Eustache not to call for me until dark. In this way, my absence from home for the longest possible period, without causing suspicion or anxiety, will be accounted for, and I shall gain more time than in any other manner. And since it is my design never to return, the gaining of time is the only point about which I need give myself any concern.'

"Dupin insists this is but his imagined thinking for Marie. He calls our attention to it because earlier in the story he spoke of the culpable remissness of his competitors, the police. Now he asserts the police may not have been remiss at all, but only dupes. He concludes, adjudging from his notes, that the most general opinion in relation to this sad affair is, and was from the first, that Marie had been the victim of a gang of blackguards. Now, he reminds us, the popular opinion, under certain conditions, should not be disregarded. Sometimes, however, we should look upon the two instances as analogous, utilizing that intuition which is the idiosyncrasy of the individual man of genius. In ninety-nine cases from the hundred the detective would abide by its decision. But here is how Dupin chooses to discern the details:

"'All Paris is excited by the discovered corpse of Marie, a girl young, beautiful and notorious. Her body bears marks of violence, and has been found floating in the river. It is made known that on the very day in which it is supposed that she was assassinated, an outrage of a similar nature to that endured by the deceased, although less in extent, was perpetrated by a gang of young ruffians, upon the person of a second young female. Is it wonderful that the one known atrocity should influence the popular judgment in regard to the other unknown? Marie was found in the river; and upon this very river was this known outrage committed. The connection of the two events had about it so much of the palpable, that the true wonder would have been a failure of the populace to appreciate and seize it. But to the philosophical detective, the one atrocity, known to be so committed, is if anything, evidence that the other, committed at a time nearly coincident, was not so committed. It would have been a miracle indeed, if, while a gang of ruffians were perpetrating, at a given locality, a most unheard-of wrong, there should have been another similar gang, in a similar locality, in the same city, under the same circumstance, with the same means and appliances, engaged in a wrong of precisely the same aspect, at precisely the same period of time. Unlikely. If not impossible!'"

"So Poe discards the blackguards to make case for a wronged lover to have committed the crime? Again, he from the first assignation, the murderer from the second."

"Just so. This, it seems, is where Mr. Poe is leading us, Papa, although the third chapter with his definitive solution remains in abeyance. When I saw my man at *Snowden's*, I asked after this final installment. He said it had been initially scheduled for the January issue, already typeset but not yet locked down. Then, suddenly, at the apparent request of the author, the story was withdrawn, and abruptly pulled from the magazine."

"Not to be ever published?"

"My imp did not know for sure. He had heard it might appear in February, after revisions by Mr. Poe."

Hays had, by this time, risen from his uncomfortable chair and was vigorously pacing the room. "Good work, Olga," he said, repeating, "February. Very good work."

🌿 29 🌿

A Bitter Reunion

The harelipped guard stood in the corridor outside Tommy Coleman's cell until young Tommy, annoyed enough, finally stood, moved over to the grate, and asked what the surly keeper wanted.

"I don't want nothing from the likes of you, hackum," the guard smirked. "Just looking."

Tommy wore a striped taupe and black prison shirt and pants too big for him. He tried his best to ignore the keeper's fat, florid face pressed to the grille. The man stood for a good long time glaring at the little gangster before finally taking it upon himself to announce Tommy had a visitor.

"Screw you," Tommy said.

"Watch what you say," the guard glowered.

"Why? What you gonna do to me? Them jack coves who run this college can only kill me once." Tommy looked the big screw square in the dorchester and laughed. "Ain't that right, Hamlet?"

"You want to see your guest or should I send ya straight to the earth-bath?" the keeper asked, not backing off. "Don't pay to give me no jabber if you want to see yer dear sweet mudder who has traveled here from dem dismal, pig-infested P'ernts where the likes of youse live ta pay her respects to you, her miserable, woirthless paddy son."

Pleased at giving as good as he got, the guard grinned, showing black-edged teeth, what there were of them.

"We're all men of one God here, captain," Tommy said. He reached for the guard's hand through the bars, gained it, clasped it. "I didn't mean nothing," he said through a leer.

The guard tore his hand away. Big as a bear, meat-faced, native-born, to his mind an American of the first order, he turned his back on Tommy and stalked to the end of the death row cell block where there was a gate.

Another keeper stood on the far side. The second guard wore his keys on a ring at his waist. He fit the key in the lock. The door swung open, letting the first keeper pass.

The second guard was about as jocose as the first. He opened the door where Mother Coleman, a soft-bosomed, white-haired woman older than her years, waited for admittance.

"Why if it ain't the darlin' fresh-faced mudder from Eyre here to pay a social visit to her condemned offspring," the first keeper said.

"So I am," Tommy's mother muttered.

"Don't it just warm the cuckolds of yer heart," the first keeper said to the second.

"Life don't seem hardly worth living. Not when one's on one's last legs like our poor little bird there," the second keeper responded.

"Bless us, but pity him, if we're not cooped up, caged day and night same as tha' black Irish boy of yers, mama," the first lamented to Mrs. Coleman.

"Ain't it the truth, b'hoyo," the second guard agreed, and laughed.

They led her down the corridor. Tommy embraced his dear old ma through the bars of his cell door. He asked after his da.

Dead-eyed, dead-faced, dead-spirited, Mrs. Coleman, already the loser of one son to the hangman's noose and five daughters to disease, fell back on her haunches. She peered at her boy, her last surviving child, her youngest, her baby Tommy, caged in front of her.

He, too, was dead-eyed, dead-faced, dead-spirited. Not so much because he wasn't happy to see her, his tortured ma, but because the two of them were crafty, wanting to give nothing away, aware of their antagonists staring at them, the blue-clad, ham-faced keepers, the high beak, Old Hays, down the prison corridor, in his office.

"God give us strength," Mother Coleman said loud enough for eavesdroppers to hear.

"I pray he will, Ma. For your sake."

The harsh voice of the harelipped guard suddenly ringing out. "What are you two Irish dogs whispering about? I don't like no whispering."

Tommy and his white-haired mother did indeed have their heads together.

Tommy looked up, said, "What do you think? I'm telling my poor old innocent ma I love her. Want her to tell my poor old innocent da at home I love him. Is there anything wrong with that?"

"My heart bleeds fer yer," the guard commiserated. "All that wasted love. No whisperin'."

"It's a death blow, plain and simple." Tommy's ma was saying to him, ignoring the guard and turning back to her son. "Yer da, he's suffering. Even if you being here don't kill him outright, he complains he got pains gnawing at his chest, gnawing at his maw, inside and out."

She glanced over her shoulder. Across the corridor John Colt was standing at his cell door staring at them.

The grizzled old woman turned back to her son, settled on the cold, dank floor, her arms folded across her chest, defiant, muttering, "They won't be hanging my last surviving son."

"I'm not afraid to be took out," Tommy told her. "I don't know how many times I have to say it."

Listening to them, the guard simply stared.

"Yer da's busy in the ward kitchen, God bless his sodden self," Mother Coleman murmured in a lowered voice. "Cooking up the scheme that will save yer soul."

"My soul don't need saving. I'm an innocent."

Tommy's da was a Fourth Ward heeler, occasionally in good standing. Heeler was in reference to nothing more than a dog commanded by his master. Da Timo Coleman was a loafer, always on the lookout for shady work. Even as his old wife and condemned son spoke, the old man was making a last-ditch effort to pull in any and all favors owed him on behalf of the ward political organization and the Democratic machine now that he so crucially needed them. He was, in truth, at that very moment (having been approached out of the blue via a local swag) at the Green Turtle's flash-drum meeting with an emissary of the powerful Colt clan, a bloke claiming to be Brother James.

Mother Coleman leaned forward toward her boy. But as she did, the truculent guard came forward and laid his truncheon on the bars.

"We'll have none of that," the surly keeper growled. "I told you that."

He fixed them with menacing pig eyes, but only momentarily. As he wandered away, Mother Coleman looked after him, she speaking under her breath what she had to say in a hurry.

"You won't be swinging," she assured her boy. "Me and your da, we won't be letting ya."

And she spat on the floor for God to hear her and give her the luck.

❦ 30 ❦

Marriage
Beneath the Gibbet

On the morning of November 18, 1842, High Constable Jacob Hays, wearing an appropriately somber black suit and dark gray stock beneath his overcoat, arrived at the Tombs' gate and waited to be admitted.

The date is the day of John Colt's execution. It is also the day of his wedding.

In the courtyard the carpenters have come at dawn to make last-minute adjustment to the gallows. As Tommy Coleman had said, no one wanted to foul up like the day his brother met his maker.

Alongside the carpenters, already some journalists from the penny papers and the more legitimate sixpenny sheets were stomping about in the early morning coolness, trying to stay warm, excited at the opportunity to write about Colt's impending marriage and subsequent demise.

That the prison authorities were permitting such pomp and ceremony sent the news brotherhood into shrill vindictive, their cry: Injustice! That those in charge were allowing, under any set of circumstance, such a circus—John Colt to marry—only hours before his scheduled execution was already a mind-boggling concession to the

Colt family and their power; a statement, as far as Hays was concerned, that emanated from way high up the political ladder.

Late that October, Samuel Colt had made one last futile run at William Seward, submitting any number of individual and group petitions to the governor, begging pardon for his brother. But word came back via the intercity wire, telegraphed from the state capital in Albany, communicating unequivocally, much to his regret, the governor could in no way in good conscience accommodate such a request. Governor Seward did send, however, final instructions to Tombs warden Monmouth Hart acknowledging that although John C. Colt would die as scheduled early that evening, in the afternoon, if the family truly wished, his marriage to his betrothed, Caroline Henshaw, might be arranged.

Old Hays accompanied Warden Hart to Colt's cell to give him the news. Upon hearing the governor's decree, Colt seemed unfazed.

"Death hath no terrors for me," he responded, addressing Hays. "There is a world above this, and I believe a just one. Man, at the worst, can only destroy my body."

THE CONDEMNED'S INTENDED, Miss Henshaw, was scheduled to arrive before lunch on the fateful day. Her arrival was anxiously awaited, but by 1:30 p.m. she had not yet appeared. Imminent vows notwithstanding, anticipation ran high amidst the gathered crowd. Newspaper accounts of the gallows nuptials, following the sensational murder and trial, had brought out scores of curiosity seekers. By noon they were jamming Centre Street and spilling into Leonard. To the newspaper publishers' delight, Caroline had been pregnant at the time of John's arrest, and unmarried. Subsequently she gave birth to a male child, naming him Samuel Colt Jr., ostensibly in honor of John's brother, the Colonel, her sole protector, in light of the soon-to-be-enacted execution of he who would soon be her husband.

Because of the pressing crowd, Miss Henshaw's carriage was forced to take the back entrance on Baxter Street, but the rear arteries were every bit as clogged as the front. Time and again the main gates opened and carriages and hacks surged in, but not the scandalized bride's.

The incarcerated, especially those in the Bummers' Cell, watched for her from their barred windows.

"Thar she is!" they cried excitedly.

"No she ain't. That ain't her!"

"Is!"

"Ain't!"

Hays saw her arrive nearly at 2 p.m., a tall, healthy young woman in white voile and white lace. While she waited patiently to enter, the crowd caught sight of her and rushed to her carriage. Her alarmed horse snorted and reared slightly in harness as Hays ordered three broad-chested, leather-helmeted assistant constables into action. They hurried from the prison waving their ash batons and helped her inside the open gate.

A couple of the gentlemen editors and writers took especial notice. The *Herald*'s Bennett, standing near Old Hays, turned to him and whistled in admiration, cracking wise to the high constable that given the inevitable conclusion to the events of the day, the nubile young widow would certainly soon enough be available for solacing, and volunteering his cross-eyed self for the unctuous duty.

Standing in the cool November sun, Hays bore witness to Bennett. He liked the editor little before. He liked him less at present, notably after such callous comment. He turned and went back inside the cell block, keeping his disgust to himself.

In front of him, Miss Henshaw was being escorted gallantly by the warden, Monmouth Hart, to a vacant cell draped with newly hung organdy in deference to the bride. She was a very young woman with cascading ringlets of caramel-shaded hair. No more than twenty-two or twenty-three years, she was of German extraction, still talking English with a pronounced accent. The warden told her she could rest here until the wedding march sounded. At that time she would be led into the courtyard to be reunited with her intended. Colonel Colt would be giving her away. Bride and groom together were to be joined by two hundred of their dearest family, friends, and staunchest allies. It had been arranged for the groom to be outfitted in the finest tailored suit and top hat of blackened water silk. The ankle bracelets were to be kept in place, and his hands would be shackled. The wedding march would be played by a family friend, the actor-composer John Howard Payne, author of the popular "Home, Sweet Home." He would be seated at a fine rosewood piano bearing the inscription of its maker, Johannes Zumpe, wheeled out into the yellow dust just for the occasion.

Priest and wedding party, consisting of the Reverend Mr. Anton, who would perform the ceremony, Colt's two brothers, Samuel and James, and the lawyer Robert Emmet, awaited the couple. John Colt's friend the poet Poe had been asked by the family to read a suitable poem for the occasion.

When word reached the crowd that Colt was out of the block and in view, there was much muttering and talk, some of it having to do with the opinion that he was wrongly condemned.

Out of respect, when the bride entered the yard the crowd became quiet. Mr. Poe had chosen a poem he introduced as "in progress, but assuredly of love." The lines were inscribed, as was his habit, on a cylinder of tightly rolled blue-tinted foolscap, secured by a red ribbon and carried in his breast pocket, close to his heart. He removed the manuscript, unfurled it, and began to read in his somber, melodic singsong:

> *"Avaunt! to-night*
> *My heart is light—*
> *   No dirge will I upraise,*
> *But waft the angel on his flight*
> *   With a Pæan of old days!*

> *Let* no *bell toll!*
>   *Lest his sweet soul,*
>   *Amid its hallow'd mirth,*
>   *Should catch the note*
>   *As it doth float*
>   *Up from the damned earth—*
>   *To friends above, from fiends below,*
> *Th' indignant ghost is riven—*
>   *From grief and moan*
>   *To a gold throne*
>   *Beside the King of Heaven!"*

As the wedding proceeded, all progress of the affair and its festivity was simultaneously relayed by prison guards to the anxious throng of eager bystanders maintaining their places outside the walls. The keepers' announcements were shouted in booming voice to be heard above the buzz of the excited crowd:

"Here comes the bride!"

"Very lovely rings have been exchanged!"

"Rice thrown!" . . .

Et cetera.

The plebeian throng happily partook in the spectacle, cheering their delight at each minute progression in the afternoon's entertainment.

Following the fractious matrimonial rite, the new Mr. and Mrs. Colt shook hands and bussed cheeks all around. More than a few fat tears streaked down the powdered faces of Gotham's society grandes dames, some, admitted, hopeless romantics.

A sumptuous meal was soon spread for the gathered guests (once again catered by Delmonico's and kept warm in the prison kitchen). Dancing to Mr. Payne's piano was scheduled to follow.

Hays watched Poe accept congratulations, watched him meticulously reroll his blue foolscap scroll and retie the red ribbon, before making point to approach him and ask, "Mr. Poe, I have read with interest the first installments of your 'Marie Rogêt' story. I beg to inquire, sir, what is to follow?"

But then the two newspaper publishers, Bennett from the *Herald*, Greeley from the *Trib*, hurried over. Standing over Poe in front of Hays, they loudly argued and jousted for the rights to his poem performed, vying could they publish the verse, Bennett offering a few cents in recompense more than his notoriously cheap other, and Hays, in sheer dismay, retreated to his office.

Within a few minutes the newlywed couple followed him inside, to spend their honeymoon (of sorts) in John's cell.

From where he sat, the shadow watched silently as they drew the curtain before retiring, calling through the fabric to the manservant, Dillback, for crystal flutes and French champagne.

❧ 31 ❧

The Marriage Banquet

In the courtyard Edgar Poe stands over the much-praised thespian and songster John Howard Payne.

As a young man Payne had acted onstage, both in Boston and New York, with Poe's mother in *Hamlet, Romeo and Juliet,* and Voltaire's *Mahomet the Imposter,* in which she played Palmyra to Payne's Zaphne.

Sitting at his Zumpe piano sipping a glass of claret, after Poe reminds him who he is and who was his mother. Payne coughs, shakes his head in disbelief, squeezes his eyes shut, flutters them open, regales Poe with how he remembers him as a three-month-old as if it were yesterday. The showman wobbles his head again, either in dismay or to clear his jumble.

"Pity your poor mater," he laughs. "As I remember, your old man was away—I beg your pardon, but as a thespian the man wasn't fit to play a footman onstage—and the lovely Eliza had all she could do to keep up with her new baby and what's his name, your brother?"

"William Henry Leonard."

Poe's older sibling, who was at the time aged two years, and the new baby, Poe.

"He's in the grave," Poe says.

"What?"

"He passed away. Six years ago or more."

"My condolences."

"Tubercular consumption. The same as my mother. And acute alcoholism."

Payne stares. His fingers never leave the keyboard. He plays on with the music.

"Your mother, poor dear, thanks to you, dear sir, rarely slept through the night," Payne laments, "and our rehearsal schedule for the three plays, not to mention the afterpiece, was enormous." He smiles, and again shakes his head in wonder. "A glass of claret, my good man?"

Poe reaches. Payne pours.

Then, behind them so they both turn, a minor commotion. The warden has arrived, escorting by the arm Caroline Henshaw back into the yard, signaling the end of her honeymoon with her new husband, to join with the celebrants and spend time, most especially, it seems, with her brothers-in-law Colt, Samuel and James, who, as Poe looks on, link their arms with hers, she so feminine, so delicate, so well-shapen, having embraced with their new sister-in-law to dance and spin to the music beneath the gibbet.

At the upright with Payne, Poe remains on the bench, their impressive heads together. A small army of colored waiters are laying the repast.

Poe sees Samuel Colt has taken over exclusively from his brother James and is dancing alone now with Caroline. Something so familiar between them, Poe senses, in a time of jubilation, in spite of the impending execution, no introspection, no mourning, no sorrow, only to dance and dance, Mrs. Caroline Colt, née Henshaw, Mr. Samuel Colt, the Colonel, inventor of the Colt patent repeating revolver, to spin her this last time before her husband's execution, through the Tombs' yard dust.

32

Preparation
for a Hanging

For the occasion of marriage it had been John Colt's manservant, Dillback, who had come up with the idea to drape elegant new silk curtains around the honeymooners' cell, a shade of peach that made the heart sing.

The groom, enjoying his lady fair, could not have but helped to hear the clatter of dishes from the prison kitchen and note the enticing smells of grilling meat and roasting fowl emanating through the cell block.

The piano, maudlin, played by John Howard Payne, continued tinkling from without, the newly married Mrs. Colt, moaning softly in her clutcher's ear, in perfect harmony to the melody.

Until, after forty-five minutes, the warden comes for her, delivers his apologies, and escorts her out.

How does a cove act knowing he is about to hang?

After his newly conjoined wife has left him, John Colt, the condemned, gives every indication of being perversely unnerved.

His last time on this earth, he means to spend at his writing desk.

He rises. Sits. Rises again.

He sits again, dips pen in ink, scratches at the paper laid out in front of him.

When finished, he shuffles the pages, picks them up, is about to fold them, then instead rolls them in a tight cylinder as he has seen Edgar Poe do, ties them with a length of black ribbon (he cannot find in his cell red), slips the scroll in his breast pocket, pats it. Then thinks better of it.

He wipes his brow with a black silk handkerchief, looks at the fine cloth, studies it. Refolds it. Puts it down, but not in his pocket, at the edge of the desk.

He stretches, mounts his cot, stares through the high window bars into the yard, catches a glimpse of the death apparatus.

It is soon after that Warden Hart arrives, flanked by two blue-clad keepers. Hart stands silent for a moment, staring through the grille into Colt's cell at the man soon to meet his maker, the condemned's chest rising and falling.

"Ready, Mr. Colt?"

A smile plays at Colt's mouth, incongruous, troubling for a man so situated in harm's way.

He says, "So soon?" but gets to his feet.

"I am taking you to a holding cell," Warden Hart announces to him loudly. "From there you will be escorted to the gallows in two hours' time."

Hearing the warden, Dillback rushes to his ward's side. He helps his young charge, brushing invisible lint from his elegant, well-tailored sleeves and shoulders.

Colt has changed into a rich velvet dark navy blue soft coat, extremely handsome of its style, a white stock at the neck.

The warden unlocks the cell with a broad key, swinging the door open.

"If you'll follow me, Mr. Colt."

At his desk Old Hays stands.

Colt pivots to see him.

The two guards clasp Colt underneath the arms, propping him up, one on either side.

Tommy Coleman looks on from his own cell.

"We're moving you to a more private cell, sir, where you can be alone in your final moments," Hart proclaims. Adding softly, almost plaintively, "At your brother's request."

Colt nods his understanding. His gratitude. The meaning of the words uttered by Hart—*At your brother's request*—has not been lost on him, nearly makes him laugh with relief, although he manages to suppress the grin working the corners of his mouth.

He does stand tall.

"Manacle him," one keeper orders the other. "We live by procedure here, man," an acknowledgment to Old Hays, who has moved into the corridor. "We don't want nothing happening."

"What could happen?" Tommy Coleman smiles.

For that one moment everything stops. Tommy is not much interested in an answer, only the devil about him. Warden Hart swings his attention around angrily.

"Watch out, you little swabbler," he snaps venomously, glaring at Tommy Coleman's evil twisted kisser. "I'll be coming for you soon enough. Just you wait and see how smart you are then."

"I'm shaking in my boots, boss."

Warden Hart glowers murderously. "I'll gladly do two for the price of one this very evening, Mr. Coleman. So don't be tempting me!"

"Me tempt you? Ha, that's a laugh!" Tommy keeps his gaze riveted on the eyes of Hart.

"You really think you're a sharp blossom, don't you, Tommy?" the warden says, glancing momentarily at John Colt. "But you are no sharpie, I can assure you that. I can take you down, young man, and I will take you down. You're nothing, you hear me? Nothing! I'll eat you up."

The tenor of such shrill outburst causes heads to turn.

Old Hays grabs his constable's staff, starts down the central corridor. John Colt shuffles in his leg irons to one side, out of Hays' way.

Hart is red in the face with anger.

"Can I help, Warden?" Hays barks, cracking his staff abruptly on the Weehawken stone, daring Tommy Coleman to continue.

Tommy returns Hays' glare, never having forgotten how the high constable forced him at the Dead House to look into the dead and milky eyes of his wife and child.

"Warden Hart, my assistance is at your command, sir."

"Thank you, High Constable, everything is handled."

Hart's face shows considerable strain, veins pulsing, turgid in temple and down the center of his taut freckled forehead. He furtively looks away from Hays, turns his outrage back on Tommy Coleman in apparent attempt to drive the young blackguard's insolence down.

Hart says, "Gentlemen," to the guards as they tighten their grip on John Colt's tailored arm. "Let's go, Mr. Colt," he growls, brushing the first guard away, adjusting his own hold on Colt, rough enough to make him wince, marching him off down the block, calling back to Hays, "Thank you for your presence, High Constable. No fear. I am in control. You may see to your duty."

With a last glance at Tommy Coleman and the retreating backs of the warden, Colt, and the guards, Old Hays turns in the opposite direction, returns to his desk, and begins to make ready.

Hays is due at the Brooklyn police commissary to pick up a prisoner, James Holdgate, a lag he knows too well, due to come in from Gravesend. From there Hays will transport him back to Manhattan.

Over the years, Holdgate, a pewterer by trade, has been a most elusive mace cove, much wanted by Hays for an extended length and breadth of time. A primary conspirator with a band of knights of Alsatia, he had been an alleged participant in the notorious Timothy Redmond misidentification involving the Howland & Aspinwall and Union Bank forgeries, along with accomplices "Bob the Wheeler" Sutton, once a scrapper of some note (documented to the fullest in Pierce Egan's fistic annals, *Boxiana*), and the figure dancer John Reed. The *Police Gazette* had certainly made much of the chase and the whole affair, including in their account, if you listened to Olga Hays, a truly unflattering steel-point etching representation of her father, and a notorious verse, another, although unsigned, recently claimed by John Colt to have been penned by him.

James Holdgate, James Holdgate, bold burglar, come out,
And unravel the train-work which bringeth about
The grasp of the law in its own proper time—
The doom of the felon—the stamp of the crime—
You may wander at large, but naught will disperse
The dark shades of your deeds—their brand and their curse,
Then shrink back, old burglar, shrink back to your den!
And pray for all Time's everlasting "amen"!

It came as a surprise, therefore, when notification arrived earlier in the week via yellow card, handed him by Warden Hart, that the screwman Holdgate had been apprehended out in the hinterlands of Brooklyn, and was now held in a hammock in the calabash there.

Even though Colt's execution is scheduled in two hours' time, Hays feels neither necessity nor compulsion to be on hand for the niceties. In his long time served at his post, the high constable has seen far too many high gaggers face the hemp necklace. The experience, long ago, lost its urgency, and any appeal (if indeed it ever held any).

To his mind, nothing more, nothing less, Old Hays, high constable of the municipality, can only wish John C. Colt peace, here on earth and in the hereafter, and deliverance from all terror.

✣ 33 ✣

A Dagger in the Heart

Night falls after five. A chill takes the air. In his cell, the bars open
to the weather, the seasonal cold rushing in unchecked, Tommy
Coleman, bundled in his thin wool blanket, knees to chest, shivers and
waits.

After watching the day's proceedings, he has conjured up an image
of himself, he and his wife under the picture frame, having a turn at
the dance, enjoying themselves, the music playing gaily, the swirling
dust rising above their shoes.

Then, suddenly, Tommy imagines, sees it in his mind's eye like it is
happening for real right there in front of him, his wife—his dead
wife—the pretty Sister of the Pretty Hot Corn Girl, in quite another
context, alive again, quiet-voiced, standing under the gallows in front
of the priest, watching as he, Tommy, is led up the board steps.

From where he stands, on his cot, looking out the small barred
window, Tommy can see the entire expanse of courtyard where the
crowd is milling, where the carriages wait, where the stone walls
stand impenetrable, where the gibbet rises, where the banquet has
been laid and eaten, where the priest brushes pale dust from his
trouser leg.

ONE HOUR LATER, it may already be two, he has lost track of time, Tommy Coleman still stares out into the courtyard through the barred high window. He has begun to hear new voices, more authoritative, murmuring in the dark. A small brigade of deputy wardens have assembled under the gallows, ready for the evening's rite. The hangman, the Jack Ketch, is there. Dressed in black, he wears no hood. He resembles nothing less than an insect, with two irregular, irritated patches of bright red skin like cankers under each pop eye, framing the sharp, twitching nose. A mournful air to him, a deathful pall.

Up above, in the bell tower of the cupola dome, Tommy is aware of the clock tolling the quarter hour.

The crowd has been gathering in the courtyard. Many who had joined in and celebrated the wedding festivities earlier in the day have returned.

Or never left.

The heavy wood and iron gate opens and a guard addresses the uneasy crowd hovering in the street beyond the prison walls, impatient and cold, awaiting news of Colt's end.

Across from Tommy's cell, John Colt's cell is now empty. The door grate stands open. The peach curtain from his honeymoon hangs limp.

Tommy stares transfixed at the empty cell, the props of the ponce's life visible in front of him: the black leather chair that reclines, the glass vase that shimmers, the overturned green champagne bottle empty, the two crystal glasses, the bouquet of pink flowers on the floor, the pen still in the inkwell, the flat green bottle of Armagnac on the bookshelf, the forgotten black handkerchief neatly folded at the corner of the desk.

Tommy gazes, unseeing, as in the twilight a somber priest walks by.

Not five minutes later, Tommy's senses seem to peak. He sits up where he has been lying on his cot.

He smells smoke.

The coal stove near Old Hays' office will on occasion belch embers into the central corridor. At such times, a sour creosote perfume assaults the nostrils, stinging the eyes of those locked on the block. Tommy knows this reek is not that.

At first wisps of black smoke, then long spindles, then clouds, begin to billow down the corridors, leak in from the skylights. Then, almost immediately, panicked voices can be heard from outside: "Fire!"

Other shouts sound from somewhere deep inside the catacombs: "Fire!"

Then, almost immediately, a cataclysmic onrush and cascade of ember, flame, cinder, smoke, and more panicked voices.

"Run for your lives!"

"I can't! I can't get out."

Against the cacophony, a single dissonant voice somewhere cries, "Let it burn!"

Prisoners screaming for their lives, gripping iron bars, begin to cough harshly.

All along the rows and tiers, up and down the blocks, from above as well as from below, horrible hacking and outright screams of terror worsen.

"Don't let us burn!"

"Please! Oh God! Please! Don't let us die!"

"Shaddup, you kirkbuzzers, burnin's no worse than hangin'." The same voice, the same dissonant voice of Tommy Coleman that shouted, "Let it burn!"

Tommy, gasping at his window for air, knowing the real night's festivities have now begun, can see on narrow Leonard Street, across from the prison, the blaze itself, the licking flames reflected in the windows of the nondescript municipal administration building, whipping and raging above in the cupola of the bell tower, atop the tomblike Justice Department building.

Prisoners are locked up, crammed and trapped all around him, coughing and wheezing as the smoke swirls and billows, permeating their cells, fed through open windows and bars, cracks in the mortar and bricks. They are wild-eyed, frightened, shouting now for cell doors to be thrown open, allow the imprisoned to save themselves.

Bright orange flames hug the building roof, lick the dark night sky, the smoke continuing to pour down corridors in acrid black clouds, giving no indication of letup.

"Somebody! Somebody let me out of here! I don't want to die."

Warden Hart rushes onto the block, his smoke-irritated sky blue eyes wide with the excitement of danger and smoke, the hue of iris bluer, the white of the sclera redder with the aggravation of quick-flowing blood.

The smoke becoming even thicker and more caustic now. Death row is engulfed in a miasmic torrent of noxious haze. The terrible hacking and coughing of the doomed and condemned has taken over.

From his cell Tommy watches the confusion almost gleefully. "We've a date with the divil we do!" he yells.

The panic-stricken are by now everywhere.

Some keepers rush up the corridors, systematically fitting keys to locks, throwing open cell door after cell door, working apace through the rows, giving the terrified, as they waited in the maddest state of agitation, opportunity to escape if they can.

Then, suddenly, at the end of the corridor, at the gallows holding cell, Warden Hart's anguished cry rings out, slicing through all other tumult, echoing back through the corridors in an unnatural falsetto staccato. "Mr. Colt is dead! Mr. Colt is dead!"

Tommy, his attention suddenly drawn, swivels in the direction of the warden's voice, everything standing still.

"Mr. Colt is dead!" clear as a bell. "Mr. Colt is dead! A dagger in his heart! Mr. Colt is dead!"

Warden Hart immobile, staring.

There the body lies: a deflated figure on a brocaded daybed. Hands folded on still chest. The dead man's two tight white fists clasp a dagger. Its bejeweled hilt protrudes from whence it has been driven home, and through clenched fingers a stream of crimson blood.

"Mr. Colt is dead!"

Warden Hart staggers backward into the main corridor, his master key held in front of him like a prod, poised dramatically as if to defend himself against any ghoulish spirit that should arise.

Hapless prisoners, still locked up, desperate to be delivered, to be saved, to save themselves, cry out in their cells for him, for anyone, their voices bearing witness to their most remarkable states of terror and flux.

"Warden! Warden! How 'bout me? Warden! I don't want to die!"

They stand at the bars, at the grates.

"Warden? Warden? Don't let me die here! Please."

Hart shoves aside a stumbling drunk, freed when the door to the Bummers' Cell was thrown open. The warden, choking on the smoke, falls to his knees, crawls on the stone slab floor, feels his way to Tommy Coleman's cell.

After two feeble attempts, he pushes key into lock, and for an instant prisoner and jailer remain fixed in time, Monmouth Hart and Tommy Coleman, on opposite sides of the bars.

Then the warden turns the key.

As the lock disengages there is an audible click, followed by Tommy's grating laughter.

"For the life of me, I should let you burn right where you stand, you little son-of-a-bitch."

And just like that, the cell door swings open and Tommy Coleman, a pressed red cotton kerchief held over his mouth and nose, pushes past his emancipator, pats Monmouth Hart's sallow cheek, and immediately disappears into the smoke and confusion.

No one of consequence or authority takes further note of him. He moves swiftly, hand out as if a blind man. Nothing is discernible. He feels his way. The thick air bites his lungs. Through his handkerchief he dares not take breath any deeper than absolutely necessary.

He hears a voice. "This way!"

The harelipped keeper, his thick finger pointing. "Your people are waitin' for ya, hackum! Put a move on."

And with that, a pat on the back, a heavy door opens, cool air rushes in, and Tommy Coleman escapes into the night.

❧ 34 ❧

The Politics of Fire
in New York City

At Burling Slip, Old Hays steps off the Fulton Ferry onto the slippery wooden dock, having returned from his foray to the hinterlands with the screwman James Holdgate shackled and in tow. At the Brooklyn House of Detention, Hays had been delayed until the prisoner was registered as having arrived from Gravesend, the paperwork a mishap, no one seemingly in charge or able to prepare Holdgate for transport back to the island of Manhattan.

The high constable suffered some annoyance, but no surprise to be put upon in such slipshod manner. Now, hurrying up John Street cuffed to his prisoner, he sees the night sky lit, the flames diffuse through the heavy mist spilling off the estuary, heavy smoke from the cupola dome blowing south and east, drifting over him toward the Narrows.

All over the east side, even before the ferry had docked, the high constable could see the sky aglow and hear the frantic cries:

"Fire! Fire rages at the prison! Deadly fire at the Tombs!"

As far back as Hays could remember, and in fact throughout New York City history, fires were fought by volunteer fire companies, most formed with political link and clout. Lore had it even George Washington, during his residence on Rose Street, chased the engines.

To the detriment of the metropolis of late, however, many of these fire brigades had become closely associated with unsavory elements, gangsters, and organized street toughs. Because of this involvement by the criminal type, firefighting had become a citywide dilemma.

Far fewer fire hydrants existed than fire companies. When an alarm first sounded, individual brigades made mad dash for the blaze lest they be blocked out by one of the other more vociferous companies. The worst thing that could occur was to be outdone by a hated rival.

The solution was to dispatch the fastest runner in each corps at full speed to the site of the inferno. Commandeering a wooden barrel from a nearby market or storefront greengrocer, this point man would quickly position his barrel over the nearest available fireplug and sit on top of it, trying to maintain his place until his fellow firefighters arrived and hooked their hoses.

If another from a rival company showed up at the same plug, a fight would surely ensue over the rights to the hydrant, and when the firefighting corps were representatives of a disreputable and violent gang, as they were more and more of late, sometimes numbering their members in the tens or hundreds, a battle, perhaps even a war, was the result, the constabulary inevitably having to be called in to break up the fray. Many a tinderbox building had been engulfed while the mortal combat on the street raged in the dancing reflection of the flames.

Each and every year for some hundred years, one of the most glorious events in the city was the annual Firemen's Parade down Broadway. Raucous crowds, made overwrought by rhum and boisterous, unrestrained celebration, lined the wide avenue and bordering sidewalks to lay excited eyes on the exuberant red-shirted brigades, handsome in pounded beaver hats, marching two by two, pulling their beloved engines to the cadence of huge brass bands blaring out "Solid Men to the Front," the bellowing cadres of firefighters coming up behind, singing and shouting the lyric to their brave anthem:

In time of need
When we succeed

The flames afore . . .
It's solid men to the front!

Their splendiferous engines clattered and rumbled down the cobble-stone thoroughfare, their names magnificently painted on their gleaming red flanks: White Ghost, Shad Belly, Black Joke, Red Rover, Dry Bones, Hay Wagon, Big Six, Big Seven, Yaller Gal, Bean Soup, Old Maid, Old Junk.

Hays knew it no jest when it was said the average Bowery b'hoyo loved his engine more than his girl.

THE NIGHT of the cupola fire at the Palace of Justice, the cobblestone streets are clotted with just such fire companies. Traffic is dense and impassable with stalled wagons and carts.

And more and more by the minute are becoming entrenched in the morass: loaded wagons and rattling trucks piled to the top post, pulled by nervous teams of steaming, snorting horses.

In front of Hays and his cuffed charge, from the piers, the low resorts and buckets of blood, the drink parlors, spas, and diving bells, hordes of people pour onto the packed east side streets.

The thoroughfares are already a high jumble, all traffic pointed toward the red glow. At clips of alarming speed, the last of the fire brigades from the car barns of Corlear's Hook and far off Boodle Hill careen through the streets.

Hays proceeds, frustrated, impatient, moving along as best he can, braceleted as he is to Holdgate, and given no transport waiting for him or his prisoner.

He is keeping west on Anthony Street when a closed, high-backed carriage rumbles off from Elm. The carriage sways at the uppermost, where the driver sits, nearly running the high constable and his charge down as the conveyance emerges from the flickering light and shad-ows onto the main throughway, racing with reckless abandon over the paving stones.

Hays stumbles out of its path at the last possible instant, pulling the cracksman down on top of him.

Hays is startled. Inside, as the carriage curtain blows back, illuminated by the chained whale-oil lamps, he glimpses a man at the window. But it is only a glimpse, and given the half-light and the state of Hays' aging eyes, he can't be sure:

Could it have been John Colt?

To Old Hays it certainly seemed it was he.

But then the carriage, a large black brougham, is gone, cutting across the intersection before diverting north at the next corner. Only the clatter of hooves and iron wheels hangs in the air.

Hays takes a deep breath, rights himself, smells the smoke, can taste the bite of it in the air. He checks his pocket watch. John Colt should have been long dead, hanged by this time. Yet somehow he would not be surprised. Money. Money in the megalopolis. John Colt not dead. John Colt not hanged. John Colt escaped.

Holdgate mumbles something at him.

Hays turns. "What?"

"Blimey! That was close," Holdgate repeats.

Hays wrenches him to his feet to continue their trek west, speeding awkwardly toward the city prison, now with the gnawing, all-but-certain, wheedling feeling that the Colt family has finally achieved its goal, reached the powers that be with their bribe money and influence.

In front of Hays a pack of young men and boys bolt across the street, down a crooked alley, through a yard, over a fence.

A tight knot of children are bunched by the kerb, minded by their cousins and older sisters. The little ones, mere tykes, clad in rags, barely notice the pack of tough boys and thug-a-lugs, not much older than they.

Preoccupied, only occasionally do these urchins peek up the street through the muddle of traffic and pedestrian confusion at the red night sky illuminated by fire.

Meanwhile they jump their length of frayed rope, joyously chanting and singing, ignoring the frenzy and wild excitement of their elders gravitating up the hill.

"Oh, I hurt, I hurt, I hurt all over," the children shout. "I got a eye ache, a toothache, a gumboil, a bellyache . . .

"A pain in my right side,
A pain in my left side,
A pimple on my nose.

Oh, I hurt, I hurt,
I hurt all over.

My face! My face! My face!"

✿ 35 ✿

Into the Five Points

As he exits the Tombs the cold air hits Tommy Coleman in the gob like a blast of attentiveness.

Behind him voices still reverberate, "Mr. Colt is dead! Mr. Colt is dead! A dagger in his heart. Mr. Colt is dead."

The streets in front of Tommy are in pandemonium. Behind him the cupola of the Palace of Justice is ablaze. Half a dozen colorful, pugnacious fire companies already vie for a corridor that does not exist through the clogged traffic. Shadowy, wraithlike figures charge through the smoke-choked confusion.

Tommy stands momentarily still outside the prison walls, beneath the high stone ramparts, overwhelmed and stupefied by the spectacle.

In every direction smoke belches.

In every direction chaos reigns.

An apparition emerges from the shadows, his left arm limp, his left leg dragging, both appendages shriveled. The chimera's clothes hang off him, filthy and much too big.

"Tom-Tom!" he hisses. "Over here."

Two leatherheads from the Night Watch, arrogant in their attitude and demeanor, both with huge ripe bellies and bloated moose faces, march back and forth beneath the Tombs' walls trying to clear the streets and make way for the fire companies. Bovine, self-important pig-widgeons, they make a big show of directing traffic, spitting on the ground, screaming at the teamsters to get their horses out of the way, punching the terrified beasts in their soft snouts as hard as they can to get their attention, get them to do what they want and move clear.

"Whatsa matta wit' ya? Ya can't git no pleasure out of that!" one indignant cartman shouts back at the stupid leatherheads after a particularly brutal blow to the driver's confused steed.

"Oh, I can't, can't I?" the big night watchman shoots back. "Per'aps you'd rather take the blows for 'em, eh, dad? Step down and permit me to give you yer whacks, ya oaf ya."

A block away, out of sight in a greengrocery, the excited and rambunctious membership of the Forty Little Thieves lie in wait. Despite the November cold they are coatless. They wear their trademark soft caps, and their shirttails are free of the restraint of their waistbands, fluttering in the night wind. They are kidders, willing and able, anxious and ready to facilitate their leader's escape.

With a signal from Tweeter (a surprisingly strong wave of his crutch), a well-chosen phalanx of these fearless, dangerous, dirty little boys charge into the already impossibly congested intersection, dragging a dilapidated red pump wagon behind them.

"Make way!" they shout, savagely pushing through, irritating everybody in their path. "Make way!"

As if any single sorry citizen would be inclined not to let them through in light of the reputation of imps like these for senseless and brutal violence.

Still, given the deplorable circumstances on the street and outside the Tombs, it is impossible to pay the slightest heed to this filthy band of lethal apaches.

The goal ostensibly sought by this virulent youthful crew is the last lowly fireplug still available. It is sequestered beneath the prison wall on White Street, but already numerous battalions of desperate men from legitimate and not-so-legitimate fire companies are participating in a very animated free-for-all of most magnificent proportion for this same such objective.

From experience Tommy knows if any of these combatants actually think they will put hose to pump this evening they will be sadly mistaken.

Taking his general by the elbow, Tweeter, half leaning, half steering, angles him through the packed streets as if Tommy were a blind man and Tweeter his cane, wedging him this way and that, whispering directions in his ear, all to keep him moving in the right direction.

At every corner, it seems, war cries are emanating from the very cobblestones. The pandemonium qualifies as riot. Hoarse voices rise everywhere to bloodcurdling crescendo, only to be met by even higher-pitched, more earsplitting cries, adding to the cacophony of the already addled mob's insanity.

"John Colt is dead!"

"John Colt is dead! Dead by his own hand!"

"Someone must pay!"

"We have been cheated!"

"More will die!"

"John Colt is dead!"

Even Tommy Coleman quivers. The grievous shouts cut through him like an unlikely augur as if it were his own funeral he would soon be attending.

"Colt is dead!"

Unsavory bands of more gangsters, scores of violent participants wearing gang outfits and colors, oft-patched suits and stuffed top hats, holey overcoats and grimy mackinaws, their eyes burning slits, dangerous men and violent boys, wade into the melee with brickbats, half-bullies, bludgeons, splintered ash batons, cudgels, slungshots, and granite paving bricks pried from the street, smashing, stomping, whacking as they plod in, ruthlessly seeking the smallest foothold.

And when gained, then another.

With grunts and groans, honest men shrink back. Terrified dray teams whinny. Drivers whip the colossal brutes, trying to somehow manage to get through the terrible morass and away.

A gaggle of exhausted leatherheads, led by a furtive-eyed Sergeant McArdel, try to enforce some perfunctory plan of action, steering traffic this way, that. And finally, one truck slips past and away, and then another. A trickle of squeaking, rattling wagons manage to eke by.

Until the perfect truck appears and the signal is given. While Sergeant McArdel of the Night Watch melts away, the rest of the gang of Forty Little Thieves emerge from their hidey-holes to pounce on it.

A large butcher cart it is, loaded with meat. It is seized and overturned by the young thugs at the corner of Cross and Anthony, its contents spilled onto the street. At the same time, swarms of street urchins appear out of every doorway and back alley, and two and three together team to carry off carcasses of oxen beef, pork, lamb, and venison while coteries of miffed citizens, knowing not with whom they are dealing, make futile attempt to shoo them, annoyed that these rapscallions should somehow be swarming in the street, partaking of this anarchy, interfering with the good citizen's view of the firestorm engulfing the cupola dome, and the pandemonium beneath.

Drivers try to escape the crush. They scream at their frightened teams, "Giddyyup, ye beast ye. Ahh, bah now! Git it on, ye damn mules, or 'tis the glue factory fer ya," and so, off, finally able to rumble, half a chance given and taken, half an inch of clearance to squeeze by, smoke and vapor pouring from the huge dray beasts' distended nostrils, horse teeth bared, while the hardened pint-sized gangsters, armed with the crudest of weapons, deal mighty blows to their adversaries and mates, whomsoever, send them tumbling under the galloping hooves of the animals, and Tommy Coleman, amidst the fury, no longer stands stock-still watching, his mouth agape, but urged forward by his old pally Tweeter Toohey, once more makes his way, following the surprisingly agile gimp, wielding his crutch as a weapon, across Franklin Street and down into their lifelong home, the worst slum on earth, the Five Points.

TOMMY COLEMAN sees the high constable, Jacob Hays, in his camlet coat, leaning on his staff, married to some kirkbuzzer, before Old Hays sees him. Tommy and his gang dash almost directly in front of the shadow and his handcuffed prisoner onto Cross Street, through the urchins jumping rope, through the streetwide commotion.

The intersection is so clogged it prevents any hope for entry to Columbia. Tommy's breath comes hard. Hastily he bolts down Little Water Street, on whose cul-de-sac loom three clapboard tenements, each in a state of horrible disrepair, each marked by a sign painter's less-than-steady hand: Jacob's Ladder, Gates of Hell, Brickbat Mansion.

The band skirts these miserable structures. All that is loathsome, drooping, and decayed is here. Tommy and his boyos run, doubling back across the southernmost boundary of this horrid patch of ground.

Had Old Hays spotted him? Is he following?

Looking back over his shoulder, Tommy no longer sees the shade. He hurries past another pocket of noisy, hell-bent six-year-olds in rags, torn between guarding their families' miserable clothing set to drying on the bits of broken spikes and rusted iron fencing of Paradise Square, and the need, the longing, to abandon their responsibility, to beat it up the hill to see what is to be seen at the cupola dome and the Tombs.

In the southwest corner of the square, Tommy finally cuts into a muddy alley behind another string of decrepit hovels and warehouses at what is called Cow Bay. It was here that his wife and child's bodies were discovered, where he bludgeoned Ruby Pearl in retaliation. The alley runs alongside a squat yellow building, an abandoned tannery on Orange Street.

A temperance board is nailed to its façade:

FIVE POINTS MISSION

OF

THE LADIES HOME SOCIETY

Tommy slips through the blue battered door, from where, inside the mission, he cannot help but hear comforting hymnal voices raised in song, sweetly singing:

"There is rest for the weary,
There is rest for you,

On the other side of Jordan,
Where the Tree of Life is blooming,
There is rest for you . . ."

❧ 36 ❧

Conjecture on the Death
of John C. Colt

The following morning, at the behest of her father, Olga Hays visited the news shed on Canal Street to return home burdened with the early-edition array of public prints, each and every one full of Colt's suicide and the inferno at the Tombs.

DEAD FOR A DUCAT—DEAD!

proclaimed the *Sun*.

WHO GAVE HIM THE KNIFE?

wondered the *Tribune*.

FIRE! FIRE! FIRE!

shouted the *Mercury*.

MR. COLT DEAD IN HIS CELL!

cried the *Brooklyn Eagle*.

A DAGGER PIERCES MURDERER'S HEART!

bellowed the *Herald,* delineating in minute, tantalizing detail:

THE LAST DAY OF JOHN C. COLT
His Extraordinary Suicide and Death

"I am reluctant to add to the misery of the Colt family," wrote eminent publisher and editor James Gordon Bennett.

> With his surviving and highly respectable relatives we can profoundly sympathize.
> But this is not the end of it.
> I have a sacred duty to perform to the public that is paramount to all other considerations. If hereafter a warden intends to allow a desperate criminal, under sentence of death, to have every facility for obtaining knives, scissors, poison for committing self-murder, why, the sooner the public is aware of it, the better for all parties.

The consensus on who might have smuggled the lethal blade into the prison laid culpability with Colt's bride. Especially after reporters, dispatched to her apartments, discovered the new Mrs. Colt not at home and nowhere to be found in society.

"We hardly know where to begin," persisted Bennett. "Or how to express the feelings and thoughts which rise up in the mind in contemplating this awful, this unexampled, this stupendous, this most extraordinary and most horrible tragedy."

> From the first moment of his trial to the last pulsation of his existence, Mr. Colt seems to have been under the influence of a false system of morals, a perverted sense of human honor, and a sentiment that is at utter variance with the mysterious revelations of Christianity, or the sacred institutions of justice in civilized society. Toward him that was, none can

have any feeling but that of pity, commiseration, and deep anguish of heart.

If Colt, the cold and remorseless killer, had not been permitted to marry in the first place, none of this would have happened! And by inference, denying the public its due, seeing him hanged.

Accompanying this phlegmic editorial and conclusion, a line drawing depicted Colt's corpse, viewed through a jailhouse window, the body lying in his well-appointed cell, the hilt of a bejeweled dagger protruding from his chest, smoke and flame, presumably from the fire in the cupola dome, licking and swirling all about the body.

The caption beneath the lurid scene read:

THE PRISONER HAD EVIDENTLY WORKED AND TURNED THE KNIFE ROUND AND ROUND IN HIS HEART AFTER HE HAD STABBED HIMSELF, MAKING QUITE A LARGE GASH.

Bennett demanded those city officials in charge be held responsible.

With somewhat less diatribe was dealt the blaze at the Hall of Justice itself. The gist: The fire burned most of the night. As a result, the building sustained substantial damage, but, thankfully, not total decimation. The blaze had been attributed to grease, for the most part held to the flue stacks, and blamed on the carelessness of the restaurant Delmonico's, using the prison facilities to prepare succulents for the Colt wedding banquet.

Warden Hart was quoted as saying that not less than twelve official fire companies, not including rogue street gangs, had participated in the extinguishment (Hart's word) of the inferno.

The fire was considered an accident, a coincidence. The cupola dome had caught fire certainly, and would have to be replaced, the warden admitted. There was much smoke and water damage.

For his part, Mayor Robert Morris declared in no uncertain terms that the building structure would be rebuilt.

"How," he was quoted in the *Mercury*, "could the city ever endure without its glorious Palace of Justice?"

THREE DAYS PASSED before the public prints saw fit to question what might have really transpired the night of the Tombs fire.

HAS MR. COLT MADE GOOD AN ESCAPE?

asked Bennett in yet another of his special editions.

Until then, somewhat to High Constable Jacob Hays' surprise, not a word had seen print to the effect that John Colt might have eluded punishment. For the most part, the follow-up accounts in the public papers had merely stated that the deceased's body was removed immediately from the Palace of Justice, an inquest soon held, the Dead House eschewed, and the corpse quickly buried without ceremony in the churchyard cemetery of St. Mark's-in-the-Bouwerie on Tenth Street at Second Avenue.

Acidly, Bennett now publicly assailed city coroner Dr. Archibald Archer, accusing him of having been in on the deception from the start, charging that an unfortunate corpse had been prepared beforehand, and the jurymen at the inquest selected for one reason, and one reason only: their ignorance of John C. Colt's appearance.

Assuming an ill-fitting stance of moral superiority, Bennett took opportunity to perch himself even higher than he was accustomed, with relish sniping down from this unaccustomed new height: "Then again a most extended system of bribery has been in operation to effect the escape of Homicide Colt from the beginning," he wrote. "Certainly, since his conviction."

Let us not forget that during his trial in the oyer and terminer, there were all sorts of rumors about the vote in the jury room, but at the time nothing certain could be proven. Last evening after the outplay of this latest debacle we were able to ascertain that the sum of $1,000 had been offered to each of three of the deputy keepers. As result all sorts of rumors remain in circulation relative to the suicide. Many doubt Mr. Colt is dead.

Bennett charged the supposed "suicide" was at that very moment on his way by private coach to either California or Texas.

Perhaps with his new wife. "Nothing is beyond the family Colt and their influence," he sniffed.

And then more.

In the next day's edition, the publisher-editor pondered:

DID OTHERS ESCAPE WITH MR. COLT?

seeing fit to name a single name:

TOMMY COLEMAN

While another headline in a follow-up edition chose to link the two, wondering:

WHERE ARE THEY NOW?

Followed by still another speculative column stating it had been assumed at first that Tommy Coleman had lost his life in the conflagration, but now, with rumor rampant about John Colt having made his way beyond the prison walls and the hangman, the fact of no body being found, the probability must be examined that Tommy Coleman, too, had taken the opportunity of the inferno to make his own escape.

Olga Hays reads to her father editor Bennett's final thoughts of that publishing day:

> As for the other rogue, I know Tommy Coleman, met him in his cell. Never underestimate the man. He is the charismatic, ruthless leader of the Forty Little Thieves, a gang that is so deeply embedded in the Five Points

neighborhood nothing short of *infestation* can suffice to describe the hoodlums' relation to their putrefic environs.

Sorry to say, now with unwarranted freedom at hand, of what might this young gentleman be capable?

I am all too fearful that we, the innocent citizenry of our great metropolis, might all too soon find out lest a savior appear who can for us undo this moldering morass.

❦ 37 ❦

A Poem Before Dying

If John Colt was dead or alive, buried or escaped, Old Hays was unable to attest. He had been most certainly absent at the time of Homicide Colt's alleged demise. Likewise, he had not been paid the privilege to view the corpse. Nor had he opportunity to be on hand when the body was put to bed with a shovel.

Still, he knew what he had seen: the gentleman in question, cloaked and curtained, passenger in that black brougham careening down Cross Street.

On the night of the cupola inferno, finally arriving at the Tombs after midnight, dragging the prigger Holdgate with him, Hays found the prison charred and reeking, the body attributed to the condemned already gone. The detective, walking slowly through the facility assessing the damage, reconstructed in his mind what must have transpired while he was absent. He prided himself on a learned skill: having spent so many years in the profession, coming upon the scene of a crime, Old Hays felt himself entirely able to smell the criminal.

Reasonably, the high constable questioned himself. What was he to make of the apprehension of James Holdgate in Gravesend after such extended period of successfully eluding police authorities? Had this not been a charade, its clever construct designed to lure the high constable away from his appointed rounds and the highly orchestrated crime scene? Had bribes been paid to facilitate the deception? And if they had, to whom? And for which reason? For Colt's suicide to proceed unimpeded, or his escape? The answers would come, Hays knew. Patience was an attribute to which long experience had paid contribution.

Still, he swore, he would not be had.

It took additional three days' time before Mayor Morris came forward, bowing to outside pressure and the outcry of Bennett and the public prints.

During that period of frustration, Hays had sought on several separate occasions (first thing in the morning on three successive days) audience with the mayor, but had been rebuffed.

Now Mayor Morris, in a noontime address to the Common Council and Board of Aldermen, professed to being merely astonished by the turn of events.

Reluctantly, he was ready to admit that something duplicitous *may* have occurred in the city's House of Detention. Yet he refused to believe John Colt had escaped.

"The man is dead," Mayor Morris declared.

Yet, he wondered, how in heaven's name had the prisoner come by the bejeweled dagger that he had plunged into his own beating heart in that final moment of what must have been unspeakable desperation?

That afternoon, in the penny dailies, names were mentioned: both of Colt's brothers, his lawyers, his minister. Even Dillback, the manservant. A horde of others, including Poe the poet and John Howard Payne the songster.

Yet Caroline Colt, née Henshaw, assumed role of the presses' general-consensus guilty party.

Monmouth Hart, under pressure from the mayor's office, now joined company and freely accused Mr. Colt's new wife.

Men were subject to close scrutiny before entering the prison, especially death row. Thorough search was required for men and women alike, Hart explained to a gathering of newspaper flacks.

But on her wedding day how closely had Miss Henshaw been examined?

On the hectic afternoon in question, the prison premises had suffered from a dearth of unoccupied guards, Hart conceded.

Had Mr. Malcolm Trencher, the man assigned the task, done his duty?

Later in the day, Warden Hart made a great show of calling the beleaguered man aside in front of Old Hays and posing the question: Had he patted her down?

"Not her bosom," Mr. Trencher, a nervous, forlorn type admitted. "I did not touch that part of her anatomy. Nor any area below the waist."

Looking on, Hays could not fault him, given the nature of their prurient society.

Trencher was the very same keeper interrogated by the English author Charles Dickens, the one who had given misinformation in regard to the origin of the name of the Tombs institution.

"I would have touched her below the waist," Warden Hart impugned. "For God's sake, man, where is your duty?"

Hart continued his foray. "So the ornamental dagger of a certain proportion might have been hidden from view?" he went on in a bluster. "Carried between the breasts, let us say, point facing down?"

Admitted.

Hays looked on but said nothing, his sympathy with Trencher, his distrust with Hart.

FOLLOWING TRENCHER'S INQUISITION, Hays returned to his desk. He sat himself heavily in his stiff ladder-back chair.

Could this spectacle have been any more of a sham than it seemed? Had Monmouth Hart really had the bad sense and audacity to stage such show, assailing the twitchy Trencher entirely for the high constable's benefit?

Old Hays had no doubt. His eyes might have grown somewhat weak over the years, but he would have to be very well convinced otherwise that it was someone else than John Colt of whom he had caught sight behind that flapping carriage curtain.

His constable's staff in hand, Old Hays made his way down the cell block to John Colt's purported place of last breath.

Seven hundred and thirty-four inmates had inhabited the Tombs that November evening when Mr. Colt had been scheduled to die. Hays prided himself on knowing virtually each and every one of these maladroits by sight. The high constable claimed never to forget a criminal face. He also was famous for touring the Penitentiary of the City of New York at Bellevue and the Women's Almshouse on Blackwell's Island at least once a week, gazing into cell after cell, withstanding the shouted insults and mutterings, so as to know the countenances of the females incarcerated there as well as he knew their jailed brethren downtown.

After the fire, all but a dozen inmates were said to be accounted for, recaptured, remanded, and transported to the women's prison at Bellevue to be held there.

Aside from a few ineffectual kirkbuzzers, shycocks, and top-divers, the notable exceptions were John Colt and Tommy Coleman.

Albeit nervously, when questioned by Hays, the warden stood by his assertion. Colt was found dead in his cell. Hart maintained he could not be certain what had happened to Tommy Coleman and made no venture. He may have died in the inferno and his body consumed by the flames. He honestly did not know, he said, and could not guess. The cell doors along the block had all been thrown open. He may have escaped. If that was the case, he would be found and rearrested.

"By whom?" Hays demanded.

"By you, sir," Hart said. "I have utmost respect for your prowess, High Constable."

Hays stalked away from the functionary. He found no necessity to mention he had no doubt seen John Colt during the course of his escape, and it was his conviction the man had appeared at the time hale and hearty.

He stood in front of the empty and abandoned cell where Colt had purportedly died, staring through the bars. The grate stood ajar. He went inside. There was no blood soaked on the cot as you might expect if someone had expired there from a fatal knife wound to the heart.

Hays returned down the corridor to Colt's cell.

Everything was relatively the same here as when Hays last saw it. Nothing much had been disturbed by the conflagration. Remarkably, the flames had actually consumed little, although the sharp smell of acridity was strong and there was a layer of black, pasty char and muck on the floor. But the reality was that most of the blaze had been restricted to the flue stacks. When Hays cursorily inspected the stone walls, it was not hard to find a series of ragged, fist-sized holes punched through the mortar from where the smoke had surely vented directly from the clay chimney liners into the prison block proper. Every indication told how the fire had been grease-fed. The fat from the broiling meats evidently had erupted in flames. Those flames had licked straight up inside the prison wall flues to the cupola dome, catching that structure on fire and eventually destroying it. The result being a spectacle of smoke and cinder that had poured into the prison through the holes punched in the flue liners and causing such panic.

He called the jailer, "Mr. Trencher? Would you mind terribly?"

Hearing his name, Trencher lumbered back down the block. By necessity he was at Hays' beck and call. Hays knew he was a man who would do anything for him. In his mind, in some part because of his embarrassment in front of Dickens, Trencher was forever diminished in front of Hays and at disadvantage.

"Mr. Trencher," Hays said, "would you mind unlocking Mr. Colt's house of solitude here for me?"

Once the lock was keyed and open, Hays stepped inside the cell and stopped stock-still. Something came over him and seized him. The consummate shadow surveyed the man's lair with its myriad appointments. He had an inner feeling, vast and unreal. The polished writing desk, the leather patent chair of Colonel Colt's invention, the multivolume library neatly lined on the cherrywood book commode, an array of unbound folios rushed straight from the printer for the prisoner's enjoyment, the plethora of pamphlets, extras, and popular magazines of the day, all stood their ground, barely touched by soot, much less fire.

Hays studied the titles of the three books occupying Colt's desk, holding them close to his eyes to better see. They were all Edgar Poe's: *Tales of the Grotesque, Tales of the Arabesque,* and a pamphlet edition, *Recent Tales of Ratiocination.*

Hays felt Trencher's eyes on him. Hays knew the man could not read. Neither could he write, nor even recognize his own name when written.

The entire prison and much of the law enforcement cadre had been taken to task by the popular press for Colt's preferential treatment. A rose on the dinner plate. Brocaded drapery. A fussy British servant attired in evening clothes. A decorous writing table, his personal library, a reclining leather chair. Conjugal visits from his mistress for the sole purpose of frolic.

For God's sake. A man condemned to death?

Rumors of bribery were in recent full circulation. The *Herald* even gave numbers: a thousand dollars each, offered to three unnamed jailers.

Trencher was a self-acknowledged lout. Hays knew him to sometimes be abusive to prisoners. But bribery?

Hays hoped not Trencher. Despite himself, without realizing, Hays lowered himself into Colt's leather chair.

John Colt had boasted to Hays on more than one occasion how his brother Sam had developed the design, had drafted the blueprint with his own hand, had even gone so far as to send the necessary paperwork to the national capital in Washington, D.C., and the U.S. Patent Office there.

It *was* remarkable how the Colt chair changed position. Indeed, an engineering marvel. When you pushed your body back in a certain manner, for a moment there, you felt almost helpless as if you were about to plummet, then the mechanism sprang into action and all went smoothly, and it was for all the world as if you were luxuriating on a fat goose-feathered divan. Old Hays took a shallow breath. For the first time in he knew not how long, the pain in his back and legs subsided. Or seemed to be diminished, if not altogether relieved.

Hays sighed deeply in comfort. He despised those who thought themselves above all else of God's creatures. Humility was a large word to the high constable. He abhorred those, like John Colt, who chose to live outside the law, those who thought themselves better than the rest of their fellow citizens, those who, by action and choice, made a mockery of all law-abiding members of society.

His mind came to Poe. He thought of Mary Rogers and wondered the connection between the two, vowed to himself it would be found out.

Trencher's voice brought Hays back from his reverie.

"Got your eye on Mr. Colt's patent chair there, Mr. High? I be glad t'he'p you carry it back to your office there. Surely is a thing of beauty. Nobody cares if you take it, sir, they surely don't."

Hays chose not to acknowledge the dolt.

It took some minutes before it dawned on Trencher that he was no longer needed.

From where he sat on the recliner, Hays glimpsed a scroll, not unlike the one he had seen with Edgar Poe, partially hidden by a folded black handkerchief at the desk corner. He picked the tight roll up, slipping off the black ribbon, and began to separate the packet of pages. Noting Colt's precise, elegant hand, one bit of doggerel written thereon caught his eye, causing the high constable to replace his magnifying spectacles on his nose to read his way with fascination through

Colt's most curious version of the aftermath to the Samuel Adams' murder in verse:

The deed was done, but one ugly fear
Came over me now to touch this thing.
There was nothing to struggle against me here
In this lifeless heap. I wished it would spring
And grasp me, and strike at me, as it did
Only a moment or two before.
I lifted the head, but it dropped, and slid
From my grasp to its bed of gore.

What will you do with this horrible thing?
Down—shove, push it in a crate!
Push! Push down hard! If you choose you may sing
That song of his. Don't start and look round!

Push! How terribly inept you are!
The dawn in the East begins to grow;
The birds are all chirping; push there, shove there
That body at once, and for God's sake go!
The world will be up in less than an hour,
And rattle and ring along the road.
Away! Away! Away for your life!

Ah, well, that o'er,
And he lies sepulchred in his last abode!

In the half-light Hays sat pondering. He realized all must for him be reduced to a simple axiom: If Colt had made escape, he would catch him and see him pay. Any and all who had seen fit to aid this murderer and abet him, they too would be dealt with the same. Be it who it may, Trencher, Colt's brothers, Edgar Poe, Monmouth Hart, whosoever. They would pay too.

He put down the handwritten verse and settled down in Colt's recliner, relaxed further. Remarkable how the supple leather molded and supported the small of the back. Colonel Colt was indeed a clever fellow. Hays had personally tried his Paterson pistol. The revolving weapon certainly had its imperfections. After the chambers were emptied, it was not a small feat to reload. But the implication of the weapon was clear to Hays. Once Colt had ironed out the kinks, the high constable had no doubt all men in law enforcement would want one of these equalizers, and it would make the profession that much easier. The real problem, however, Hays thought just before he fell into sleep, was that all villains and blackguards would desire one of Colt's revolvers as well, and that acquisition would make their profession that much easier, and lethal, just the same.

❦ 38 ❦

Colt's Patent Chair

Later that evening, a grave cartman arrives on Lispenard Street, an irregularly shaped object of some size wrapped in thick gray blankets, bound with strong blue braided cord, and posited in the carry-bed of his two-wheeled wooden cart.

The man struggles to unload the bundle, drag it to the door, and knock. After some moments, Olga Hays answers, drying her hands on a dish towel. She has been cleaning the kitchen following dinner: clearing the dishes, scrubbing the pots, wiping down the table of its crumbs.

Lately, directly after dinner, her father has seen fit to abandon her. Already upstairs in his bed, under the covers, fueled by a cup of brewed black tea, a magnifying glass in hand, he would read, and reread, Poe's strange and eerie tales, "MS. Found in a Bottle," "Maelzel's Chess-Player," "The Fall of the House of Usher," "The Masque of the Red Death," "The Pit and the Pendulum," "The Murders in the Rue Morgue," "The Black Cat."

Meanwhile, downstairs, Olga asks of the cartman, "What is this?" to which he wipes his spongy nose with the back of his hand before responding.

He pulls an envelope, twice folded from his back pocket. "A gif' fer 'igh Consuble 'ays from Cunnel Sam'l Colt," he manages, clearly uncomfortable with speech. He hands over to Olga the folded communication, which he has managed to unfold in a manner.

Olga takes it, scrutinizes the soiled envelope, but does not open it.

"Does High Constable Hays know about this?" she asks. "He mentioned nothing of it."

"I dun' know, ma'am? Mind if I bring thu bun'le in, be on m'way?"

She tells him to wait, excuses herself, goes to the stairs, the soiled envelope in her hand, calls, "Papa?"

When there is no answer, she hurries up.

By the time she comes back down, the chair is in the center of the parlor, the cartman standing over it, sawing away on the final strand of rope by which it had been tethered.

A few moments later her father follows her down the carpeted stair, the envelope torn open, the letter in his hand. He offers the folded page to Olga:

My Dear High Constable Hays:

Sir, please excuse this presumption on your privacy, but I have been made aware by one of your colleagues of your admiration for my deceased brother's patent chair.

Since tragedy has rendered it impossible for John to be here with us to enjoy this chair as intended, I would be remiss not to offer this object to you as a gift. In recognition of the respect you paid my brother in his last months, I would be honored if you, sir, saw fit to accept.

My brother always spoke highly of you. And I too in our meetings, both social and business, have found you a highly moral man, a true and capable gentleman.

Signed with sincerity,
Sam Colt

"Take it back."

But the cartman is already heading for the door, not hearing, not understanding, or just plain ignoring the high constable.

His protest unheeded, the cartman gone, Hays sits himself heavily at the dining room table, glowering, purposely not looking at the chair positioned in the middle of the parlor floor.

"Olga, have you done with your chores?" he asks.

"I have."

"I have been reading author Poe's 'Purloined Letter.' Again the detective Dupin. I ask you, Olga, in all my years, I have never heard of such a thing. What is a *chevalier* anyway?"

She tells him. "A French term. A man of honor. One of some nobility."

He grumbles at that too.

She asks about the chair, the gift from Colonel Colt, why does it upset him so?

He refuses to answer.

She sighs. "Make use of it, Papa. At least as long as it is here you might as well. Especially if it is as comfortable as you have told me it is. Don't be so stubborn."

"I shall not have it," he snaps. "And for your information, the last thing I am being is stubborn, Olga."

"Don't be silly, Papa. You are too being stubborn. You told me over dinner Colt's chair was the one thing you have found that in any way makes your legs stop their ache. Don't spite yourself."

Hays snorts, puffs his pipe vigorously, glances at the chair with scorn, then relents, sits back down in it, and reclines.

"Would you like me to read you the rest of your story?"

"Yes, that would be very nice."

She goes upstairs to his bedroom and comes down with the pamphlet volume, *Recent Tales of Ratiocination.* As she picks up from his bookmarker, he listens tight-lipped to her pleasant, authoritive enunciation.

"'And then came, as if to my final and irrevocable overthrow, the spirit of PERVERSENESS. Of this spirit philosophy takes no account. Phrenology finds no place for it among its organs. Yet I am not more sure that my soul lives, than I am that perverseness is one of the primitive impulses of the human heart—one of the indivisible primary faculties, or sentiments, which give direction to the character of Man.'"

Her father's voice interrupts her.

"The deeper we descend into Mr. Poe's writing, Olga, the more my instinct tells me to strong-arm the man once and for all, get him to tell me what he knows exactly of Mary Rogers and her death." She then hears him mutter, "I'll give him a well-disturbed mind."

But long listening is not what Old Hays can endure this evening. His pipe still clamped between his teeth, it is not long before he has closed his eyes, and in the comfort of Colt's gift patent chair, and in the bascom of his daughter's comforting voice, he has once more succumbed to sleep.

39

Grave Robbers

Tommy Coleman's father, the ward heeler Timothy Coleman, had made his life doing his masters' bidding. Timo Coleman lost his first son to the hangman, but the nature of politics in the Sixth Ward, part of it comprising the Five Points, has changed. The Irish now walked arm in arm with the hall of St. Tammany, and had begun to learn how to tether some Democratic might.

When it became apparent that John Colt would not outdistance the hangman, Samuel Colt sent his delegate, his brother James, to approach ward heeler Coleman, pointing out to him that it had become abundantly clear that both families, the Colts and the Colemans, were in the same boat, Timo's son Tommy no more likely to escape his own jerk to Jesus than their John.

Timo Coleman sat in awe of such a rich and powerful man as this James Colt, come to talk, paying special attention to what he had to say to him.

Immediately following he went directly from that reverential meeting, hat in hand, to his taskmasters.

As a result, a fruitful parlay occurred between those parties involved, where overtures were discreetly proposed and reached, ample and generous payoffs assessed, a plausible escape planned and eventually hatched.

First, of course, the arson needed to be engineered as diversion, a body procured, some poor besotted soul married to that harlot Alcohol, found lying facedown one cold midnight, drowned in the open sewer of Canal Street, eventually to have a jade and ruby encrusted dagger implanted in his drink-sunk chest.

As predestined, fire broke out. The body discovered. An inquiry fixed, jurors bribed.

The final act, perhaps the most crucial, would by necessity be to arrange for the rhum-pickled corpse to disappear from the cemetery where it had been interred, laid to quick bed with a shovel, so as to at least temporarily prove unavailable to be identified as not that of John C. Colt.

Here, Tommy Coleman learned after his escape, his part would come into play. If there was no body to bear witness to the duplicity, all future investigators would forever be silenced. Who cared what the rumormongers and croakers might say? No one would ever (could ever) be the wiser. What had become of John Colt—was he alive or dead—could never be proven if there was no body to give evidence, no squelcher to tell the tale.

To this end (and with substantial added monetary sweetener proffered by the fair-minded family Colt), Tommy Coleman, called to account, trailed by a half dozen of his most trusted and strongest cohorts, left his hidey-hole at the Five Points Mission, setting out on his scurrilous way along these scurrilous streets.

Anticipation of the night's activity chilled all hearts. Fear and wretched glee pervaded. The lot of them Forty Little Thieves, sitting silently in the chilly flatbed truck, alone with their private thoughts as the four hide-bare mud brown horses leaned into their traces, smoke pouring from their runny nostrils, steam from their rib-studded flanks. The horses' hooves clattered and sparked along the cobblestones in the cold night air. Behind Tommy, at the gang's feet, lay shovels, pry bars, pickaxes, rope, an evening's accoutrements for an evening's hard toil.

Across from the St. Mark's-in-the-Bouwerie church there stood a stable near the corner of Second Avenue and Eleventh Street. Opposite, Tommy drew rein underneath a spreading chestnut tree, denuded by the cold and wind of all leaves. He waited there until the bobbing heads on the avenue grew few and fewer with impending midnight. Until the tradesmen and recreationers died away altogether and went home to their beds. Until all was silent and black and soulless.

Tommy finally saw what he was waiting for—a sign: a guarded flash of lantern, relayed from across Eleventh Street, and a boy in a filthy Joseph coat stepped out from the stable to signal all clear. Tommy flicked the long reins, the leather cracking over the team, and the truck rolled forward, lurching to a halt outside the iron gates and stanchions, where Tommy dispatched his broader-back boys, Pugsy O'Pugh and Boffo the Skinned Knuckle, laden with picks and shovels.

A faint wind moaned through the trees, and Tweeter Toohey voiced his crazy fear it might be the dead making complaint upon being disturbed. The boys talked little, and only under their breath, for the silence, time and place, and the pervading solemnity oppressed their spirits.

Pugsy and the Skinned Knuckle found the sharp new heap of fresh earth they were seeking and ensconced themselves within the protection of three great Dutch elms that grew in a bunch within a few feet of the grave they knew to be designated as John Colt's.

As wet as it was, the ground, newly dug up and turned on top of it, gave softly as Tommy watched from his perch while the strong core of his boyos worked to uncover the remains of that unlucky rhum lushington from his final earth-bath.

The pugnacious Pugsy swung his pick enthusiastically, relishing the project, the frightful grin on his face counterpoint to the frozen frown affixed to the terrified sour throbbing gob of the bigger Boffo. For some time there was no noise but the grating of spades discharging their freight of mold and gravel. Finally a shovel struck upon the coffin with a dull woody accent. Then, within seconds, carried on the night breeze with pungency, reaching their nostrils, the first whiff of m'lady Death.

Each and every night, past this particular boneyard, a roundsman, his lantern bobbing, would follow his appointed rounds, looking in on the grave of Peter Stuyvesant, died 1672, the watchman's voice ringing out solemn and clear over the silent St. Terra: "By the grace of God, one a.m., in peace!"

By previous pecuniary arrangement put in place by certain trusted servers of that political society of Tammany, fueled by funds from the family Colt, never did such constable peer through the fence that night. Neither through the fog to where Van Rensselaer lay, nor to where Trumbell's stone barely obscured the gaping maw of John Colt's ground sweat.

Standing about the open grave, one at each corner of the pit, Tommy's boyos dropped ropes of braided red and blue hemp into the hole and reached down to slip the weave around and through the brass coffin handles, and, as one, they made attempt to tug and heave and coax the dead weight of the polished mahogany crate up and out.

With no luck.

Head down, downtrodden, Pugsy came trudging back to the wagon where Tommy Coleman still sat.

"We need another hand," he said to Tommy.

So Tommy trailed him nervously back over the slate path, back over the flat marble tombstones, past the white limestone family crypts. Four at a post they stood, each at their corner, each at the ready, and leaned in, pulled with all the strength God gave them.

The coffin sucked mud and groaned and came loose and slowly rose, the voices and nervous laughter of them, "Oh heave-ho! Oh heave-ho!" cojoined in unison, like the pirates of yore about whom they had heard so much thrilling tale while standing an evening around a drum fire.

As they worked together, the faces of the boys were etched with the task, and when they felt the give, the sudden delight of success, it was only somewhat tinged with ghoulism. Yet as the coffin finally gave forth from the moist earth, the band of them broke into unseemly grins, taking air into their lungs shallowly because of the offensive odor of human rot.

"Any of you boyos wanna open 'er up?" Tommy's eyes glinted playfully. "Who's dying to see the dead looby, gone a week, face to face?"

Tired eyes, red with fatigue, widened wildly.

"Beware!" Tommy murmured. "Lest he rise up and jump yer bones!"

Pugsy gulped, Boffo shivered, Tweeter gaped, and they, the night's pallbearers, stumbled with nervous trepidation.

They struggled to carry the death trough back to the truck. There they tossed it into the bed, clamored up themselves, and anxiously awaited Tommy to strike up the sorry horses, the four dozing on their feet.

Under his breath, to appease himself, Tweeter softly hummed a sour "Rock of Ages."

But Tommy Coleman made no move to stir the horses, his attention momentarily caught in the distance, across the graveyard, where he had seen something move. The long leather reins remained poised but failed to slap the snuffling nags. Their thin flanks did not budge save an involuntary quiver against the cold.

Tommy nudged Tweeter next to him and murmured, "Shhh, d'you see a watcher across the way?"

With that, as if on cue, a shade moved, slinking through the gravestones and hocknobby, slipping by the boneyard, beneath the oak tree from whose stout limb Tommy had once heard an ancient evildoer by the name of Lemuel Peet had been hanged two hundred years before for just such an offense as this passel had just committed— necrophilia.

But who can be sure what is seen in a night so dark, so charged?

Still Tommy cried out at the real or imagined augury. "They're coming after us!"

Gagers bulged, straining the darkness, across the way, in the trees, they all saw it, a bit of reflection, a face, indeed, a glint of light on an expanse of forehead, and then a shape, fully illuminated at the opposite end of the cemetery for the briefest instant in the pale, flickering gas streetlight before disappearing.

"See it? Spectre or squelcher?"

And with that the shade tremoloed, and Tommy cried out his own answer, "Spectre!" and everyone jumped in fright, and Tommy snapped the long reins with terrified abandon, the strops slapping down on the snuffling horses' bony backs, and the team veritably leaped forward, jolting the lot of Little Thieves as they cowered in pure fear.

🌿 40 🌿

Following Poe

From the building shadows across the street on Second Avenue, Old Hays watched the nervous team hitched to the truck stamp their splayed hooves in the dark and obscured cemetery copse. The coffin had now been loaded in the back, the huddling mass of urchins in the bed, clutching and cackling in the night at each other to keep off the spirits of the dead.

It was then Hays saw a phantom ghost reveal himself, emerging almost directly in front of Tommy Coleman and his land crabs, a hundred strides away from where Hays stood, the shadow across the street from the cemetery plots.

In response to the phantasm's presence, Tommy cracked the traces down on the nags, demanding speed lest the devil himself get them, and the wagon began to roll out the iron gate from whence it came onto Tenth Street, loping at first, faster than a canter now, steering sharply onto Second Avenue on two wheels before the wagon righted itself with a clatter, left again, on Eleventh, cross town, again two wheels, and then righting itself once more, continuing on Eleventh to turn again up the Fourth Avenue at a full gallop.

The spirit stood stock-still momentarily, ephemeral, before making labored attempt to follow horses and wagon. A bandy-legged man, he was dressed in black, of poor build.

Hays immediately saw there was no hope for such person to keep up. He was struck by the man's physiognomy. He had impossibly large head to the point of misshapenness. As Hays continued to watch, he stumbled along on Eleventh Street, bent over grotesquely, his cranium seemingly an undue weight, a veritable burden. This individual's eyes were trained down at the sidewalk and the muddied manure-slickened road. The man remained unmindful at worst, unaware at best, of the high constable behind him, a shade to his own shadow.

Hays recognized him now, knew the phantasm for who he was. Yes, it was he. None other. Edgar Poe, the poet.

He signaled for his police barouche. Balboa rolled up immediately from across the road, reins in hand, waiting as he was by the kerb at Second Avenue and Ninth Street.

With an arm up from this colored gentleman, the high constable climbed heavily aboard the carriage, taking his well-worn place in the rear.

"Hurry!" he shouted aloft to his aide-de-camp, who had resumed his place in the raised driver's seat. "Our suspects have left at something other than a funereal clip."

Balboa snapped the reins, and the fine pair of geldings leaned into their traces.

In his accustomed seat, although the carriage had its detachable top in place for the oncoming winter, Hays arranged a coarse woolen blanket over his legs against the biting midnight cold as Balboa made his attempt to keep up with the casket wagon by now racing blocks ahead along the deserted night streets.

At Fourth Avenue and Twelfth Street a crush of drunken pedestrians stumbled into the intersection on their way north from the beer gardens of the Bowery. Balboa made vain attempt to cut sharply in front of them, nearly running the lot down before coming to a forced stop.

The group squealed, first in terror, then in rage.

Hays, about to lean out the carriage window and shake his fist at the whole besotted bunch of them, there glimpsed the writer Poe. He had straggled up and was now standing directly behind the drunken group, under an awning, in front of the plate-glass window of a dark shop, shifting his weight uneasily from one foot to the other. He was wearing the military-style greatcoat Hays had seen him in before. The huge garment flapped about him in the stiff north wind shooting violently down the wide avenue. Hays silently studied him as Poe pulled the heavy garment tight, his thin body wracked by an audible, ratcheting cough before he gagged and expectorated on the ground, sighing dismally when it was over. Hays thought once more of Mary Rogers, of this man's involvement, and wondered what was he doing here. Was it mere ghoulism or something more? Hays watched as Poe looked around him and ran his fingers through his disheveled black hair. He frantically patted himself all over as if he were searching for a misplaced pocket wallet or his keys. He peered ahead, up Fourth Avenue where the Forty Little Thieves and their hearse had all but disappeared, and then stepped closer toward the shopwindow, and here Hays observed the establishment was, of all things, a bookseller.

Poe peered through the glass behind where were displayed any number of volumes Hays could not possibly discern as to title or author from this distance.

After a few seconds, Poe broke off his entrancement and moved away, muttering to himself, took a step in one direction, then a step in the other direction. He acted bewildered, unable to decide where he was going. A pang of vague sympathy struck High Constable Hays then. He saw him, the broken man, perhaps drunk, perhaps intoxicated on opium. (Hays had taken note the night his daughter read him "Ligeia," reasoning rightly Poe the conqueror worm.)

Whatever Poe's queer mandate that evening (the inexplicable attraction of the grave?), it now seemed lost on the gentleman himself, and on Hays.

For God's sake, man, get a grip, Hays nearly bellowed at him. *Stop wasting time. If you are going to follow, follow!*

Tommy Coleman and his boyos were lost in the distance, three blocks north at the least, and more than likely lengthening that gap.

Hays found himself calling out to him. "Mr. Poe!"

Poe turned and peered about him, confused as to who might call his name.

From the carriage window, Hays signaled him, and Poe stepped closer.

"Mr. Poe, do you know me?" Hays asked.

Poe's eyes blinked once, twice, then seemed to snap into focus through a self-made mist. "Indeed, sir," he said. "You are Jacob Hays, high constable of the metropolis."

Hays was once more struck by the man's lyric lilt, the charm of his southern accent.

"Get in!" Hays ordered.

Poe cocked his head ever so slightly. "Why are you here, High Constable?" he said. "And where might you be going?"

"There are few persons, even among the calmest thinkers, my dear Mr. Poe, who have not occasionally been startled into a vague yet thrilling half-credence in the supernatural," Hays replied, pushing the door to the barouche open from the inside. "I, sir, am but a weak and weary wanderer in pursuit of whatever ghosts and ghouls that might abound this ebon night."

These words had been purloined by Hays directly from "The Mystery of Marie Rogêt." Unlikely as it was in this cold night air to have them regurgitated back at him, the afflicted author's dark eyes softened with recognition. Hesitating only for an instant, Poe struggled aboard, taking the proffered seat opposite the high constable.

Old Hays turned his attention, barking the straggling Bowery drunkards out of the carriage's way. Already, as far as Hays could see, the truck of the Forty Little Thieves with their casket load was long across Fourteenth Street and past the Union Park. Hays called to Balboa to lay leather to horseflesh. As they rolled past the inebriates at a lope, the stragglers did not even look up.

With Balboa bent at the reins, the barouche rushed up Fourth

Avenue. The Negro driver cut around the park, as had presumably those of whom he was in pursuit. They followed the tracks of the Haarlem Railroad before veering off at Thirtieth Street onto Middle Road, reaching Fifth Avenue and swinging north on this steeped piece of roadway, as the pursued hopefully had, eventually to come to the Forty-second Street, where lay in a most pleasant copse of wood and hill, illuminated by icy moonlight, the new municipal distributing reservoir, tippling with water funneled from Croton.

Here again there was no sign of the grave robbers. Balboa pulled the reins and shouted at the matched horses, "Whoa!" and he and Hays, talking rapidly, weighed their options (High Bridge or Kings Bridge?) before deciding to continue northeast with plan of eventually cutting due east in the nether reaches toward the Haarlem River, to cross above Hell's Gate, where they hoped they might intercept Tommy Coleman and his gang, surmising their flight up Broadway and the Bloomingdale Road anticipated a dash east to the Bronks (even Connecticut), presumably to rendezvous.

As the barouche continued its way through the night, past the Irish pig farms and German vegetable gardens, through the irregular terrain of swamps, bluffs, and rocky outcroppings that studded mid-island, Hays first launched his questioning what was Poe doing at the graveside of John Colt.

Poe, sitting facing the high constable, stared at him peculiarly. He shook his head slowly as if it were indeed a painful weight. "I was holding vigil at the final resting place of a friend," he said.

"And when you saw those rough lads digging up his grave only to abscond with the coffin?"

"I felt outrage. I had every intention to follow and redeem the remains of my associate."

Hays gauged him. "Admirable notion on your part, Mr. Poe, if improbable," he said.

"It is true my best intentions proved implausible," Poe responded. "It did not take long to come to the realization the cause I had undertaken was hopeless."

"So you allowed yourself to become distracted at that bookshop?"

"We all have our weaknesses, High Constable."

"And might I ask what exactly was displayed there in the window of the bookman that caught you strongly enough to distract you from your initial intention?"

Poe's eyes watered. "Dickens," he muttered. "Dickens, Dickens, and more Dickens. Ah, the omnipresence of that blessed individual. His *Barnaby Rudge*, that cursed crow Grip."

In Poe's voice Hays heard the tinge of sad lamentation, if not envy. "Your volumes were not visible?" Hays asked. "Not even the *Ladies' Companion* with your 'Marie Rogêt' story?"

Poe blinked several times. He laughed mirthlessly. "See, High Constable, already you know me too well."

AT EIGHTY-FOURTH STREET, near the colored enclave of Seneca Village, the steeples of its three churches ghostly in the night, Balboa swung the barouche onto a muddy lane, following northeast for more than half an hour, the deserted, well-worn cow path on its meandering way to the water's edge. Here he reined the carriage. Standing still, the snuffling of the horses subsiding, surrounded otherwise by quietude, they listened to the lapping, stared at the choppy current of the East River, and then Balboa again whipped the horses, now due northward, this time all the distance to High Bridge, where they started to make their way over the rock outcroppings and across the tidal strait into the villages of the eastern shore.

Already it was nearing four in the morning. Hard pressed to the Manhattan shore rather than the Bronx, a flatboat passed near against the current. The waters shimmered from the whale-oil lanterns of the barge, towed along the towpath hugging river's edge by a team of sorry-looking mules.

The only sound Hays heard at this point was the fast flow of the river itself rushing by the broad barge flank, mixed with the soft slap of waves as they smacked the vessel head-on.

Hays sat stolidly, watching the swirl of water below. Poe remained opposite him, perhaps a little more hunkered into himself than before, muttering under his breath as he stared down at the water, the current's gyre.

"Nevermore," Poe spoke, Hays knowing not why. "Evermore." Then again, "Nevermore."

In this manner he continued until Hays interjected. "Mr. Poe," having to repeat his name not once but three times before finally gaining the troubled man's attention. "Mr. Poe? Mr. Poe, please remember. Some short time ago, during his incarceration, John Colt paid me the service of extending a copy of the first installment of your story 'The Mystery of Marie Rogêt.' My daughter later went out and procured the second. I must say I read both with fascination, and await the final chapter and your solution to the crime; a crime and solution that vex me to this moment. Mr. Poe, please, sir, you knew the maiden Mary Rogers?"

Hays awaits reply, considering this man, his puzzlement, his apparent trouble. Finally, when no answer comes, he says, "Mr. Poe, I am warning you, when I find myself in need to ascertain how wise or how unwise, how good or how wicked is a suspect, or what might the thoughts of this nemesis be, in accordance with that expression of his, I fashion that individual's expression on my own face, as close to the real as possible, and then I exercise the patience to wait to see what thoughts or sentiments might arise in my mind, or better still, my heart, as if to match, and sometimes even to correspond with he whom I wish to know."

Poe looked up at him then through forlorn eyes. His head still hung, and the hurt emanating from those exposed windows did not escape Hays.

"I did," Poe murmured. "I did know her."

"And my daughter tells me you have made claim to reveal who murdered Miss Rogers in the third installment of your story."

Poe now struggled to sit up straight.

"I repeat, Mr. Poe, you and Mary Rogers, you were what to each other?"

Poe stammers. "We . . . M-Mary . . ." he struggles. "I . . ."

It is then and there that the high constable hears gunshots ringing out. At least a dozen, if not more. Distinct, echoing over the countryside. Distant pops and cracks, muffled by miles, reverberating over wooded land and flowing river, carried by the wind on the water, the crispness of the predawn air.

Hays turned his keenest attention in that westerly direction from where he surmised the shots had emanated. There was absolutely no telling, no seeing, nothing.

The night returned to stillness and silence, little more than the lapping of the river.

Hays looked back from where he had been peering into the utter blackness of tree and woods, trying to see that which was unseeable, what was miles away and invisible, as the barge on the river carried listlessly toward Spuyten Duyvil, the name, bastardized, Hays knew, from the first Dutch more than two hundred years before: "in spite of the devil."

❧ 41 ❧

Ambush Below the Heights

From inside the barouche, racing alongside the Haarlem River, past the Macombs Dam, through the dark and tangled woods of upper Manhattan Island, Hays shouted up his instructions of direction to Balboa, given the dark road and breakneck speed, Hays, who knew every nook and cranny, hell-bent to reach the source of that gunfire, to atone for that which he had been delinquent.

Opposite him, Poe remained, muttering to himself, doubled over into his own lap, his head covered by his arms.

Hays ignored him.

Eventually the high constable shouted for the carriage to cut sharply west until they attained the oft-traveled route, the Kings Bridge Road. Below and to the south he espied the sparse, flickering lights of Haarlem Village.

"South here!" Hays cried to Balboa.

Poe stirred with the sound of the high constable's bark, but made no further discernible move or action, not rising from his bent and fraught position.

At this juncture, from what seemed far away but may have been closer, Hays thought he could hear the faintest indication of the shouting of men working in concert, their voices raised so as to be carried faintly on the wind.

Balboa slapped the horses with the reins. The carriage continued in its singular direction until the high constable, listening with all his concentration, cried abruptly, "Left here!"

A hundred yards off the main road, they took up an eastern path through the woods toward the Morningside Heights. Ten feet from the precipice edge, Balboa reined the matched geldings and lit from the carriage.

He returned almost instantaneously. "Mr. High, come see quick, suh," he said, and offered his broad brown hand down to Hays.

Following Balboa, the high constable made his way through the shrubs and low growth to a vantage point at the cliff crest.

Far below Hays could make out Tommy Coleman's wagon being righted. On the rocky ground John Colt's empty mahogany coffin lay askew, its lid torn off, battered and splintered.

"Hardly seem real, Mr. High," Balboa said.

A twisted corpse lay on the ground. A group of boys stood to one side beneath a rogue growth of ailanthus trees, their backs to the cliff, hugging themselves against the wind and cold. From this distance, Hays could not make out who they were for sure. A group of armed men stamped and milled about in front of them, occasionally joking and laughing among themselves, but for all intent ignoring the golgoths.

Even from this elevation and distance, however, Hays was able to recognize at least one of these armed individuals. Hays despaired what Sergeant McArdel, too familiar by his gait and manner, would be doing down there with this array.

A lone voice carried up on the wind. "Shoot the wid a few more times in the mummer."

Hays knew it McArdel's order.

Three men stepped forward and aimed their muskets point-blank into the dead man's obscured face. The loud blasts resounded. The corpse jumped.

Then, as Hays watched, the now-faceless, disfigured body was fitted back into its wooden coat. The lid was replaced, the brass fittings
of the coffin twinkling, and the box lifted, then tossed by two oafs
back into the righted flatbed.

Hays nudged Balboa. "Let's go," he whispered, "I've seen enough,"
starting back through the undergrowth before turning one last time to
catch the armed men grouping, the procession forming presumably
for return to the city.

In the carriage, Poe had not moved. His head remained cradled in
his arms. "Nevermore . . . evermore . . ." He had resumed his incessant
chant.

Balboa called softly to the horses and they nudged into motion, the
black barouche following the comparatively easy path of the Bloomingdale Road due south toward town.

As they rolled, Poe began to speak, although his voice was garbled
and unclear.

"From the first, High Constable," he mumbled, making no attempt
to meet Hays' eyes, "I have viewed you that *rara avis en terra*—a kin-
dred soul. I beg you, sir, do not abandon me now."

"Abandon you?" Hays answered, very nearly astonished. "How so,
sir?"

Poe's long and delicate fingers clutched at his black and matted
hair. He did not lift his head. "I loved Mary Rogers," he said. "I did
not abandon her. She abandoned me."

Poe's great head bobbed and fell. Hays made attempt to inquire
further, but Poe failed to respond.

At Eighty-fourth Street the carriage came upon a farm with several
barns in the rear, a small rudimentary shed, a silo, and a number of
other outbuildings hedging the back acreage. A phalanx of farm
trucks stood, their dray teams tied at several of the yard's numerous
hitch rails. The animals pushed with their muzzles at random bales of
hay, thrown for them on the hoary, cold ground.

Even at this early hour there was activity, the farm a livestock and produce depot, the truck farmers and jobbers engaged already with their morning pickups and deliveries.

Hays called to Balboa to pull in.

Dutifully he obliged. He reined the horses, sliding the carriage in skillfully among other vehicles where it might not so easily be singled out by any casual viewer passing on the road.

It was not long before Hays heard the clatter of horses, the iron wagon wheels riding the ruts.

The processional of armed men had ascended the Heights, regained the main thoroughfare of the Bloomingdale Road, and was now rolling by. All in line were grim and silent. Hays had opportunity now to see more than some were militia, others police. No one saw or noticed the high constable's barouche where it sat hidden under a swamp maple.

Hays had indeed recognized his sergeant from the Night Watch. It was McArdel all right, standing the column lead.

Tommy Coleman and his cohorts were nowhere in evidence, under custody or otherwise, although the wagon carrying the casket was undoubtedly theirs.

Poe stirred from his oblivion. His eyes twitched.

"If you don't mind, Mr. Hays," he coughed, struggling to sit up, "I find necessity to bid adieu."

Hays turned, "Wait!" but before he could restrain him, Poe had pushed the carriage door open and stumbled to the hard ground.

"Mr. High, should we follow, suh?" Balboa called from above, motioning after McArdel and the line of wagon, casket, horses, and men already past.

Hays stared after Poe as he disappeared, stiffly hobbling behind the white farmhouse.

"Yes," the high constable said, his stomach hollow. "By all means, follow."

🌿 42 🌿

The Band Undone

Having, for whatever reason, slept fitfully, wracked by worry, Olga Hays sits at the kitchen table at noon, awaiting her father's return, nursing her third cup of Javanese of the morning, when she hears the deep tones of Balboa's voice in the street, directly outside the door.

"Guh'night, Mr. High," Balboa says. "Or should I say guh'day, suh?"

The kitchen door opens with Balboa's tired laughter, and Old Hays enters. Olga hurries to help him out of his cloak, off with his boots, but he is in no good mood, and does little talking.

Instead, after sitting for a minute or two, he exhales heavily, kisses her, and takes the stairs, turning at the top of the landing to say, "Olga, the day's prints, I need them all, and your opinion, when I wake."

Later, after a solitary midafternoon luncheon of vegetable soup, bread and butter, Olga dutifully dons her Persian fur coat and matching Persian hat, both once her mother's, and walks through the brisk, cutting air to the corner for the afternoon papers requested by her father.

At the news shed it is not hard to see. In 48-point type the *Herald* headline proclaims:

COLT UNDONE!

Even before arriving back home on Lispenard Street, Olga is engrossed. She reads fixedly as she walks, only taking time out to manage the doorknob.

The byline is an accustomed one, that of James Gordon Bennett.

Late last night below the Morningside Heights a small caravan was observed proceeding due north at swift rate of speed by local sheriff authorities, including Haarlam Village and Manhattanville office deputies, a contingent of militia soldiers, and representatives from the Night Watch and city police.

The police received anonymous tip that a band of ghouls had robbed a fresh grave in the city and were out to blackmail the grieving family.

Little did the authorities suspect that the grave robbed was that of the Homicide, John C. Colt.

Surprised by the confrontation, the gang turned out to be a cutthroat band representing the Forty Little Thieves, a notorious Five Points collective of wild boys and apaches, none more than seventeen years old, known for their wanton viciousness.

Until recently this group had been led by Tommy Coleman, younger brother of the infamous, now deceased, gangster Edward Coleman, who met his maker three years ago on the gallows in the Tombs, perpetrator of the murder of his wife, the well-known, in this metropolis, and much-admired "Pretty Hot Corn Girl."

This Mr. Coleman, too, had been condemned to death. In his case, for the murder, ironically, of the very sister of the very Pretty Hot Corn Girl his older sibling had seen fit to murder, a young woman, not much more than a girl, who had, much to her credit, according to all credence, spurned her brother-in-law's first advances.

Mr. Coleman had also been charged and convicted of killing his wife's alleged lover, one Ruby Pearl, a butcher at the Centre Market, and her small daughter, aged four years.

But before said sentence could be commissioned, Mr. Coleman engineered his escape.

It has been surmised this roué fled the prison the night the cupola
dome of the Palace of Justice was set ablaze, the same night Mr. Colt was
found dead in his cell, the hilt of a jewel-encrusted dagger protruding from
his lifeless chest.

Olga reaches for her tea, having switched after lunch from the dark,
thick coffee. Lifting cup and saucer, seated at the kitchen table, she
thinks she hears her father stirring now in his bedroom.

For some seconds she listens intently, but hears nothing more.
After another sip of Ceylon leaf, realizing him still asleep (due to the
clarity of his rather loud snoring, penetrating through the floorboards
from above), she resumes reading Bennett's depiction of the last
night's activities:

> All ghouls, including Mr. Coleman, were reportedly killed in the
> ensuing conflagration with police authorities and militia.
>
> The bodies of the others were reportedly taken to Haarlem Village or
> various nearby enclaves. The body of Mr. Coleman was returned to this
> city, much mutilated by musket balls, especially in the area of the face, sus-
> tained during the foray.
>
> Fittingly, for this last journey, Mr. Coleman was transported in the
> same coffin set aside for the remains of John C. Colt, the Homicide.
>
> This band is now considered undone.

Of late, in Olga's scornful observation, Mr. James Gordon Bennett has
seen fit to take it upon himself, in a brazen exercise of sinful pride, to
have himself identified in the city prints as the singular practitioner of
what he so readily liked to call the new, "objective" journalism.

Olga snorts her utter contempt at the mendacity of the man for the
very notion. In reality Olga knows Mr. Bennett, through a series of
meetings at the Harper Brothers and close scrutiny of his newspaper

forays, to be a callous cur, a mere retailer of scandal, profiteer of vulgarity and sensation, purveyor to all who delight in the misery of others.

Still, Olga admits to having been drawn back, and back again, to the wide spectrum of Bennett's exposés. The man's particular brand of charlatanism manifest in print held its own particular delights. The brutal murder of the prostitute Helen Jewett and ensuing sensational acquittal of her conspicuously guilty murderer, a young pansy christened Richard Robinson but self-named Frank Rivers, comes to immediate mind.

"A journalist's duty," Bennett lectured her (and others, presumably) from the podium of the *Herald*'s 5 p.m. edition, his self-revelatory third extra of the day, "is to gather the facts, independent of prejudice, preconception, pressure or personal agenda, and present them, in order to reproduce the world as it is."

If it is not in keeping with what we might like, so be it. You, Dear Reader, are entitled to know every last fact and conjecture connected with the Homicide Colt case, and only I can provide them. But need I remind you, facts don't necessarily add up to reality. Especially when the possibility of justice is sat upon by the privileges of power, the inequities of class, the consequence of sin, the very nature of evil.

My *Herald* is equally intended for the great masses of the community—the merchant, the mechanic, the working person—the private family, as well as the public hotel—the journeyman and his employer—the clerk and his principal.

I hold no favorites. I attack rich or poor, religious nut or agnostic, high society or low, police or criminal. I am an editor. I am your editor. I am fearless. I am candid. I am honest. I am independent. All my reporting is dedicated to serving the legitimate interests of you, the people. My questions are asked in this capacity, and this capacity only.

Olga is beyond herself with disbelief, caught between outright disgust and delight. Compulsively, she finds herself following every fleck and nuance of the extravaganza through the rest of the afternoon until her father wakes in the early evening. In spite of the hour, she brings him a breakfast of two fried eggs, two pancakes, two chicken legs, and a basket of warm buttered rolls and places the tray on his lap in bed.

With the tray she carries what she can only hope wearily is Bennett's final ejaculation of the day, the one wherein he conveniently sums up the melodrama and addresses what he now has come to call:

THE COLT QUESTION

"Papa, while you slept Mr. Bennett has taken it upon himself in the most extraordinary way to sound quite a loud noise. He now charges John Colt not dead, but having made good an escape, solely owing to the cooperation of the Watch, the warden, certain prison authorities and guards, and that even Dr. Archer was aware of the deception, in on it, too, his jurymen carefully selected for their ignorance of Mr. Colt's physical appearance."

"What exactly does he say?" inquires Hays between ravenous bites of pancake and egg. "Has he implicated me, dear?" his old eyes twinkling with his facetiousness. He has awakened famished, and is grateful to his daughter for providing such bounty in such timely manner.

"Not you, Papa. Even he knows in this city you are beyond reproach. Your implication would not sell newspapers. The opposite. His readership would only see through him, and abandon him in disgust." She winks. "Papa, what I loathe about Mr. Bennett is not his doggedness, but how he so shamelessly plays to his readers. He is the worst sort of demagogue. He claims the populace entitled to know every fact, every conjecture, yet he disdains them. He proclaims himself nothing less than an editor on public duty, yet again, he makes like it is he, and only he, who can provide the goods, flailing this way, flailing that. All geared to the single, purposeful, deplorable bottom line of making money."

"It is the American way. If Mr. Bennett is crass, you, my dear, are not the first to point at his fallacy. Now what is it he does allege? Please tell me."

"His allegations are as follows, Papa," she fumes. "A body had been looted from the Dead House, substituted for John Colt's, replacing the privileged murderer in his coffin after the corpse had assiduously been prepared for the occasion. The famous bejeweled dagger, he alleges, has undoubtedly been plunged into the innocent's heart by conspirator or conspirators unknown. The hapless victim's clothes removed from the corpse and more than likely carefully destroyed in the ensuing inferno at the prison. None of this could have been carried out, according to Mr. Bennett, without the cooperation of certain officials and men in charge. Here, I'll read to you from his latest and, I hope, final screed of the day:

> "We now know Mr. Colt's suicide to be an untrue make-believe. Presently, it is assumed the two, Mr. Colt and Mr. Coleman, escaped in concert, leaving another body in Mr. Colt's stead to be mistaken for his own.
>
> Authorities further speculate that Mr. Coleman was paid to rob Mr. Colt's grave in order to curtail a rising tide of rumor, gossip, and out-of-hand speculation, in this way preventing city authorities from exhuming the coffin to see once and for all if it really was Mr. John C. Colt sepulchred in said crypt.
>
> At first blackmail seemed the game, and it still might have been, because after ambushing the gang of ghouls and upon unlidding the box, sheriff's deputies said they discovered the coffin empty.
>
> If ever a corpse was interred within may now never be known. The bones of Mr. Colt may have indeed lain there, to be ransomed by his family, or, perhaps, as is the consensus at this writing, the body was not (and never was) that of Mr. Colt, but that of another, a derelict, laid out in his stead, until last evening, no one the wiser."

Olga continues. "Mr. Bennett further charges the cupola dome fire to be neither accident nor coincidence, Papa, but deliberately set, also with cooperation, while Colt's clothes were soaked in the dead man's blood and then fitted to the body. He runs on at the mouth ad nauseam with his opportunist onslaught, claiming he has no doubt that Governor Seward of New York State, as well as New York City Mayor Morris, will order an investigation at once into this most unheard-of, most unparalleled, travesty.

"According to Bennett," she moves on spitefully, "lending credence additionally to this nefarious conspiracy is the disappearance of Colt's bride, Caroline Henshaw, now, he claims, substantiated. The rival *Sun*, he alleges, speculates she has traveled out west, to California or Texas, in the company of her husband. Mr. Bennett writes, unequivocally, this is untrue. He has learned from unknown source, he says, she is on her way to Europe with her infant son, specifically to Germany, having booked passage using the name Julia Leicester."

"None of this is news, Olga. All of this information, including that in regard to Miss Henshaw, is known, and has been available to the constabulary. Go on, please."

"Grudgingly, I will admit, the man has a certain capacity, Papa. He finishes masterfully. You, Mr. Hays, of all people, I fear, will appreciate Mr. Bennett's salient point. Prick your ears and prepare yourself, sir."

She clears her throat and once more begins to read:

> "On the plus side, our city is now spared the cash outlay, in this time of relative recession, of hanging the likes of Mr. Coleman, killed in the resultant shoot-out with local police and support authorities.
>
> Now if only to recapture Mr. Colt and hang him, even in these hard times, dash the expense."

Old Hays smiles, albeit tightly, at his daughter as he wipes his lips with the napkin she has provided.

"Mr. Bennett has indeed developed the knack to extract good from small things," he offers.

Olga agrees.

"In a more sober moment, Papa, Citizen Bennett concedes the likelihood of such possibility, Mr. Colt being returned to New York to face his punishment, scant at best."

"Yes, but Mr. Bennett has missed the most salient point, Olga."

"And what is that?"

"Tommy Coleman is no more likely dead than John Colt."

❧ 43 ❧

A Visit Paid by Old Hays to the Colonel, Samuel Colt, at His Paterson Arms Manufacturing Company

Sergeant McArdel was not to be found at any of his haunts, although Old Hays would have dearly loved to have a word with his underling. He failed to show for work. His home on Murray Street, near the Columbia College, stood unoccupied. The proprietor at his favorite drinking spot on Dey Street said the sergeant, a usual customer, had not been in his establishment for some three or four days.

Hays took McArdel's actions as nothing less than testimony to his betrayal. He held no doubt this man, whom he had trusted, had turned corrupt under the influence of money, and in all probability had fled.

In accordance, trying to get to the bottom of it, Hays sought substantiating audience with the harelipped keeper and another jailhouse guard, but these two, highest on his list, too, had failed to report to their posts.

Trencher, however, was present.

"Mr. Trencher," Hays said after summoning the man to his office.

Trencher stood uneasy in front of him. "Yes, sir, Mr. High," he managed.

"Mr. Trencher, your fellow guards, you have not seen them?"

"Which ones would be those, sir?"

"I think you know."

Trencher's gaze slipped to the floor. "Yes, sir," he mumbled.

"Mr. Trencher, I do not tolerate betrayal well."

"Nor should you, sir."

"What do you know of your fellows, sir? Tell me!"

"Not much, Mr. High. I speak the truth."

"And Sergeant McArdel?"

"Not much either there, sir."

"I have heard talk of bribes paid."

"Yes, sir."

"Were you offered money, Mr. Trencher?"

"If I were, sir, I didn't take it."

"But you were offered?"

"Yes, sir."

"By whom?"

"Sergeant McArdel spoke with me, sir."

"I see. Would you know the source of these funds offered you?"

"No, sir."

"Could you guess?"

"I'm not very good at guessing, sir."

"Come now, Mr. Trencher. We have worked together often over the years. I expect nothing less of you, speak the truth! Tell me what you know."

Trencher looked back up from the floor. He puffed his chest and it swelled the blue serge of his keeper's uniform. "Mr. Colt faced the gravest jeopardy," he said. "The sergeant did not say where the reward was coming from, but a thousand dollars is a lot of currency. It weren't hard for me to surmise."

"No, I imagine it weren't. Good lad, Mr. Trencher."

By Friday of that week, with still no word of McArdel and without consulting Mayor Morris or any other superior for that matter, the high constable took it upon himself to enlist Balboa and travel with the barouche on the vehicle ferry to Paterson, New Jersey, to pay visit to Colonel Colt at his revolver factory. Over the last months, Hays had heard some vague talk circulating that Colt's Patent Manufacturing enterprise might be on the verge of financial failure, by some accounts even leading to bankruptcy.

At the old mill where stood the plant, the high constable was announced. He found Mr. Colt in his office, behind his desk, smoking a well-formed segar. The two men shook hands. Old Hays had met Mr. Colt on any number of professional and social occasions, including several at the Tombs during John Colt's prolonged incarceration. Nevertheless, Sam Colt again took the opportunity to speak expansively how he was an ardent admirer. He offered one of his dark-wrapped segars, not failing to mention that it was from Anderson's top shelf. Hays declined.

The Colonel shrugged and resumed his desk chair, puffing tenaciously at his own smoke, achieving a bright red ember glow, gazing across his desk, over the segar ash, nodding slightly at Hays, an acknowledgment before inquiring had the high constable received the patent chair that had been sent to his residence.

Hays met Colt's gaze evenly, said he had, expressed his gratitude, remarking the chair in question an uncanny instrument.

Colt grinned, pleased. He said he had much enjoyed in the pink pages of the *Police Gazette*—"Huey," he called it, using the argot—the story of the Timothy Redmond bank fraud case from years past, where an innocent publican had been implicated, identified, and then arrested to face a life term for forgery. Hays had unmasked the true gang of scratchers, including the pugilist Bob the Wheeler, the screwman James Holdgate, and the figure dancer John Reed, after carefully studying the physiognomy of Redmond in his Tombs cell.

"The part I liked the best was when, in the courtroom following his acquittal, the hotelier—what was his name?—Redmond! turned to you in front of the entire procedural and cried, 'Thank God for you, sir, and men of your kind!' Was this true?" Colt asked.

The Colonel carried himself in such manner, thrust forward—his ponderous weight and bulk applied in a condition very nearly a threat—that might rankle a lesser man. Hays told him the account had been embellished, but intrinsically the facts were fairly depicted.

Colt nodded thoughtfully as if he concurred wholeheartedly with Redmond's assessment of the high constable.

"Now what can I do for you, sir?" asked Colonel Colt. "I am at your service."

"That is very kind of you. I am here to know, sir, what you may or may not know of your brother's suicide."

"Suicide?" Colt repeated slowly, his look guarded. "From all I am reading currently in the prints, do you not mean escape, High Constable?"

"I was hoping you might tell me."

A laugh like an animal yelp erupted from Colt. His eyes twinkled. His big belly shook.

Ultimately Colonel Colt insisted he had no knowledge of how a dagger might have been smuggled into the Tombs for his brother to use on himself, if indeed he had committed such an act of self-annihilation. It was hard to believe everything read in the newsprints, especially the pennies. If John did not commit suicide but had escaped, Sam Colt said, he had no idea how this might have been managed. He himself had no culpability in such antics, he assured Hays. He had not heard from his brother, and assumed him dead. He had no presumption of any other scenario. He refuted any rumor that he had tried to pay bribes to any single individual employed at the Men's House of Detention. Nor, he said, had he received any blackmail attempt to reclaim his brother's remains. He said he did not know Sergeant McArdel.

Hays considered this. He thought it curious that the Colonel had seen fit to single out and mention the Timothy Redmond case of so long ago. Most especially as it evoked the name James Holdgate, the very man Hays had been dispatched to retrieve from Gravesend the night of the cupola dome fire and his brother's undoubted escape.

"On parallel note," Hays changed course in his inquiry, "what do you know of Mr. Edgar Poe, and how did you and your family come to him?"

If Colt thought the question queer or the change of subject vexing, he gave no indication. "I know nothing really of Mr. Poe," he said. "My brother mentioned his name, calling him a colleague, someone he desired to be in concert with during his final days. Out of courtesy I followed through with Mr. Poe in my brother's name."

"Did you ever talk to him?"

"To Poe? I had several conversations, mostly about money and increasing his fees."

"What was your impression?"

Samuel Colt smiled, almost as if Hays was a conspirator. "In all honesty, I found him a strange bird," he said. "My brother never failed to call him a genius, but I had my doubts."

"Was the name of Mary Rogers ever mentioned by your brother in conjunction with Mr. Poe?"

The Colonel seemed to consider. "The segar girl?" he said deliberately, as if to ruminate. "No. Never. Not that I can recollect." He stood. "Excuse me for a second." He left the room, to return almost immediately. With him he now carried an elegant book-sized cherrywood box. He laid it on his desk and opened it in front of Hays, revealing the box's red felt lining. Within lay a magnificently crafted and hand-etched blue steel Paterson revolver, laid out with all its accessories, rammer lever, powder flask, bullet mold, and multifunction tool.

"Please excuse me for not having this pistol personally engraved with you in mind, High Constable. I would have preferred to present an offering more personal and representative of your station, but your visit is unexpected and I am ill prepared. I'm afraid my armament venture on the verge of poor failure. All the same, I wonder if you would not honor me by accepting another small token. It is, of course, a repeating pistol of my design: forty-caliber five-shot percussion cap, capable of firing ten shots in forty seconds."

🎋 44 🎋

The Wake and Funeral
of Tommy Coleman

O ld Hays departed Colt's office without the gun. Back home, he sits over an all but silent luncheon, prepared by his daughter, of stewed chicken and parsley dumplings, until suddenly, with no provocation, he says,

"I asked Colonel Colt if his brother John knew Mary Rogers. If John had ever mentioned her in context with the name Edgar Poe."

Olga put down her fork. "What did he say?"

"At first he did not even answer. Then he said, 'The segar girl? No. Never.'"

Olga asked, "Papa, do you think we shall ever know what befell her, what befell Mary Rogers?"

He now too put down his utensils. He declared to his daughter it was his honest conviction that with an open mind the individual has opportunity to learn, to discover. "With a closed mind? What is there?" He spoke rhetorically. "Nothing. Olga, when first I joined the constabulary, I was oft reminded on the first day Europeans set foot on this island, seven men lost their lives. Two red, five white. Since that day the killing has not stopped. Death and violence is the mere tapestry of life in this city. I accept this, Olga. You must as well."

SOMETIMES DURING THE winter months it became so cold on lower Broadway that the ice forming in outhouses could not be broken, and the roaring fire in a fireplace was no guarantee that in the next room a penman's ink might not freeze in its well.

The Lord's Day, the second Sunday in December, was the day set aside for the funeral of Tommy Coleman. As it dawned, blue and crisp, the harsh wind roaring down the Hudson from the north country, howled its last, and by midmorning a new breeze, rising off the saline tidal river, billowing from the southern reaches across the harbor, gently insured it being the balmiest and most transcendent of December days.

Old Hays set forth from his home on Lispenard Street. In front of him the sun shone down on the sidewalk. Above him the sky transformed, and the warmth carried on the southern currents erased any hint of chill from the air. The ink in the well of the lowly priest Father Patrick O'Malley, scheduled to hold forth at Tommy Coleman's funeral, finally thawed, assuring he would, praise to the Almighty, now be able to set about his Sabbath work of composition.

Meanwhile, at the funeral home on Mott Street, an Irish wake of phenomenal proportion was concluding. As Hays arrived, four of Tommy's boyos stood sentries at the door in honor of their downed leader.

How young they were! Yet already they displayed the countenance of their elders. Hardened, inured, their rag caps pulled low on sloping brows, sure sign of studied stupidity. Greasy hair hanging, ragged at the edges under their grimy caps. Flat noses, mouths mere cruel slashes, crooked, downcast lines of insolence. Chins? Hays found them skimpy and weak. And necks? Ha! Scrawny and black with necklaces of dirt. The dirt rising like a vapor, extending and staining behind the fleshy, unwashed ears. As young as they were, the cauliflower ear was not remarkable among this set, and when they talked it was out of the side of their mouths with more than a modicum of "dims" and "does."

Inside the oft-used funeral parlor, whiskey flowed, and had flowed over the last week.

Through the window Hays could see Tommy's ma and da presiding over the mourners.

Both Coleman faces were red with drink and heat. Both their handsome heads, crowned with snowy white manes of silken hair, were abob with grateful acknowledgments of stricken sympathy and heartfelt good intent.

How many people attended this wake? Of mourners and curiosity seekers, gang members, adjutants, and well-intentioned neighbors? Family and friends? Pushy newspaper flacks, publicity seekers, and the semiliterate? Of louts and prigs? Good people and the compassionate? The plain? The simple? Those who knew Tommy Coleman and were personally devastated? The callous and devoid?

As far as Hays could tell, thousands, if there was one. All come to pay their respects in their own personal way to the too-soon-taken-from-their-midst young gangster.

They stood in line, waited their turn to enter.

Hays would not venture who came out of legitimacy and who out of perversion.

Eventually, after everyone was suitably rip-roaring drunk, the mourners carried the closed casket (Tommy's face said in whispers to have been literally shot off in the fracas with the police and militia below the Morningside Heights) from the wake site to a basement resort happily owned by Petey O'Malley, nephew to the funeral home proprietor, Seamus O'Malley, and the curate, Patrick O'Malley, then one block to the church, Our Lady of Contrition, directly south of the Mulberry Bend on the north beat of Paradise Square, later the coffin to be heaved a-shoulder by Tommy's favored companions and compatriots to be paraded through the streets more than a few blocks away via gala fete, muscled up through the Bend and on to the consecrated ground of the holy cemetery.

The pallbearers were indeed a well-soused yet still upright crew in mourning coats and black stove hats, culled from the ranks of the fraternal Irish gangs, one from each brotherhood in a symbolic gesture on the occasion, in the face of tragedy, of newly found unity and good trust.

The streets surrounding Paradise Square all along the parade route were teeming with curiosity seekers. But only those calling themselves "blood relatives" and "honest folk" could be welcomed into the chapel proper.

Many more "close acquaintances" and "well-wishers" clotted the narrow streets starting south from Canal. The crowd swarmed the park and hundreds infested the roofs and windows and outer stairways of the buildings surrounding the church.

At one point the rickety wooden outer stairway providing access to upper stories and roof, tacked precipitously to the face of Sweeney's Feed Warehouse & Distillery, groaned and creaked before loudly cracking, like a cannon shot, then crashing outright, sending some seventy-odd viewers to the sidewalk and street below.

Rubberneckers, giddy with joy and horror, seeing and hearing the commotion, ran will-I, nill-I, but even they, this dissolute mass of onlookers, became quiet when the bells finally tolled, signaling the start of the funeral mass proper, the sanctuary of the church so very well filled to the apse, the high constable relegated to standing uncomfortably in the rear behind the holy water.

Prayers were said, and on the pulpit from inside Our Lady of Contrition the priest, Father O'Malley, began his eulogy in voice loud enough to be heard by those nearly gathered right there in the chapel and through open door outside in the street, while for the benefit of those farther away the prelate's words repeated and amplified by another, the crier, yet one more relative of the O'Malley clan, this one a third cousin, thin and pinch-faced, in shabby but soulful black robes, his voice of incongruous, ponderous deep timbre, blaring nothing but a misheard semblance of what his eponymous kin was saying to those poor shattered and shuttered inside, to those out there in the street, feet dangling from the tin rooftop cornices or bearing witness from the surrounding tenement windows, straining if only to listen from tanneries and ash houses, and comprehend all God's mysteries.

"Many tombstone of a miller reads: 'Killed in his mill!'" intoned Father O'Malley from the pulpit. "The same may right be said of our young son and brother, Tommy Coleman."

With the high constable watching from the back of the church, the father, he who Hays knew had baptized infant Tommy and had known him personally through his short and misspent life, looked up, as if scrutinizing the assembled, gauging their reaction (not a dry eye in the house), and pressed on.

"Killed in his mill? What mill had he? This was a boy of seventeen, nay, eighteen years. He had no mill! He had nothing. Absolutely nothing. So I'll answer this inquiry myself. *What mill had he, he was!* I warn you one and all, and I repeat: *Stay away from evil!*

"I knew the lad well, and said the same to him often. Our dearly departed, enough is enough! *Stay away from the evil that infests our streets and our minds. Save yourself!*"

As Hays shifted his weight uneasily, this steadfast, earnest man of God looked over his overflowing, overzealous audience and congregation and continued.

"What's more to be said?" he inquired.

Hays waited with the rest of the assembled for the answer.

"What more indeed? . . . Nothing. Not a thing. Take not another breath. Nothing more need be spoken. But speak we must. Cry out we must.

"He who lives by the sword, dies by the sword," continued Father O'Malley. "It is our own stark reality, and so be it for what it is."

The accepted code of conduct being, Shoot twenty poor citizens of the Points in the scragg and expect twenty bullets in your own boke in reprisal.

But the priest was not finished yet.

"Young as he was, we all looked up to Tommy Coleman," the father continued with his oration. "That is to say, young as he was, we all looked up to him at the same time we all looked down upon him. He was a boy. How old was he? I ask again. Eighteen? Then he died. A shame. A real shame. A mere mite. Yet how many more immutable movers of men have we known more astute than he? Our Tommy's was a rare gift. To be admired, to be mined, to be put to use. But not to be killed. To be killed is a sin. Crime does not pay!" Father O'Malley intoned loudly, his voice quivering now with even more charged melodrama.

"Listen to me, one and all, inside and out, all about. All who can hear me, I implore you, pay attention! I beg you, pay attention! Humanity needs you! Pay attention! Do not waste yourselves! Pay attention! America needs you. Pay attention! New York City needs you. Pay attention! Your family, your friends, your brothers, your sisters, your children, they all need you. Pay attention!

"We all need you. Strangers, admirers, confess! Brothers, sisters, mothers, fathers, pay attention! We need you. Heed the warning issued here today. Study the example extolled so clearly for us all this day. Mourn your loss, one and all, and repeat after me: *Crime does not pay!*"

Credit must be given where credit is due, Old Hays noted to himself. Father O'Malley was, if nothing else, persistent. The priest fixed with a hardened blue eye his congregation.

Then all those massed in Our Lady of Contrition, and all those gathered outside on the sidewalks and on the cobblestones, and all those perched on the rickety fire escapes, and all those pressed together, shoulder to shoulder, in the alleys, breathing tannery fumes and privy stench, all those crowded stomach to rump, shoulder to maw, took up the chant.

"*Crime does not pay!*" went the reverberate through the holy building, through the streets.

From windowsill to lamppost, from tenement flagging to tree limb, wherever citizenry hung within earshot, scarred and unscarred, Irish-

American or the most recent greenhorn immigrant from Kerry, scathed or unscathed, he or she, child or man, boy or girl, they reached deep and repeated, crescendo and bravado, pure and deeply felt: "Crime does not pay!"

"*Crime does not pay!*"

"Crime does not pay!"

What joy to the ear!

Who could deny?

"Crime does not pay!"

IN THE OUTSIDE BREEZE many Irish pennants and Stars and Stripes flew. Pretty young girls marched out from the church in solemn file. Tommy's grieving ma exited the building, staggering under the support of two burly boys, holding her weight up at the armpits. Her eyes red as her nose, her cheeks as red as her eyes. Hot tears streaming, splattering on the board sidewalk.

Her life mate, Tommy's old white-haired da, Timo Coleman, needed, nor accepted, assistance. He was of the task and mind rather to stumble along on his own steam. He managed to stand tall, or at the least as tall as his frame allowed him. Diminutive at an inch south of five feet, he stared straight on, his eyes as blue as the clear blue sky overhead. Unruffled by the commotion surrounding him, with his every step he stepped lively, spry in black suit, emerald green neck stock, his hair as white as new potato shavings, his face every bit as red as blood, most especially the outsized and lavishly veined proboscis.

Somewhere in front of Hays, a brass band started up. A slow procession began tramping through the streets, their sad song sung, what Hays had heard Da Timo Coleman proclaim his favorite at the O'Malley family funeral home, "Whiskey, You're the Divil."

✸ 45 ✸

Aftermath to Obsequies

O ut of respect for the deceased, all pallbearers at the funeral of
Tommy Coleman wore red satin stripes down their pantaloon
seams, as did all brethren Irish gangsters.

The idea derived after one of the most powerful and admired Five
Points gangs, the Roach Guards, had taken to wearing a blue stripe
down their trouser legs, and the red stripe, in imitation of this, or
some misconstrued homage.

The high constable watched the funeral procession snake through
the winding streets, until onlookers could be heard beginning to whisper in hushed voices.

Hays could now make out, still blocks away, what he took to be the
muffled upraised voices and grumbling of the native-born bands
approaching out of the Bowery from the east.

Across Paradise Square, the Irish gangs, the Chichesters, the Plug
Uglies, the Dead Rabbits, the Shirt-tails, the Forty Little Thieves,
among others, grew quiet to better listen.

Hays hurried to a vantage point. Where he stood, above Mulberry,
he watched while the Bowery gangsters, a remarkable thousand and a
half strong, neared the heart of the Points and hesitated at Cross

Street, ready to meet their adversary gathered in front of them, fifteen hundred belligerent Irish coves.

In recent years a system of police had been suggested by certain political factotums and civilian factioneers, featuring multiple station houses, one to a ward, which might in time of crisis work together in consort, but although Hays found it a fundamentally sound idea, the proposal had been defeated by those fearing a standing army controlled by local government.

Instead, the United States Twenty-seventh Regiment had been repeatedly relied upon of late by local government to quell riots and suppress unrest. Stationed near the Narrows in Fort Hamilton, Brooklyn, and led by a newly appointed Captain Robert E. Lee, the troops, what was being called a National Guard, with the knowledge that Tommy Coleman's funeral would afford an occasion for unrestrained racial unrest and belligerence, were put on the ready, but not yet officially pressed into action by Mayor Morris.

By this Sunday afternoon, every Bowery gangster had come boiling out of his hole. The Butcher Boys, the Atlantic Guard, the American Guard, the True-Blue Americans, were all in full assemblage, all in club costume and colors. Something beautiful to behold, they stood at attention, dressed in their spotless undershirts and taut suspenders, gazing down upon Paradise Square.

The day remained crisp; the sky blue. If Hays had been asked, he would have said the sun surely seemed to be smiling down on the remains of Tommy Coleman's stand-in. A breeze wafted off the East River, another gentled off the Hudson. The trees in the square had lost their leaves. Their brittle remains crunched underfoot.

As Hays watched, having dispatched Balboa to go for the standing reinforcements, the Irish gangsters doffed their funeral attire as quickly as they could, stripping down to their own undershirts and suspenders so as not to spoil their special mourning clothes, with which they took pride.

Suddenly bullies were in hand, slungshots at the ready.

The two forces faced each other on Bayard Street.

The brass band stopped its playing.

The black-dressed women ceased their mournful wail.

Past Hays, fearful civilians scurried to seek higher ground on Cross Street from where they might watch the battle unencumbered, uninvolved, safe.

Below, as the grieving watched, the Bowery b'hoyos took up a cadence rhythmically slapping their truncheons and neddies into their meaty butcher palms, one, two, one, two, in anticipation of battle charge.

AFTER HER SON WAS KILLED, Mother Coleman had received word at her airless basement apartment from High Constable Jacob Hays to report to the Dead House behind City Hall to identify her boy's body.

When she arrived, however, Hays abruptly refused to allow Mrs. Coleman to view her son. Speaking softly, he took her hand in his and told her the boy's body was in no condition to be seen. It would be too difficult, he said, for a grieving mother to view such carnage under such circumstance.

Instead, like Phebe Rogers before her, Mrs. Coleman identified her child, passed on to a better place, by his clothing. By no means was it lost on Old Hays that Tommy Coleman had escaped death row in his striped prison taupe, and any clothes he might have been wearing on the night he was said to have been killed would have been borrowed or stolen, and certainly not his to be identified.

Still, he allowed Mother Coleman to bawl. "Yes, these are his," tears staining her creased fat red cheeks. "God rest his miserable soul."

Even as this charade played out, Old Hays was still half waiting against his better judgment for Sergeant McArdel to reappear his post. When he did not, McArdel's evident betrayal weighing heavier by the minute hand, the high constable nevertheless took the initiative among his men to speak to them about that Sunday night's ambush reportedly by the Watch and local constabulary beneath the Morningside Heights.

"Who among you was there?" he asked, too aware he had been reduced to being unable to trust any single one of them.

As he more than suspected, no one raised his hand.

"Who among you knows by whom or how information regarding the ghouls was relayed?"

No one offered to this either.

He inquired did anyone know the whereabouts of Sergeant McArdel.

No one did.

Sitting at his desk in the Tombs earlier that day of Mrs. Coleman's visit to the Dead House, the high constable had had the opportunity to read in the *New York Herald* the results of the Great Census of 1842, conducted by the Five Points House of Industry. Identified in the survey were 3,435 Irish families living in the Five Points. Next in number were the Italians with 416 families recorded. Of the English? Only 73.

Hays was not surprised. According to the report, punctuating Paradise Square and its immediate environs were 270 saloons, with several times that number of dance halls, diving bells, blind tigers, buckets of blood, shanghai palaces, houses of prostitution, suicide halls, sporting houses, and greengrocers selling more fermented wet goods of local confection than vegetables or fresh fruits.

So while the battle of Irish and native gangs raged on the streets in front of them, the vast majority of Tommy Coleman's mourners understandably repaired to one or another of these local Paradise Square emporiums to eat and drink while keeping in view the pitched brawl.

The general alarm had by now been most thoroughly sounded. Old Hays considered wading into the fray, as he once had, the brash maneuver for which he had once been renowned, but he was not that young man any longer. He did have his constable's staff in hand, but he chose, at least for the moment, to stay the high ground and wait for the support of guard and his constabulary.

After fifteen minutes of bloody clashing, the Bowery Butcher Boys managed to break free from the pack and circumvent the flank of the Plug Uglies, overwhelming these hated toughs and pushing them back with one sweeping effort.

Eventually the natives rushed the Irishers' clubhouse on Mott Street with every intention of rendering maximum destruction and harm to this abhorred brotherhood's residence. But the resilient papists, with the help of the surly Dead Rabbits and Chichesters, beat the natives into retreat, and by means of a brilliant counterattack forced their fierce and detested adversaries north on Orange and east down Hester, out of the Points and back into the Bowery, where they took refuge deep in the bowels of a building on Rivington Street.

The Irish horde charged in behind the Rabbit standard (on this day the corpse of a snow-shoed hare held aloft on a twelve-foot pole), wrecking the place, angrily tearing apart seventeen apartments in two separate tenements.

Reports reached Hays. One city marshal, he was told, had come on the scene. Recognizing his duty, the man had waded into the fray. The Irish ruffians were on him in an instant. They stripped him naked and beat him to the sidewalk. Ultimately he managed to get his assailants off him. He staggered all the way to the station house on North William Street, there to raise the alarm.

The constabulary responded in force to drive the warring factions back to their respective neighborhoods, but it did more harm than good. The fighting was broken up but the gangsters, both Irish and native-born, now spread, and instead of venting their anger and frustration on each other, they became indiscriminate and began to waste the city at large.

At the beginning of the day the sun had been out and an unaccustomed warmth had been in the air. Citizens were tempted to doff their coats and shawls to revel in the mild air. But suddenly and without warning the weather changed. Whereas it had been warm, now it grew cold. In the space of little more than four hours, the temperature plummeted forty degrees. And by the next day had dropped to a bone-numbing seventeen below zero.

In the hands of criminals, the Second, Fourth, Sixth, and Seventh wards burned as unrest raged. The rioters turned their fury on all they encountered: stables, car barns, private homes, tenement apartment buildings, offices of public finance, wagons, hacks, drays, carryalls, trucks, omnibuses, even fellow citizens.

For the general public there was no recourse, because the very gangsters who were burning the city manned the fire companies whose charge it was to put the fires out. Even honest folk found themselves milling about, marauding and looting. In a car barn on Catherine's Slip one ginger-haired individual, said to be a hod carrier apprehended in the act of torching a hayloft, was hanged from a streetlight arm, and the police proved unavailable to cut him down, or even to make an appearance on the scene. The man's thoroughly frozen body, stripped of clothing save his blue woolen pants, bunched at the ankles, dangled there for three miserable days.

❧ 46 ❧

Sergeant McArdel

Edgar Poe, since slipping from Hays and his barouche at the farm depot on the upper Bloomingdale Road, had wandered for a week through woods, pastures, and shantytowns in the city's upper reaches, finally blindly finding his way back to the city proper, sick and hungry. On Doyers Street, at the crook of Murderers' Bend, he had managed a small bottle of ether from a half-Chinese, and now, through a hangover haze, stood in front of the hanged man's desiccated body.

As he watched the dead man sway, Poe recalled vividly the most frightening thing he could imagine when a boy was to feel an ice-cold hand laid upon his face in a pitch-black room.

At the time the image had so terrified him he would often keep his head buried under the covers until he nearly suffocated himself.

His stepfather, John Allan, had little sympathy for his shenanigans. He scolded the lad, lecturing that the boy picked up such nonsense from lazing about the slave quarters with his friend, the house nigra, Dabney Dandridge, listening to the foolish ghost stories stupidly regaled by the Negro slaves while sitting about in the dark around their dying cookfires, scaring themselves, and him, half to death

Allan, a Scots mercantilist, scoffed and told the child, a laddie he would never consider his son, to cease and desist from such nonsense or face the consequence.

Yet even now, so many years removed from his boyhood, he stood remembering those days, distraught in the icy cold, shivering and ailing, unable to rid his mind of another time, when passing a graveyard, he jumped into his stepmother Frances Allan's arms, begging, "Save me! Save me! They will run after me and drag me down."

Powerless to tear his eyes away, he moaned. In front of him swung the deep-frozen body of an individual he could not imagine ever having known; yet something about the dead so familiar. Still, on that spot identification seemed beyond his fevered ken as the body, suspended from its rope, twisted in the ghastly gale.

Icicles hung from the dead man's closed eyelids, from his splayed nostrils, from his twisted blue lips. Hoarfrost pocked his cheeks and chest. Urine and feces, the bodily fluids frozen solid, ran from shriveled member and mottled purple marbleized haunches down thick, hairy, naked legs.

Like the twin blades of scissors, the cold sliced off the East and North rivers, converging on the lower island, snipping off far below the root all hope for human comfort. Poe pulled his old West Point greatcoat tighter to his emaciated body. He coughed up sputum, green and black, hawked on the hardscrabble ground. The wind blew the expectorant back into his face. He wiped himself with his coat sleeve.

"Time to go home," he addressed the aggrieved body of the dead man, and suddenly remembered him, Sergeant McArdel of the Night Watch, from the Tombs. Of course. The man had oft escorted him through the corridor to John Colt's cell. The ginger hair was the giveaway. "If Muddie will have some soup, Sergeant, it will surely be our body guard," Poe addressed the corpse. "I feel a bout of ill health coming on. Do you?"

He broke away from his transfixion, leaving him of the frozen-stiff ginger hair and grotesquely stretched neck twitching in the wind, and started north, hugging the East River docks.

The city had become quiet in the aftermath of the last days' melee. The Twenty-seventh Regiment was now in attendance on the streets and corners. The rioters had finally gone home. Along the waterfront, a splintered wake of broken slats and rowboats in dry dock, smashed windows of warehouses and feed bins, overturned barrels, and whinnying horses, stood the legacy of urban warfare. But this evidence soon gave way only to frozen swamp as Poe made his plodding pilgrim's progress.

He had set his destination as Weehawken Street, to an inn he knew called the Lubber's Friend, where he had a recollection someone, an acquaintance (could it have been John Colt's brother Sam?), had vouched him a room.

Was it not here, at this destination, the Lubber's Friend, where he had once stayed with she who was no longer of this earth?

Could he remember? For the life of him, could he?

Upon first setting out, every few steps he turned, peered back over his shoulder, heard the creak of the rope as Sergeant McArdel of the Night Watch slowly spun. Then it was gone, out of earshot, out of sight, and he was beyond the river bend where it turned west-northwest at Houston Street.

He took Lewis Street, past the shipyards, reached Eighth Street via that route, continued due west, and soon was crossing the expanse of land once the farmstead of Peter Stuyvesant. He cut up two blocks and looked in at the St. Mark's churchyard, the spot where seven nights before he had laid watch beneath the twin Dutch elm trees, his eyes trained on the still-open grave of John Colt, holding his breath lest the spirits of the graveyard enter his body.

In self-absorption the poet thinks everything is known. His eyes aglow, a fire beyond malnutrition burns, madness, imbalance, within.

When finally he reaches a place of warmth, the poor inn on Weehawken Street (indeed there is a bedstead reserved for him, and paid in full besides), he slumps immediately at the writing table and composes a letter to his Muddie in Philadelphia.

"Oh my dear, darling Mother," he writes, clutching his brow. "It is now three weeks since I saw you, and in all that time your poor Eddie has scarcely drawn a breath except in intense agony. My clothes are horrible and I am so ill."

❧ 47 ❧

For His Soul

For his soul he could not have told you what he was doing on the riverbank. By a path obscure and lonely he made his way, until he stood on the rocky shore, gazing out on the water.

To the south the harbor lies, molten liquid pewter.

In the pit of his stomach he feels something—a queasiness—an unease.

He wades out into the low reeds, soaking his shoes, his wool trouser legs. The waves rise and fall, the river a chop. Nausea descends, momentarily dispelled by the relentless cold water lapping. The unrest returns, seizing his intestines, twisting them.

He closes his eyes, and he has a vision. He sees a hand, a woman's hand, his Mary's hand, break the water, reach out, beckon.

Hatless, dressed in black, he stumbles back into the woods, trying to remember where he is going, but cannot. He remembers his once-fiancée, Mary Starr, from Baltimore, but now married, with the name—he has learned—of Jenkins, and living somewhere in Jersey City. He has already crossed the Hudson three times that day looking for her. When he knew her, she was going by the name Mary Devereaux. He finds the path along the shore back to the ferry quay, past the Sybil's Cave, past the lovely Elysian Fields.

At the dock, the ferryboat is waiting. He crosses back to the city again, pacing the deck, asking everyone he meets, do they know the lovely Mary Devereaux? do they know where the lovely Mary Devereaux lives?

He has already been to her husband's place of business once that day to find her address, but now the information has wriggled from his mind and he is at a loss. The boat arrives at the Courtland Street docks in New York City. He rides it back to Jersey City without getting off, then back to New York, then back to Jersey City, with him still on board, still inquiring of anyone and everyone, do they know Mary Devereaux, he means Mary Jenkins, mumbling he will go to hell for the address of his Mary whateverhernameis, if he must.

Finally, he finds a deck hand who takes him at his word (later, when Mr. Jenkins, the husband, a merchant tailor, shows up on his way home from work, the navvy will tell him a crazy man was looking for his wife) and says he knows the place where she resides.

No one is at home. Mrs. Jenkins is shopping in the city with her sister when Poe arrives. Upon their return, from inside the house the door opens as if by its own volition, and Eddie stands beneath the jamb to greet them.

Mary, who has not seen him in a number of years, since she visited him and his child wife in Philadelphia, immediately sees he has been out on one of his sprees. His eyes do not focus, and his mouth is awry.

"Well," she says, "Edgar, so nice to see you."

His eyes flash, and he spits the words. "So you have married that cursed man!"

She is taken aback. "Yes, I have married," she admits, "but he is not cursed. No, he is kind, and he is attentive."

A slow smile creeps on Poe's face. "Do you love him truly?" he asks. "Truly?"

"Did you marry him for love?"

She is affronted. "That is nobody's business. That is between my husband and myself."

"You don't love him," he persists. Then his voice takes on a different tone, almost pleading. "You do love me." He very nearly weeps. "You know you do. Oh, Mary!"

They stand and stare at each other.

Finally her face softens. She asks him if he would like to stay for tea.

He takes his seat at the table but eats nothing, and becomes so distracted by a bowl of radishes he seizes a table knife and with quick, hacking strokes so that pieces fly all over the table, reduces the red radishes to mincemeat.

At first Mary and her sister are stunned, but then Mary laughs, and her sister follows, and then so does Poe.

He insists she sing the song she knows to be his favorite, "Come, Rest in This Bosom," penned by the Irish poet Thomas Moore, and so she does:

"I know not, I ask not, if guilt's in that heart?
I but know that I love thee, whatever thou art.

Oh! What was love made for, if 'tis not the same
Through joy and through torment, through glory and shame."

Almost immediately upon completion of this canticle, Poe gets up to leave. He compliments her, telling her she still sings with wondrous sweetness, and it is only a few days later his aunt, Mrs. Clemm, shows up at her door looking, she explains, for "Eddie dear."

Mrs. Clemm tells Mrs. Jenkins she has tracked her son-in-law from Philadelphia to New York to New Jersey, and now finally to her home. She says Virginia is beside herself with anxiety and worry. "If he does not write her twice a day," she confides, "my poor daughter begins to fret and descend into a state until she is nearly crazy, refusing to eat or drink, despite anything I can do."

A search party is organized. Within hours Poe is found with twigs and leaves in his hair, and moss and brambles stuck to his clothing, not far from the Sybil's Cave, wandering in the woods on the north-ernmost outskirts of Jersey City.

"What a thing it is to be pestered with a wife!" he gripes when told of Sissy's concern.

Undaunted, Mrs. Clemm corrals him to take him back to their home in the City of Brotherly Love, where she puts him to bed. He remains in delirium, distraught, for the better part of a week, moaning one word, the proper name "Mary," over and over again, through his fever.

A Year and a Half Later

APRIL 13, 1844

❈ 48 ❈

The Hunt for the Murderer of Mary Rogers Resumes

What was it?

Images of her death never left him.

But of her murderer?

He could not picture him. Was it Poe? Was it another?

Some fourteen months before, in February of 1843, the third installment of the author's "Marie Rogêt" story had appeared after a month's delay in *Snowden's Ladies' Companion.*

Olga had impressed on the same printer's imp of her acquaintance, even before that number hit the newsstand, securing proofs in January, only hours after the type had been locked down.

She returned home that day and pored over the galleys.

But what had come of it?

Hays, awaiting his daughter's scrutiny, had hovered over her.

There was no real way to know what had been cut or added to the original text. It was clear Poe had afforded no real answer to any murder.

After much close scrutiny Olga made case at least for the final two paragraphs having been tacked on.

"I venture the original story stopped right here"—she pointed out

the words "With God all is Now" to her father. "The following paragraph after this sentiment takes up, 'I repeat, then, that I speak of certain things only of coincidences . . .'

"Papa, here, at least in part, I would wager, is last-minute addition.
To my thinking, this passage is out of character for Mr. Poe. Repetition of a nature so crude and poorly executed is not his style. He is far
too elegant for such self-conscious stumbling. Not to mention, within
the context, he digresses from Marie, names Mary Rogers, and labels
her fate 'unhappy.' To my judgment, he has made sloppy work of his
emotions and uncertainty, evidencing his confusion."

Hays considered. "Is there more, Olga?" he had asked.

"He names no murderer," Olga answered, "if that is what you are
asking, Papa. He makes only sketchy reference to Marie dying in an
aborted attempt to terminate a pregnancy. It would seem in the previous draft he made claim of a lover killing her in the clearing. I doubt
Mr. Poe was in much condition to do much additional. Nor does it
seem that he had the time. A single paragraph earlier where he makes
clumsy case to charge, then excuse, the clearing as the scene of the
crime. But, truthfully, even this is misconstrued. In my opinion, Papa,
Mr. Poe has been taken up short by Mrs. Loss's admission during her
delirium that Mary Rogers died during the administration of a premature delivery."

Hays hesitated. "So in the end, Olga, would you say Poe has exonerated himself or implicated himself?"

"By tone alone, his own ineptitude exculpates the author. If pressed,
Papa, I would declare Mr. Poe an innocent. His crime not one of
secret insight and murder, but of short time and poor writing."

Studying his daughter, Old Hays noted the skill of her delving, the
certitude of her thinking, the concert of her personal emotion.

He took her wisdom; his investigation, for what it was, going elsewhere (and nowhere) until some fourteen months later, in the early
afternoon of April 13, 1844, sitting at his Tombs office, the high constable received official summons instructing him to report without
delay to the office at City Hall of the newly elected mayor of the

metropolis, the Honorable James Harper, the same James Harper of the Harper Brothers publishing firm.

THE NEOPHYTE MAYOR-ELECT sat large and lugubrious behind his polished black teak desk, carried over from his publishing house. He stood when Hays entered and extended his hand. "Good to see you again, High Constable," he said.

"Sir," Hays replied, taking James Harper's hand and finding it, not for the first time, soft. "I offer my congratulations on your successful campaign."

"Thank you very much, High Constable Hays. Please be seated."

Hays lowered himself into the padded chair indicated and awaited his summons.

"Can you imagine why you are here, High Constable?" the mayor complied.

"You are putting the kibosh on me?" Hays answered without hint of a smile, and only half in jest.

James Harper laughed. "Very good, very good," he said, his own grin wide. "But I would not dare, sir. Your daughter would have my head. Turn Old Hays out to pasture?" Harper shook his large head and chuckled more at the absurd humor in it.

In his election campaign Harper had portrayed himself the average working stiff, as if he were nothing more than some ordinary guilds- man plucked direct from the ranks of the General Society of Mechan- ics and Workmen. The Harper Brothers publishing concern was the city's largest employer. Olga Hays continued to maintain her position as a copy editor at the firm, working from home, sometimes more than sporadically, on some Harper Brothers manuscript or another. Notwithstanding, as far as Old Hays apprised, James Harper was about as far cast from a regular workaday lout as one might possibly be.

"A man held as high in the public trust as you, High Constable?" Mayor Harper continued. "You are much too well-loved and feared; I might add, much deserved. Still, I admit to having an agenda, sir. But

I'll confess it's not quite so foolhardy as seeing you on the chopping block. Not yet, at any rate." Harper chuckled once more, this time with the pleasure of his own lightheartedness.

He went on. "If I might so mention, and Lord knows I am sorry to draw attention to it, and be the unenvied bearer of such news, but even before I was able to assume this, my elected post, the state legislature already had usurped me, sir. In a clandestine maneuver, High Constable, last evening they have voted in Albany to put an end to the city's force of police as it now stands. In so doing, these unseemly politicos have tried, for all intents and purposes, in one fell stroke, to put an end to your constabulary and the Day and Night Watch in favor of a new, professional regime of their own design, modeled, according to them, on the magnificence of the London Metropolitans. They have further, in an effort to make a neat package of it, and at the same time render me entirely impotent, seen fit to fold into this proposed democratic troop of theirs all the city's fire wardens, health wardens, dockmasters, street inspectors, lamplighters, bell ringers, and every last one of the rest of our miseried city servants. I have been informed a law to this effect has now been signed by the governor."

Hays said, "Mr. Mayor, in this city crime has never failed to keep its pace with commerce and culture. That the criminal element has infected the legislature comes as no surprise. The political machine of Tammany has made deft success of harnessing the ignorant and indigent. You Whigs will have a hard time in any quest to keep up with the postulants, more or less quell them."

"Hear, hear, that is so, Mr. Hays, and certainly a concern. Yet the most erudite of my advisors tell me I am not bound to follow this state mandate. I am assured if I do not ratify the Democrats' plan, the city's present system, by law, must remain in effect."

Hays maintained his gaze directly into Harper's red-rimmed eyes and waited for the upshot.

"With my apologies, let us follow the opportunities afforded us," Harper continued, looking away through the window where the omnibus station on Broadway at Ann Street could be just seen loading passengers into a line of caravans. "This is, therefore, the course I find I must pursue, sir. Rather than follow the state's lead, to offset them and render their hostile act harmless, I shall legislate in their sour faces so that I might hire two hundred men of my own choosing to comprise an existing force of my own. One and all, they will be native-born and loyal to my patronage. Not a papist, I daresay, will stand among them. Additionally, for the purpose of morale and to connote a new day, all officers will now wear uniforms."

"With all due respect, sir, my men will object to uniforms."

"I care not a whit for their objection. But might I ask, why is that, High Constable?"

"This is not the first time the discussion of uniforms has been engaged, Mr. Mayor. The feeling of the men is uniforms make them look like butlers."

"As I have previously stated, what your men object to holds no consequence to me, High Constable. Your men have no say. I must not have made myself clear. All your men have been sacked, sir. Not by the state, but by me. You are hereby notified the city constabulary is dissolved, as well as the Day and Night Watch. A new police force will be put immediately in their place under my direction, and, with no disrespect meant, unlike your leatherheads, all will be professional, full-time officers, and all, sir, will wear uniforms as I see fit, acknowledging their allegiance and their professionalism."

Hays did not flinch. Instead he said, "Yet, Mr. Mayor, you say your plan is to keep me in my post as high constable?"

"Precisely. At this point in time, I am not prepared to relieve you of your position, the position the public—and, I might add, sir, even if you find it hard to believe, I count myself among this number as well—feels you have occupied so ably for so many years. Again, with all due respect, how aged are you now, sir?"

"I am in my seventy-third year."

"Seventy-three! Good for you. And you have stood your post since when?"

"1802."

"Forty-two years. Through thick and thin. I admire you, sir, but when you step down—and given your longevity, I am going to make the assumption that will be sooner than later—your post will be necessarily consolidated."

"Whatever my title, kept of my post of high constable at the whim of politicians or not, I am here to tell you the bloods and hooleys on the street will have a field day with *your* men in uniforms."

"These officers will have to bear the brunt of any disrespect. They will be trained, and they will be armed. I am considering new Colt repeating revolvers for each man. I have already spoken with Colonel Colt on this matter, and each and every officer will be properly outfitted."

Harper stood from his padded chair, rose to his full height, taking, as it were the high ground over the still-seated high constable. "I have seen fit to have a prototype of the intended dress tailored," said the mayor. His chest expanded, he strode to a gleaming wooden armoire pushed against the wall in the room's northeast corner. Opening the twin doors, he removed the garment in question.

"As you can see, the uniform is constructed from stiff, durable twill. It will consist of a frock coat, vest, and trousers. All will be this deep shade of blue. All buttons will be covered with matching blue serge, and each man will wear on his standing collar the letters *MP* embroidered in gold silk thread, signifying his affiliation to the force of Municipal Police. A number singular unto each individual will be assigned and also embroidered with bold silk thread on the collar for the purpose of identification of each officer, one from the other. In addition, pinned to each individual officer's chest will be an eight-pointed, star-shaped badge, the prongs meant to honor each of the first eight Dutch officers to police this city in its infancy. The star will be made from copper, and is meant to signify the bearer's allegiance to his duty." Concluding with pride, Mayor Harper so stated, "They shall be known as none other than *my* Star Police!"

Here Harper saw fit to flip Old Hays a prototype of the proposed copper badge, which Hays managed to pluck out of the air with some dexterity given the poor quality of the toss and the high constable's ever-degenerating reflexes.

"By my order, the main concern of this new police concentrate on temperance, and all its implication," continued the new mayor. "My feeling is that if we shut down the Irish groggeries and drinking emporiums, we have good chance to regain control of the greater metropolis, and for once put the papist immigrants in their place. First and foremost, from now on, High Constable, by my municipal decree, all Irish groggeries will be closed on Sunday Sabbath."

"To what effect, sir?" Hays asked. "For many years, Mr. Mayor, I have fought the criminal element in this city. By foisting such pointed and discriminatory law upon a singled element of the general public you will serve only to further empower the very criminality you seek to disarm."

"My office will be not altogether heartless, Mr. Hays. To prove it so, commencing on July Fourth, Independence Day, of this year, in City Hall Park, I plan a gala celebration for all city inhabitants, loathsome papist Irish included. At that gathering, for refreshment, icy cold Croton water will be served exclusively. Public scrutiny has reached a pitch, High Constable. Pardon me, but we both know the reality. Those on your Watch, both Day and Night, have in no way been in the business of preventing crime. You must admit that unfortunately most of your standing force has joined in gleefully with this very criminal element of which you speak, for their own personal pecuniary reward. Need I mention the name John C. Colt, High Constable? Need I mention your Sergeant McArdel?"

"Given the type of man I have been empowered to hire, the laggard cousin of this like politician, the dallying uncle of that, does this come as any surprise, sir? How many times have I been to the Common Council with my petition for funds sufficient to hire a proper breed?" Hays pointed out. "We do our best with what we have. And as for Sergeant McArdel, I make no excuse."

"Understood. Still, need I tell you, Mr. Hays, your police, whoever they may be, whatever their mettle, have come to the habit of turning their backs on capturing thieves and the rest of this city's queer roosters, and instead readily join in with the criminals' venture and take their cut of plunder from them. Or, at best, to make clandestine arrangement to return those goods stolen for whatever recompense offered by the merchant, then to turn around to split their revenue with the thieves themselves. In the end, all concerned, save the merchant, are eager to do it all over again. Rarely, sir, do I see an actual thief apprehended. So let's you and I anticipate a good and thorough revamping, shall we?"

A newspaper lay on the mayor's desk. The mayor tapped it. "Which brings me to this," he said. "Have you seen it?"

Hays peered across the desktop at the sheet. "Is there something specific I should note?" He took from his inside coat pocket his magnifying spectacles.

The mayor indicated the front page. It was the *Sun,* its bold banner headline declaring:

ASTOUNDING
NEWS!
BY EXPRESS VIA NORFOLK!

THE
ATLANTIC CROSSED
in
THREE DAYS

Signal Triumph
of
Mr. Monck Mason's
FLYING MACHINE!!!!

FULL PARTICULARS TO FOLLOW!

"We reside in a new world, High Constable," said the mayor. "The Atlantic has only yesterday been crossed by air in three days' time, man. Quite by accident, as it turns out, but it makes no difference. You have not seen this, Hays? The aviator Monck Mason seemingly was heading across the Channel for France. The wind shifted violently, and the rudder on his airship incapacitated. As result, the balloon was catapulted in the opposite direction over the pond on the greatest air voyage of all time, landing down within seventy-five hours in South Carolina. Although unsigned, I have on good authority the author of this article is none other than Edgar Allan Poe. If I am not mistaken, you are familiar with this man, are you not, if only in passing, Hays?"

Hays stared at James Harper, trying to read the man. He was a large individual with full muttonchop sideburns and florid complexion. His cheeks were red, his brows furrowed, his eyes flinty, small, and calculating. Hays would not want to underestimate him.

"I have had conversations with Mr. Poe. He was a somewhat infrequent visitor from his residence in Philadelphia to John Colt during his imprisonment in the House of Detention. So I know him, if vaguely. Of what interest is Mr. Poe to you, sir?"

"He is returned to this city. Talk is you work from some instinct, Mr. Hays, from some inner voice. I too have heard an inner voice. The voice is whispering to me the name Edgar Allan Poe, High Constable. It is a woman's voice, the voice of Mary Rogers, and she is saying Mr. Poe is responsible for her death."

Hays leaned forward in his chair, his gaze direct into Mayor Harper's eyes.

"I am familiar with his writing, including his take on the Mary Rogers murder. In the course of my investigation, Mr. Mayor," Hays said after pausing momentarily to gather his thoughts, "Mr. Poe has been tied in my mind at one time or another with both John Colt's escape from punishment and peripherally with the death of this aggrieved young woman. Over the last two years I have had innumerable conversations and followed innumerable clues to concretize any and all suspicions, no matter who the individual, no matter how out-landish or specious the speculation. None have come to bear, including those implicating Mr. Poe."

"At this time do you feel everything needed to be known about the death of Miss Rogers has come to light and been pursued?" asked Harper.

"Of course I do not. The murder has not been solved. No murderer has been punished. So there is no satisfaction. After the proprietress of the Nick Moore House, Mrs. Frederika Loss, was shot by her son a year ago last November, she became delirious. She mentioned several crucial bits of information which had not to that point been revealed. One was the mention of a young doctor called to her establishment to facilitate an early delivery on Miss Rogers. According to Mrs. Loss's ravings, the girl died during that procedure. Who was the doctor? Who was the beau? The investigation has never been able to ascertain, although I can assure you every line of inquiry has been arduously pursued."

"Exactly! And here is the revelation, Hays, to put your investigation back on track and make it that much easier: knowledge has reached me that none other than Mr. Edgar Allan Poe put the unfortunate young lady in question in such compromised state and it was he, and only he, Mr. Poe, who has catalyzed the ensuing outrage. I have it on authority it was he, none other, on the premises of the Frederika Loss inn at the time of Mary Rogers' tragic death."

Hays held rigid. "On whose authority and what certainty is such accusation based?" he asked.

Harper lifted a fashionable white clay pipe off its cradle on his desk and, with what Hays took as a noxious air of victory, began stuffing the bowl from an oval canister beside it.

"Anderson's," the mayor deferred. "Do you not find it as peculiar as I do that the man calls his tobacco 'Solace'? I'll give him, man is a genius. He has cut the leaf with a bit of dried cherry fruit. Wonderful aroma and a nice, sweet bite. Help yourself."

He pushed the container across the desk, offering the tobacco to Hays.

For a brief moment the high constable considered declining the blend in favor of his own personal sock, Solace or otherwise.

Then, thinking better of it, he reached for Harper's cherry leaf and packed his bowl. "I grant you this, Mr. Harper, Mrs. Loss, on her deathbed, had no reason to lie. I have no doubt Mary Rogers, in the company of some cur, calling himself gentleman, repaired to Nick Moore's inn to facilitate an early birth. A young doctor was brought in to help her with this procedure, but whatever his skills, this operation went awry, leading to her death; if not during the procedure, then the day after. Three questions remain to be answered. As said, who was the doctor, who was the knave with the unfortunate young lady, and why was her body ravaged so?"

"Poe was very much smitten with her." Harper puffed a half dozen consecutive billowing clouds of smoke from his pipe and leaned forward. "I daresay the fellow uses his tragic air to ingratiate himself to all people, but especially women. Candidly these barely disguised tactics of his drive me to utter madness. Women feel sorry for him, Mr. Hays. I know Miss Rogers did. She spoke of it often enough."

Hays' eyes narrowed. "You knew her beyond the counter, Mr. Harper?"

"Let us say I admired her. We all did. She was like a daughter. My brothers, our associates, any casual visitor to Anderson's establishment. Poe is married. His wife is sickly, yet he uses the continual suffering of his spouse to implement his repeated seductions of caring ladies."

Hays held the mayor's glare.

"You could not possibly know this, High Constable, but Mr. Poe is presently shopping a manuscript. It is a collection of tales, not by accident numbering sixty-six, the devil's number, if you see my meaning. Included in these pages is the story he calls his 'Mystery of Marie Rogêt.' In my opinion this particular tale is nothing less revelatory than an admission of guilt and cry for help on the part of the author. I will tell you this final detail divulged to me, why I know him to be guilty of this crime, and then you, too, may be convinced, Mr. Hays. Earlier you referred to, said you were familiar with, this story author Poe has concocted, the subject thereof, without question, Mary Rogers and her death?"

"I have read his effort. With my daughter's able assistance, I have been over every sentence, every detail."

"I myself rarely read," Harper stated. "I have no time for it. But my clerk has outlined the cogent points for me. As I say, the tale had been offered to my firm in conjunction with sixty-five others this author hopes to see published as his all-encompassing collected prose work. For my own reasons, I passed on it. You are aware that Mr. Poe has gone back and made changes in the original work? He has irrefutably tailored his conclusions to fit his needs and lead the delving mind away from him as suspect. I have heard Poe distastefully boast often of his astuteness in matters of rational thinking and reason. Granted, he has become adept at following logic in one direction, or reversing it in opposite direction, to suit his mood, in order to give the illusion of some brilliance. Believe me, High Constable, Mr. Poe is guilty of the crime of which he writes. The original story, as he constructed it, was to be divided into three segments. The first two appeared on schedule in *Snowden's,* but before the third could see print, with the revelations and death of the charwoman Mrs. Loss, he withdrew it. A month later, after a hectic scramble, he resubmitted a now-altered third chapter. This saw print a year ago last February. I assume you saw it then?"

"I did," said Hays. "It pointed to Miss Rogers dying at the hands of an abortionist."

"It did. Now to consider, what had Mr. Poe changed in his supposed fiction, from one version to the other. Therein would lie key to his crime. No, High Constable?"

"Go on, Mr. Mayor." Hays held his own, content to see where this would lead him.

"Against my advice, my colleague George Palmer Putnam, a man I much admire, is publishing an edition of Poe's tales at his house. Thankfully, much pruned down, I'm told, to the no less irksome number thirteen, again a telling number. Mr. Putnam can, in all likelihood, provide you with the exact details, and before and after manuscripts of the Mary Rogers story. If you need introduction to Mr. Putnam, I will furnish it. Apparently there is yet another revamped version of the story. Mr. Poe has made certain alterations now alleging the wronged young lady's rejected suitor of the past is the scoundrel of the present, the very individual Miss Rogers entertained on the occasion of her murder."

"In all probability his point is well taken, sir," spoke Hays. "I myself might not argue with him."

"Precisely! There you have it, High Constable. It is a confession, don't you see? She was with him, man! With that infernal Poe! He was on lecture tour along the Hudson at the time of the first instance. In the town of Poughkeepsie. She was his intimate companion. They were as lovers in a hotel there."

"You know this as fact?"

"I tell you they were seen. I have made habit of knowing my enemies." Mayor-elect Harper rose, signifying Hays' dismissal.

"I am an excellent assessor of men, as, I am assured, are you, High Constable. Now, good day, sir, and all good success as you pursue your unencumbered apprehension of this most wretched individual."

❧ 49 ❧

George Palmer Putnam

"It is all a hoax, Papa!" Olga Hays exclaimed, indignant upon her father's return to Lispenard Street, if only briefly, following his meeting with the new mayor-elect. "The Atlantic crossed by air balloon? Trust me, Papa, pure twaddle."

"How do you mean?" Hays asked, amazed by his daughter's certainty. "A hoax?"

He retrieved the offending print from the kitchen table, picking it up, searching for some as-of-yet-overlooked (by him) clue in the finer print.

"My deductions are as follows," Olga said evenly. "As always I take my methodology and lead from you, Mr. High Constable." She smiled with some private glee, if only to be one step ahead of her father. "Although the notice is unsigned, I don't need to be told the author: Edgar Poe. Papa, I have recently read a story by Mr. Poe entitled 'The Gold Bug.' This story is a brilliant puzzle, unlike his 'Marie Rogêt' foray, wonderfully told, delightful for its intellect. It is set on the outer coastline of South Carolina and mentions Fort Moultrie, notable to me this day because it is the very same particular locale where the flying machine of this news account is said to have set down. As I have read, it does not escape me this tale of the balloon crossing, as related by the author, is remarkable, but full of quasi-science and math: this propelling principle, and that warm air current. In my estimation, it is, in its entirety, orchestrated claptrap. Nothing more, nothing less, than another shallow, transparent maneuver on the part of the unseemly *Sun* in order to ensure elevated sales and increased circulation."

"I have discerned none of this, Olga. Please, go on, and allow me to continue once more the pleasure of following your thinking."

"Some time ago, at a lecture I attended with my dear friend Miss Annie Lynch, Mr. Poe spoke of having been stationed at Fort Moultrie during the course of his military enlistment, again the very setting of his 'Gold Bug,' and again illuminated in this newspaper account of said airship emprise. A coincidence, as Mr. Poe himself would undoubtedly underscore, once recognized, too great to be anything other than unlikely; more emphatically, nigh on impossible."

Hays thought with some satisfaction to himself, *Remarkable girl*, although all he said to her was, "I see."

She went on unfazed. "Additionally, to this bit of chimera add again that it is the *Sun* of which we speak, and there you have it."

"There you have what?"

"Come now, Papa: meaning the *Sun* can escape neither its reputation nor its history for putting over on her gullible reading public. This is without a doubt the same stroke of editorial genius that stoked the Moon Hoax."

Hays elevated an eyebrow. There was no denying to what his daughter referred. Ten years before, the same *Sun* was a struggling penny paper when it achieved unfathomable fame and fortune after foisting on the city's readership what became known as the "Moon Hoax," wherein it was reported that the famed English astronomer Sir John Herschel had set sail for South Africa with a gigantic telescope in order to study the galaxy from an entirely new perspective than it had previously been observed.

In sensational editions over the course of the next week, further dispatches, ostensibly sent from Capetown, went on to reveal that the preeminent scientist, through his insistent peering, had spotted actual living human-like beings frolicking amidst the moon's lakes and forests. The beings were approximately four feet tall, and were said to have wings consisting of a thin, hairless membrane.

Sir John reportedly described these moon creatures as yellow in color. It was difficult, he admitted, to describe them as entirely human. They were more like pelicans or giant bats, although the renowned scientist allegedly went on to explain they did exhibit some humanoid traits, spending happy hours eating, flying, bathing, and loitering about.

The remarkable accounts made an immediate sensation, and overnight the struggling *Sun* became the best-selling *Sun*, the most successful daily newspaper not only in the city, but also in the nation. Moon frenzy raged for ten full days until the sixpenny *Journal of Commerce* exposed the story as a complete hoax.

No matter, a book version of the folly, *The Moon Hoax; or, A Discovery That the Moon Has a Vast Population of Human Beings*, written by the *Sun*'s clever, entrepreneurial editor, continues in print even to this day, more than ten years later, its sales remaining nothing less than brisk.

"It is entirely within reason," continued Olga, "that Mr. Poe seeks to emulate the Moon Hoax's enviable example, enrich himself with the resultant hummer, and promote his name."

Old Hays saw his daughter's logic for what it was, and considered himself agreed.

FOLLOWING A QUICK TEA, Hays returned to the Tombs. Here he immediately arranged to have a card sent on his official stationery to the offices of Wiley & Putnam, Publishers, requesting an interview with proprietor George Palmer Putnam. In regard to what affair precisely, the high constable did not specify in the note.

Return reply reached Hays within the hour. "Come when you will." The publisher would see him at the high constable's convenience.

Old Hays entered the premises of Wiley & Putnam at 155 Broadway later that same afternoon. Although not as opulent as the Harper Brothers' block-long Ann Street book publishing empire, the fiefdom of Putnam and John Wiley was still very well-turned with thick oriental carpets, subdued gas-lighting, and, lining the plastered walls, hand-carved mahogany bookshelves stocked with the firm's handsome publishing efforts.

Hays knew Putnam as two men-about-town would know one another. They shook hands, having met before, perhaps two dozens times over the years. Putnam was a man in the prime of life, full-bodied, with straight nose and russet chin whiskers, and an unmistakable intelligent cast in his warm, clear brown eyes.

Quietly making studied assessment of the publisher's regular features and well-formed brow, Hays judged Putnam, as in the past, a man of forthrightness and honor. No reason arose to amend his previous impressions of his physiognomy now. He looked to Hays to begin his inquiry.

The high constable, therefore, began without further preface or small talk. "What are your impressions of the author Edgar Poe?" he asked.

For his part, Mr. Putnam did not express surprise at Hays' question. "Indeed, sir," said he, "are we talking as a literary figure or a man? To what context would you like me to speak? I'll give you the likes of Mr. Edgar Poe is a strange but impressive individual."

"Strange? How do you mean?"

"Strange is strange, High Constable," the publisher answered with a half smile. "Given any close scrutiny of the author's writings, one does not necessarily want to underestimate anything of which the eminent Mr. Poe might be capable. No?"

Hays considered this. He told Putnam he was very much cognizant of the macabre in Poe's work, but inquired in his opinion was this simply creative guile, albeit an eerie and peculiar one . . . "or is it some other, more foreboding manifestation of the man's personality?"

Putnam pursed his rather full purple lips. "Foreboding granted," he said, adding, "Perverse even. But mind you, Mr. Hays, not without interest. I have through the years worked closely with the man. Poe is the most ambitious author of whom I am aware. His writing style is full of a strong, manly sense. Yet as I know him, he is the loneliest individual in the world. There has never been a more perfect gentleman than Mr. Poe, High Constable, when he is sober. When he is drinking, however, he would just as soon lie down in the gutter as anywhere else."

Hays stared at Putnam momentarily. "Have you read the story he has composed based on the murder of Miss Mary Rogers?" he inquired.

"Indeed I have."

"And, of course, there is no disguising his protagonist, Marie Rogêt, is Mary Rogers."

"There is no contention on this point, High Constable Hays. Certainly not from the author. Not as far as I know."

"Have you ever considered that Mr. Poe might know a bit too much merely to serve an innocent bystander in the tragedy of this young woman?"

"I am not quite sure I understand the direction of your question. Are you making assertion in order to implicate Edgar Poe in some way in the death of this unfortunate girl?"

"Not at all. I am simply keen to know from exactly where Mr. Poe might have culled his information on this most specific matter."

Putnam coughed. "According to him, harvested straight from the public prints. By his conversation with me, the weekly *Brother Jonathan* and James Gordon Bennett's *Herald* in particular. Nowhere else as far as I know. This is what he has told me, and this is what I believe to be true."

George Palmer Putnam puckered his lips once more while he

mulled through his thoughts. As his eyes locked with Hays, he said in a low voice, barely audible, "We all knew her, High Constable. She was a lovely girl. Sorely missed. The abomination stays with all of us."

Hays paused, allowing Putnam's sentiment to hang in the air.

"Are you aware of any love affair between Mary Rogers and Edgar Poe?"

Putnam did not hesitate. "I may have heard something, I try not to put too much stock in such talk."

"James Harper told me you are contracted to publish Mr. Poe's collected tales."

"I am."

"He said there were an original sixty-six stories, but these have been trimmed to thirteen."

"Twelve is the number we have agreed upon."

"Just so. And is the story of which we speak, 'The Mystery of Marie Rogêt,' to be included in this volume?"

"It is."

"Might there be a copy of this volume with this described story that I shall be able to take with me?"

Putnam assured him if there was not a bound book, at the least there would be galley pages. He rang a bell for his clerk to come, dispatching the young man to find a sample of the proofs.

While they waited Hays continued his questioning. He asked Putnam the nature of any noticeable differences between an earlier version of Poe's story published in *Snowden's* and this version. Putnam furrowed his brow and inquired where the high constable had heard mention of such actions, and Hays said again, from the mayor, James Harper.

After momentarily pondering this turn, Putnam responded that as far as he knew there were some seventeen counted changes between this version and the last. Additionally, he said, there was a plan afoot to also include footnotes. "The Mary Rogers case has been out of the public's mind," he explained, "and it is our judgment the casual reader might need reminding."

Hays asked him to delineate what were the changes effectuated.

"I cannot tell you that specifically. There are those in my employ, notably the editor Mr. Duyckinck, who worked closely with Mr. Poe, but, frankly, this is not my position in the house."

Putnam did say, however, he thought the changes had been made from one version to the next, solely to present Mr. Poe in a more favorable light to his readers, as a more astute observer of the facts governing the actual murder; given, "like the rest of us," the author had only been made aware from Frederika Loss's deathbed confession that neither a group of gansters nor an aggrieved lover had killed Miss Rogers, but that she had actually, tragically, died during the implementation of a bungled premature delivery.

"Mr. Putnam, in all candor, from what I've read, much of Mr. Poe's self-impressed narrative seems to center on trivial discourses involving body hair, mildew, the physics of drowning, elastic garters, whether criminals carry handkerchiefs, the growth rate of grass, and the shape of rips made in fabric by thorns. Despite Mr. Poe's contention that he has laid out the true principles for which all inquiry should be directed in future cases of this nature, I must say I am not so much impressed with his insight. Logic, as core to this gentleman's presented technique of choice, might prove fine, but instinct, over all else, is my credo, sir. Mr. Putnam, carefully consider this before answering," Hays said. "Do you believe that Edgar Poe in any way may have been involved in the death of Mary Rogers?"

Putnam's mouth fell open. "God no," he replied immediately. "Do you think that, sir? Does Harper? The death of Mary Rogers is a tragedy, sir, surely not a crime. And Mr. Poe's involvement? What aspect possibly do you believe can his involvement take?"

"I ask you."

Putnam made a noise deep in his throat, considering for several seconds before speaking.

"Mr. Poe has received inordinate public attention of late. I'll grant you, not all of it in good light." Putnam turned his soft white palms upward in a gesture of supplication. "Mary Rogers was well loved. There was resentment directed at Mr. Poe that the two were at one time close. But that fell away. Poe was married after all. As far as I know, they had gone their separate ways. You are certainly aware of Mr. Poe's recent arrival in New York from Philadelphia? The man has reputation as pure troublemaker, I'll give you that. He is the most feared critic in the nation, taking on any and all comers. Many of his fiercest adversaries feel his vehemence stems simply from jealousy and pique. Knowing him the way I do, I am prone to agree. The only time it seems Mr. Poe has anything nice to say about anyone is when he needs something from them, me included: a job, money, a favorable review. The man is the consummate careerist, sir, there is no denying that. I regret to tell you he is only interested in himself. But, High Constable, if you are asking me if I believe him a murderer, the murderer of Mary Cecilia Rogers, I must say, No!"

❧ 50 ❧

Stopping in at
the Tobacconist's Shop

In his younger days High Constable Jacob Hays nightly patrolled afoot the streets north to south from the Bayard Mount to Castle Garden, west to east from the North River to the East. The offices of Wiley & Putnam were located on Broadway at Cedar Street, five blocks below the leafy environs of City Hall Park. Hays undertook to walk his way back to the Tombs after leaving Putnam, thus vesting himself opportunity to exercise his lungs and air his mind.

Meanwhile, as quitting time grew nigh, a tribe of young clerks and steady old fellows emptied into the broad avenue and lesser lanes to mix with the porters, sweeps, and piemen, the coal-heavers, organ-grinders, umbrella makers, balladmongers, ragged artisans, and exhausted laborers of every description already crowding and jumbling the byways. Avoiding the press of them as all turned dark yet splendid in light spewed from the gas lamps, the high constable paused as he passed at the segar store where the unfortunate Mary Rogers had once been employed.

He was surprised when he stepped inside. Hays had not seen John Anderson for more than a few months. The proprietor, a relatively young man, certainly in comparison to the aged high constable, showed visible signs of having aged, and not well.

The tobacconist stood behind his counter, hunched over, shoulders stooped badly, transferring aromatic leaves from one canister to another. Seeing Hays, he immediately straightened up, but Hays signaled for him to continue with what he was doing, watching the gentleman silently for some minutes while he worked. Some pleasantries were exchanged after the completion of Anderson's duties, before Hays eventually steered the conversation in an alternate direction: "Mr. Anderson, are you of the acquaintance of one Mr. Edgar Poe, a gentleman, I am given to believe, who has over the years patronized your establishment?"

Indeed the segar man did know Mr. Poe. "He stops by from time to time when he is in New York," he told Hays. "More in the past than in the present, but plainly put, rarely has he money. Often another customer, taking pity on him, will buy him a sock of tobacco for his pipe, and he might sit with the others and talk their lofty literary talk, perhaps drink a mulled cider or port wine."

"Would you know if Mr. Poe is presently in the city?"

"If he is, I am not aware," Anderson replied.

"Let us say Mr. Poe *is* in the city." Could Mr. Anderson venture where he might be found?

"No, I could not."

"I see," said Hays. "Mr. Anderson, as far as you have observed, does Mr. Poe get along with his fellows?"

Anderson shrugged. "With some. With others—no. Like any man."

"With whom does he not get along?"

"I could not say in good conscience."

"Understood. And with the late Miss Rogers, what was the nature of Mr. Poe's interest in her, if any?"

Anderson's eyes narrowed proportionally.

"Like the others. Everyone was enthralled by my Mary," he said flatly.

"Mr. Anderson, did Mr. Poe ever make overture to Miss Rogers that you observed?"

Anderson flushed before addressing Hays' question. To Hays the shopkeeper looked like he had swallowed a hard chaw of his own Solace tobacco, before admitting hesitantly there were times when he thought them close, but he could not remember specific instances. He concluded he would not be surprised if Poe had.

"Had what?"

"Been intimate with her. They were all trying to make their assignations with her. As a whole they are not such a likeable lot, these literary types. Such a beautiful girl. Such unpleasant, self-involved men." He coughed wetly, a rather prolonged, grating jag. "A pity," the tobacconist finally managed. Tears had brimmed in his eyes, Hays assessed, either from the violence of the gagging or merely mention of the man's Mary.

As was the custom of the shop, there was a small coterie of gentlemen seated around the low-slung table in the rear partaking in their share of mulled cider and sharp yellow cheese. At some point, the bulk of James Gordon Bennett, of the *Herald*, emerged mightily from their midst.

"So you are back on the scent of Mary Rogers, High Constable?" Bennett said without endorsement of "Hello" or even "Excuse me."

"I'm unhappy to tell you I've never left the pain of it, sir," replied Hays. "Progress moves its own slow pace, Mr. Bennett."

"I am embarrassed to admit that I have inadvertently overheard you mention to Mr. Anderson the name Poe. Is that the author Poe of whom you speak?" Obviously knowing full well it was. "Surely, sir, after all these years," Bennett continued, "Mr. Poe is not implicated in some manner in this horrid case?"

"No, not implicated." Hays returned Bennett's oily smile. "I am simply making my inquiries. Is there something you would like to tell me, sir?"

"What could I tell you that you do not already know, High Constable? Let me see. Surely you are aware of Mr. Poe's latest three efforts, all of which have set the sharp tongues of our local literati to wag. The first is entitled 'Thou Art the Man.' The second, 'The Oblong Box.' Both, as I am sure you know, make rather perverse reference to the John Colt murder affair."

A third story, Bennett added rather gleefully, "The Spectacles," involved, according to him, some kind of demented affair of love and dalliance between a young man and his elderly mother. "Some acerbs are commenting it is not unlike the realm of reality in which Mr. Poe finds himself in real life: married to his child cousin, his own aunt his mother-in-law. Spurious rumors, surely unfounded, I hope, are that Mr. Poe has chosen to lay down with his own elderly blood relative," Bennett finished.

Hays said he had heard nothing of such aspersions. "Who would level such charges?" he wondered.

"Who can say where rumors begin?" answered Bennett.

"Is there any other loose talk involving the author you need to share with me, Mr. Bennett?"

"Of Mr. Poe?" the editor spoke, making pause for dramatic effect, with little or no heed for any deprecatory tone he might himself have detected in the high constable's voice. "I can tell you he is not well liked. I can tell you he is a drinker of some repute and a drug taker of equal repute. A womanizer who likes them young and dreamy, and a gentleman of somewhat inflated ego. Other than that . . . who can say, High Constable?" Bennett shrugged. "But I can tell you this: If you truly seek him of whom we speak, I know of a woman who may be able to help. As I recall, her name is Mrs. Mary Jenkins, and she was once fiancée to Mr. Poe back in his youth in Baltimore. Some years ago, you might recall, after the woeful John Colt breach against society, the confused Mr. Poe was found wandering the woods near this woman's home in Jersey City, muttering of his love for Mary. If it was this Mary, Mrs. Jenkins, or some other Mary, an individual by happenchance sharing the same Christian name, say Mary Rogers, I am not the one prepared to say."

❧ 51 ❧

Mary Devereaux

James Harper proved a man of his word. The next morning, following the meeting in his office in City Hall, in no way taking Hays by surprise but disappointing him, the high constable learned, indeed, his constabulary had been dissolved by the new mayor. Only Balboa remained for him, the one trusted soul left under Old Hays' auspice to be sent forthwith on the ferry to Jersey City to ferret out Mrs. Mary Jenkins. Referring to the voter and taxation rolls, Hudson County justice of the peace Merritt provided Hays' envoy with her address, informing him she lived near the north wood, and was married to a fellow who worked as a merchant tailor not far from the Wall Street countinghouses.

Balboa returned by the Courtland Street steam ferry with a woman aged approximately thirty years, fit and hale, with a healthy complexion to her, and rich, bright auburn-colored hair.

When she was escorted onto the prison floor, Hays stood, trying to be as affable as he might. He introduced himself, and told Mrs. Jenkins the purpose of her visit to him.

She half curtsied. "I have been informed what this is about," she said. "Justice Merritt has spoken with me briefly, but as I told him, I have no information to afford about Mr. Poe, and know not his whereabouts."

Hays did not argue with her. He did remind her, "Mrs. Jenkins, good citizens, be they of the male gender or female, will tell the truth," adding that he appreciated her cooperation and honesty. He apologized for inconveniencing her.

"How well do you know him?" he inquired.

"He was in love with me once, and I with him."

"Forgive my intrusion on these personal matters, Mrs. Jenkins, but what happened?"

"It was when I lived in Baltimore," she said. "My maiden name was Starr, but I was using the name Mary Devereaux in those days, imagining it romantic. I was just a young girl, seventeen. I had a friend, Mary Newman, who lived next door on Essex Street in Old Town. She was quite nice, and we used to love to sit on the stoops in front of our houses, with only the balustrade between us, and watch the world pass by. Edgar was living next to me at the Clemm house. I knew who he was. He was a young soldier, and a poet. His brother had written a tragic play about him and his love affair with a girl in Richmond called Elmira Royster, and it was the talk of the town. He cut quite a romantic figure for a young girl such as I. He spent his time in the third-floor attic writing and from my own back window I could see him at his desk composing. One day our eyes met, and he waved a white handkerchief at me. After that it became a frequent occurrence, waving our handkerchiefs, him at me or I at him, or blowing kisses back and forth, using our hands as rackets and the kisses our shuttlecocks. At one point he sent his little cousin Virginia, who at the time was a sweet schoolgirl, plump and hearty, no more than nine, to my house, requesting a lock of my hair. Of course, I never told Mary Newman any of this, but then one day we were sitting on our respective stoops, as I say, and all at once we both saw Eddie approaching from across the street. Mary asked me in a rushed whisper if I knew him. I lied and said no. 'Why, that's Edgar Poe!' she said in a gush.

'And who might Edgar Poe be?' I asked. 'He has recently come from West Point,' she told me. 'He writes poetry too. Why, I declare! Here he comes across the street. Oh! Isn't he handsome!'"

Hays smiled. "My own daughter certainly thinks so," he said. "She has been to several of his dramatic readings, and thinks him not only a stunning exemplar of this nation's manhood, but also the possessor of a wonderful voice and manner."

Mrs. Jenkins returned Hays' smile. "To a young girl at the time, even more so. He said hello to Mary but sat down next to me, and immediately he began about my hair. I confess I swooned for it. He went on how I had the most beautiful head of hair he had ever seen. He said I had the hair poets always raved about. From that day on he visited me every evening for a year."

"He must have been veritably smitten. If you don't mind me asking, Mrs. Jenkins, how did he comport himself during that period?" Hays' eyes shone with interest. "Was he affectionate?" he inquired.

"Affectionate, sir? He was so passionate in his love that most of my girlfriends were afraid of him and forsook me on his account. He made a great show of despising ignorant people and held no stock for trifling or small talk. He would say when he loved, he loved desperately, and I found this to be true."

"I suspect things have not changed on his part."

"To this I cannot vouch. I must say, though tender, he had a quick and passionate temper. He was very jealous. His feelings were always intense, and he had little control over them. He was not well balanced. These failings, in all likelihood, continue to this day. I often joked he had too much brain. But he saw nothing funny about it. He scoffed at everything sacred, and never went to church. He often lowered his voice and declared that there was a mystery hanging over him he never could fathom. He swore he believed wholeheartedly that he was born to suffer and this embittered his whole life. We were young and only thought of love. His darling little cousin Virginia always carried his notes to me. He repeatedly told me his favorite name was Mary.

My family was not in favor of him. When my brother heard Eddie was coming around so much, he took me aside and said, 'You are not going to marry that man, Mary? I would rather see you in your grave than that man's wife. He can't support himself, let alone you.' Being as romantic as Eddie, I replied that I would sooner live on a crust of bread with him than in a palace with any other man."

"Was your brother furious at such response?"

"He most certainly was."

"Please continue, madam. What happened?"

"Well, one day a gentleman came to the house and Eddie became very jealous of him. The man's name was Mr. Morris. I can recall it as if it were yesterday. He was a friend of my father's and he knew Eddie somewhat, and took pleasure to tease him by pretending intimacy with me and calling me by the familiar 'Mary.' Having surreptitiously learned Eddie's favorite song was 'Come, Rest in This Bosom,' Mr. Morris asked me to sing it for him. The whole time I sang, Eddie paced the floor biting his nails. After Mr. Morris left, Eddie stayed. We quarreled. He stormed off, saying he would return. I waited for him, but he did not come. I cried, and then he appeared, drunk, the only time I ever saw him drunk in that year I knew him. He said he had been out walking and, while crossing the bridge, had run into some old friends, cadets from West Point, where he had once attended, and they had gone out to Barnum's Hotel, where they had supper and champagne. I went and opened the door and sat on the stoop with him in the moonlight. We then quarreled further and I jumped up and ran around the house weeping and into the room where my mother was doing her sewing.

"'Mary! Mary!' she said. 'Whatever is the matter?'

"Eddie had followed me into my mother's room, and I was much frightened by his state of mind. My mother told me to go upstairs and I did so.

"Then Eddie said to my mother, 'I want to talk to your daughter. If you don't tell her to come downstairs, I will go up after her.' My mother was a tall woman, and she placed her back against the stairway door and told him outright, 'You have no right; you cannot go upstairs.'

"Eddie answered, 'I have every right. She is my wife in the sight of heaven!'"

Here Mary Jenkins shook her head, apparently half in disbelief, half in amusement. "Can you imagine?" she laughed, her eyes brimming, to Hays unclear whether from pleasure or pain.

She collected herself. "My mother had had enough," she went on. "She scolded him, saying he had better go home and get to bed."

"Did he do as your mother ordered?"

"He went away. After that I didn't see him much. Frankly, I was lucky to get away from him. He was not a man of much principle, and valued the laws of neither man nor God. He was an atheist, and would just as soon have lived with a woman being married to her as not. I made narrow escape in not marrying him."

"I suspect you might be right."

"Oh, I know I am. After such a bitter quarrel I broke off all communication with him. He wrote me a letter, but I returned it unopened. He wrote again and again and then finally, against my better judgment, I opened his letter. He addressed me formally. 'Dear Miss Devereaux,' he wrote. He upbraided me in satiric terms for my heartless, unforgiving disposition. I showed the letter to my mother, who in turn showed it to my grandmother, who shared it with my Uncle James.

"As head of the family, my uncle was very indignant, and sent Eddie his own cutting letter, without my knowledge. At the same time, Eddie published in a Baltimore newspaper a poem of six or eight verses, entitled 'To Mary.' The poem was very severe and spoke of fickleness and inconstancy. All my friends and family saw it, and knew the verse was directed at me.

"Eddie was incensed by my uncle's letter. He bought a cowhide and went to my uncle's place of business and after a short conversation struck him with this implement. My uncle was a man of over fifty years at the time. My aunt and cousins rushed to my uncle's aid when they saw Eddie beating him, and in the struggle to defend my uncle tore Eddie's black frock coat from collar to skirt at the back. Eddie then put the cowhide up his sleeve and, with his torn coat flapping, went out into the street, followed by an excited crowd of boys. He came to my house, pulled out my uncle's letter, said he resented the insult, and announced he had been to see him at his store and had cowhided him in response. He then pulled the weapon out of his sleeve, threw it down at my feet, and cried, 'There, I make you a present of it!' With that, he stormed off, and since then, frankly, I have seen very little of him."

"He came around last year to your house in Jersey City, did he not?"

"Last year? No, the year before. He was in a terrible state. I worried for him."

"But to no ill result, assuredly? He is all right today."

"I cannot say. I have not seen him."

"But you have heard?"

"Heard what?"

"That he is in New York. Do you know where he is, madam? Do you know where I can find him?"

"No," Mrs. Jenkins said, looking away, staring off as if into the past. "No, I do not."

❦ 52 ❦

The New York Sun, the New York Moon,
and
All the Stars in the New York Sky

"What we have learned," stated Hays to his daughter, joining her at the stove where his luncheon, a quartered capon, stewed in an iron pot under her watchful eye, "Mr. Poe is capable of love and he is capable of violence. If that means he is capable of murder as our mayor charges, I cannot know or say."

"I care not for nuance," Olga seethed. "If Mary Rogers in fact died during a premature delivery, does that not already qualify as murder, Papa? Not only her murder, but also the murder of her unborn child as well. I beg of you, Papa, had this poor girl already felt the quickening? Had she already felt the life of her child inside her?"

It was obvious to Hays that his daughter was already settled on her opinion. He watched her move the bird from pot to table. "Olga, I could not agree more," he told her, taking his place, from where he continued to study her. "I do not need to be convinced. Even more disturbing, the troubling fact is that not only did she die during this illegal procedure, but also, and arguably worse, the perpetrator chose to disguise the heinous act by desecrating his victim's body to make it appear as rape and murder."

Olga had neglected to make a setting for herself. She sat down to watch her father eat. "And why would he do that?" she asked.

"I have wondered myself the same. The answer, perhaps, to deflect attention away from himself."

"Yet your purported prime suspect, Mr. Edgar Poe, seems too eager to attract that very attention!" Her eyes gleamed.

"Olga, I know you revere him, but the man is a suspect, and he could be a murderer," said Hays.

" 'Could' is a very large word, Papa. It remains to be seen. There might be a scenario wherein we consider the violence only a ruse."

Hays sat up. "How so, Olga?"

"I have said it before. For the moment, think of these terrible actions against Mary Rogers as a cloak, Papa. To have died during the shame of an abortion is one thing in our society, to have died at the hands of a murderer—a monster at that, or monsters—another. But the violence perpetrated on the victim might very well be taken as a crude and horrific disguise, committed entirely to salvage her virtue. Papa, is it only me, or do you not find Mayor Harper's attitude toward Mr. Poe at the very least—curious?"

"Again, I have made my consideration just the same, Olga. Tell me, strictly with Mr. Poe's defense in mind, is there any reason you know why Mayor Harper might entertain vendetta directed against Mr. Poe?"

"I can think of several reasons, Papa," she said. "Firstly, let us go to the most obvious: outright jealousy. Over the years, if all is as you say, Mr. Harper has been frequent visitor to Mr. Anderson's tobacco haven. He told you he called Mary Rogers daughter, did he not? I would describe the distilled emotion he carries as something else, something more potent, even lecherous. If Mr. Harper is spewing the brand of fury you describe, if he is accusing Mr. Poe in this manner of an indigestible, clandestine, loathsome, supposed, just-now-discovered liaison with Miss Rogers, true or false, I must say I would not be unduly surprised if Mr. Harper himself was the nurturer of some deep-seated, unrequited infatuation for Miss Rogers."

She continued. "Mr. Harper, no doubt, blames Edgar Poe for nothing less than just being Edgar Poe: handsome, talented, acerbic, brilliant, tainted. But I daresay there is a second, an economic aspect to Mr. Harper's accusation as well. Only a few years ago, the Harper Brothers were on the verge of bankruptcy. Today they are quite healthy, far from the brink, the single largest employer in the city. Mr. Harper's recent success, it can be argued, in no small part is due to the lack of laws governing international copyright, and the enormous profits enabled by depriving certain authors of what some might see as their fair share. Mr. Poe has continuously positioned himself an advocate and vociferous supporter of native literature and copyright legislation. Mr. Harper, on the other hand, is vociferous supporter of his own profits. Which by the way, Papa, I understand, as a businessman he should be, although his tactics clearly make it that much more difficult economically for writers emanating from our own native soil. Thus, Mr. Poe has enjoined Mr. Harper's enmity, and, in turn, Mr. Harper Mr. Poe's.

"Some years ago, Mr. Poe wrote a volume on conchology for the very well-respected firm of Haswell, Barrington & Haswell. This publisher came to Poe—despite what James Harper has frequently charged, Poe did not go to them—eager for a text on this very specific, if esoteric, subject, and the resultant work was exclusively at their behest, solely for Poe's monetary advantage, and strictly for hire. But in the end, in a time of uncertainty and economic unrest, Poe's book served to drive a previously lucrative, similar volume of the Harper Brothers out of print. I have heard many times over, Papa, that Mr. Harper has never forgiven Mr. Poe for such indiscretion."

"And conchology is what, Olga? Pardon my ignorance."

"The science of seashells and mollusks et al., Papa."

Hays eyes widened. "And there is market for such a work?"

Olga shrugged. "There must be. Wouldn't you agree? Because Mr. Harper certainly seems to remain vexed enough on the matter in regard to Mr. Poe. Eventually Poe's hackwork, entitled *The Concholo-*

gist's First Book; or, A System of Testaceous Malacology, attracted some
attention. The cover was a very lovely illustration, as I remember, with
stamps of shells, weeds, and grasses. As it turned out in the end, a similar book had been published some years before in Scotland, and
apparently Poe, having gotten hold of the manuscript, took this as his
easy master, barely changing a word or sentiment of the basic text,
introduction, or even elemental phraseology. When the transgression
was inevitably uncovered, blatant charges of plagiarism were leveled
against Poe. Harper seemingly has never forgiven him."

"And is this the all of it, Olga? Is this why Poe is so disliked by
Harper and his fellows?"

"I would not say he is disliked," she answered. "You must understand, Papa, people are more afraid of him than they dislike him. And
for good reason. He is a formidable presence. A wicked critic. It is the
risk he takes with full knowledge. He attacks and attacks. He cannot
perceive there will be no consequence. Worse, he charges others with
transgressions of which he himself, it turns out, is guilty."

"You refer back to his plagiarism with Harper's mollusks?" Hays
said.

"I do. After that bit of scandal, it was discovered that Poe's much-
discussed and grudgingly admired theory of poetry, cited over and
over again in American magazine essays, articles, and monographs,
was directly lifted—virtually word for word—from Samuel Taylor
Coleridge's own published theory on verse."

"Is this serious?"

"My word, yes, Papa."

"And how was this discovered?"

Olga shook her head. "Let it be enough said that Mr. Harper is the
American publisher of Coleridge. He was not about to let Poe get
away with it, not, as you say, after the mollusk book. He went after
him, and since that day, as a trigger defense, Mr. Poe is quick to point
his own finger at others, guilty or not, for the very same transgression
of which he had been himself humiliated. Most recently he has gone

after Longfellow, the New England poet. The two have feuded bitterly in the journals, although I must say it is decidedly more on the one side of Poe's than on his counterpart."

"And what is this about?"

"For the most part the charges began and involve themselves with a comparison of Longfellow's poem 'The Good George Campbell' with a Scots ballad, 'The Bonnie George Campbell.' Frankly, it is all minor and ridiculous, Papa. More recently, Mr. Poe has charged Mr. Longfellow with lifting his poem 'The Beleaguered City' from Poe's own 'The Haunted Palace,' vehemently labeling the sin first gross plagiarism, then nothing less than undetected palming off."

"Have people conviction for this sort of besmirching?"

"They do indeed," Olga said seriously. "The *Boston Atlas* has responded to Mr. Poe's histrionics against their native son by labeling Poe nothing less than a 'dunderheaded critic.' In addition, I cannot help but vividly recall him called as well a 'dancing dog' and a 'somersaulting monkey.' The New England press has enjoyed themselves immensely, mocking him as 'Poo,' which I have been graciously informed by my good friend Lynchie is a direct and not unsubtle reference to his father, a failed actor, who was booed off the Boston stage under denigrating circumstances with similar unkind calls."

"And how has Mr. Poe reacted to this onslaught?"

"He has simply reiterated his countercharges. He is quick to blame James Harper, and any and all of his enemies. In retaliation, Harper has risen up and bitterly repeated his allegations that Poe had made up citations in much of his criticism, as well as reading texts in translation rather than in their original language. Poe then recharged Harper with passing up American authors in favor of foreign scribes to whom his firm would not be required to pay royalties because of the lack of an international copyright law."

"Is that true?"

"The way Harper's argument goes is that literature, like all imaginative creations, should not be ruled by law and commerce. His point is that the free availability of authors' works to publishers is an absolute imperative to nations such as ours. He maintains that the citizens of this nation, being both undercapitalized and underculturized, without access to public libraries and collections, need inexpensive access to ideas and entertainment. These, it is obvious, our citizenry cannot generate for themselves. Therefore, providing the public with access to native authors' works affords more to advance reputation and long-term earning potential than the restricted circulation created by the higher price of books on which a copyright royalty is paid could ever."

Hays smiled tightly. "This is Harper's thinking?"

"It is. So expressed. And he is not alone. Far from it, Papa. As I say, Mr. Poe is as strong and vociferous an advocate of an international copyright law as any of our native authors. Many more publishers than James Harper could do without him. Yet to think James Harper that perturbed, that vindictive, to accuse Edgar Poe of this heinous crime against this poor young woman and her unborn child, I find such action unfathomable."

"We shall see," Hays said. "After I speak with Mr. Poe, hopefully I will be better able to judge. All I can say for sure, Olga, if he is guilty, he will stand in front of the court."

"Yet you have no idea where the man is?"

"A number of individuals, including our mayor, swear he is in the city. I was hoping that Mrs. Jenkins might afford me the exact location, but she did not."

"Then how will you find him?"

"If you have no objection, you will find him for me, my dear. Do you think, Olga, you might do me the good service to go to the offices of the *New York Sun* and have a word with their editor in charge of Poe's balloon hoax, and perhaps ascertain from him where the author in question thereof might be found. I would send one of my assistant constables, but, as you know, they have all been sacked ruthlessly by your old boss, my new boss, our honorable new mayor, Mr. Harper. You, of course, Olga, have not been sacked, have you?"

She gave him a sidelong look, going for his constabulary staff as if to bash him, but eventually said, "I don't mind, Papa. I shall go gladly."

She took off almost immediately after lunch, leaving him to clear the table and wash the dishes, and returning some hours later that afternoon.

To Hays' inquiry she replied the *Sun* offices crowded, but not unduly so. She swore there was no frenzy to gain hold of the Atlantic Crossing broadsheets, nor to read breathlessly fomented and contrived extra edition accounts of the alleged daring aviation feat. The prints were selling briskly, no doubt, she conceded, but nothing like what she remembered as a girl of the frenzy surrounding the Moon Hoax.

She informed her father (who remained sufficiently reclined in Colt's leather patent chair) she had spoken with the chief editor, Moses Beach, directly. In accordance, she handed Hays an address on Greenwich Street, not far from the Barkley Street pier, two blocks off the river, one of the very last places where Mary Rogers had reportedly been seen alive with her dark-complexioned gentleman of military or naval carriage. The residence number proved to be that of a small, nondescript boardinghouse. It was a two-story brick building with dormer windows and a slant roof.

Not an hour later, with Balboa at the reins, the police barouche parked at the kerb, the landlady, dressed in a well-worn housecoat, opened the door, a fat woman with pop eyes that became even more pronounced with the recognition of High Constable Hays at her entrance, his hand still on the rapper.

She told him, upon his examination, that Mr. Poe was indeed in residency there, that he had initially arrived at her doorstep alone. He had first arranged to occupy one room on her premises at the rear of the first floor, but recently, over the last few days, with his big success (she spoke behind her hand that he had bragged something awful about some confabulation, something involving a flying balloon, she did not know how, of which he said he was the author), he had sent for his wife, her mother, and their cat, and taken an adjoining room for their comfort.

Although Mr. Poe was not at home, she said, smoothing her faded housedress, his mother-in-law and wife were. "The poor dear seems sickly," the landlady whispered. "Such a young thing."

The door to the rooms occupied by the Poe family was then pointed out to him by this landlady, and it was she, the young, infirm wife, who answered the door when Hays knocked.

❧ 53 ❧

130 Greenwich Street

An elderly woman appeared from behind Mrs. Poe. Hays assumed her to be the mother-in-law, Mrs. Clemm. She was severe and manly, square and heavyset, dressed in a plain black dress with a stark white bib collar and apron.

"Can I help you?" she said, stepping in front of her daughter, who literally fell back behind the broad obstruction of her mother before catching herself.

Hays introduced himself, touching the brim of his bowler hat. "I am High Constable Jacob Hays of the New York City Day and Night Watch," he said, failing or ignoring to remember the crucial bit of knowledge that the Watch had suffered most recent dissolution, and in fact, even if he needed reminder, he now represented that newly birthed body, the New York municipal force of police.

No matter, Mrs. Clemm gave no indication of being impressed.

"I am Maria Clemm," she said evenly.

Hays glanced past her at Poe's wife. She looked a child, but Hays knew her to be at least twenty years. She had a full flush to her cheeks, which if he did not know better would have bespoken health.

"This is my daughter, Virginia Poe," Mrs. Clemm introduced her.

"Pleased to meet you both." Hays bowed slightly to each. "Is the man of the house at home?" he asked.

"Mr. Poe is about town, seeing to his work," said Mrs. Clemm.

"I see."

"Can I help you in any way? If this is about funds owed, Eddie has had some recent success, and I know he is currently at work on an article already promised. You can be certain consideration will be coming, and all bills will be paid."

Hays shook his head. "I am not here about accounts," he assured her.

A shadow passed over Mrs. Clemm's suspicious eyes that did not escape the high constable. He registered her concern, and felt more than a small amount of empathy for the elderly woman, alone and fearful for the well-being of her children. "I am unaware of when he will return," she said.

She turned to her daughter then, and asked wouldn't she feel better to go back into the apartment out of the chill. It was not a question and the girl smiled at Hays, but without a word obediently stepped back from the threshold and retreated into the interior, repairing to a small sitting alcove where she took up some handwork. From the angle and distance Hays could not quite be sure if it was crewel point or crocheting she was about.

From what he could garner, behind the broad and severe obstacle of Mrs. Clemm, the boardinghouse apartment seemed to be composed of two rooms. There may have been an additional small closet or sleeping alcove. There seemed to be no kitchen, although there was a cast-iron stove that must have been stoked despite the already mild spring temperature, because the rooms, even from where he stood, were very warm.

He had remained standing in the public hall. Flock wallpaper adorned the walls, and worn carpet stretched down to the corridor end.

"Were you expecting to come in and wait for Edgar, sir, because my daughter is not quite well, and I fear your presence . . ." Her strong but febrile voice trailed off. "That would be impossible."

"No," Hays stated, "I would not be so bold, nor would I want to impose on your hospitality, madam. If you would simply inform Mr. Poe that I was here, and that I need to have a word with him. I can be found at my office on the ground floor of the Men's House of Detention on Centre and Leonard streets. If I don't hear from him, please let him know that I will return."

"I shall do that."

"Thank you."

"Thank you, High Constable."

"He knows who I am, Mrs. Clemm. Please say Old Hays needs a word with him."

❧ 54 ❧

What Song the
Syrens Sing

"Note well, Papa," Olga Hays forewarned her father, "his first tale of ratiocination, 'The Murders in the Rue Morgue,' begins with a quotation, the words of Sir Tom Browne: 'What song the Syrens sang, or what name Achilles assumed when he hid himself among women.'"

"And who is this Sir Tom?"

"That doesn't matter, Papa. A seventeenth-century English author who concerned himself with Christian morals. We are here to discern Mr. Poe's intent, not Sir Thomas Browne's hidden meaning."

"And what are you supposing this hidden intent of Mr. Poe to be?" asked Hays.

She looked her father straight in the eye. "Mr. Poe is likening himself to the strongest and bravest of men, one not even to be outdone by such of a magnitude as a Greek hero. Yet through his authorial voice he is telling us of his vulnerability, that he is not above hiding behind the skirts of females."

"I see," Hays said.

Olga was not totally convinced that he did.

Both Olga and her father had dishes of China tea in front of them at the kitchen table. Olga had not touched hers. Hays had both his thick hands woven round his, warming.

Some nights before, he had returned from Wiley & Putnam's laden with books and page proofs. These he had turned over to his daughter. Since then she had taken up her chore. For the intervening three days and much of the three nights she had kept bent over at her desk perusing Poe's well-worked words in what had once been her mother's sewing room.

"It is a tantalizing puzzle he presents," Olga observed. "As you have described the scene at Greenwich Street, it is not beyond all conjecture."

"That he hides behind his wife and mother-in-law?"

She cocked her head at her father. "That he obfuscates behind them, his women, just so."

She saw him wince, almost imperceptibly, at her use of his phrase.

"And what of the alteration of text in the 'Marie Rogêt' story from its first appearance in the *Ladies' Companion* until now?" he asked. "What of that?"

"There are fifteen changes that I have counted. Three are deletions, the rest additions."

"Putnam said he thought there were seventeen."

She shrugged. "Maybe so. But I only counted fifteen."

"Do these fifteen change the story perceptibly?"

"They do. As before, they make a case for the possibility of an accidental death at the hand of an abortionist performed at the innkeeper Madame Deluc's roadside house, rather than outright cold-blooded murder by a scorned lover. These alterations are designed to make it appear that right from the start, the author was kerrect in his exercise of deciphering the crime."

"And what precisely are these alterations?"

"The deletions first. As I stated, there are three. The first two refer to the thicket as the scene of the crime. The third made reference to an individual assassin who purportedly made confession of the murder of Marie to the gendarmerie. By these three cuts he exculpates himself from his initial implication that one man, ostensibly a lover, committed this sordid crime perpetrated against the innocent Marie in a thicket near the Parisian woods."

"Can we imagine the one man mentioned, he, the author, trying to draw attention to himself?"

Olga shrugged. "As you wish, Papa. I would think not, but you are free to think what you will."

Hays chose to ignore his daughter's implication. "And the additions?" he inquired.

"As I said, the additions are crafted to insinuate Marie's death occurred during a premature delivery at Madame Deluc's roadhouse, rather than in a lover's fit of jealousy or rage. There are twelve instances of text added that I have counted, and in all they encompass something less than one hundred and fifty words in a story that spans some twenty thousand words."

Olga continued. "Twenty-four footnotes have also been added to the story. Most simply identify the author's research, the true-to-life participants, the newspapers cited, the varied venues. For example, Madame Deluc is noted as Frederika Loss, the Seine as the Hudson, Jacques St. Eustache as Payne, Monsieur Beauvais as Crommelin, et cetera. Allow me to read this to you, Papa." She referred to her notes, proceeding to a place in the text.

"'Ultimately,'" she begins her reading, "'let us sum up now the meager yet certain fruits of our long analysis. We have attained the idea'—and here is perfect example of Mr. Poe's calculated change, Papa—'either of a fatal accident under the roof of Madame Deluc, or'—and here he resumes from the original *Snowden's*—'of a murder perpetrated, in the thicket at the Barrière du Roule, by a lover, or at least by an intimate and secret associate of the deceased.'"

"I see. And there you have it: if one chooses to believe Mr. Edgar Allan Poe, as author, perhaps as criminal, not about to get caught; not in one role, not in another."

"Let me read you, additionally, the first footnote, because that is really the only one of any interest. As far as I can ascertain, each of the fifteen changes made in the manuscript by the author, from one version to the next, are simply designed to absolve Mr. Poe of some kind of self-perceived ignorance to the true nature of the crime. In other words, Mr. Poe had it wrong to start, but now, with no reference to the first published draft, he desires for his reader to hold no other belief than he has had it right from the start and always. It is all about him; it is about no other; in my opinion, nothing more nefarious. Here it begins: 'Upon the original publication of "Marie Rogêt," the footnotes now appended were considered unnecessary; but the lapse of several years since the tragedy upon which the tale is based, renders it expedient to give them, and also to say a few words in explanation of the general design. A young girl, *Mary Cecilia Rogers,* was murdered in the vicinity of New York; and although her death occasioned an intense and long-enduring excitement, the mystery attending it had remained unsolved at the period when the present paper was written and published.'"

"It bereaves me it is so. Does Mr. Poe provide a date for that, Olga?"

"He does. November 22, 1842."

"Four days following the date of the Colt execution."

"Yes."

"Go on. Excuse me for having interrupted. I was under the impression it was his editor who insisted these changes upon him."

"Knowing the way a publishing house works, doubtful," Olga said. "His editor, Mr. Duyckinck, might have made suggestion, but ultimately it is the author's choice, Papa. It is Mr. Poe's name attached, not his editor's. Again, I quote: 'Herein, under pretense of relating the fate of a Parisian grisette, the author has followed, in minute detail, the essential, while merely paralleling the inessential, facts of the real murder of Mary Rogers. Thus all argument founded upon the fiction is applicable to the truth: and the investigation of the truth was the object.'"

Hays made a sour face. "Is there more?"

"Indeed there is. The author continues in what might be seen as an effort to exculpate himself. This is interesting, Papa. I must say, almost as if Poe finds necessity to provide himself alibi. Here is what he writes: "'The Mystery of Marie Rogêt" was composed at a distance from the scene of the atrocity, and with no other means of investigation than the newspapers afforded. Thus, much escaped the writer of which he could have availed himself had he been upon the spot and visited the localities. It may not be improper to record, nevertheless, that the confessions of *two* persons (one of them the Madame Deluc of the narrative), made at different periods, long subsequent to the publication, confirmed, in full, not only the general conclusion, but absolutely *all* the chief hypothetical details by which that conclusion was attained.'"

"Is it so much he is providing alibi for himself, or, rather, does he make gesture to pat himself on the back? As I am coming to see it, first, above all else, his intent was to appear to his readers as if he had special knowledge, but now, with Old Hays breathing down his neck, he wishes me to think his information all comes from the public prints."

"He protects himself. He knows your reputation."

"Perhaps," he said.

"He has employed you in his latest story, Papa."

"What?" Hays stared at his daughter. "How so? What do you mean?"

"He has absconded with some very select but recognizable attributes of your personality and added them to the fictional chevalier Dupin."

"Attributes of personality?"

She could see from her father's face that he was perplexed.

"Such as what?" he very nearly growled.

"For one, from the 'Rue Morgue' to 'Marie Rogêt' to this third tale to which I refer, 'The Purloined Letter,' Monsieur Dupin now blows his clouds of smoke from a pipe. But more than that bit of all-too-familiar idiosyncrasy, let me again cite from his text. This is Dupin himself speaking:

"'When I wish to find out how wise, or how stupid, or how good, or how wicked is any one, or what are his thoughts at the moment, I fashion the expression of my face, as accurately as possible, in accordance with the expression of his, and then wait to see what thoughts or sentiments arise in my mind or heart, as if to match or correspond with the expression.'"

She looked up from the written word and grinned at her father, whose hard countenance registered both annoyance and confusion.

He glanced away. Outside in the night air, rain seemed to be pelting off the window. "Mr. Poe is an expressive writer. He listens well."

"Yet he perceives himself above all others. To prove to be anything less than all-seeing would strike him an enormous personal failure. I verily admire his power of observation, his clear, calculating approach. As an author he is masterful. In his three tales of mystery and logic thus far, 'The Murders in the Rue Morgue,' 'The Mystery of Marie Rogêt,' and now this new effort, 'The Purloined Letter,' he uses the clever device of a seemingly simple character, employed as narrator and foil, a veritable everyman, to bring out his sly detector, the chevalier Dupin. In each of these works, he illuminates the pointing finger of unjust suspicion, and the detective's penchant for deducing, by putting himself in another's position, concealing by the obvious, posing an ever-enticing puzzle which we cannot possibly unravel. Papa, this is an exceedingly shrewd individual. From my perspective, Mr. Poe cannot possibly conceive that he is *not* somehow integral to Mary Rogers' death, and this self-importance leads to feelings of guilt and paranoia—each and all, part of his grandiosity."

Hays had listened. Now he spoke, wondering, "Since when, Olga, does grandiosity preclude murder?"

✣ 55 ✣

A Carman

If Mrs. Clemm had given her nephew Old Hays' message, delivered to her by the high constable himself for the author at their Greenwich Street boardinghouse, no matter, Poe never saw fit to appear at the Tombs as requested.

Hays returned to the rooming house after waiting patiently three days. When he did, the landlady informed him the Poe family had moved out. She claimed she did not know where they had gone, only that they had hired a carman to carry their belongings. She suspected, she whispered, not for the first time, behind her hand of bent fat fingers, from something she admitted she had (not entirely) inadvertently heard, that the family had left the city.

It took Hays three days more to locate the carman. He made yet another request of Olga, this time to make the rounds, to place an advertisement in each of the penny prints and sporting papers seeking that individual who had moved a family from 130 Greenwich Street to some location outside the city, giving his address at the Tombs for respondents.

A gaunt man came forward to claim the reward, although no reward had been offered. A Scandinavian with long, stringy yellow hair, wearing much-battered canvas pants, he said he had taken several bags, a trunk, and some wooden boxes containing books for a family of three: a gentleman, suited in black, his young invalid wife, and her mother, a mannish woman, her plain dress, as he remembered, fronted by a white bib, to a farm on the Bloomingdale Road at Eighty-fourth Street. He said he had been paid a pittance for his trouble. At the last, the black-clad gentleman claimed to be short of funds. The carman said he accepted what trifling was offered. The pecuniary indignity of thirty-seven cents, he spat, better than nothing.

❧ 56 ❧

The Brennan Farm

In his time as high constable, Jacob Hays had given considerable thought to the manner in which a suspect was to be approached. If Old Hays had settled on Edgar Poe as a true murderer, a simple abetter, or just some tormented sam-rip, he had vacillated enough. All he felt of himself was his frustration, his concentrated desire to come to resolve what had befallen Mary Rogers. The crime had eaten at him enough. So it was on a late Sunday afternoon that he appeared at the rear door of the Brennan family farmhouse, some feet off the Bloomingdale Road, without benefit of strong-arm, but leaning on his large ash staff, knocking politely. When a child answered, he asked in his most even tone, "Good day, young lady. I am seeking a family by the name of Poe. Do they reside here?"

He waited patiently at the door, facing west, staring out at the river, recalling his first time here with his suspect, Poe, the night of the Morningside Heights debacle, while the little girl, gay pink and white ribbons in her caramel-colored hair, went off in search of her mother.

Between the house and the Hudson spread the proliferation of outbuildings. A number of hearty men worked the busy produce depot. Behind the curtained window Hays saw the rear door led into a mudroom through which one entered the kitchen of the downstairs apartment. Hays could smell pie baking, apple with cinnamon, if he was any judge, and for a moment it made him mourn his deceased wife, and he found himself imagining, and even longing, to live with his daughter Olga in a setting safe and outside the city proper where an apple cinnamon pie so baked and placed to cool on such a windowsill would not be purloined, and a young woman, innocent and hardworking, would not be subject to the sordid and criminal. His thoughts then went to his daughter specifically, and he felt an uncomfortable hollow and longing to deliver her from him, her own overloving and protective father, to whom she was inordinately loyal. He felt compromised by age. He tormented himself why Olga had never married. He worried why she had chosen her father over a life with husband and children of her own. He wanted, once and for all, to solve the mystery of the murder of Mary Rogers, and then he would stop, quit the city force gladly; he and Olga would go away, move to the Hudson Valley, far from the nature of evil and the consequence of sin.

Patiently he waited with his thoughts so engaged. The lady of the house, Mrs. Brennan, eventually came to the door, and to Hays' inquiry made her explanation.

"Mr. Poe is in the parlor reading to the family," she said, her little daughter in her ribbons, matching pink dress and crinoline, hiding behind but peeking past her mother's apron.

Hays asked Mrs. Brennan would she not say to Mr. Poe that Jacob Hays, high constable of the city of New York, was here to speak with him.

She fixed him with a curious eye before saying that she would indeed, at first opportunity, although making it clear she could not interrupt Mr. Poe unduly.

He told her he would be grateful.

She left, returning a few moments later.

"There is no way to disturb him in mid-breath," she apologized. Would High Constable Hays like to come into the parlor and listen to the recitation until Mr. Poe is through? "It is from a poem he has only lately written and works on still in his upstairs study," she gushed. "Also there will be tea and cakes afterwards."

She led him inside. Through the kitchen (he left his boots in the mudroom), through the dining room, a big plank yellow pine table, a cherrywood breakfront displaying the Sunday family dishes, yellow-glazed with painted blue enamel flowers, very sunny, the floor scratched, and in some spots even splintered where chair legs had marred the soft yellow pine as the farm men must have pulled away from the table or leaned back in their bentwood chairs, patting their full bellies after finishing up their Sunday supper.

The scene he encountered in the sitting room took Old Hays up short. What exactly he was expecting, he probably could not have said. He was a quick-witted man, prideful, cagey, he thought somewhat cultured. But an author reading his work on a Sunday afternoon in such an idyllic setting as this sunny living room presented, what was that? He had not seen Poe since the night of the grave robbery at St. Mark's churchyard. Consequently, what remained in Hays' head in regard to the man after the verbal character attack on him by James Harper, not to mention the workings of his own insinuated imagination, might have been just that, mere conjury.

In the Brennan parlor the listeners sat enraptured in front of the fire, immersed in the spell of the literary work. The black-clad poet, a pearl gray stock at the neck, stood with his back to the blaze. The room was not the least chilly. Poe's young wife had been given a seat of honor, closest to the warmth. The assembled surrounded the reader. They were fully attentive. In circles of society and even in law enforcement conversation there was of late much talk of the Viennese medical physician Franz Anton Mesmer. (Olga was certainly fond of mentioning this radical medical practitioner, regaling her father, telling him even Poe was said to be a fanatic.) The expressions on the faces in this room qualified to Hays as nothing less than "mesmerized." The attendants in the parlor were that well entranced. Even the children.

In his hands, Poe held a long, partially unfurled roll of blue foolscap on which was penned in neat and exact script his text. On the floor at his feet, temporarily discarded, was a snippet length of red ribbon used to hold the manuscript in a tight cylinder before it was unrolled.

Hays stood quietly motionless in the arch leading from dining room to parlor until Mrs. Brennan, touching his elbow, ushered him to be seated.

Mrs. Clemm, alone, occupied a rose-hued velvet love seat. Now, from across the room, as she registered the high constable, the color drained from her face. She shot him a look that bespoke a certain panic, but as Mrs. Brennan ushered him into the room, she moved over uncomfortably to make space.

Hays silently half bowed and mouthed apology. He sat carefully, his intelligent eyes quickly taking in the other adult listeners, all female, all enraptured.

At the same time, Poe looked up from his recitation and saw him, Hays, perhaps without recognition.

Six children, including the one who had answered the door, were present, the youngest fidgeting, but not the most mature, an open-faced teenaged girl, who sat as utterly transfixed as her elders by the fascinating, if macabre, poesy of Mr. Poe, a gentleman she must have thought quite romantic from the starry look in her eyes.

Poe's wife sat quietly, her delicate hands folded in her lap. Upon seeing her in this light, Hays was again struck: she was indeed so much younger than her husband, a mere child, not much older than the Brennan girl who sat with such excitement permeating her countenance.

The wife coughed.

Hays shifted slightly as she pulled from her sleeve and used a delicate lace handkerchief to dab her mouth. Her eyes momentarily lifted and met his, then lowered. Hays switched his gaze, following her adoring eyes back to drinking in her husband as he recited. A young bride, the high constable observed, absolutely loving and devoted.

❧ 57 ❧

Mr. Poe,
Do You Remember Me?

In the Brennan parlor, the high constable waited until the wan poet finished reciting; his final word, charged yet familiar to Hays from that night on the Heights, hanging in the air: "Nevermore." After that Poe's wife Virginia rose unsteadily from her chair, came to her husband, and fell to her knees, scrambling to take up the unfurled foolscap scroll and reroll it. The good Mrs. Brennan came up to the writer then and whispered to him, and he looked toward the detective, and then he nodded ever so slightly that he understood, and Hays took this as a signal and rose himself.

Having regained his boots, Hays stood at the kitchen door waiting to be joined by Poe. While he waited he surveyed the backyard in the late afternoon sunlight. In front of him stood a cluster of three small sheds, excluding the privy, and a larger barn to the right. Holding pens for livestock, some with a few stray beasts, stood behind the barn. The orchards extended down to the railroad tracks. A line of trees, a windbreak, stood at a right angle at the far side near the river's edge. In the crisp light Hays could see clear to the water, and in that entire expanse on this Sunday afternoon at this hour no one was to be seen, although earlier the place had been teeming with busy men.

The high constable's mind wandered. He mulled over how, at another time, he might have found it pleasant to sit, as he just had experienced, in a sunny and cozy farmhouse parlor, listening to a forlorn poet read his curious poem about a talking black bird in high dramatic voice intoned, to sip strong East Indian tea and munch hot scones, fresh from the oven, slathered with jams boiled from fresh fruit culled off the backyard orchard trees. For a moment he was taken off guard by the resounding loneliness and emptiness that had suddenly come over him in such setting, the debilitating sense of loss and uneasy despair he felt all at once for his departed wife.

Hays trudged down the rickety boardwalk from the kitchen door, listening to the resonance of his own heavy feet on the tread in the still air, the faint bleating of a sheep from the pens—or was it a kid goat?—despondency and utter fatigue having taken the animal over.

He stood still for a moment and it was in this brief interim, with the unseen beast keening, that he sensed Poe approaching. He turned. Yes, here he was, dressed in black, traipsing heavily through the barnyard muck toward him.

When they faced each other, Hays apologized. He said, "Mr. Poe, it was not my intention to interrupt your Sunday." Adding, "Mr. Poe, so good to see you again. You remember me, I'm sure."

"Most assuredly, High Constable."

They stood together in the yard, a number of chickens pecking at the dirt between their feet, Poe's gaze fixed in the distance on some indiscernible object or site (the sun-dappled cliffs of Weehawken?) whilst Old Hays' gaze remained fixed on him.

"Why, sir," Hays asked finally, "did you choose to avoid me in the city?"

Poe seemed to have no idea of what Hays was talking. "I did not realize I was avoiding you," he said.

"I came to call at your rooming house."

"No one told me," Poe said.

"I spoke with your mother-in-law, Mrs. Clemm. I told her I needed to see you."

"It must have slipped her mind. She said not a word to me. My sincere apologies for any inconvenience. My wife is in delicate state, you see, and is much fatigued. My family has only just arrived from Philadelphia. They find the city noisy and dirty. We are all unsettled . . ." He made vague motion to take in all around. "Here the air is cleaner. For all our sake, we decided to move to this farm. Remember, Mr. Hays, it was with you I first came upon this site."

"I remember," Hays said, "as if it were yesterday."

"So there is nothing more insidious," Poe answered, his voice tinged with melancholy. "Avoidance was the last thing on my mind. Why, sir, should I avoid you?"

"Exactly my question to you, Mr. Poe. Can you explain to me, sir, why your name comes up repeatedly in my ever-ongoing investigation into the murder of Mary Rogers?"

Poe did not answer immediately. He stared at Hays almost blankly. Behind Poe, at the kitchen window, the high constable could make out Mrs. Clemm, pressed to the glass, staring at her put-upon son-in-law, and him, the villain, Old Hays, her Eddie's poor shadow nemesis.

"I am fully aware my name is denounced by James Harper. For what transgression, I am confident you will soon tell me, High Constable."

"Why, sir, would a man such as he entertain a vendetta against you?"

"Revenge," Poe said without hesitation.

"Revenge? Revenge for what?"

"Revenge for my infringement on his bailiwick! Revenge for standing up! If I were to tell you, High Constable, the most popular writer in America is the Englishman Charles Dickens, and he makes not a shilling from his work here, I promise to you, my good Mr. Hays, *I* am your good citizen telling *you* the God's truth. Same for the likes of Thackeray, Walter Scott, Bulwer-Lytton. Not a sixpence. And I, just for your enlightenment, make not a sou in Britain, and barely a sou here. It is why I write short stories, sir, and not novels. At least the magazines pay. American book publishing houses find neither need nor desire to fork over royalties, or any fee whatsoever for that matter, to we writers. Especially we natives."

"No? And why is that?"

"Because, as I have said, there is no recourse. There is no international copyright compelling them to do so. Mr. Harper has gallantly, most vociferously, most conveniently, adopted the credo, bellowing loud and long over this wide and vast young country: Why should we as an American people pay for a literature of our own when we can have it for nothing?"

"And this is why you contend he denounces you, implicates you in crime and the avoidance of punishment?"

"Exactly. To be sure. He seeks his revenge for my support of an international copyright law, sir. Because I myself am after him, sir. This gentleman accuses me of what? Infringing on his God-given right to make money? Let me tell you something, Mr. Hays, even though Mr. Harper mints flying eagles hand over foot, Mr. Harper finds within himself no need or want to defend a national literature, sustain our men of letters, uphold our dignity. You know what his standard practice is, Mr. Hays? His Honor our mayor, this dignitary, stations a man in London and pays him a substantial wage, certainly more than he pays any wordsmith. This secret agent is usually an employee of a prestigious English house. As soon as the latest literary volume hits the streets, or better still returns in galley form from the printer, this scoundrel will pirate the manuscript and rush it to the docks. There the book is jettisoned across the Atlantic on the swiftest sailing vessel available. While still miles off the Montauk Point of Long Island, a ready schooner is dispatched. The schooner will meet the English ship mid-swell, the English literary work transferred, and the schooner races back to New York City and our publishing megalopolis. Here the volume is torn into a hundred sections, each consisting of four or five pages, no more. Then each of these is distributed to a printer, who will labor through the night to have his bit typeset, proofread, and complete by morning. At which time all the printers come together each of their contributions assembled to comprise the whole. The volume, now complete in folio form, sans cover, will be on the street by noon ready for purchase, not a cent destined for the embattled author of the work."

Hays was about to make comment but Poe, so self-dramatically engaged, waved him off.

"Because the profits are enormous, sir, the risks negligible, because all concentration is turned toward such business, our American publishers have no need, nor inclination, to print writers from our own shore, and if they do have said inclination, they pay miserably for the favor. The most popular native writers of our day—who would you say?—Irving and Cooper, both talentless curs, mind you, are lucky to receive even one thousand sovereigns for their latest output. And a writer such as myself is left begging to eat."

From his countless professional encounters, Hays knew suspects to have a certain way of comporting themselves when they felt the onslaught of threat. Their faces light with an unnatural distorted smile or turn dour with self-absorption. Their eyes may have a certain cast, a certain intensity. Their backs are straight or stooped, their hips sway with the shifting of an uncomfortable weight. Emotions may well. You look into their eyes. You see something chilling—what is it?

Hays had no doubt Olga was right: Poe considered himself above any man in intellect. In power of deductive reasoning, he must have thought himself unsurpassed. Even now, in confrontation with him, high constable of the city of New York, a grin Poe seemed not able to suppress played under his mustaches. But was it a villain Hays saw, or something else?

"And now, sir, Mr. Hays," Poe said, "now that you understand the motives of Mayor James Harper directed toward me, such as they are, here *we* are. What exactly is it that you would like, sir? How may I help you?"

Hays took it a given, as he had heard, that women would take to this man without respite, and that men would not. The high constable's frank, steady eyes fixed on Poe's penetrating eyes, pupils and irises concentric circles, dull black disks.

The realization came to Hays the man had not a clue why he was here. He pulled out his tobacco, tapped his pipe against his shoe, and filled the bowl. He proffered his leaf to Poe, saying, "Won't you join me? This is from a sock, first rate, purchased from Anderson's."

Poe refused, saying he carried no ready bowl.

But then he reconsidered. He removed from his inner breast pocket the foolscap cylinder of manuscript from which he had read earlier, retied with its red ribbon length. Without a word of comment, he tore off a corner and held out the small rectangle. Hays, seeing Poe's intention, filled the slip with a healthy pinch of blond cut and watched him roll his smoke.

"Ingenious," Hays said as Poe licked the neat cylindrical package tight.

"It is nothing more than a tiny segar. Quite appealing really," Poe said. "What is being called a segarette."

"Just that indeed."

Hays made himself comfortable by the side of the barn, sitting on a nail keg, the smell of manure in his nose, not unpleasant. "I sympathize with you, Mr. Poe, for what you did," he elicited, firing a locofoco with a thumbnail. "Sometimes in a court of law a man does not always get justice. Sometimes a man is sorry for what he has done, contrite, but the court is unable to see his remorse. If the young woman was pregnant, if she died accidentally during the procedure, I tell you, vouchsafe, I can help. I am here to beg your cooperation, and if we are successful, sir, I shall be of both moral and mortal assistance to you to the best of my ability. Would you like that?"

Poe stared straight ahead. On the nail keg Hays puffed his briar until it glowed red. "Forgive me, High Constable, but what have I done again?" Poe asked.

"You have acted nobly to save your wife embarrassment. What have you to do with the death of Mary Rogers, sir?" Hays sternly inquired.

"Mary Rogers? Nothing, I tell you. Is this the game in which Mayor Harper implicates me? I thought you were talking palming off.

The man's audacity is boundless. Mary Rogers! I . . . My God, I wasn't even in the city at the time of the crime against her . . . I would never . . . and I was living in Philadelphia at the time besides."

"Living there, yes. But it is my understanding you frequently traveled to New York to visit publishers and editors and the like. And the occasion of Miss Rogers' death coordinates with such a time."

Poe coughed but could not deny it.

"Mr. Poe, I expect nothing less than the truth from you!" Hays persisted.

"I knew her. I did. You know that."

"You admired her?"

"I admired her, yes. She was a young woman of extraordinary beauty and bright spirit."

"And this is why you held her in such esteem?"

"Please, Mr. Hays, disingenuousness is not your strong suit. I am a poet, sir. Beauty attracts me. But as to anything else . . ." He hesitated. "I am a married man, sir," Poe managed.

"Need I remind you such status has not stopped others before you, sir."

"This is true," Poe conceded.

"You loved Mary Rogers," Hays said. It was not a question.

"And what, sir, if I did? I have already admitted as much to you."

"And you traveled to Poughkeepsie with her at the time of her first disappearance."

This, too, not a question.

"And what if I did that, sir?"

"In your own clever tale and indictment of we police, entitled the 'The Mystery of Marie Rogêt,' Mr. Poe, you have charged whosoever was with Mademoiselle Marie at the time of her first disappearance must have been the villain in her second disappearance. What can you tell me, Mr. Poe, that will convince me you are not the assassin of Mary Cecilia Rogers?"

🎋 58 🎋

Poe, Poe,
a Thousand Times Poe

P oe returned to the Brennan house in a state of extreme agitation.
Trudging heavily up the outside stairs, he wrestled with the idea
of alcohol as solution, momentarily considering a glass of sherry
might do much to settle his nerves.

Before the arrival of the high constable, Poe had been relaxed, content with his recitation. His new poem had been the singular thought
on his mind, a work years in progress. He had persuaded himself it to
be the bit of doggerel to change everything for him—the verse of the
black bird—a crow or raven, he still hadn't quite decided which.

While he was reading to the Brennans, to Muddie and Sissy, the
poem's intrinsic power coursed through his blood and psyche, engendered his hopes. He knew what he had. Listening to himself recite, he
felt privileged to witness the excitement reflected on the faces of his
listeners, and with the unexpected appearance of the high constable,
he actually relished the opportunity as well to watch the reaction of
this man with no link to him, save as antagonist.

Although perhaps at first confused by his presence, Poe certainly
knew immediately who the police constable was when he entered the
room, after his eminence had been shown to his seat by Mrs. Brennan,

after he had excused himself to Muddie and settled beside her on the red love seat. Poe had looked up at a moment when he was most impressed with himself, as he pronounced a pilfered phrase he had heard uttered by a little boy while he, Poe, paced the paths of Rittenhouse Square in Philadelphia some years before with the same poem occupying his mind, reciting to himself, repeating, trying the lines, the meter, the foot, and the boy, not more than eight or nine, minded by his guardian, preoccupied in the grass with a hoop, had overheard the poet's mutterings and turned to him, saying in the most extraordinary childlike chirp something to the effect that he, the boy, "had never heard bird or beast with such a name as Nevermore," and Poe, flabbergasted by the innocent, inadvertent poetry of the child, had immediately incorporated what the boy had said into the line, and here he was thinking now how beautifully his poem was playing out in all its song, as the scroll slowly unfurled to the floor, and there—out of where?—out of nowhere, was this police constable, this broad man of imposing figure, with large, powerful block torso set upon dwarfish legs, and a decidedly Semitic cast, being shown by the lady of the house, Mrs. Brennan, to the vacant spot next to Muddie.

Poe looked up and Hays' boring stare caught his own eyes, and held. For a moment Poe flustered. Their looks were locked, and Poe felt an unsettling, the words of Muddie reaching him out of the near past that Old Hays was after him, had paid a visit to 130 Greenwich Street looking for him, but then Hays sat heavily and Poe fell back into his reading, the long paper scroll continuing to unfurl from his hands, all things considered, the poet undisturbed in a course that must inevitably lead to his triumph, and Poe smiled to himself in his secret heart, eternity to come in this guise of carefully crafted words with black bird.

So now Poe was returned to the parlor following his disturbing outdoor tête-à-tête with the detective, visibly agitated, in spite of himself, as he watched his dear aunt bustle about, helping Mrs. Brennan clean and straighten after tea and cakes, dinner preparation to follow, his face ashen when he entered the room and paused in the threshold.

Upon his reappearance, pleasant conversation ceased. Sissy from her seat, warmed by a crocheted coverlet against her ceaseless inner chill, fluttered her fingers in his direction, motioned to him, her Edgar.

He came to her immediately, dutifully.

"What is wrong, Eddie dearest?"

A pure white handkerchief, certainly not silk, but pounded cotton, twice, or even thrice, darned, yet so neatly and carefully pressed giving the illusion of perfect newness, was clasped to her mouth.

He took his spot next to her on the brocaded sofa. Mrs. Clemm joined them. His two women now having taken their familiar spots to either side of him, his protectorate, each with one of his hands in theirs. Muddie with the left, Sissy with the right. Sissy stroking the soft hairs on the back of Eddie's hand, admiring his long, sensitive fingers. Muddie patting his other hand reassuringly, lovingly, loyally.

"Everything will be all right, Eddie," Muddie said. "All will be fine. There, Eddie, rest your humours. You are all a-boil. Everything will find its proper level. Is that horrible man gone?"

Poe stared at her for some seconds before answering. "No, he is not gone," he said finally. "I fear he will never be gone. And he is not horrible, Muddie."

Mrs. Clemm's look bespoke her alarm. Then she collected herself. "Don't worry, Eddie," she tried another tack to soothe him. "This too will pass. Your magnetic fields are simply in a state. Now what in the world does he, this not-so-horrible man, want with you?"

On the divan, Poe abruptly pulled away from his aunt, snatching his hand back from his wife. He clutched his head and murmured to himself, rocking back and forth, before requesting salts of Mrs. Brennan to relieve the terrible ache encapsulated in his skull.

❧ 59 ❧

Poe Makes Overtures
to His Doomed Wife

Mrs. Brennan prepared dinner of freshly killed lamb shank and
boiled potatoes for her family and the Poes. High Constable
Hays was graciously invited to this meal. He took his place at the near
end of the table along with the cojoined families of landlord and
boarders and three weathered farm depot workers, already seated.

From his place the high constable ate moderately while occasionally, unobtrusively, observing Poe.

When it came to attending to his ailing wife, as far as Hays could
tell, Poe was beyond reproach. He made himself sensitive to her needs
and, invested in her health, made overtures to all her comforts.

She, in turn, seemed indeed a delicate creature, very pale with
feverish consumptive eyes, eyes that in their infirmity appeared to
Hays almost otherworldly.

After supper, a substantial meal despite its simplicity, there came a
time when the poet called on her, his wife, to sing. He clapped his
hands once to gain the attention of the assembled, and announced it
was in honor of his guest, High Constable Hays of the New York City
Municipal Police, that Sissy would sing, and so she, somewhat
abashed, rose unsteadily.

Hays immediately protested, saying he felt no necessity to be entertained.

"Sit, child. Sit," he instructed her. In his mind he was verged on volunteering himself in her stead. He had only a half-bad voice, as Olga fondly at times reminded him.

But before he could launch into his treasured rendition of "Tiddly Aye-Aye for the One-Eyed Reilly" or the absolutely riveting "Widow McGinnis's Pig," Martha Brennan, the eldest of the comely Brennan children, sprang to her feet and eagerly offered herself up instead.

Sissy would not have it. Whatever her ailments, she made a few tentative steps to the sideboard, picking up the concertina with a sidelong look of smug satisfaction toward this rival for her husband's affections, Martha Brennan, that fervent, robust, healthy farm girl, four years her junior.

Hays had to admit Mrs. Poe made a striking figure, round-faced, pouting lips, arguably a forehead too high and broad for beauty (must this not have been a Poe family trait? he wondered), big, dark eyes, raven black hair, contrasting, almost startling, with her white, translucent, virtually colorless complexion.

She was outfitted for the evening in a simple white dress when she stepped to the middle of the warm little room and announced proudly, "My husband's favorite."

So began her rendition of the hymn "Come, Rest in This Bosom," sung in that very high-pitched manner known as trilling, which struck Hays' ears in such a curious way as to almost cause pain. Yet the high constable certainly sat in stark admiration of the sheer range of human sound of which the young woman was capable.

> "Thou hast call'd me thy Angel in moments of bliss
> And thy Angel I'll be, 'mid the horrors of this,—
> Through the furnace, unshrinking, thy steps to pursue,
> And shield thee, and save thee,—or perish there too!"

With the exertion of this caliber performance, her face now took on color. Earlier Mrs. Poe seemed to Hays a ghostly presence, but here in front of him as she performed she began to transform, to turn uncannily red.

Unsuitably red.

The hue became very deep indeed. Truthfully, it was the first time Hays had seen such progression of shade in a human being.

When she reached the part of the song that went, "Rest your head on my bosom, my warm comforting bosom . . ."at the start of the second refrain it became evident that all was not right. She gagged. Her eyes became wild, and a gummy eruption of bright blood suddenly spewed from her mouth in forceful projection. She moaned and collapsed on the floor.

All leapt to their feet.

"She has burst a blood vessel!" Poe cried, looking to Hays helplessly. "Her left temple," he sobbed. "My God, don't you see?"

Evidently, right then and there, Mrs. Poe had suffered some kind of stroke. Hays pushed the panicked, ineffectual husband out of his way and began to massage her temple, then applied direct pressure to what was pointed out by Mrs. Clemm as the point she took as the prime locus of disturbance. The horrified girl was conscious. She looked up into Hays' eyes momentarily, murmuring his effort a comfort, but her skin was so very transparent that Hays could nearly see through the thin veil of flesh, blood flowing seemingly with no outlet, pooling from the pulsing ruptured vessel beneath the epidermis.

Almost apologetically, as the high constable knelt over his wife and continued his work, Poe tearfully admitted that something similar had happened once before. His panicked explanation, the cause of this catastrophe being her choral effort, his contention his wife's meticulous high-pitched trilling an absolute exertion of a magnitude sufficient to put her down.

"Then why let her do it?"

"I do not know. Forgive me."

Poe could not take his eyes off her. He wiped the blood from her lips and chin, tearfully swabbed it from where it ran in red rivulets down her white dress front.

In return, she gazed up at him, her eyes wide with love and fear.

The thought came to Hays then that if this is what it took, if Mrs. Poe had ever been in danger of losing him to any woman, the healthy teenaged Brennan girl, the beautiful and spirited Mary Rogers, whomsoever, any other game coquette, she had learned to use her illness as love's elixir, she had won him back with this tactic—if illness could in any way be called tactic.

In the confusion and panic of the moment, despite the blood running from the corner of her mouth and the dreamy look in her eyes, by Hays' judgment, Virginia Poe seemed very much aware of her victory.

🌿 60 🌿

Beneath a Bust of Pallas

Poe and Patrick Brennan, Mrs. Brennan's husband, with Old Hays directing their movement, carried Virginia upstairs, where she was put to bed in her room. Within a few moments she had lapsed into a state of unconsciousness, and remained therein, occasionally moaning softly.

Hays' family physician Dr. John Francis, who had administered to Old Hays' wife Sarah at the end of her life, was sent for immediately from his home in Greenwich Village, Balboa dispatched to fetch him.

Poe paced the room, not for a moment leaving his wife's side, while Muddie applied cold compresses to keep her daughter's temperature down.

Hays eventually left the vigil, shown to sit in Poe's study through the center hall by Mrs. Brennan, where he made himself relatively comfortable in a stiff horsehair chair under a small shelf nailed to the wall displaying a plaster bust of Pallas Athena.

"It was left by a previous renter," Mrs. Brennan explained to him when she saw Hays observing the curious object of sculpture. "A French lieutenant who had served under Napoleon."

In addition, the walls were decorated with assorted French military prints and hangings of the Empire manner, also the detritus of the Gallic militarist. There was a clock on the wall and books and magazines on the shelves. The remaining furniture was covered in cloth. Two windows looked out over the yard with a view of the river and the New Jersey Palisades across it, the very bluffs of Weehawken where the body of Mary Rogers had been recovered.

After Mrs. Brennan's departure, Hays remained seated for a long period before picking up a folder from the desk labeled in neat, near-calligraphic hand: THE PACKET OF STORIES NUMBERING 66: TALES AND LETTERS TO EDITORS. He held the folder briefly, weighing its heft, and then opened it. The stories were listed and numbered on a sheet within the folder. The letter on top of the pile was addressed "Dear Bennett" and expressed this sentiment: "Can you not send me $5? I am sick and Virginia is almost gone. Come to the Bloomingdale Road and see me. Word is you suspect me of a cruel deed. I hope you know this impossible. Please bring your open mind along with you when you make the visit you promised to Mrs. Clemm. I will try to fix the matter soon." It was signed "Yours truly, E.A.P."

It was some two hours later when Hays became aware of the arrival of his friend John Wakefield Francis, entering through the downstairs mudroom.

"Where is the patient?" Hays could hear the medical man's booming voice as he crossed through the kitchen.

Dr. Francis was led up the carpeted stairs to Sissy's room. From the open door Hays observed him, a wise, florid fellow, in steel-rimmed spectacles, with white flowing locks and high boots.

Within a few moments Poe, head hanging, trudged into the room. He showed surprise to find Hays in his private sanctum in his favorite chair at his study desk. "Oh, you," he said, glancing at the manuscript letter laid out in front of Hays. "You are still here?"

"Is she all right?" asked Hays.

Poe shrugged. "From what ails her, I do not think there is reprieve."

"So the doctor has diagnosed what it is?"

"I do not need a doctor to tell me. It is death in life, sir."

"I see," Hays said. "I am sorry."

"The doctor said he would make his examination and then speak with me. Muddie is with her. I should never have asked Sissy to sing that song."

"It's good that her mother is there. Mrs. Clemm seems devoted to her daughter."

"She is."

"And she seems devoted to you as well."

Poe looked at him. "She is as well," he said slowly. "To each three of us, family is everything."

"I appreciate that. For me, the same. Family takes precedence over all things."

Poe sighed.

"Something more worries you, Mr. Poe? What is it?"

Poe shook his head.

Hays waited.

"I do not have money enough to pay the physician."

"Don't concern yourself with that right now. I will pay the doctor's charge. He is an old friend, and you can repay me when you can."

"Under the circumstance, your visit here, I could never accept that," Poe muttered, but both he and Hays knew this was only to uphold whatever fragile semblance of personal honor to which the man held. That he would accept Hays' offer, nothing further need be said in regard to this matter.

"Only a few moments ago I was standing there at the window, gazing out at the river, thinking this must be your daily view," Hays said. "It is there, nearly directly across, where the body of Mary Rogers was discovered. Back then, when it happened, I thought the puzzle would be easily solved, but here we are nearly four years later, and nothing. I have had some discussion with my daughter. As I may have told you, she is an avid reader, and so much admires your insight and obvious intelligence. She has explained to me how in your three stories of reason, 'The Murders in the Rue Morgue,' 'Marie Rogêt,' and now 'The Purloined Letter,' the puzzle that you have invented as author, and the clear, precise manner in which you unravel it for your readers, this is something not seen before in the annals of literature."

Poe stared at him wearily. "That may be so," he said slowly. "I never thought about the antecedents of my process. I am grateful to your daughter for her kind words and cognizance."

"I must say, however, Mr. Poe," Hays continued, "from my own particular vantage point, there is great gap in solving a puzzle purposely set forth to be solved by a calculating literary practitioner, from unraveling a mystery, taken place in a true reality by a criminal mind specially hell-bent to deceive."

Poe blanched. "Point granted. I could not have said it better myself, High Constable. You wouldn't happen to have some more tobacco, would you, sir?"

Hays patted his pocket, searching for his leaf. When he found it he held the sock to Poe. Poe reached to his desk and took a cheap corncob pipe from a ceramic mug. He filled it from Hays' pouch while Hays struck a locofoco and lit both Poe's bowl and his own.

They sat smoking. The voices coming from Virginia's bedroom were infrequent and muffled.

"You have family?" Poe asked him.

"I have the daughter. I think you must know her. Olga Hays. She works sporadically for the house of Harper as a proofreader."

Poe nodded. "We have spoken a few times. She has attended some of my lectures, I believe."

"My wife died some four years ago. We had four sons, but none survived."

"I am sorry to hear that. My sincere condolences."

"My daughter is an ardent attender of your public presentations. She much admires you."

"I am flattered." He half smiled. "She shows good taste," he added facetiously.

"She tells me you have a new story in *Godey's Lady's Magazine*."

Poe's eyes narrowed again with added suspicion.

"I'm sorry, I'm sure my daughter told me, but what is the title?"

" 'The Oblong Box.' "

"That's it! 'The Oblong Box.' Veritably the coffin. If I'm not mistaken, in some ways inspired by the John Colt murder affair, no?"

"Only insofar as the offender sepulchres a corpse in a crate, here the oblong box of the title."

"As did Mr. Colt sepulchre the body of his victim, Samuel Adams, in a similar crate."

"As did Mr. Colt."

"And 'Thou Art the Man'?"

"You are indeed an ardent follower of my work, High Constable. You keep up surely."

"As I said, my daughter reads assiduously. She funnels to me all matters of interest. The manner in which the corpse of Mr. Shuttleworthy is nailed into the crate, only to burst forth, it again brings to mind Mr. Colt's unfortunate treatment of Mr. Adams."

"Yes, I admit I thought of John Colt as I wrote it."

"You have had no recent correspondence with Mr. Colt, have you, Mr. Poe?"

"Correspondence with John Colt?" Poe smirked with some slyness. "Since his suicide you mean?"

"As you wish."

"No, none," he said. "In my imagination I may communicate with the dead, but in life, I daresay, I have had none."

"Come now, Mr. Poe, neither of us believes John Colt to be dead, do we? These two stories of yours, followed by 'The Premature Burial' . . ."

"This is the time, High Constable Hays, where you should be again admonishing me: 'Good citizens speak the truth.' "

"Good citizens speak the truth, Mr. Poe."

"No, I have had no communication with Mr. Colt, dead or alive. And 'The Premature Burial' speaks of my own fears to be mistaken for dead, and prematurely entombed. I have nothing more to allay, and furthermore, sir, for your information, no matter what you might think, I did not in any way murder Mary Rogers."

🎐 61 🎐

Murder for Pleasure

"Please believe me, sir," Poe said, gazing out at the still night, at the two hundred or so silent acres of the Brennan farm, at the flowing river beyond, at the place where Mary Rogers died. "I have not killed her. Nor have I partaken in her death."

"I have not said that you did, sir," Hays responded. "Not yet, in any event."

"I loved Mary Rogers," he breathed softly. "I would not have harmed her."

"But did you disguise her death to preserve her honor?"

"How do you mean?" Poe turned from the window, toward he who was his pursuer and accuser; he who had remained seated but was watching him. He exhaled. "I make admission," he said, "she, Mary, was with me in Poughkeepsie. I was visiting river cities, lecturing and reading poetry at local halls. She joined me as companion on my tour. Of that I am guilty. I betrayed my wife. But, again, I am not Mary's murderer."

"When was the last time you saw her?"

"I was at Anderson's, some weeks before her death, with John Colt."

"John Colt? Was he a frequent visitor to that establishment?"

Poe grimaced. "By all means, yes," he said. "The tobacco shop is only across the street from his office on Chambers. What with the free port and free food, not failing to mention the companionship of those he admired and envied, I daresay Mr. Colt virtually lived in the establishment."

"And you went there to see Mary, and John Colt accompanied you?"

"Mary no longer worked for Anderson. Surely you know that, High Constable. She had stopped employment some two years or more before. Her name came up, however. I cannot remember the context exactly."

"So you went to see her?"

"John Anderson gave me her address. Mary had put an end to our liaison. Truthfully, under difficult circumstances for us both. It was shortly after our sojourn to Poughkeepsie. I was married. She desired a life for herself free from the rigors I offered. I did not begrudge her. That day at Anderson's, there was some talk of difficulties she was having. I went to the boardinghouse on Nassau Street to see how she was faring."

"Faring?"

"Was she well? Was she happy? Was she fulfilled?"

"And was she?"

"A new gentleman had entered her life after me. I knew not who he might be. At Anderson's that was the talk in her regard. That her gentleman had abandoned her, but when I asked her, she said, no, they were still together, and that there were prospects of marriage."

"This must have been disconcerting to you?"

"I was relieved, for her sake."

"Yet she gave you not his name?"

"No."

"And you did not insist?"

"I did not."

"There are those who suggest that gentleman was you, sir."

"It was not."

"Were you still in love with her?"

Poe did not answer this question directly. "She told me she was pregnant," he said instead.

Hays glared. "Why didn't you say this before?"

"I promised I would not tell. I gave my word."

"But she told you she was going for an abortion?"

"No, she did not. And if she did, it could only have been against her will. She had already felt the quickening. God knows I knew her, she never would have put an end to that life."

At that instant Dr. Francis, looking tired and haggard, entered the study. Poe's voice broke off. From beneath the bust of Pallas, both he and Hays faced the humbled physician.

"I am sorry to say," said the doctor in a subdued voice, "I can hold out little hope."

Poe asked few questions. There was little to ask that he did not already know. Consumption, the white death, was on hand. The blue-veined eyelids, the rouged-looking cheeks, the bright-eyed flush, often mistaken for loveliness, were all alight. The tubercle bacillus killed without disfiguring the body or destroying the mind.

"It will not be today," said the doctor quietly, "and it will not be tomorrow. But her days are in short supply. She may have as long as a year, but surely not much more than that."

Mrs. Brennan held her position in the kitchen, at the plank table, when the men came downstairs, moving slowly. A kettle was on the stove. She rose and offered both Hays and Dr. Francis beds for the night. She assured Hays his man—she referred to Balboa—could sleep comfortably enough in the barn on fresh hay, and there were stalls in the same building enough for the horses.

Hays thanked her for her kindness but refused, saying he would prefer to return home that evening for the express purpose, if nothing else, of sleeping in his own bed.

"My old bones," he apologized.

Mrs. Brennan smiled, said she understood. Again she offered tea. Again she was refused. Hays and the doctor left the house through the back door. Balboa was standing under a solitary willow tree, gazing out at the dark river. The carriage was nearby, the more slender of the matched steeds stamping his left front hoof impatiently in the soft, moist ground, ready to be back in his own familiar stall.

Balboa helped both Hays and Dr. Francis up. At that moment Poe hurried out of the house. He said he found himself in dire financial straits, necessitating him traveling immediately to the city. He inquired if he could not ride with them. Hays answered that of course he could.

They rode for some time, each man staring straight ahead, lost in his own thoughts, before anyone spoke. It was Poe who broke the silence.

"I loathe to leave my Virginia ailing so. From my infancy," he said, "I have been noted for the docility and humanity of my disposition. My tenderness of heart was even so conspicuous as to make me the jest of my companions. I married my wife early, and was happy to find in her a disposition not uncongenial with my own. My uncomplaining wife, my adoring wifey, alas! is the most usual and the most patient of sufferers. Forgive me, gentlemen, I know not what to do."

Both Hays and Dr. Francis commiserated with their carriage companion's anguish. Both men, eldered and vulnerable to chill, had wool blankets thrown over their laps, but Poe, where he sat opposite, facing them, shivered, and refused the offer of cover.

He continued. "Do you know that modern discoveries in what may be termed 'ethical magnetism' render it probable indeed that the most natural, and consequently the truest and most intense, of human affections are those that arise in the heart as if by electric sympathy?"

He began searching in his pocket, taking out a pencil.

"I dwell alone," he suddenly blurted, "in a world of moan . . ."

He fell silent then, before beginning to scribble in an unsteady hand on a small assemblage of paper scraps rummaged from his coat pockets. In the east the dawn gave evidence of breaking. His inspiration suddenly broken off, the poet now stared into space for some minutes before falling back to the bits and tears.

Referring from one to another, he began a recitation anew in lilting, murmured voice: "And my soul is a stagnant tide . . ." he said.

> *"Till the fair and gentle Virginia became my blushing bride—*
> *Till the raven-haired young Virginia became my smiling bride.*
>   *Ah, less, less bright*
>   *The stars of the night*
> *Than the eyes of the radiant girl,*
>   *And never a flake*
>   *That the vapor can make*
> *With the moon-tints of purple and pearl,*
> *Can vie with the modest Virginia's most unregarded curl—*
> *Can compare with the bright-eyed Virginia's most humble and*
>   *careless curl.*
>
>   *Now Doubt—now Pain*
>   *Come never again,*
> *For her soul gives me sigh for sigh*
>   *While all day long*
>   *Shines bright and strong,*
> *Astarté within the sky,*
>
> *And ever to her dear Virginia upturns her maiden eye—*
> *And ever to her young Virginia upturns her violet eye."*

Staring at him as he ended, Hays asked, "Have you only just composed this?"

Dr. Francis by this time was snoring softly, his head lolling.

"What inspires the poet," Poe enounced, "what inspires me, is a prescient ecstasy of the beauty beyond the grave, High Constable. It is through the music of poetry that we reach out to those departed, those beyond life."

He glanced at the sleeping Dr. Francis.

"The mere thought of my wife's departing drives me wild. Forgive me. There can be no barrier against the fear of death, because death knows no limits. Darkness and decay and red death hold dominion over all. My wifey is victim for an early grave. I know that. I know the darkness can devour us. I know it can annihilate us. Yet the darkness is astir. I hold that the dead in some form survive and return. I like to tramp the woods. I detest the dirt of the city, the din of the wagons. I loathe the insufferable noise of traffic rumbling over round paving stones, the loud-throated voices of clam and catfish peddlers. Who can blame me? Ah, broken is the golden bowl, the spirit flown forever! Let the bell toll for a saintly soul, let the burial rite be read. A dirge for the most lovely dead that ever died so young. For my Virginia, weep now for me, sir, or nevermore."

In the first glinting rays of dawn, a tear glistened in Poe's eye.

WHEN THEY FINALLY REACHED the city, morning was at hand. Hays gently woke the doctor and they dropped him at his home not so far from the once home to John Colt on the Washington Square in Greenwich Village. Hays and Poe then continued south below the open sewer of Canal Street to the high constable's own home on Lispenard. The hour had now reached half past eight.

"Would you not like to come in for a cup of Javanese before proceeding on your way?" offered Hays.

Poe had announced his intention to find his way to his magazine publisher's (a place of previous employ). He had the idea (he said, brought on by necessity) to try to sell his poem of the black bird.

Poe acquiesced feebly to the high constable's invitation. He was enamored with coffee, he admitted, and the prospect of a brimming cup at this early hour, after a night of sleeplessness and emotional upheaval, seduced him. He stepped down from the carriage, following the high constable, and with him entered the comfortable home of Hays and his daughter.

The early hour notwithstanding, Olga Hays was already fully awake and busy in the kitchen at the stove. The house was warm and the smell of bread, freshly baked, and brewing coffee prevailed.

"Ah, our preeminent reader and critic," Poe smiled at first glimpse of Olga, his voice soft and alluring. "Miss Hays, we meet again."

Olga was a woman with even, symmetrical features. She was now approaching her thirty-third birthday, but thanks to her bright, intelligent eyes and smooth skin looked younger than her years, save for her chestnut hair, which was streaked with three prominent tresses of a gray, so pale as to be almost white. Her father, hard on his own blood, thought her striking, if not beautiful.

"Mr. Poe, this is an honor as great as I have ever enjoyed, to have you in our home. As I have told you on previous occasion and you might even remember, there is no greater acknowledged fanatic of your work than I, sir."

She held out her hand to be shaken.

Poe bowed in acknowledgment before slumping at the kitchen table.

She brought for her father a porcelain basin and filled it with warm water, heated on the stove. Hays washed his face and hands at the sink stand, using strong soap, and rubbed them dry with a coarse towel.

"Papa," Olga said, noting her father's red-rimmed eyes, the deep black stain beneath, "you need sleep. Why not off to bed with you?"

"No, no," he protested, "I am fine. Is the Javanese ready yet, dear?"

She rose to the stove. With a thick blue potholder woven years before by her mother, she removed the coffeepot from the heat and poured out three large cups.

"Cream?" she asked Poe.

"Thank you. And, if possible, sweetener, please, miss."

She placed the creamer and bowl in front of him. He drizzled in a mere drop of cream, but three brimming pewter teaspoons of brown crystal sugar.

Father and daughter watched him as he dumped the third spoonful in the cup and stirred.

"Your father is after me," Poe said to Olga, offering a sly, very nearly grotesque wink with nod. "He pursues me. He thinks I have murdered."

"And have you?" Olga asked her guest evenly.

Poe lifted his cup to her and gingerly sipped before answering. "Only my soul, my dear good woman. I am sorry to say, I have murdered only my own soul."

❧ 62 ❧

If Not He, Who?

For a long while after Poe's departure and her father retired to bed, Olga remains at her mother's former sewing table, now functioning as her desk. Above her on the shelf, where once stood stored needles, brass thimbles, tape measure, and variety of threads, now resides her library. As she gazed upon these volumes, her eyes lit on her well-worn childhood copy of Susanna Rowson's novel *Charlotte Temple*, and she remembers vividly, as if it were now, her Sunday afternoon pilgrimage, at her persistent insistence, with her father, hand in hand, to Trinity churchyard to visit Charlotte's grave.

In her mind, she recalled the day chill with no rain but much moisture in the air. The sky dark, black, with low, ominous clouds, yet a large crowd, mostly stony-faced fathers and bemused mothers accompanying impassioned little girls, had assembled in front of Charlotte's grave. Much weeping, many flowers, a plethora of handwritten notes, each of endearing love, sympathy, and support, suffused the grave bed and stone.

"I am so sad," little Olga had uttered, looking up into the broad, dark face of her father, dark as the sky, dark as the clouds. His expression was set, and as she began to sob softly, he took her hand more firmly and led her off some distance.

"Young lady," he said sternly then (she must have been nearing nine, no more), "it is the duty of a good papa to tell the truth to the daughter he loves so much and treasures."

She waited, damp eyes wide and expectant.

"You know who Charlotte Temple is, Olga?" he said.

"Yes," she answered dutifully.

"And who, might I ask, is she?"

"She is a girl who was done wrong. She suffered and died for her sins, and she is buried here at Trinity Church."

"No," he said. "Charlotte did not live. She did not die. Charlotte is not real, Olga. She is a figure out of the imagination of Mrs. Rowson, the authoress."

"Charlotte *is* real," Olga had emphatically corrected him. "And she has been laid to rest here. It is a tale of truth," she insisted, evoking the novel's oft-repeated subtitle.

"No, no," her father said. "Not truth, dear, merely an apocryphal tale. It is made up, Olga. It is a story. Granted, a pointed story with strong moral, meant to instruct, nothing more."

"Then who is buried here in Trinity churchyard in Charlotte's grave?" asked Olga.

Her father shook his head. "No one is buried here," he said. "This grave is empty. It is but a mockery, a stone unveiled at the insistence of Mrs. Rowson's readers, those who adored her creation, your Charlotte Temple."

Back in her study, Olga cringes, almost felt embarrassment to have ever been so heartfelt and passionate, so naïve. She ran her hands through her hair, considering Edgar Poe, recent visitor to her home, his weakness for women, for love. She thought of the murdered segar girl, Mary Rogers, her first disappearance, her second, the circumstance of pregnancy, of virtue. She wondered of her father's motive in bringing Mr. Poe home. She knew her father. He wanted her to see something, be aware of something, judge something.

Here Olga pauses for a moment. Why did she pause? She was not sure.

Who had killed Mary Rogers? Under what circumstance?

Then, shaking herself free from this torrent of formless impressions cascading down upon her, she rises from her makeshift desk and enters the kitchen. From the counter she takes a full head of cabbage, places it on a planked board, and begins to chop with an unexplained vigor. Earlier that morning she had made egg dough. Finishing with the cabbage, she flattens the dough, dips her knife into water, and cuts long, half-inch-wide lengths for noodles. When finished, she dices an onion, freshly stokes the fire, and sets the onions in a pan to lightly brown. She then adds the green chopped cabbage leaves, a good deal of dark red paprika, damp gray salt, and coarse black pepper. She pours in a cup of Croton water and stirs a few times with a wooden spoon as the cabbage, water, and spice begin to cook down.

When the cabbage is evenly stained orange-red with the paprika, she returns to her mother's sewing room. Revisiting her thoughts, she asks herself again could this man she knows somewhat vaguely but admires, this most curious fellow, this brilliant gentleman some seem so ready to condemn (including her own father?), this Mr. Edgar Poe, truly have performed so heinous an act on such a girl as Mary Rogers?

And if not he, who?

❦ 63 ❦

Grip the Raven and
We'll All Have Tea

Meanwhile, sometime later that morning, he, the author and poet in question, and under suspicion, appears at the New York office of *Graham's Lady's and Gentleman's Magazine,* his former employer in the Quaker City, now resituated on Manhattan's lower Broadway, with the idea to sell, in his estimation, the only thing he has worth anything, his new poem of the black bird.

The present number of the magazine was in production and the noise of the handpresses was overwhelming. George Rex Graham was a native of Philadelphia. He had been publisher of that city's *Casket* when he bought out Billy Burton and changed the name of his periodical from *Burton's Gentleman's Magazine and American Monthly Review* to *Graham's Lady's and Gentleman's Magazine.*

The new owner had sought Poe out specifically and retained him in his capacity of editor. For his part, Edgar had eagerly gone to work for Graham at his newly located offices at Third and Chestnut, earning a satisfactory, renegotiated yearly salary of eight hundred dollars.

Up until then, Poe had been known more as a critic than a poet, but he had a newly burgeoning reputation as a fiction writer, approaching his notoriety as a critic. To his detriment, Poe began to moan in print that the effect of his personal analytic brilliance was illusory.

As a result, critics maligned him, charging he was on a mission to subject the whole of American letters to his own personal critical authority.

Bewildered Graham ordered his editor to soften his stance.

Trying to appease his boss, Poe argued his need to defend himself. "I would never allow my personal feelings in regard to literary personalities to cloud my critical judgment about their work," he protested to Graham's counsel.

Poe declared ruthlessly he could neither tolerate nor work under such subjugation. He said he had already been put in a place where he was forced to praise ninnies. He quit in a fit, although some observers, less generous, claimed he was fired over matters of drunkenness and ineffectuality. Making matters worse, hired in his place was his rival for arbiter of American poetic taste, the pinch-faced Reverend Rufus Wilmot Griswold (sometimes called "Rufe," sometimes called "Griz," sometimes called "Animal"), at a salary of one thousand dollars per annum, two hundred dollars more than Poe had been getting paid.

No matter. On this day, as he received entry into the inner sanctum of Graham's newly located magazine publishing facility, head bowed for fullest dramatic effect, all would be forgiven and forgotten in Poe's mind.

After being warmly greeted by his ex-employer, Poe took Graham aside and whispered he had something most pressing to reveal. He admitted tearfully that he was destitute of funds, his wife ailing, both she and his aunt home, starving. Brightening somewhat, he announced he had a copy of a new poem he would like Mr. Graham to see and consider for publication in his magazine. From his breast pocket he pulled the same script from which he had read the previous afternoon at the Brennan farm. The scroll, carefully copied out in his own neat hand, was passed between Graham and his fellow publisher, Louis Godey of the *Godey's Lady's Book*, who happened to be present in the office at the time. Thankfully, Griswold was not.

After reading, one over the other, neither man was much

impressed, both saying the poem was evocative of Dickens' work in *Barnaby Rudge*, where like *avis*, the raven named Grip, is mentioned.

Godey nimbly quoted from that popular work, his face lit with boyish glee: "'Grip, Grip, Grip!'" he cried. "'Grip the clever, Grip the wicked, Grip the knowing—Grip, Grip, Grip!'"

Graham laughed with his fellow publisher's cleverness. "'I'm a devil,'" he yelped in his own feat of memory, exercising what Poe considered a rather pathetic imitation of a raven's caw. "'I'm a devil I'm a devil. Never say die. Hurrah! Bow wow wow! Polly put the kettle on and we'll all have tea.'"

Godey then guffawed heartily with this rather spirited spectacle, to be joined by Graham, although Poe failed to see the humor in it, he, too, being perfectly capable of reciting the bird's nonsense lines verbatim.

Seeing Poe's pained and confused reaction, Graham shrank back and tried to right himself. He pronounced Poe's poem "eerie," but if he meant this as a compliment remained unclear to Poe. He who considered himself word master felt in the unenviable position of having to defend himself.

He rose up, insistent on the verse's merits. Again he mentioned (he said, reluctantly) his financial difficulties. "It would not do to let us poor devil authors absolutely starve," he bitterly argued, "while you publishers grow fat on our backs."

"Poe—" Graham protested.

Spiritually wounded, Poe waved him off to continue. "That a man has any right and title either to his own brains or the flimsy masterly firmament that he chooses to spin out of them, I ask you," he begged. "How can I endure?"

In recognition of the poet's state and in deference to his stature, the rest of the magazine's staff was called in and Poe, seizing the manuscript out of Godey's hands, angrily read the verse to Graham's gathered ink-fingered imps, printer's devils, and abused office clerks after having agreed to abide by their decision.

Poe was shocked and outraged when Graham's staff concurred with the opinion of their boss and his visiting associate, Mr. Godey.

Poe's entire countenance darkened. "A young author," he spoke morosely, "struggling with despair itself in the shape of ghastly poverty which has no alleviation—no sympathy from an everyday world, or from the likes of you that cannot understand his necessities—this young author is politely requested to compose and read in hopes that he will be handsomely paid. But with no result. Is that it? I ask you: Is that how you want it, sirs? Is this the sum of a literary life?"

Never might he have imagined that those gathered would not give him their full attention. He tried to have them listen again, this time more carefully, but Graham said they had all heard quite enough for one afternoon, they were on deadline, and it was time to get back to work.

With some embarrassment a newsboy's hat was passed among those still present, and although the black bird poem was not accepted for publication, Poe was awarded a sum of fifteen dollars for the benefit, he was told, of his wife and his saintly auntie, Mrs. Clemm.

🌸 64 🌸

The Black Bird

New York Mirror:

PUBLISHED EVERY SATURDAY MORNING.

THREE DOLLARS A YEAR}   {PAYABLE IN ADVANCE

OFFICE OF PUBLICATION, CORNER OF NASSAU AND ANN STREETS.

VOLUME 1. NEW-YORK, SATURDAY, FEBRUARY 8, 1845. NUMBER XVIII

We are permitted to copy (in advance of publication) from the 2d No. of the American Review, the following remarkable poem by EDGAR POE. In our opinion, it is the most effective single example of "fugitive poetry" ever published in this country; and unsurpassed in English poetry for subtle conception, masterly ingenuity of versification, and consistent sustaining of imaginative lift and "pokerishness." It is one of these "dainties bred in a book" which we *feed* on. It will stick to the memory of everybody who reads it.

THE RAVEN.

Once upon a midnight dreary, while I pondered, weak and weary,
Over many a quaint and curious volume of forgotten lore—
While I nodded, nearly napping, suddenly there came a tapping,
As of some one gently rapping, rapping at my chamber door—
"'Tis some visitor," I muttered, "tapping at my chamber door—
            Only this and nothing more."

Ah, distinctly I remember it was in the bleak December;
And each separate dying ember wrought its ghost upon the floor.
Eagerly I wished the morrow;—vainly I had tried to borrow
From my books surcease of sorrow—sorrow for the lost Lenore—
For the rare and radiant maiden whom the angels name Lenore—
            Nameless here for evermore.

And the silken sad uncertain rustling of each purple curtain
Thrilled me—filled me with fantastic terrors never felt before;
So that now, to still the beating of my heart, I stood repeating
"'Tis some visitor entreating entrance at my chamber door—
Some late visitor entreating entrance at my chamber door;—
            This it is and nothing more."

Presently my soul grew stronger; hesitating then no longer,
"Sir," said I, "or Madam, truly your forgiveness I implore;
But the fact is I was napping, and so gently you came rapping,
And so faintly you came tapping, tapping at my chamber door,
That I scarce was sure I heard you,"—here I opened wide the door;—
            Darkness there, and nothing more.

Deep into that darkness peering, long I stood there wondering, fearing,
Doubting, dreaming dreams no mortal ever dared to dream before;

But the silence was unbroken, and the darkness gave no token,
And the only word there spoken was the whispered word, "Lenore!"
This I whispered, and an echo murmured back the word, "Lenore!"
      Merely this, and nothing more.

Back into the chamber turning, all my soul within me burning,
Soon again I heard a tapping, somewhat louder than before.
"Surely," said I, "surely that is something at my window lattice;
Let me see, then, what thereat is, and this mystery explore—
Let my heart be still a moment and this mystery explore;—
      'Tis the wind, and nothing more!"

Open here I flung the shutter, when, with many a flirt and flutter,
In there stepped a stately Raven of the saintly days of yore;
Not the least obeisance made he; not a minute stopped or stayed he;
But with mien of lord or lady, perched above my chamber door—
Perched upon a bust of Pallas just above my chamber door—
      Perched, and sat, and nothing more.

Then this ebony bird beguiling my sad fancy into smiling,
By the grave and stern decorum of the countenance it wore,
"Though thy crest be shorn and shaven, thou," I said, "art sure no craven,
Ghastly grim and ancient Raven wandering from the Nightly shore—
Tell me what thy lordly name is on the Night's Plutonian shore!"
      Quoth the Raven, "Nevermore."

Much I marvelled this ungainly fowl to hear discourse so plainly,
Though its answer little meaning—little relevancy bore;
For we cannot help agreeing that no living human being
Ever yet was blessed with seeing bird above his chamber door—
Bird or beast upon the sculptured bust above his chamber door,
      With such name as "Nevermore."

But the Raven, sitting lonely on the placid bust, spoke only
That one word, as if his soul in that one word he did outpour.
Nothing farther then he uttered; not a feather then he fluttered—
Till I scarcely more than muttered: "Other friends have flown before—
On the morrow he will leave me, as my Hopes have flown before."
        Then the bird said, "Nevermore."

Startled at the stillness broken by reply so aptly spoken,
"Doubtless," said I, "what it utters is its only stock and store
Caught from some unhappy master whom unmerciful Disaster
Followed fast and followed faster till his songs one burden bore—
Till the dirges of his Hope that melancholy burden bore
        That sad answer, "Nevermore."

But the Raven still beguiling all my sad soul into smiling,
Straight I wheeled a cushioned seat in front of bird, and bust, and door;
Then, upon the velvet sinking, I betook myself to linking
Fancy unto fancy, thinking what this ominous bird of yore—
What this grim, ungainly, ghastly, gaunt, and ominous bird of yore
        Meant in croaking "Nevermore!"

This I sat engaged in guessing, but no syllable expressing
To the fowl whose fiery eyes now burned into my bosom's core;
This and more I sat divining, with my head at ease reclining
On the cushion's velvet lining that the lamp-light gloated o'er,
But whose velvet-violet lining with the lamp-light gloating o'er,
        She shall press, ah, nevermore!

Then, methought, the air grew denser, perfumed from an unseen censer
Swung by Seraphim whose foot-falls tinkled on the tufted floor.
"Wretch," I cried, "thy God hath lent thee—by these angels he hath sent thee

Respite—respite and nepenthe from thy memories of Lenore!
Quaff, oh quaff this kind nepenthe and forget this lost Lenore!"
            Quoth the Raven, "Nevermore."

"Prophet!" said I, "thing of evil!—prophet still, if bird or devil!—
Whether Tempter sent, or whether tempest tossed thee here ashore,
Desolate, yet all undaunted, on this desert land enchanted—
On this home by Horror haunted,—tell me truly, I implore—
Is there—is there balm in Gilead?—tell me—tell me, I implore!"
            Quoth the Raven, "Nevermore."

"Prophet!" said I, "thing of evil!—prophet still, if bird or devil!
By that heaven that bends above us—by that God we both adore—
Tell this soul with sorrow laden if, with the distant Aidenn,
It shall clasp a sainted maiden whom the angels name Lenore—
Clasp a rare and radiant maiden whom the angels name Lenore."
            Quoth the Raven, "Nevermore."

"Be that word our sign of parting, bird or fiend!" I shrieked, upstarting—
"Get thee back into the tempest and the Night's Plutonian shore!"
Leave no black plume as a token of that lie thy soul hath spoken!
Leave my loneliness unbroken!—quit the bust above my door!
Take thy beak from out my heart, and take thy form from off my door!"
            Quoth the Raven, "Nevermore."

And the Raven, never flitting, still is sitting, still is sitting
On the pallid bust of Pallas just above my chamber door;
And his eyes have all the seeming of a demon's that is dreaming,
And the lamp-light o'er him streaming throws his shadow on the floor;
And my soul from out that shadow that lies floating on the floor
            Shall be lifted—nevermore!

❦ 65 ❦

Miss Lynch's Conversaziones

Minutes after seven, a brown hansom cab left the soft gaslight glow of Lispenard Street with High Constable Jacob Hays and his daughter Olga aboard.

"It will change everything for him," Olga was saying to her father. "He has outdone himself. Believe me when I tell you, Papa, in one stroke Edgar Poe has transformed American letters. You will hear for yourself. It is quite chilling. His voice takes on such omnificence. The women are all taken by the performance, and if I am any judge," she added excitedly, "this pleases him greatly."

"And the men? How does Mr. Poe's performance strike the men?"

She sighed as if her father truly was without hope. "He does not really pursue the society of men, Papa," she answered. "Rather that of highly intellectual women with whom he likes to fall into peculiar, eloquent monologue, half dream, half poetry. Men, Mr. Hays, like you, are intolerant of such performance, but women are transfixed. To this starry sisterhood, reports of his domestic tragedy are all too consuming. His beautiful but doomed young wife, his poverty, his until-now-unrecognized genius, these are the themes of much fascination and relished gossip among those of the female gender."

"You included, Olga?"

She smiled. "Me included, Papa."

"So heed me, O my daughter," Hays turned to her, his face a tight mask, "quoth the ancient papa: Just beware."

"Stop, Papa," she laughed in spite of herself, half amused, half annoyed.

"Need I remind you, dear, I have had the pleasure of hearing Mr. Poe's iteration and have witnessed his poem's effect firsthand. I remain under the impression the verse has taken the nation by storm."

"Papa, you must keep in mind he is loathed. His raven has brought out his enemies, and they are multiple."

At that moment the hack veered off Sixth Avenue and came to rest in front of number 116 Waverly Place. Old Hays pulled from his overcoat his pocket purse in order to pay the driver the fifty-cent fare, and, upon completion of this transaction, followed after his daughter.

She and the high constable arrived this Saturday evening in early April, of the year 1845, at the home of Olga's friend and colleague from the Brooklyn Female Academy, Miss Anne Lynch, Hays sharing Olga's invitation to Miss Lynch's renowned weekly salon, the most sought-after of all sophisticated Gotham's glittering conversaziones, regularly well-attended by gents and ladies from the highest stratum of social and cultural life.

Three handsome young gentlemen of this elite echelon, in silk stovepipe hats, two in black cloaks, one wrapped in a dark gray shoulder shawl, sat smoking on the interior stairs. The man in the shawl recognized Old Hays, alerting his mates, and the three immediately rose as one to make way. With his daughter on his arm, his constabulary staff held in hand stoutly, with a nod of the head for their consideration, the high constable maneuvered past them to Miss Lynch's rooms on the second floor.

The three-story pitch-roofed red brick building, only a few doors off Sixth Avenue, occupied a lot, twenty-five feet by one hundred, one block west of the northern boundary of Washington Square. At the top of the landing a varnished yellow oak door stood open leading into the apartment of Miss Lynch.

As Hays entered the lively room, he immediately heard himself called out. "High Constable!"

He turned.

Samuel Colt stood in front of him, his face bright. "Good to see you again, sir!" Colt exuded.

The Colonel had taken a post just inside the door. A suppressed smile strained his wind-roughened face under his whiskers. He did not seek to disguise his avid surveillance of the womanhood in abundant attendance.

The men shook hands. "I understand you are coming out of your financial difficulties. Good for you," congratulated the high constable.

After Colonel Colt had gone bankrupt with his Paterson repeater, he had cast about for some months, eventually embarking on an enterprise to manufacture marine explosives, a type of water mine he liked to call "torpedo."

In one apparent exuberant and effective public display (to which Hays and his new municipal force had received more than one frantic call), the Colonel had succeeded in blowing up a ship in the lower harbor from five miles away using an electric submarine cable to set off the blast.

When commented on by Hays, Colt granted he was gratified by his success, but not completely satisfied. "As result, I did manage to procure a fifteen-thousand-dollar government grant. No small potatoes. But I admit my first love remains the revolver business." He moved closer, speaking directly, in subdued voice, in Hays' ear. "Recently I have been approached by a young Texas Ranger by the name of Samuel Walker, a veteran of the Seminole Indian War in Florida, now fighting in Texas against the Mexicans under Zachary Taylor. In both Florida and Texas, this young man has made good use of my Paterson repeating firearm on the battlefield. He told me riding with fourteen fellow combatants, all equipped with Colt five-shooters, they went up against eighty Comanche warriors, leaving thirty-three dead Indians on the battlefield. Ranger Walker has come to me as a representative of the United States Army, and in this role has contracted for one thousand new weapons to be manufactured and delivered."

Colt told Old Hays each weapon was to be priced at twenty-five dollars. A nice windfall, but at present, he confessed, he had no factory at his disposal. So in turn he had been forced to approach Eli Whitney Jr., son of the famed inventor of the cotton gin, and in his own right a successful armaments maker, boasting a government contract for the manufacture of military muskets.

"We're in it together now," Colt said. "We've a factory in Whitney-ville, in Connecticut, and, God bless us, on the verge of signing up a thousand more weapons for the army."

"So all sounds well. I am sure you must feel relief to be back on your feet again," Hays said. "In my estimation, Colonel, your invention of the repeating revolver has only been outstripped this century by Howe's invention of the sewing machine."

"Thank you, sir," Colt said slowly, not sure how to take this commentary. "I am indeed back on my feet."

"And have you received word from your brother?"

Colonel Colt blinked, then grinned.

"You make this same inquiry each time we have the pleasurable fortune to see one another. You know he is dead, High Constable."

"Yes, yes, so he is. It totally slipped my mind." Hays grinned back at him. "Still I have had several cards with word that he is reincarnated in Texas. It wouldn't have been his apparition who has put Ranger Walker onto you and your munitions enterprise, would it, sir?" Hays shook his head as if only now catching on to himself. "No, no, no, impossible," he admitted. "I forget myself yet again. A mere phantasm, wouldn't you say, Colonel?"

"Speaking of phantasms," Sam Colt responded, taking opportunity to change subject and drift, "Mr. Poe has certainly garnered some renown of late."

"Indeed. He is our man of the hour."

"Notwithstanding, poor fellow seems to be suffering somewhat mightily for the sins of a lifetime, wouldn't you say?"

"Indeed."

"I tried to help him when last we encountered each other. I suggested he keep his bowels open, pay his bills, and trust in God," Samuel Colt spoke, his voice tinged with dire. "I told him these were my three rules for living, and he might find success employing them as well."

"And how did Mr. Poe respond to such consideration?" asked Hays.

"He said he might very well do."

Each man forced his false smile upon the other. Meanwhile, next to Hays, having approached from his rear, Olga cleared her throat. Her radiant russet hair had been arranged for the evening in a Greek style with a band of exquisite cameos representing Roman emperors encircling her crown. Her gown, with waist seven inches across, had been made of palest pink tulle, embroidered with cut-steel beads. Both gentlemen turned toward her with pleasure. Hays took his daughter's hand and made the introductions. "Colonel Colt, my daughter, Miss Hays."

Sam Colt gazed upon her with obvious appreciation. "Fortunately for you, Miss Hays, our most merciful Protector has looked down upon you with utmost benevolence, given the most evident fact that you do not in any way take after or resemble your father, most specifically in the realm of beauty. I daresay you are a striking presence, Miss Hays." He bowed. "Miss Hays, my distinct pleasure."

She smiled demurely and thanked Colonel Colt, who, for his part, continued to study her with the eye of a shrewd appraiser. "Papa, you must say your hello to Annie. She is beside herself awaiting your approach." She took her father's hand, made rudimentary excuse to Colonel Colt, and led her father away.

Hays saw the mistress of the house, his daughter's friend, as slender and dark as ever, dramatically framed, dressed to her advantage in indigo taffeta, at the far end of the dark brown room, standing in front of the black-manteled fireplace. Two women, who proved to be Miss Lynch's mother and younger sister, were positioned at her side.

"High Constable Hays, my mother has been looking forward to this honor," Annie Lynch gushed. "Welcome, sir, welcome to our home."

A second fireplace occupied the wall at the opposite end of the room. There, a slightly smaller parlor adjoined the first. Over Mrs. Lynch's shoulder, Hays noted on a couch nearby the open coal fire in the outer parlor sat Mayor Harper and G. P. Putnam, heads together, engaged in what appeared private talk.

The drawing rooms fairly glowed with an abundance of satin-upholstered furniture. Marble-topped side tables with copper and zinc fittings, reproduced to replicate gold, or inlaid with glass and ceramic tile, were appointed and strewn with various silk-bound volumes of the latest poetry. Several embossed, leather-covered editions of the Reverend Rufus Griswold's lately published *The Poets and Poetry of America* had been made prominently visible to Miss Lynch's guests.

Anne Charlotte Lynch kissed her friend Olga on both cheeks in the French style and took Hays' hand up in both of hers.

"How delightful, High Constable Hays," she insisted. "When Olga sent her most elegant note to say that she would like to bring you, I could only think what have I done to have Old Hays after me. But seriously, what a terrible failing on my part. My dear sir, you must think how remiss of me not to have extended invitation to you on my own."

"Not at all, not at all." Hays returned her charming smile. "It is only for pure pleasure, and my own edification, that I asked Olga to inquire if there might not be a place for me at your function. I am very glad to be here, young lady. Thank you for having me."

"Friendship is my mental sustenance," she explained, holding his hand tightly in her own and smiling into his eyes. "If you could only know how happy and fortunate I am made by personal relationships such as these, Mr. Hays. I thank the good Lord every day for your daughter. I find the act of friendship as absolutely necessary as the material, yet infinitely higher. But I must confess, sir, I give no entertainment except what my guests find in each other."

By this time there were about thirty-five people in attendance in Miss Lynch's parlors, not including those smoking on the stairs and those standing in the hall, accounting perhaps for an additional ten. Olga had mentioned that on a good night, sometimes as many as eighty might attend Miss Lynch's function. With Poe invited to again repeat his "Raven," Olga estimated at least that many were conservatively expected.

And indeed, still more guests, in a steady stream, found their way into the warmly lit living room through the course of the early evening. Lynchie's mother had abandoned her daughter's side to serve tea and cookies with the assistance of the younger Miss Lynch.

Some of the new attendees Old Hays knew to be quite illustrious. All, illustrious or not, were filled with visible expectation. Olga pointed out the New England transcendentalist Ralph Waldo Emerson, in the city, she said, to visit with his dear friend and like-minded thinker Miss Margaret Fuller, also in attendance, a mechanical paragraphist for Greeley's *Tribune* as well as author of a newly favorite tome of Olga's, the feminist study *Woman in the Nineteenth Century*.

Young and bold author Herman Melville, sporting big boots, strode in with the daguerreotypist Mathew Brady, eager, he informed everyone and anyone who would listen, to talk to Mr. Poe about a proposed sitting at his studio at 205 Broadway.

The great Norwegian virtuoso violinist Ole Bull arrived with his instrument, quickly unsheathed it, and began to saw away.

During Bull's recital, Horace Greeley himself, not dressed like the other men, he an iconoclast, trudged up the stairs alone, in a grimy white coat, his canvas pants tucked into his boot tops. He arrived at the entrance, wheezing loudly, trying to catch his breath, surveying the crowd before he caught Hays' eye. At once he inserted himself past several people to shake the policeman's hand.

"I am surprised to see you here, High Constable," he said in a hushed voice underneath Bull's mad fiddling.

Still huffing for breath, Greeley turned to Olga, confessing to her, "I used to be a vegetarian, but of late I find I need meat more and more to keep up my energy." He mumbled something additional, unfortunately (or fortunately) lost to both her and her father. "Although this might sound unduly cynical," Greeley freely continued, "in my view, the purpose of a gathering such as this can only be singlefold: to bring together the two aristocracies of 'brain' and 'pocket.' What in your erudition say you to that, Miss Hays?"

Without waiting for an answer, but with a comforting departing pat to Olga's forearm, the former vegetarian wandered away in search of what he loudly announced as a link of blood sausage or a satisfying Cabernet.

All about Annie Lynch's rooms were adorned with the strong and perfumed personae of those women of the literati, those whom Olga had referred to as the "starry sisterhood."

For the most part, these eager young women wore elaborate evening ball dresses, each skirt bordered with triple embroidery of gauze and colored silk, gold upon a white background; the professional gossip Mrs. Ellet, her hair parted in the middle with cascading thick water curls, was dressed expensively in bird-of-paradise yellow satin upon which were mounted embroidered flowers of lace, encircled with light silver thread, producing an effect calculated and very beautiful when worn over a skirt of shimmering silver, as it now was. Whereas Mrs. Oakes Smith, a would-be poetess whose husband had paid Poe one hundred dollars to instruct his wife, favored a light blue hoopskirt with ostrich-plume headdress, her hair immaculately arranged beneath in heavy, taffy-like loops.

"So what do you think of all this, High Constable?" The mayor had come up unnoticed upon Hays. He waved his hand to take in the general direction of the ever-growing crush of visitors, crammed now into Miss Lynch's parlor. "It all seems perfectly glorious, wouldn't you say, Mr. Hays, if you are a poet, of some compromised character, and all these proper gents and ladies have come to hear you recite your latest effort. It warms my heart to see so much attention foisted on one so deserving."

"Mr. Harper, your sarcasm aside, with all due respect, I was telling my father how two weeks ago, in these very rooms, we sat as a group, you included, and listened to Mr. Poe recite as if transfixed, did we not?"

Harper cleared his throat. "We did, Miss Hays."

"And tonight finds you back! You must have found the evening enjoyable despite your snide cynicism toward Mr. Poe. As I recall, that evening the good poet's voice took on a charm, an absolute and remarkable resonance that bespoke the intervention of something more than mere man."

"I'm afraid, young lady, you will soon find it requires more power to raise a demon to heaven than to drag an angel down to hell. I have it on good authority Poe's poem is written for people who don't like poetry. It is a poem calculated and insincere."

Although the author under discussion still had not made his appearance, by this time many of the city's most illustrious publishing concerns were well represented. Not only the mayor, with his three brothers in tow, and the estimable Mr. Putnam, and his chief editor, Mr. Duyckinck, but also the accomplished Messrs. Scribner, Wiley, Van Nostrand, Dodd, and Mead were present, among still others, including James Gordon Bennett of the *Herald* and Moses Beach of the *Sun*, Ned Buntline of *Buntline's Own*, Mr. Graham from *Graham's Magazine*, Clark from the posh *Knickerbocker*, and Mr. Park Willis and Mr. George Pope Morris of the *Mirror*.

"Poe is a pathetic critic mad with love and hate," enjoined Joseph Harper as he stood not far off at the end table pouring for himself a fresh glass of port. "His jealousy of other writers has grown to a mania."

"I shall not say no to that," agreed the unctuous Bennett.

"You only agree, sir," Olga glared at the cross-eyed editor, "because Mr. Poe has taken his occasion to attack you personally, Mr. Bennett. What is it that Mr. Poe said? Dear me, allow me to recall. Oh yes!

That you, Mr. Bennett, are noticeable in the world except for the markedness by which you are known for nothing?"

Old Hays took surprise at the blunt vehemence of his daughter's retort, yet knowing her well enough to fully understand she felt compelled to defend Poe, who was not present to defend himself.

There was more than one nod and laugh from the gathered at Olga's cleverness, and by the time of this progression still many others seemed all too eager to join the discussion, including the Reverend Griswold, compiler of the much-in-evidence *Poets and Poetry of America* anthology, who had not so nimbly inserted himself close enough to the center of the oral fray to have trod painfully on the bunions of the feet of Old Hays.

"Not a whit of the author's true emotion is involved in his raven poem," Griswold commented through his rather long nose.

The culprit was a thin, lanky man with a scruffy beard and an unbecoming stoop to his shoulders, giving off an unpleasant (repellent to Hays) soured-milk odor. "The repetition in the verse forms nothing more than a singsong," he continued. "True, it enforces the words to stick in one's mind, but it is merely a bit of trickery, chicanery really, on the minds of all who read it."

"Ah, pish on you!" Olga's anger at the lot of them was rising by the second. She stood face to face with the reverend. "Give Mr. Poe his due, Mr. Griswold. In the realm of the imagination he has been able to create something new and unique."

"You can't be serious, Miss Hays?"

"But I am, Mr. Griswold."

Griswold glared at Olga, ostensibly for her sheer audacity at having disagreed with him. "Dear girl," he said haughtily, "there is no realism in his work, no resemblance to anything in the real world. An ogre lives in his pages with a trough of dead ladies."

At this comment, some of those very ladies, standing nearby, presumably neither quite stone-cold yet nor at trough, blushed and tittered.

T. D. English, a lawyer Hays knew from the police court, and counted by Poe as a friend, rose from their midst. "Miss Hays is right," he declared. "Edgar Poe has created nothing less than a new Nowhere in the empire of literature. Like it or not, my dear Griz, the man is the Shakespeare of America."

"As a poem his damnable crow will not bear scrutiny," the Reverend Griswold whined back. "It might do well as a song, a unique musical piece, but as poetry it will not stand."

The assembled were growing impatient for Poe (or "the Raven," as more than some of their number were pleased to call him) to arrive.

At the hour of nearly nine-thirty, the lithe and childlike poetess Mrs. Fanny Osgood arrived alone, somewhat flushed from either the weather or exertion. Seeing her as she entered, Olga nudged her father. They watched as the overstuffed Bennett jumped up, abruptly abandoning a much-animated conversation with the equally over-stuffed Buntline in mid-sentence to run to greet her, bending to whisper conspiratorially in the lissome little woman's ear, the gesture striking Hays as overly familiar.

For her part, Mrs. Osgood laughed, looked up into the unpleasant editor's broad and harried face with seeming adoration, and took his arm, whereupon he led her into the excitement and confusion of the room. They crossed to where Mr. Bennett settled himself dramatically back down on the silk divan he had only moments before abandoned. Mrs. Osgood fell on an ottoman at his feet in front of the coal fire, laughing gaily, but almost too loudly.

She was a striking, delicate creature. Her gown, tight-laced at the waist, was colored an attractive ethereal blue. Her hair had been so arranged with flowers and loops of ribbon worn over the left side of the coiffure and face, so placed as to almost conceal her left eye. A gold heart-shaped locket glistened in the hollow of her neck. If Hays were pressed, he would have to say her appearance, not to mention her laughter, designed singly to attract male attention unto herself. She appeared slender, almost fragile because of her small height, graceful, with pale black glossy tresses and clear, large, luminous gray eyes, showing a wide capacity for expression.

"Papa, if you have not already surmised, Mrs. Osgood prides herself a worshipper of the *beautiful*," Olga confided in her father's ear, observing him closely studying Mrs. Osgood. "By her own estimation, dear girl, so ardent! So sensitive! So impulsive!"

"You sound very nearly bitter, Olga," he remarked. "If I didn't know better, I would say you jealous."

She met her father's gaze of inquiry, retorting acidly "No, Papa. Not bitter. Not jealous. I acknowledge the woman, the very soul of truth and honor, present recipient of everything Poe, arbiter of all—"

He nudged her. "Hush, Olga, she comes."

And indeed Mrs. Osgood approached, on the heavy arm of the newspaper maven Bennett.

"High Constable Hays, my dear friend Mr. Bennett has only just pointed you out to me, and I insisted he introduce me at once to a man of such renown and courage. So here I am, monsieur. *Enchantée*."

Following these icebreaking cordialities, Mrs. Osgood soon began to speak in a veritable gush of the guest of honor. "Edgar Poe is the most gentle, sweetest, most poetic of men," she proclaimed.

Hays inquired how she had come to know him, she spoke so familiarly, and she said it was through the kind auspice of the very generous Mr. Willis, Mr. Poe's onetime boss and patron at the *Evening Mirror*. She said that shortly after the publication of "The Raven," she had been told (by Willis) that Poe had spoken of her favorably at a public gathering at the New York University. She had promptly sent a thank-you note to him, and he in response had written back, including a copy of his poem and requesting her personal views of its merit. She beamed with the acknowledgment.

"I shall never forget the morning when I was summoned to the Astor House by Mr. Willis, to the hotel's drawing room to meet him," she said. She spoke, gazing directly into Hays' eyes as if into a crystal ball, her hand gripping his forearm, not unpleasantly.

She had by now sent Bennett off, shooing him in search of wine. "You can only imagine his magnificence, sir," she continued after her devotee's departure. "With his proud beautiful head erect, his dark eyes flashing with the electric light of feeling and thought, an inimitable blending of sweetness and hauteur in his expression and manner, he greeted me that memorable afternoon calmly, gravely, almost coldly, sir. Yet with so marked an earnestness that I could not help being deeply impressed by it."

Falling back, she smiled, first at Hays, then made a peculiar face, so childish, at Olga, as if to swoon.

Frances Sargent Osgood, known to her intimates as Fanny, Hays knew, was wife of Samuel Osgood, the portrait painter. A number of people in the know had remarked right now her husband, on commission, was painting a likeness of Poe for the New-York Historical Society.

Olga had informed him Mrs. Osgood's poetry had often been maligned—labeled bombastic, rhetorical, sentimental by her more strident critics, and even her peers—but Olga did admit there was a certain grace, and it was with that grace which Poe evidently seemed to have been taken.

She was author not only of *The Poetry of Flowers and Flowers of Poetry,* but also of a reworking from the French of Perrault's classic *Puss in Boots,* as well as what she admitted to be a slightly sentimental collection entitled *The Casket of Fate.*

"At the very least," Olga explained to her father as Mrs. Osgood abruptly showed them her back, "deservedly or not, he has taken up her defense and praised her." Because now, finally, Poe had made his entrance into the apartment. He was in the company of a tall gentleman outfitted in a long black swallow-tailed coat. Hays recognized him at once from the stage, the dramatic figure Mr. Edwin Booth, the actor.

Poe's eager admirers gathered around him quickly, but not Mrs. Osgood, who started to approach but, seeing the crowd, seemed now to make a point of remaining off to one side and aloof, before ultimately returning to hold her ground with Hays, taking up his hand.

Both stood silently, watching Poe pass pleasantries among those who pressed so eagerly to be near him. His slender form, intellectual face, and uncommon expression of eye never failed to arrest the attention of even the least observant. His storied associations with various women appeared tantalizing to some, and now many, a veritable bevy—Mrs. Ellet, Mrs. Oakes Smith, even the transcendentalist feminist Miss Fuller—gathered around him and vied for his attention.

He made the round of the room, offering his greetings and obvious good feelings. When he reached Hays, his eyes may have widened slightly in surprise, seeing him, the high constable, unexpectedly present at this venue.

After a moment's hesitation, however, he nodded before greeting Mrs. Osgood, who had remained with Hays, hand in hand.

"Hello, so nice to see you again so soon, Mrs. Osgood," he said to her.

"Hello, Mr. Poe. So very nice to see you."

Why did this seemingly innocent exchange strike Hays as so disingenuous? He noticed at once there was something more than familiar transmitted between them, something complicit, even conspiratorial.

Mr. Bennett sauntered back, two brimming goblets in hand, excused himself for the delay, said something innocuous to Poe, nodded to Hays, and pressed Mrs. Osgood away.

Upon her departure, Hays had the opportunity to take Poe aside. He shook hands and asked how was his health and state of mind, and how was his wife?

"Frankly, for all my popular success, the devil himself was never so poor," Poe confided bitterly. "I have made nothing but twenty dollars from this infernal black bird, and for the first time in my life I am having trouble writing. As for my wife," he paused in his proclamation, "she remains sick, and surely shall die."

Hays was somewhat taken aback by such ardor engendered by such response, straightforward as it was, but before he could react, Annie Lynch stepped forward, come to ask the poet if he was ready to begin his recitation, but having overheard Poe's torment, and most eager to express her own sympathy and concern in regard to his despondency, she told him certainly whatever demons he saw, they were probably only a chimera of his imagination. "All success and adulation due you," she assured, "will surely come your way in time."

Kindly, by Hays' estimate, she offered her services to come to his apartment to sit and talk with the ailing Sissy, keep her company. "If you think it will help, I shall be glad to," she said.

Surprising Hays, his own daughter offered likewise.

After thanking these ladies for their consideration, Poe took a place in front of the fireplace. From his inside breast pocket he withdrew the familiar, although decidedly more battered than Old Hays remembered, scrolled manuscript on which was written his raven poem. But instead of taking the scroll up himself, he handed it to his companion, the actor Booth.

"I'll have it read," he announced, "by one whose voice is like the chime of silver bells."

But the starry sisterhood, and some of the more drunken male revelers, would not have it. They wanted Poe, and by shouts, hisses, and huzzahs, expressed their want for only him. Hays could see he was pleased, although he made a play to relent reluctantly. The room immediately became quiet. Those who had been standing on the landing or sitting on the stair came to the door and tried to push through. The parlor could only hold so many. Those who could not gain admittance remained at the threshold, straining to see but content to listen.

Hays was taken how Poe's style of public expression had changed from that Sunday afternoon at the Brennan farm. Olga had commented after hearing him recite at the New York University, "His voice has become quiet," she had said, "almost like a knife falling through water."

Indeed, in its quietude his instrument had taken on an ominous, stirring quality.

Afterwards, as Hays watched, the poet accepted congratulations from the men, and adoration from the women.

Some called to him for comment, and he accommodated, addressing the crowd *tout ensemble*. "The day I published 'The Raven' and sold away the rights was the blackest day, blacker than the bird," he declared. "As we all know too well, New York is the most overstocked market for writers. Only yesterday, Mr. Greeley, of whose company I see we have the pleasure tonight, said to me, and I quote this gentleman, 'You write fair verse, my friend Poe, but not such as the public will buy with any regularity!'"

The crowd laughed.

Poe waved them off. "Dear friends," he said, "we live emphatically in a thinking age. Indeed, it may very well be questioned whether mankind ever substantially thought before. How many times have I been admonished: An American author should confine himself to American themes, or even prefer them. I return to Mr. Greeley, and our conversation of last night. 'Do you not realize, Poe,' he said to me, 'how little the mere talent of writing well has to do with success or usefulness? There are a thousand at least in this city who can write very good prose or verse, while there are not fifty who can earn their daily bread by it. Haven't you realized, my dear Poe, what it is that is wanted of men who live by literary labor here, at what dreadful cost any distinction must be purchased!'

"Unfortunately for all of us, my friends, I do realize, and it is to the magazines we must go. And although a magnet, I am sorry to say, this institution can only represent a degeneration of taste. Yet we are all forced there to make a living because of one thing, and one thing only—the lack of an international copyright law. We who are writers have all been forced to embrace this true magazine spirit at the expense of the more expansive novel. The fact cannot be argued that the work of American authors can be copyrighted, but not the work of our counterpart Europeans. This reality is what drives we native scribblers to the short form of the magazines. But here in this quaint realm we find it even worse, because publishers, some of them, right here in this room—Mr. Harper, I address you, sir—pirate not only English writers but we American writers as well."

The cited James Harper rose rapidly to answer back. "Mr. Poe, publishers oppose copyright laws for good reason. Cheap literature is an essential to our nation, sir. The absence of copyright law makes it possible to provide literature affordable to your average countryman."

"I remind you, Mr. Harper, young America is a young nation," shouted back Poe. "And we young Americans continue within aim to free American literature from English influence. That an American writer should confine himself to American themes, or even prefer them, is a political rather than a literary idea—and at best, sir, a questionable point."

"Then why do you malign Henry Longfellow so?" a woman's voice rang out. "Who is more American than he?"

Before answering, Poe drained his third glass of port. "If you truly want to know, Miss Fuller," he addressed the voice, "your good friend Mr. Longfellow's poetry is exceedingly feeble. I find it singularly silly, utterly worthless, scarcely worth the page it occupies. I myself have never seen a more sickening thing in a book!"

"Yet you opine yourself beyond brilliant?" Margaret Fuller had heard enough. She shook her head. "Perhaps to your own thinking, sir, but, I assure you, to few if anyone else's."

"As I have said before, madam, the effect of analytic brilliance is illusory. I bow to you and all those like you."

Meanwhile, as the mood in the room degenerated, the waiflike Mrs. Osgood had risen, having abandoned Bennett, and was now at Poe's elbow, her face upturned, sparkling tears of admiration in her eyes. It was not much longer before she took up his hand in her own. Many eyes noticed them begin to leave. This couple said good night to few, but Poe did approach Hays, and led him aside near the doorway out.

"I am not who all these people think I am," he said.

"No? Then who are you?" asked Hays. "Are you worse, sir?"

"I am better," he whispered, glancing at Mrs. Osgood, waiting patiently for him in the hall. "Have pity on me, Mr. Hays. I am in the damnedest amour you'll ever find a fellow to be in in all your life."

🐚 66 🐚

Back in the Lair
of the Green Turtle

With hope held for the success of his black bird (he contended the raven would supplant the eagle as America's national emblem), Poe moved his family back from the Brennan farm to the city, taking up residence in a small two-story building below Washington Square on Amity Street, he said, to be closer to his work, but some meddlers claimed it only to be closer to Mrs. Osgood; that summer they had been espied by gossips together not only in upstate Saratoga Springs, but also in the cities of Providence and Boston.

A street urchin knocked at the front door of the Amity Street dwelling, and when Poe answered asked if he were the Raven. The boy then handed over an envelope bearing Poe's name but no postmark.

When opened, the envelope contained a letter, unsigned, but in precise pen, begging him to appear at the establishment known as the Green Turtle on Prince Street, and there to retrieve a sealed package left waiting.

By late afternoon Poe had found his way beneath the arch on Prince Street to said realm. A sign, recently nailed to the door outside, poorly written, painted, and spelled, warned:

```
HE WHO HATH NO
BUSINES HERE
KEEP OUT!
BY
ORDER OF
THE GREEN TURTLE!
```

Inside, down the long, dark hall, the front room stood empty, the air stale. Poe found his way to a table and slumped there, staring at the black walls. In front of him on the much-scarred wood tabletop lay that day's newspaper, in this case the morning *Sun*, containing a list of New York's wealthiest citizens. In order to make it into this rarefied air, the criteria employed, each individual must have self-worth exceeding $100,000. Number one, no surprise there, stood John Jacob Astor at $2,500,000. He was followed by his son, William B. Astor, his personal fortune estimated at one-fifth that of his father's. Peter Goelet, the merchant, was third at a not-paltry $400,000; Cornelius Vanderbilt, the self-made steamboat magnate, followed in fourth place at $250,000; and bringing up the rear was ex-mayor the Honorable Philip Hone, at the not-so-shabby cutoff of $100,000.

Poe was contemplating the astronomy of these numbers, not entirely without envy, when that immense woman known to him indelibly from a past visit (it was here John Colt had sent him to procure opium) entered from the back room, passing through a thick curtain.

Mistress of the inn, her accustomed two blue Colt revolving guns in her waistband and this day a jeweled dagger in a sheath between her ample breasts, she made her way a few feet into the room, where she stood in front of a portrait of Benjamin Franklin, a hole torn in the canvas beneath his eye.

Poe made feeble request from her of a glass of spirits. His eyes were clouded. Much white showing beneath the iris, to some, with a knowledge of the ways of folk medicine, a certain sign of failing health. She looked upon him with scorn (or was it pity?) before moving slowly behind the zinc bar and pouring him his drink, served in a bowl.

He shot the cloudy liquid down and felt an immediate increase in pulsation to his magnetic system inspired by this elixir, quickly quaffed. He asked to borrow a piece of brown butcher paper from the proprietress, digging a nub of lead pencil from his pocket, mumbling to himself the cryptic phrase, "She's warmer than Dian," watching her. He then took note of his words, recording them in studied hand on the butcher paper before reiterating:

"And I said—'She's warmer than Dian.'"

After another swallow of demon rhum, he again took the stub, continuing up from where he had left off:

"She rolls through an ether of sighs—"

Then, "She revels in a region of sighs," before again putting down the pencil.

But not for long.

He murmured again to himself, took another draught from the bowl's dregs, picked up the lead nub, and once more hurriedly began to scribble.

Seemingly exhausted by this exercise, the poet turned away from the table and signaled the mammoth, so black as to be almost green in hue, still standing her post behind the hammered flat zinc-surfaced bar, her arms akimbo, the dagger nearly rising to her chin on the sea tide of her bosom.

"More spirits," Poe commanded in a mind-sick tone, strangely coated.

The writer, fearing death by thirst, it seemed, became sorely con-

cerned and agitated when the huge woman gave no indication whatsoever of movement.

He almost said something more, but then, taken on by the muse, a
spirit otherworldly, picked up his pencil to add additional sentiment
to his effort:

> *She has seen that the tears are not dry on*
> *These cheeks where the worm never dies—*

As a gentleman from Virginia, he bowed slightly to her, the vast presence that was the colored proprietress, tippled what little was left in
his rhum dish, licked his chops, and reapologized for his thirst.

He shifted his blurred vision to face some formless apparition
across the room's sawdust floor, then, again shifting, addressing the
Green Turtle once more, implored, "My good woman, could you see it
in your heart . . . please."

From beneath her black hat and drooped black feathers, she stared
before pouring a fresh portion of rhum into a fresh cracked bowl and
bringing it to his table.

Poe said, "Thank you, my good lady. Thank you. This city, if not the
world, is a corrupt place. Justice and politics are available within her
confines for a price. Pettifoggery is at no premium."

"Suh," she responded, "my philosophy, after many years of observation, go somethin' like this: *All men is dogs,* colored or white, but
mostly tipplers. I don't see you as no exception." She set the swill
down with a bang while sneaking a surreptitious look at what the
tired-looking gent was writing, although she could read hardly anything more than her name.

"I have received notice you hold something for me."

She now looked at him somewhat more carefully.

"Indeed I do," she said finally, "if you are the fellow known about
town as 'the Raven.'"

"Rest assured, dear lady, I am he."

"In that case, I'll have to see to it, won't I?"

She smiled tightly, showing strong teeth between her meaty lips and round, prodigious cheeks before exiting the room through the back curtain.

Poe now became sure he heard voices emanating from the back room. He deciphered the name "Ossian," shouted, followed by someone rebutting in return something to the effect, "Screw you, boyo, do it yourself."

After a few minutes the curtain rustled, but it was not the Turtle who slipped back into the room. Rather it was a stringy-haired youth, quite drawn and misshapen, hampered by one withered leg and one withered arm. He limped his way to the metal-planked bar, where he sucked a quick draught of swill straight from the holding vat through a much-chewed red rubber tube, all the while his sharp eyes never leaving Poe.

"Do I know you?" Poe asked, uncomfortable with the lame boy's stare. "Because, if you don't mind me saying, you seem somewhat familiar to me."

"I don't think so," the stringy-haired youth answered. "Don't reside in this burg, do I. I make my home in Baltimore, I do. I'm only on a mission here in the old Frog and Toe."

"Baltimore!" Poe exclaimed. "Then that's it. I hail from that city myself. I still have family there."

"Don't you say."

"I do say. Where do you live, friend? Whiskey to crab cakes, I know the place."

"The Fourth Ward it is then, sir."

"Fourth Ward! Gunner's Hall. Ryan's Tavern."

"There you have it," the boy grinned. "Good for you. Sir, if you don't mind me saying, I'd watch myself. This likker served here by the mistress works as well as embalming fluid as it does beverage."

At this point the curtains parted once more, and the Turtle, having retrieved said sealed parcel, reappeared. "Away, vast Tweeter," she ordered, her voice now harsher than before, "I need a word with this jack cove."

She shooed the lame boy off and for his part he retreated dutifully.

"Now," she said to Poe, stepping close and slamming the parcel on the table in front of him, "this has arrived to me to be delivered to you the Raven."

"What is it, dear lady?" he asked, lifting the package off the table, checking its heft. "Do you know?"

"Some kind of book," she replied, glaring at him. "Been tole on good authority worth nothing."

Ten Months Later

MARCH 23, 1846

67

My Dreams Are of the Unknown

Olga Hays rushed into the parlor, stamping snow from her shoes. Her father had been dozing in front of the fire, stretched on Colt's leather recliner, wrapped in a tartan wool blanket, but her return had awoken him.

"Papa, I was at the Jefferson Market, hoping to get home and out of the snow, when Annie Lynch approached me as I was haggling with the butcher. She took me aside and said, 'Have you heard?' to which I, of course, responded, 'Heard what?' and she proceeded to tell me Mrs. Osgood has separated from her husband. It is said she is with child, and not necessarily the child of Mr. Osgood."

Olga continued in a rush. "There is more," she said. "It is all coming out."

Hays was by now wide awake.

"The prattlers are all saying how Fanny's condition is only one in a series for Edgar. Popular talk is it was he who put Mary Rogers with child, and it was with him, none other, that Mary Rogers traveled to the inn of Nick Moore to secure her premature delivery; that he offered similar solution to Mrs. Osgood."

Hays felt the weight of sadness and frustration descend. "The tongues of wagging women can be lethal as a dirk," he sighed before inquiring of Olga if she knew Poe's most current address.

"Eighty-five Amity Street," she replied.

NEARLY A YEAR HAD PASSED since James Harper had suffered crushing defeat. Running for his second term as a Nativist, he had been voted out of office by nearly seven thousand votes of forty-nine thousand cast.

As mayor Mr. Harper had failed to foresee that the mayoralty might so quickly be done with him. He had portrayed himself nothing less than a staunch populist, an advocate of frugal government, supporter of low taxes, limited city service, and social control. But he never fathomed how his vituperative posture directed against the papists assured him only defeat. He had deluded himself, failed to recognize dismally the new face of the city, the force of the slums, most of all, the ever-increasing voting power of the poor and downtrodden.

Since the turn of the decade the city's population had mushroom-grown from three hundred thousand souls to five hundred thousand, largely Irish and German immigrants.

And most, if not all, ably harnessed to Tammany.

Within days of taking office, the new mayor, William Havemeyer, a Democrat, dissolved his predecessor's Star Police (those who had become known on the street as "coppers" or, for short, "cops") if not their copper-star badges, bringing in a man of his own choosing, George Washington Matsell, to oversee a new, handpicked municipal force of eight hundred.

Summoned to City Hall the day after elections, Old Hays had taken the news stoically that he would be out of a job.

Truth be known, Mr. Jacob Hays himself had cast his ballot for Havemeyer, knowing exactly what his resulting fate would be when the wealthy sugar merchant took office.

Having reached his seventy-fifth year, the encroachment of age enjoyed a palpability not to be denied in the high constable. Aches and pains (a gumboil, an eye ache), Hays had not taken his sacking personally, and he was urged by the new mayor and new police commissioner, Matsell, to keep attached to his name for as long as he wished the rank and nomenclature of high constable.

Notwithstanding, since that day and before, his ire and frustration had not abated, his absorption with the name Mary Rogers had not desisted, but had lent his every day a source of remorse and inconsonance; yet indignation by itself had led him no closer to solution.

HAVING REACHED the address on Amity Street provided him by Olga, a small three-story structure off Sixth Avenue, Old Hays learned from the landlady, a thin woman manning a straw-bristled broom, the Poe family had moved yet again, and left no forwarding address.

Since he was only a few blocks from the residence of Annie Lynch, Old Hays decided to go there to inquire if she perhaps knew what had become of the Poes.

His knock found her in.

"What a surprise, Mr. Hays!" she exclaimed.

Made aware of his mission, without much encouragement she corroborated and, if anything, embellished the sordid tale circulating, told by Olga, in regard to Mr. Poe and Mrs. Osgood.

"Miss Lynch, do you know where I might find Mr. Poe?"

She did. "He is living on East Broadway. I have only yesterday been there to commiserate with his aunt and wife, if not with him. He claims the building once the residence of a wealthy merchant, but I think not. It is a common tenement. I must say he is living with his family in a sorry state on the third floor in the rear. If I am not wrong, let me see, yes"—she referred to her daybook—"here it is right here, the number is 195."

"Thank you, Miss Lynch."

"Thank *you*, Mr. Hays."

Balboa had been summoned from his home along the Minetta Brook, and it was he this chilly day who had been ferrying Old Hays about the city, taking time out from his own life (having married three years before the Rogers family's colored maid, Dorothea Brandywine, and presently being the father, despite his rather advanced age, of two little girls, with a third child on the way).

In the light carriage, the streets and buildings sparsely dusted with snow, they proceeded east on Waverly Place, turning right on the wide expanse of the Broadway, proceeding down to reach the back side of City Hall before turning east.

The home was as Annie Lynch had described: a low tenement squabble, not a great distance above Chatham Square. Hays made his way down the dark corridor to the rear of the building where the stairway rose. Gripping the banister for support, in the dim light he proceeded to the first landing, rested there, made his way to the second, rested there, cursing his age, his painful legs, his nagging back, and then on to the third, catching his breath in the hallway before knocking.

Mrs. Clemm answered his short, curt rap, inviting him in without enthusiasm.

Almost immediately Poe emerged from a back bedroom, his face flush, his hair wet as if he had been holding his head under a pump.

"Mr. High Constable," he said, some confusion curtaining his features, "what are you doing here? Have you not retired from the force?"

"I have, sir. I am here as a private citizen, with some concern for you as a gentleman."

Hearing this, Poe dismissed his aunt. Before she could leave the small room, however, he called her back, asked where his wife was, to be informed that she was sleeping in the front bedroom.

Once Mrs. Clemm had departed the room, Hays, mindful of his words and their volume, told Poe of the reason for his visit, asked him about Mrs. Osgood, if not about the pregnancy, and not yet mentioning the name Mary Rogers.

"I assure you. No need to worry," Poe said. "It is evident there is a conspiracy among all other authors of America to belittle my genius and smother my work. I vow it will not stop me. I announce to you today, High Constable Hays, I am on my way to England where I shall read 'The Raven' to none other than Queen Victoria and the royal family. Of course, I am more than a little cognizant that this can only further incite the jealousy of my brother and sister writers. Even so, I shall persist. It can only be posterity that will judge my work. Future generations will sift the gold from the dross and then my black bird will be beheld, shining above all else, as a diamond of the purest water."

"Mr. Poe," Hays said gently, "are you in any way aware of how this all appears to the discerning eye, sir? I have been your defender, but more and more you presume a position untenable. I implore you, sir, as a good citizen of this city of New York, are you responsible for Mrs. Osgood's state of pregnancy?"

"I am not," Poe stated adamantly, if a little confused.

"You are not?"

"As I say."

"I am troubled, because I have heard otherwise. And again, sir, I warn you, not only have I heard you are father to this child, but also, to my sorrow, your name arises again from the unseemly murk entwined with the name of Mary Rogers."

"Do you dream, sir?" Poe deflected, as if he would have Hays believe he did not hear.

Hays puffed his cheeks and blew out a breath of unrestrained exasperation. "I do, sir," he replied. "As do we all, I fear."

"I mean sleeping dream," maintained Poe.

"What other kind of dream is there, man?"

Poe stared at him as if he were trying to put the high constable in sharper focus. "My dreams are of the unknown," he finally said. "If you must know," Poe continued, unsullied, "I reside in the great shadowy realm of dream whose music is hidden from mortal ears, swells through all space and gleams of more than mortal beauty. Ravish the eyes, come to me! That, sir, is to dream spiritually."

"Do those sweet, shadowy faces to which you refer wear to you an expression of pain, sir?" inquired Hays.

Poe blinked. "Not so much pain as grave thoughtfulness—tender sympathy."

"Ah-hah," Old Hays rejoined, "so that is your mind, sir?"

"No, no, no," the poet responded quickly. "Because, you see, Mr. Hays, even if my dreams are populated by the same ghosts as yours, I say to you, only mine wear a look of suffering—patient suffering— almost an appeal, sir—and I spread out my hands to reach them. I call to them in my dreams. I implore them. I am more to them than they to me. I call to them, sir, to speak, but they are silent and float away, pointing forever onward . . . but your spectres, Mr. Hays, I maintain when they call to you, sir, those spirits, your spirits, can only be looking backward."

❧ 68 ❧

Turtle Bay

Three days after his visit to the Poe home, Hays returned to East Broadway, only to once more find the family gone.

No word or sign of this family's whereabouts reached him for some time until Olga received word from Annie Lynch, over tea and cakes one afternoon on Elizabeth Street, that Mrs. Clemm had been seen in the city. She apparently had approached the poet and editor William Cullen Bryant, begging that gentleman for help, saying her son-in-law was crazy, his wife dying, and the whole family starving.

Bryant reportedly related to Miss Lynch how the countenance of this lady struck him simultaneously as both beautiful and saintly. He regarded himself, he conveyed, in the presence of one of those angels upon earth that women in adversity can be, and although he admitted he may have been a little astonished by this good lady's request ("But not unduly so," he stressed), he gave her twenty dollars with the understanding she need not pay him back.

During the course of their encounter, Mrs. Clemm stated to him that her family had left the city under the most undesirable of circumstances, the torrent of cruel gossips pursuing them, Sissy's health in a continued torment of downward spiral, Eddie in a state of despair and unable to write. They had found a place, Mrs. Clemm said, on the shore of the East River at Turtle Bay, and were now living in a home they could scarcely afford, even if they rented it for a pittance, from a kind farmer by the name of Miller, a friend of the Brennans.

The house was situated at the foot of Forty-seventh Street, she had told Bryant, a decidedly country district with fresh air, unlike the heavy, fetid stench they had endured in the cloistered city. The home itself was neat and freshly whitewashed, with lovely fruit trees and cows and chickens grazing and pecking by the riverbank.

Upon receiving this information, Hays once again enlisted Balboa. But from where the carriage sat now, a quarter-mile distance inland from the aforementioned Turtle Bay, Old Hays was unable to spot Poe about the property. To Hays' instructions, Balboa eased horse and buggy out of sight, under a copse of crab apple trees, welcome shade from the sun's strong rays this spring day.

It was not long before Hays observed the door to the white clapboard house open and Mrs. Clemm come out onto the porch. Hays watched as this broad, staunch old woman, her face set square and impassive, remained momentarily on the porch, her slash mouth clamped tight. Then, apparently seeing not at all what she sought, she trudged to the riverfront, looked up and down the bank, scanning the little islands that sat midstream. After a few moments of so viewing, her lips moved, she muttered something to herself before hurrying off, back and shoulders bowed, in the direction of a second house, a larger version of the first, a nearby neighbor, Hays judged Farmer Miller's.

Hays delayed some moments before descending the carriage. He used his constable's staff as he moved purposefully along the muddy path, approaching the Poe house. He climbed the stair, stood on the porch, peered in the window.

Inside, through the glass pane, all stood still, all silent. He could see Poe's writing desk, pen and inkpot, books piled on the floor.

He knocked on the door, called softly, "Hello?"

No one answered, and he heard nothing.

Then a cough, wet and ratcheting.

Virginia Poe emerged from the back room wearing an ill-fitting red felt dress, decidedly homemade, with curious yellow ribbon piping. Her hair appeared stringy and damp, less glistening than previously observed, her complexion more peaked.

"High Constable Hays," she murmured. "I thought I heard someone calling."

"Forgive me for disturbing you, Mrs. Poe. I seek your husband."

She forced a smile, fidgeted with her fingers. "I know not where he is," she said. "I was asleep. My mother? Is she not here?"

He indicated outside in a westerly direction. "I saw her go in the direction of the neighbor's."

"Ahh," she said, as if that explained all. "Forgive me, sir, for being so bold as to ask, but I am at a loss why you pursue my brother so doggedly."

"Your brother?"

"As I call him, Eddie, Buddy, I'm sorry, I refer to my husband."

"Dear lady, I do not pursue him so doggedly. But my duty remains my duty, and in the course of conversation with Mr. Poe, I have become aware of your husband's acute power of reason. I seek only his capable aid in my investigation, that is all."

"What investigation is that of which you speak?"

"The death of the segar girl, Miss Mary Rogers."

"I assure you, sir, Eddie has nothing to do with such horror."

"I do not say that he does, dear lady." His eyes had wandered to Poe's writing table. A leather-bound binder lay atop a pile of manuscript pages.

She mistook his gaze. "I wrote that," she said. "For Eddie on Valentine's Day."

"What?"

"The poem you are looking at."

It was pinned to the bottom shelf of the bookcase, overlooking his desk. The phrases were neatly penned in her girlish hand. He put on his spectacles, the magnification increased recently by the increment of three, in order to decipher the sentiment.

> *Ever with thee I wish to roam—*
> *Dearest my life is thine.*
> *Give me a cottage for my home,*
> *And a rich old cypress vine,*
> *Removed from the world with its sin and care,*
> *And the tattling of many tongues,*
> *Love alone shall guide us when we are there,*
> *Love shall heal my weakened lungs;*
> *And oh, the tranquil hours we'll spend,*
> *Never wishing that others may see!*
> *Perfect ease we'll enjoy, without thinking to lend*
> *Ourselves to the world and its glee—*
> *Ever peaceful and blissful we'll be.*

"Very nice," he said, nodding his encouragement. "You wrote this?"

She grinned, obviously pleased by his solicitation. "There is a secret message hidden within. See if you can decipher it, High Constable."

He looked but saw nothing.

"What is it I am looking for?"

"Read the first letters of each line in progression down the page," she said. "It spells out Eddie's name: E-D-G-A-R A-L-L-A-N P-O-E. Don't you see?"

"So it does."

"And you a detective!" she teased.

He smiled back at her. A mere child, grinning, so taken with herself and her accomplishment. Her violet eyes shifted. He looked where she looked.

Through the window glass he could see Poe out on the river a short way off, standing in a rowboat, wending his course toward shore, using an oar to push himself through the reeds.

Evidently the poet had been on the other side of one of that group of small islands midstream. As Hays came out of the house, Poe had reached the shallows. Seeing the high constable, he remained in the boat as it bobbed at the rocky shore.

Hays came down the front stair, making his way to the bank. "Mr. Poe, how are you?" he called. "Are you coming ashore, sir? I need a word with you."

When no response came from him, Hays said, "Mr. Poe, I have come a distance from the city to speak with you."

The boat continued a few yards offshore. Poe stood the gunnels. "How have you found me?" he said.

"Have you tried to elude me, sir? I would hate to think it so."

"Elude you? My intention was nothing of the kind. Poor Sissy suffers. I do anything I can to ameliorate her pain."

"For all our hundreds of thousands of citizens, we both know Gotham to be a curiously small place, Mr. Poe. It is no great accomplishment to find what one seeks here. How is your health? How does your work go?"

Poe now navigated the last few yards of river to achieve land.

"I have been too consumed to write," he said as he leaped, somewhat unsteadily, from boat to rocky shore, grabbing Hays' solid forearm for support, "although the idea for a new masterwork plays about in my head. I am going to explain the universe. For the here and now, however, I am sorry to say only a few pathetic words do I find cascading from my brain to my pen: 'The moaning and groaning,'" he recited, his dark eyes gleaming. "'The sighing and sobbing, quieted now with this horrible throbbing. And, ah, of all tortures that torture, the worst has abated, the terrible torture of thirst. The sickness, the nausea, the pitiless pain, have ceased with the fever that maddened my brain.'" He grinned tightly with his performance while remaining somber. "You see, High Constable," he admitted, "it's not all bad."

They stood together gazing out at the river, an estuary really.

"I was a champion once," Poe said. "As a youth I swam six miles against the current in the James River. And once I held the nation's record for the standing broad jump."

"You don't say." Hays nodded.

Poe paused. "I have known an inordinate number of young women to whom the master, Death, has come all too soon. At that exact moment where their life comes into blossom, they are taken. What am I to believe?"

"Is Mary Rogers one you count among these?"

"You know what my darling little wifey told me?" he said, seeming for all intent and purpose to discount the question. "She promised me that after she is dead she will come back to me as my guardian angel and protect me."

"If she is in any way able, I am sure she will," said Hays.

He looked through Hays in an unearthly manner, and after securing the beleaguered watercraft on the bank, trudged past the marsh grass and reeds, up the flagstone path to the little white house, Hays following him.

"Do you think it true, High Constable? Do you think I need protection from beyond?"

"I cannot answer that. Only you can know. Have you sinned under such circumstance whereas you will need protection in the hereafter? For your sake, sir, I hope not."

What struck Hays most upon reentering the house was not the cramped quarters, but the order and cleanliness of the living space, the dignity of Mrs. Clemm's dogged determination to keep a spotless and decent home for her children.

The parallel, he felt unexpectedly, to his own deceased wife's predilection toward orderliness overwhelmed and saddened him.

The elderly woman responsible for such scrupulousness came in soon after, her apron full of turnips and dandelion greens from the field. Upon her seeing Hays, her expression hardened, but she was cordial and polite, apologized, said these were meant for Eddie's lunch, but she would go right out again and pick more, her not knowing the high constable coming for luncheon.

He begged her not to bother, protesting it was impossible for him to stay.

Out of politeness she asked after his health and the health of his family, having met his daughter Olga on occasion at Amity Street during several supportive visits to Sissy from the starry sisterhood. She made no mention of her distrust of Old Hays, too polite to press on in recrimination, insisting on taking to the field in search of more dandelions, saying no matter, it was no trouble, the greens and turnips both meant for the cows, not human consumption.

Hays pressed on her that she did not. Finally acquiescing, she returned to the stove, where her preparation had begun for what she called dandelion soup, although as far as Hays could see she had no chicken broth, nor salt pork.

On her straw bed Virginia must have fallen asleep, but as he prepared to leave, Hays heard her stir in the back room, her heartbreaking cough muffled somewhat by space and distance.

Because of her illness she had been given the choice room for her own in the rear of the house, the family cat, Caterina, mewing for affection at her bedside.

Muddie and Poe shared a room with a single bed in the front, adjacent to the kitchen. A small pallet had been set out for Poe in a closet of that room.

Virginia was calling, "Eddie. Eddie, darling brother, come see me."

Mrs. Clemm insisted on dismissing them. "Go, Eddie. Attend to your business with this man. Your sister knows how deeply you love her. I'll see to her."

He kissed her. "My Mother," he said, looking at Hays as he said it, "without you, I am nothing."

Together he and Hays returned outside and stood briefly on the porch watching the ships steam up the East River on their way to the Long Island Sound, or down, from Hell's Gate to the harbor.

"I want you to know there is no way in the world I would have endured even as long as I have without my mother," Poe said to Hays, once outside in the fresh air. "The trials and tribulations brought to bear on me, on our Sissy, our longtime suffering. She of all of us, our dearest Muddie, she is the truest sufferer. My own mother, who died early, was but the mother of myself; but she, Muddie, is mother to the one I love so dearly, and thus is dearer than the mother I knew. What can it mean, High Constable," Poe asked, "that my grandfather, father to my beloved, and his fellows fought the Revolution some seventy years ago with the queerest idea conceivable, that all men are created free and equal?"

"That book on your desk," Hays said, "it is from John Colt, is it not?"

Hays momentarily saw lucidity in his eye. Then the veil dropped again.

"What do you mean?"

"I recognize the penmanship on the frontispiece. John Colt's hand. Where did you get it? Do not think of lying! Need I remind you once more: Good citizens tell the truth, Mr. Poe, and despite all that I see and have heard, I want you to know I count you, sir, as a good citizen of our city."

"I received notice that a package awaited me at an address on Prince Street," Poe said. "Nothing more sinister is involved. I went there. A package was indeed waiting. I was told it was a book worth nothing. I picked it up, and it was the manuscript. I too recognized the hand. The poems inside as well."

"How was the package postmarked?"

"It was not. It was simply addressed to 'the Raven.' To be hand-delivered, as it was."

"What did you think?"

"At first nothing. Occurrences of this stripe have become common in the course of practicing my profession. Everyone thinks they can write. Everyone wants to be published. I dismissed any notion until I had had a look at the hand."

"And then?"

"Then I thought, John Colt should never have left such trace. Here is proof that he is alive."

"Indeed, just so. What establishment was it on Prince Street?"

"That of the Green Turtle."

"The Green Turtle?" Hays considered a moment. "Are you aware of who Tommy Coleman is, Mr. Poe?"

"Certainly. He occupied the cell across from John Colt on death row in your Tombs."

"Would you recognize him if you saw him?"

"By all newspaper accounts, he is dead."

"As dead as we would have John Colt. *Would you recognize him if you saw him, Mr. Poe?*"

"Stepping up from the grave, I'm not sure. Perhaps."

"Was anyone there in the groggery you recognized?"

"The Turtle herself. She is quite unforgettable."

"Was it she who gave you the manuscript?"

"Yes."

"Was there anyone else?"

"As you mention, another member of the Tommy Coleman gang, the lame boy with the withered arm and leg. I have not seen him for so many years. He is no longer a boy, but it was he."

"Tweeter Toohey?"

"Is that how he is called?"

"His sobriquet in the underworld."

"There were others there as well. I heard voices. Another name called. I don't remember what." He snapped his fingers. "Ossian! That is what it was."

"Ossian?" Hays considered. "Mr. Poe, could you fetch the Colt manuscript, please?"

From the Plumed Pen of One Who Must Remain Unnamed

Even peering through those bothering magnifying spectacles at the title page, Hays found himself needful to squint in order to fully decipher. There was no doubt: here was the same poetic effort in regard to

Samuel Adams he had puzzled over in Colt's cell at the Tombs that day following his escape.

> *The deed was done, but one ugly fear*
> *Came over me now to touch this thing.*
> *There was nothing to struggle against me here*
> *In this lifeless heap. I wished it would spring*
> *And grasp me, and strike at me, as it did*
> *Only a moment or two before.*
> *I lifted the head, but it dropped, and slid*
> *From my grasp to its bed of gore.*

> *What will you do with this horrible thing?*
> *Down—shove, push it in a crate!*
> *Push! Push down hard! If you choose you may sing*
> *That song of his. Don't start and look round!*

> *Push! How terribly inept you are!*
> *The dawn in the East begins to grow;*
> *The birds are all chirping; push there, shove there*
> *That body at once, and for God's sake go!*
> *The world will be up in less than an hour,*
> *And rattle and ring along the road.*
> *Away! Away! Away for your life!*

> *Ah, well, that o'er,*
> *And he lies sepulchred in his last abode!*

When Hays returned to his barouche, Balboa was sitting on the warm spring ground beneath a swamp maple tree finishing his own lunch, brought from home, of cold suckling pig and equally cold roasted potatoes, the greasy newsprint in which he has carried his meal spread on his lap.

"One last thing, Mr. Poe." Hays turned back to Poe, who had only taken a few staps toward the house. "What concerns me are certain similarities between the circumstances of Mary Rogers and Mrs. Osgood. I do not want to believe you guilty of heinous acts, Mr. Poe. Your name has been associated with both women, Miss Rogers and Mrs. Osgood. I would ask Mrs. Osgood herself, but she has apparently fled the city, and as of yet I have not made inquiry to ascertain her present whereabouts. But if I were to pose this question to her, 'Did Edgar Poe suggest to you the idea of a premature delivery to put an end to your difficulty?' what would her answer be?"

"I would never, sir, make such recommendation to Fanny. Even if I had mentioned such action, she is already the mother of two small girls, and the idea of putting an end to the life of an innocent child before it has had opportunity to draw first breath would certainly be anathema to her, and I did not push it."

"Listen to me, Mr. Poe, because this is very serious. I never had opportunity to pose questions to John Colt in this regard: When you befriended Mary Rogers, or after, did you ever consider, did you ever have a clue, there might have been some clandestine bond between her and John Colt?"

Poe hesitated. "I did not. How so?"

"Sir, could it in any way have been possible it was John Colt to whom you lost the affections of Mary Rogers? Please, do not answer just yet. I want you to consider the possibility that it might have been him, John Colt, none other, who arranged this criminal action. If he had been the lover of Mary Rogers, it would follow. If he had been the laggard who put her with child, he might have seen it as a necessity to arrange the premature delivery that ultimately led to her death, given his own personal circumstances with Caroline Henshaw. Let us for a moment imagine: following the tragedy, the loss of this girl, whom he may or may not have loved, the confusing matrix of emotion enjoined in his own home. Under this tragic scenario, Mr. Colt finds himself out of grief, mind you, or immense displeasure with himself, in a state of flux that he cannot control. His humours have brewed, simmered, and raged, now to escalate until they have erupted, leading to the otherwise unwarranted, unrelated, senseless murder of Samuel Adams."

Poe peered at Hays.

"I am asking you as a professional, Poe. Your acumen and your insight are called upon. My daughter scolds me continually that instincts are the precinct of an old world, that logic rules the modern day. She calls you master of ratiocination. I am asking you to ratiocionate, man. In your opinion, could John Colt be guilty of the murder of Mary Rogers as well as Samuel Adams?"

Again Poe hesitated, stammered. "I-it is possible. I don't know. It is possible."

"You had lost her, sir. Lost her undoubtedly to her murderer. Do you have any inkling to whom?"

Poe began to cry. "I do not."

"Could it have been John Colt?"

"Truly, I cannot say," Hays studying him as he turned away, stumbling back to his mother-in-law and ailing wife, his family.

❧ 69 ❧

The Dead Are but for the Moment . . .
Motionless

Notice first appeared in Bennett's *Herald*. "Edgar Poe has lost his sanity," stated the dispatch. "He has become deranged. His friends, with little choice else, have seen fit to have him confined to the Insane Retreat in Utica, New York."

"Can this be true?" inquired Olga Hays of her father, her concern in evidence.

Old Hays said he did not know. The last he was aware, he said, Poe was still living in Turtle Bay. At the time of his visit he had seemed sane enough.

Olga took it upon herself to travel immediately to that last known locale on the East River, only to find the Poe family departed, the small white farmhouse empty once more, and the farming family, the Millers, even if they had knowledge, refusing to divulge their whereabouts.

A day later a second disturbing announcement appeared, this in the *New York Evening Mirror:*

> We regret to learn that the gentleman Edgar A. Poe and his wife are both dangerously ill with the consumption and that the hand of misfortune lies heavy upon their temporal affairs.

> We are sorry to mention the fact that they are so far reduced as to be barely able to obtain the necessaries of life.

And then, not a day more gone, a third mention, an alarming chastisement, this emanating from Greeley, printed in his *Tribune:*

> Great God! Is it possible that the literary people of the Union will let poor Poe perish by starvation and lean-faced beggary?

Upon reading this, without delay, Olga traveled south from her home to Publishers' Row in order to seek Horace Greeley out at his offices.

"From what I hear from Bennett," he told her, "the three of them are all currently dying under the most strident and tragic circumstance. Apparently no proper medical care is attainable due to their state. Poe himself is said to be entirely compromised, in the throes of utter and desperate insanity."

"Do you know where they are?" asked Olga.

"I have heard Fordham Village."

"Fordham Village?"

"In the Bronks."

Said village was situated sixteen miles from the city heart proper. There were stagecoaches, and a new line of the Haarlem Railroad had recently been opened.

Without returning home to Lispenard Street, neglecting to inform her father of her plans, Olga rushed to catch the caravan north from Canal.

RENT WAS ONE HUNDRED DOLLARS for the year. The house was small, and again white, situated atop a gentle hill. Twenty-five years old, it featured a tiny upstairs attic, divided into three minuscule rooms. Downstairs there was a sitting room, small kitchen, and an additional functioning bedroom. No more than a bungalow, Olga found it tucked away in a dingle of woods in the far reaches of the Bronks borough.

The cottage itself was very humble, but Olga noted an air of refinement.

She found Poe certainly ill, suffering delirium. Muddie told her he had been demanding morphine, but she said she had scoffed at his desire. She had no morphine and there was no way to get it.

Once more, as he had in his youth, he called himself "Israfel."

Israfel, the angel who will sound the trumpet announcing the end of the world.

"The moon never beams without bringing me dreams," Poe told her. "And the stars never rise, but I feel the bright eyes . . ."

Virginia was quarantined to a neat, scantly furnished room, lying on a straw mattress with snow white sheets, shivering with the cold and final primal fevers caused by bronchial consumption. Against the chill Olga found her covered by Poe's old military cloak, the cat, Caterina, on her chest for added warmth.

"I have not endured suffering beyond my limits," Poe assured Olga. "I have any number of friends to whom I might turn. I still have a future, dear lady, and I have resolved myself not to die until it is done."

He took her hand in his and added, "To just disappear into the countryside, to stand on the cliffs of this rural village and peer across the Sound to the blue-hued land of Long Island, hoping, praying in some way the fresh clean air will revive my Sissy, bring her back."

In a loud, crazed voice he clamored that the French boasted in their reviews of him that there is only one faculty of inspiration in his work—reason—and only one muse—logic.

"I see too well," he said, "that the world regards wretchedness as a crime."

From there on in, Olga traveled to Fordham almost every day. When Hays objected, she said to her father, "I cannot let them suffer so. I cannot find it in my heart."

Old Hays thought to protest further, but did not.

She took over the family, ministering to all. She brought a goose-down comforter and a box of wine, which Virginia never failed to drink, smiling even when having difficulty getting it down.

"Surely, dearest Olga, you must possess a heart for loving all the world," Sissy whispered.

As the end grew nearer, and each knew, Virginia kept a picture of her husband under her pillow. She expressed deep concern for him.

On the penultimate day of her life, she took Olga's hand.

"Olga," she said in a small voice, "always be a friend to Eddie. And don't forsake him; he loves you so—don't you, Eddie?"

Poe, sitting nearby, looked from his wife to Olga Hays. Tears brimmed in his eyes. He wept heavy tears. "I will be calm," he proclaimed.

Virginia Poe died on the afternoon of January 30, 1847. In the twenty-fifth year of her life, she had been twelve years married.

Following her death, Olga sprinkled Sissy's room with perfume before going out to Fordham Village to buy her proper linen grave clothes and a coffin. She also purchased Edgar a new black suit, suitable for mourning.

Returning home to Lispenard Street for her own mourning clothes, Olga confided to her father that at her passing the dear girl died painfully, unable to speak, with much expression in her eyes.

At the funeral, held on February 2, three days following Sissy's death, Muddie approached Olga and Old Hays and took Olga by the hand in front of her father. "Forgive me, but if it wasn't for you, dear lady," she said, "my darling Virginia would have been laid in her grave in cotton. I can never tell my gratitude that my darling was entombed in lovely linen."

Women of a fashionable sort, detritus of the starry sisterhood, streamed to Fordham for the interment. They were, for the most part, done up in bonnet and dress and tight-bodiced jackets suited for a day of rough travel and unknown adventure. After all, Olga observed to her father, with little tolerance, these autumn-cacklers were here to see for themselves the straits of the great Raven, to see just how down-trodden such a man might be, and in the process enjoy fresh air and proper amusement for a day's outing while at the same time giving service to their civic, charitable, and Christian duty.

Over his new suit, Poe wrapped himself (as if in swaddling) in his old West Point greatcoat, the very same that he had worn all these years, and most recently had been utilized to shield Sissy from the cold while she lay on her deathbed.

Olga gently objected to this cloak, calling it both unsuitable and inappropriate, but Poe shunned her opinion and wore it all the same, having rooted out the worn garment from where Olga had hidden it from him.

Prior to the burial, Virginia lay on Poe's writing table in front of the window in the little parlor of their cottage.

Poe followed the body of his beloved cousin and wife through the aisle of trees to the burial vault at the Dutch Reformed Church, one-half mile through the wood from their bungalow.

Upon returning from the service, Poe gave evidence of having entered a state of numbed collapse. Later that night after everyone in the little house had gone to sleep, he snuck out in his stocking feet and tramped through the freshly falling snow to visit his wife's grave.

In the morning Olga, who had spent the night, saw he was suffering from a raging fever and outright delirium. At her own expense she retained a carriage and driver, rushing the ill Poe to see Dr. Francis in Greenwich Village.

The physician took immediate alarm, diagnosing brain fever. A midwife (in lieu of a nurse) who had administered to Poe in Fordham had expressed fear he might have a lesion on the left side of his brain, and Dr. Francis conceded it might be so.

He prescribed a cure, but emphasized without qualification Mr. Poe's strict cooperation was needed to effect it.

"Edgar," Dr. Francis ruefully instructed, "you must sit away from the stove with a soapstone by your feet. In addition, it is all-important that you replenish the phosphates lost by your mental exertions. In order to facilitate this end, you must eat fish, clams, and oysters every day. I would also urge you eat exclusively bread made from Hosfords yeast so that the phosphates in the wheat might be preserved."

Taking Olga aside, the physician (the very man who had delivered her and her late brothers) instructed sedatives were to be administered to the patient, but carefully lest the remedy excite the ill one to madness.

Olga took to Poe's care as a dedicated volunteer.

Hays worried at the influence such close quarters with Poe might have over her. He considered saying to his daughter, *You are forbidden*, but the sentiment of it sounded too ridiculous, and he knew even if he uttered such phrase, she would not obey, and he would not blame her.

At the cottage in Fordham, she took Poe's pulse continually, waiting for a moment when he would calm so that she could administer the sedative. Under her careful ministration he not only rallied, but was also able to work again.

She came often to him at his refuge in the village, and when she didn't come she sent flowers by train. He was deeply grateful to her.

He called her "my sacred sun."

Muddie confided tearfully to Olga she did not know whatever they would have done without her.

"So here I am," he told her one day in an unaccustomed fit of the loquacious, "and this is what has become of me. It is the beginning of time for me, the end of time. When I was fifteen I fell in love with a local girl in Richmond, Virginia, where I lived with my stepparents. She, too, was fifteen years old, a neighbor, Sarah Elmira Royster, the daughter of a man from whom my stepfather, John Allan, had borrowed money on his personal account for his business. I called her Myra.

"How can I describe her? She had a trim little figure, an appealing mouth, large black eyes, and long chestnut hair that fell in a gaggle of dark curls. At one time she lived directly across the street from my school. I loved to take walks with her along the quiet streets of old Richmond or in the woods and fields nearby, and I loved to sing to her.

"Our favorite spot was an enchanted garden tended by a trusted slave of my father's business partner. Within its leafy and hedged confines, I would quote to her Giles Fletcher the Elder: 'The lawn stretched away in a green and flowered vista of slumbered delight. The myrtle and azure leaves, sparkled with dew, and shown like twinkling stars in the evening blue.'" He smiled, the pleasure of remembrance of the poem. "We were entranced with each other," he continued. "In love. We planned to marry.

"When I was seventeen I was sent off to university. At the time, my naïveté boundless, I had every expectation to return to my stepfather's home in Richmond, marry my Myra, and work hand in hand in my stepfather's concern, eventually to take my place in the countinghouse, to assume all entitled wealth, privilege, and responsibility of daily life as heir.

"How sadly mistaken I was.

"In my studies I achieved highest honors in Latin and French. I was an able debater and an outstanding athlete, leaping downhill, twenty feet in the running broad jump.

"Still I became increasingly morose. I wrote frequently to Myra, but received no reply. I had no clue back in Richmond her father, in collusion with my stepfather, was intercepting my letters to her and destroying them. I never imagined John Allan had merely waited his advantage. His pecuniary pettiness proved stultifying. He gave me not even enough money to subsist. He would send me thirty-nine dollars to cover forty dollars in debts. I began to drink mint slings and play high-stakes whist in hope of financing my education.

"I failed miserably. I threw myself into the cards with a recklessness of nature and abandon which acknowledged no restraint. By Christmastime, when I returned home for the holidays after not yet even one full semester, I estimated my indebtedness to my stepfather as approaching twenty-five hundred dollars.

"His reaction bordered on apoplexy. He immediately informed me that he was removing me from the university. If he had ever had an ounce of respect for me, he told me, he had none now.

"That night, my first back at my boyhood home, I attended a party at the residence of the Royster family, only to find the celebration in honor of Elmira's engagement in marriage to another, an individual much older than she, a man called Shelton.

"I attempted to have a word with her, but found myself rudely blocked by her father, and removed bodily from the dwelling.

"Once home in my room, dejected and betrayed, I made the decision to no longer abide by the law of my stepfather, John Allan. I went downstairs to confront him. A fight of enormous proportion ensued. Although it did not start that way, my debts now became the focus of this disagreement, and I found myself threatened with prison by a man I had once trusted and called 'Father.'

"'You have misled me,' I remember shouting at him. 'You have restricted me. You have rejected me. You have betrayed me. And now I have heard you say you have no affection for me.'

"And so with no choice I left."

Because of his indebtedness, Poe told Olga, he was forced to use aliases. He told how he masqueraded as one Henri Le Rennet from Boylston Street in Boston, or when to his advantage, Paris, France. Eventually he enlisted in the army as Edgar Allan Perry.

During this time his brother, William Henry Leonard Poe, dying from acute alcoholism in Baltimore, wrote an unflattering ostensible fiction, a story entitled "The Pirate," in which he had seen fit to plagiarize Edgar's affair with Elmira Royster and the frustrating outcome.

This fiction met with surprising success, even seeing the stage; the result a great deal of notoriety, Poe saying it was at this juncture, noting the accolades afforded his elder sibling, where began his own immersion into short-form tale-telling, the short story, and the transcendence (or not) that such tale-telling has brought him.

"But for my life, although married to my darling wifey, the undeniable thrill I felt for Mary Rogers"—tears welled in his already red-rimmed eyes—"the vibrance of Mrs. Osgood, I never knew a love as was my first love of Elmira."

WORD REACHED POE at his cottage on February 22 that although he had been unable to testify on his own behalf because of his grief in a lawsuit for libel (unfounded reports of insanity and institutionalization) brought by him against the *New York Herald,* he had nevertheless prevailed, and been awarded judgment of $225.06 in damages, plus $101.42 in court costs, to be paid immediately by the *Herald's* owner and publisher, James Gordon Bennett.

With this news Olga commented to her father she saw an immediate change come over her patient. Upon the arrival of the funds, his health immediately began to respond. Poe said he felt not only vindicated, but rich. Visitors to the cottage now found him much rejuvenated, even amused.

A new rug appeared in the house. The table was suddenly laden with delicacies. A bright and shiny silver-plated coffeepot stood on the stove.

Taking a walk with Olga and friends in the woods, the men engaged in a jumping competition in which Poe split his pants. He grew sideburns and waxed his mustache. He wore his elegant mourning clothes with newly found dignity.

He declared himself well. Better. Best.

Visiting Olga on Lispenard Street, he offered Old Hays unasked-for advice based on recent personal experience.

For his part, Hays kept private his own thoughts about his visitor and his daughter.

"I now rise early," Poe announced to him, "eat moderately, drink nothing but water, and take abundant and regular exercise in the open air."

He glanced at Olga, then leaned close to confide in her father that in retrospect he now knew what had driven him mad. It was nothing less than the impending and prolonged death of his wife, the interminable fear of losing Sissy. This fear led him to drink, and out-of-control behaviors.

"She died time and time again," he explained. "I was subjected to unfathomable torture, long oscillations between hope and despair. It was," he said, "an unceasing, constant source of anxiety that only alcohol could subdue."

He stared at Old Hays, his eyes blinking rapidly, then at Olga, as if waiting for their judgment. "Truth be told, I did become insane," he concluded, "with long intervals of horrible sanity."

Later that afternoon when it came time for him to return to Fordham, he claimed to be unable to move. He was put to bed, with Hays looking on, and Olga again administering to him.

Wiping his brow in the course of nursing him, Olga warned he must learn to live a more prudent and settled life. She urged him to find a woman fond enough and strong enough to help him manage his work and its remunerations for his best good.

Through his dyspepsia, Poe suddenly sat bolt upright and swore on his oath that if he sought a righteous woman, she, Mary Olga Hays, was the one he sought.

Although Olga smiled at his absolution, she swore she was not.

He would not take no for an answer. He reiterated his realization: she, most singular and worthy exponent of her gender, could only have been put on this earth for him, Edgar Poe, and only him.

"I tell you, beloved, when I love, I love desperately, and know no other way. I can only remind you my favorite name is Mary, and Mary is your name, dearest Mary Olga."

Again, this time with increased deliberation so that even he, who she recognized as diminished, might hear her and understand, Olga stressed, although gently, then stressed additionally, that this savior of whom he spoke, his savior, put on this earth by grand plan otherworldly or otherwise, for him or not for him, was decidedly, emphatically, not she.

That evening, Poe finally asleep, Olga shared with her father what Poe had said, the words familiar to him from his deposition of Mary Jenkins and unsettling.

Hays stressed to his daughter that although he deeply hoped not, there still might be chance that individual lying ailing upstairs a murderer. Hays implored his daughter to send him on his way, the gentleman unsupportable, cerebrally damaged, no prospect, to which she responded, as much as she loved her father, respected and revered him, she would do what she saw fit, and there was nothing in this world that would see her influenced any differently.

❧ 70 ❧

The Bells

The next morning Poe called to Olga from upstairs. She came and
he said he needed to talk to her. He confided he had come to
realize "crying will do no good."

Discordant, he claimed he was broken by Olga's resolve to remain
estranged from him, taking it upon himself then to get out of bed at
least, and, with some newfound strength and apparition of good
health and optimism, to travel to Albany, paying fifty cents to board
the steamship *Henry* at the Ossining dock.

Word had reached him that Mrs. Osgood had delivered her baby. It
was a little girl, and she had named the infant Fanny Fay, "fay," a Middle English singleton for faerie, a reference to a poem, "The Diamond
Fay," they had endeavored to write together for an ill-starred presenta-
tion in Boston. The child was said to have come into this world unwell.

> *The wealth of sick feelings—the deep—*
> *the pure. With strength to meet*
> *sorrow, the faith to endure*
> *Fair Lulin, listen while I sing*
> *Thee legend of this diamond ring*

I found this story quaint and old,
In fairy archives, where it's told
Of a mortal maiden heed
A quiet heart your soul may need.

Mrs. Osgood had seen advantage in resuming residence with her husband. She and Mr. Osgood had been estranged, but now they were back as man and wife, residing in Albany, New York, although not everything was entirely comfortable between them, and Mr. Osgood was not present at the time of Poe's visit.

Arriving at the Hudson River dock, Poe proceeded straightaway to Mrs. Osgood's home to get down on his knees and beg her to be with him.

"I love you," he said, "and you must love me."

Fanny knew not how to respond to such entreaty after such ruination, the calamitous public spectacle of their most intimate and innermost feelings.

At that moment a nurse brought the infant child into the room, interrupting them. Poe scrambled to his feet and looked at the little girl. Extremely small for her age, she was crying, inconsolable.

Her mother lamented that she did not know what was wrong with the baby, nor did the doctors. She took nourishment, but none of it seemed to nourish, and she could not gain weight. Fanny told Poe, her eyes glistening with emotion, to see her daughter suffer was the most grievous punishment a woman could bear.

Within a week of Poe's return home, news reached him at Fordham the infant had died. He went outside and paced the porch. As he drifted from one end of the cottage's little portico to the other, his overcoat draped over his shoulders, he contemplated the passing of this baby girl, his innocent child, undersized, undernourished. He observed the stars, remaining on the porch until long after midnight, his mind shaping something, a treatise that would transform human thought, revolutionize the world of physical and metaphysical science.

He felt himself ready to unveil the mysteries of being and nothing-
ness, baring nothing less than the secret of eternity.

He hungered for the companionship of women. He could not bear
to attend the funeral of little Fanny Fay. Again he approached Olga
Hays. "I swear," he implored her, "I believe wholeheartedly, that I have
been born to suffer and this suffering has only served to embitter my
whole life," telling her he despised ignorant people and held no stock
for trifling or small talk. He told her in the presence of her father,
once again echoing words Hays had heard from Mrs. Mary Jenkins,
that she had the most beautiful head of hair in the world. "They are
the locks poets rave over," Poe said, smiling weakly. "They are the
tresses I adore."

Again he was rebuffed.

Saying he was humbled, after pining alone for several weeks, he
decided he must try once more with Mrs. Osgood, beg her to be with
him. He traveled by train back to Albany, where he intended to throw
himself on her.

When he appeared at Fanny's door, professing love, she acted not
surprised at all to see him. She said he was expected, that a local seeress had foreseen his coming. With all that had happened, they
embraced and she wept for their departed baby. She spoke wistfully,
recalling their first meeting in the Astor House. They sat on her front
path, under the garden trellis, bathed in moonlight. She said she had
composed a poem for him, and she recited it from memory whilst they
sat amidst the honeysuckle:

> *Oh! Thou grim and ancient Raven,*
> *From the Night's plutonic shore,*
> *Oft in dreams, thy ghastly pinions*
> *Wave and flutter round my door—*
>
> *Romeo talks of "White doves trooping,*
> *Amid crows athwart the night,"*
> *But to see thy dark wing swooping*

Down the silvery path of light,
Amid swans and dovelets stooping,
Were, to me, a nobler sight . . .

Then, oh! Grim and ghastly Raven!
Wilt thou to my heart and ear
Be a raven true as ever
Flapped his wings and croaked "Despair"?

Late that evening he proposed marriage but admitted confusion, confessing he still suffered grief over the loss of Virginia.

She swore it mattered not to her, after all, she was still married to Mr. Osgood.

"I shall speak to your husband." Poe rose, clasping her hands in his.

"No, no," she insisted, "I shall see to him," and again she began to cry.

HE RETURNED JUBILANT to Fordham to inform Muddie he would shortly be returning to live in their tiny cottage with a new bride.

Mrs. Clemm was so alarmed by this crazed and abrupt declaration, suspicious of the circumstance and unsaid implication of the forthcoming union to an already married woman, the stark revelation that Mrs. Osgood, as Eddie's new bride, would now be coming to live a penniless existence to which she could be in no way inured, a life of deprivation and hardship that to Muddie's mind had led to nothing less than the forfeiture of the very life of her own daughter, upon hearing the news, collapsed in the cottage's *petit foyer.*

Poe dismissed his aunt's apprehension. He swore to her Fanny would present no problem. "Mrs. Osgood loves me too deeply," he contended.

Muddie retreated. Regrouping, she urged her son-in-law, if he must marry, to thoroughly warn Fanny of his circumstance, and what the reality of an existence lacking necessary funds for even ordinary sustenance would soon mean.

He scoffed at her but bussed her cheek, his aunt who remained very cold to him, and, saying goodbye, swore he had a plan and would make all well.

He left Fordham by rail but did not proceed directly to Albany and the arms of Mrs. Osgood. Instead, he made a side trip, heading east and disembarking the train in Hartford, Connecticut, to proceed directly to the newly founded factory works of Samuel Colt on Pearl Street.

In Whitneyville, where the Colonel had shared enterprise and premises with the junior Mr. Eli Whitney, he had chosen to take no cash profit out of their revolver business, but rather shrewdly took his end in the new machinery procured by him and his partner in order to see to the manufacture of the firearms in the first place.

Before the delivery of the second batch of government orders, Colt broke the partnership with Whitney and moved his share of the factory works, including this new machinery, from Whitneyville to Hartford. It was here on Pearl Street where Poe came.

With no wait whatsoever, he found himself ushered into the Colonel's office, an amalgam of rich Central American woods and fine East Indian carpets.

"Poe!" Samuel Colt exclaimed upon laying eyes on him and clamoring to his feet. "My God, man," he shouted, clapping him on the back like a long-lost brother and seeming genuinely pleased. "After what I've read in the public prints and heard tongues wag, I was not sure I would ever see you again alive."

"I am well," Poe smiled, adding what had become something of his easy mantra, "Better. Best. Mr. Colt, with all due respect, I need to talk to you, sir," he said.

"You are here, my good man. You have my ear. Please have a seat."

"Thank you, sir." After arranging himself, Poe said, "Although not on me at present, I have in my possession a manuscript with which I think thou must be interested. I am sure it is penned by none other than your brother, and I am sure it is of recent vintage. Do you know anything in regard to this matter, sir?"

Colt pursed his lips sourly. "My brother is dead," he said softly yet firmly. "I am hoping you have no thought otherwise. In no way should you be in receipt of any proof that he is anything other!"

"No, no," Poe stammered, and coughed. Colonel Colt's eyes were indeed intent upon him. "What I have in my possession must surely have been written before John's tragic passing, a poor replication, and I shall swear to that at any inquisition, to any inquisitor. I am only looking for your reassurance and support, sir. This work has most assuredly only now come to me. From whence I cannot be sure. I thought it was you, but perhaps his wife."

"I am hopeful you are not going to be a problem, Mr. Poe. My brother's widow has returned to resume her life in Europe. She may have sent it. I cannot say."

"I swear to you on the soul of my own poor wife, I shall do my best to see"—he cleared his throat—"the memory of your brother John well protected. My assessment is there can be but one reason these poems have reached my hands, and that is to see them well published. But if this is not the case, in his best interest, or in the best interest of you, sir, and your family, I am here to abide by your decision, an individual so strong-willed and clearheaded. We all shall see justice done, sir. In all actuality, Colonel Colt, that is what has prompted my visit, why I am here. I don't know if you know this, sir, but my darling wife, God rest her soul, has died."

"I'm sorry for your loss," Colt said, his eyes steady on Poe.

"Thank you. I am now engaged to be married to someone else. A wonderful woman, I might add. A poetess, charming and intelligent. Sissy, my departed wife, I know, would be pleased with my choice."

"I'm happy for you." Colt crossed and uncrossed his legs. He had clearly grown impatient with this conversation, although Poe was not aware enough to perceive anyone else's discomfort save his own.

"Thank you again, sir. I regret to be forced to tell you, however, that I have a problem. I see how efficient and well you are doing here in your munitions factory, and I sit in admiration of you and your prosperity. The life of a writer is something else entirely. I know you desire to keep your brother's legacy bright. To this most estimable end, could you see fit to advance me funds against royalties of any publication of his work, only so that my family and the family of my intended will not look upon me with such skepticism and loathing? You see, all concerned seem to be unsure of my financial situation and distrust me. I have assured my auntie and wife-to-be many times over that I am solvent, but, not unreasonably, they have all voiced their doubts. Funds from you in my pocket would surely cure all of this ill will."

"You want money?"

"Only against my editorial skills as rendered on behalf of the manuscript in my possession, sir. Mine is in no way the venture of a highwayman."

"I see. I am relieved, yet confused. And what exactly is your intent, Poe?"

"As you wish, Colonel. I shall see your brother's admirable efforts well published in an acceptable manner, as I perceive my charge to your brother's estate and memory . . . or, if you prefer, I can make the manuscript disappear and it shall never be heard from again. It's entirely a decision I make yours."

Colonel Colt remained momentarily motionless. "I see, Poe," he finally said, nodding ever so slightly. "I see what you have in mind, and I see, sir, what must be done."

UPON ARRIVAL in Albany, Poe found much licentious talk going round that city in regard to him and the prospects of any upcoming marriage ceremony to Mrs. Osgood, fueled in part by malicious tales that he had, already since his arrival, been seen drinking red wine in the company of several friends at the River House in downtown Albany. (He claimed them to be Sergeant Bully Graves from his days at Fort Moultrie and some old West Point comrades up from Bear Mountain.)

As part of the agreed marriage arrangement, Poe had promised Fanny to forevermore eschew drink. Now rumor had it here he was already partaking. Finally, convinced by a claque of concerned and wary friends that her influence would matter to naught over her new husband, Mrs. Osgood agreed to rethink her engagement, as it were, come to her senses. Poe was summoned from his hotel by embossed letterhead to the Osgood family home, where he was informed by Mrs. Oakes Smith, who had hurried on such mission up from the city, of Fanny's change of heart.

From his breast pocket Poe removed the currency procured from Colonel Colt, and waved the bills about the air as proof of his liquidity.

Staring across the parlor, unbelieving, he approached Mrs. Osgood and begged her not to deem this a final interview. He fell upon his knees, imploring her to reconsider.

"Say that you love me!" he begged.

Mrs. Osgood was worn out, about to faint and near hysteria. A handkerchief soaked in ether and supplied by Mrs. Oakes Smith was clasped to her mouth.

"I love you," she murmured before Poe was rudely seized by Mr. Osgood, he who had been biding his time out of sight on the back porch at the ready for signal, his coattails full of pistols.

With Poe in iron hand, Mr. Osgood roughly escorted him to the station with the aid of several burly gentlemen, where a southbound train awaited.

RETURNED TO NEW YORK in such circumstance, Poe once more assumed a state of nervous agitation. By the end of the day he appeared on Lispenard Street, at Olga Hays' doorstep, on the verge of collapse. Old Hays answered his knock and was shocked to see the condition of the caller. He ushered him inside, but before calling for Olga as requested, told the man there was no chance he would be allowed to stay in the house or in the company of his daughter, where-upon Poe crumpled to the floor.

Over the next days, despite her father's objections her patient should be remanded to the care of the hospital at the Northern Dispensary, Poe stayed in Olga's study. He was subject to spells of delirium and hours of wandering, sleeping twelve hours a day yet near the limits of exhaustion. Seeing him this way, Olga became truly alarmed, and again called in Dr. Francis from his home in Greenwich Village. The doctor examined Poe and quickly ascertained that his heart was beating irregularly. Observing that Poe's sleeps resembled comas, Dr. Francis warned his patient that unless he gave up all stimulants and excesses, the end was near.

Poe dismissed Dr. Francis's prognosis without denying his death might be imminent. Once more he took up Olga's hand in his, Hays looking on, resigned to silence. "Unless some true and tender and pure womanly love saves me," Poe swore, "I shall hardly last a year longer alone."

The Hays home was not far from a church. That afternoon Olga and her patient sat in the pleasant little backyard overlooking the well-maintained garden where she enjoyed drinking her tea.

Poe complained that he had been contracted to write a poem but had no inspiration. Olga, in hopes of helping him, went for paper, steel pen, and ink. For a moment or longer they sat in silence, then the bells from the nearby church began to sound. To Poe's jangled nerves the ringing was like an assault on his ears. He pushed the paper away harshly, declaring, "I dislike the noise of bells tonight. I am exhausted. I cannot write. I have no subject."

Olga, exasperated with him, then took it upon herself to seize the blank paper from his hand and write:

The bells, the little silver bells

Poe, seeing what she was about, pulled back the paper and with the same pen, snatched from her hand, finished the stanza, but in so doing his eyes rolled back in his head and he almost lapsed into a state of trance.

Olga then took the paper back from him a second time, upon which she wrote:

> *The heavy iron bells*
> *From the jingling and the tinkling of the bells.*

Fluttering his long, almost feminine eyelashes, Poe once more grabbed from her pen and ink and now finished in a scribble the verse, continuing through to end the two stanzas:

> *From the bells, bells, bells, bells,*
> *Bells, bells, bells—*

Following supper, Olga took the poet upstairs and installed him on the feathered mattress in her own bedroom, where he appeared to lapse into a very deep sleep, his breathing labored.

She returned downstairs. Her father wore a sour expression. "What?" she said, but Hays said nothing save he thought Dr. Francis should again be summoned.

Upon arrival the medical man sat at Poe's bedside, Olga watching, noting his symptoms. "His pulse is weak and very irregular."

Afterwards, downstairs in the kitchen, Dr. Francis spoke quietly to Hays and his daughter the caregiver. "He has heart disease, and will die early in life."

Two days later, alone in the rear garden, Poe tried to kill himself by ingesting a large quantity of laudanum, more than an ounce. (He claimed to have procured two ounces of the elixir, mumbling to Hays, who found him prostrate on the blue stone, he planned to save the second dose to administer while in the presence of Fanny Osgood should he survive the first.) The ingested narcotic, something more than thirty times a normal dose, did not take fatal effect. With the help of a mustard mixture, poured down his throat by Hays, he vomited, thus saving himself.

"Forced to endure," he forswore to he who had saved him, "the awful horrors which succeeded."

His reason gone, in a state aghast, his hand trembling, with Hays standing behind him encouraging him, the high constable's two strong hands on his shoulders, the poet somehow managed to take pen to paper and write his beloved auntie, although disguising his true affliction from her. "My dear, dear Mother, my dear Muddie," he began. "I have been so ill—have had cholera, or spasms, or something, quite as bad, and can now hardly hold a pen."

Still, he engendered hope, telling Muddie, again at Jacob Hays' insistence, he was to undertake a change of air, one last expedition. In receipt of an invitation from the *Southern Literary Messenger,* a magazine for which he had worked as a young man, he was to travel to Richmond, Virginia. His days may be numbered, and he may have been regressing, but he would make his way home again to the city where he had been brought up by John and Frances Allan.

On the steam train heading south, in a state of the occult or paranoia, he thought he was being followed, although each time he turned around abruptly, he could catch no one lurking.

Upon arrival in Richmond he hurried to his hotel and mailed a second missive back to his aunt at the Fordham cottage:

My dear, dear Mother, my dear Muddie,

I arrived here with two dollars of which I enclose you one.
I fear, Oh, God, my Mother, shall we ever meet again?

In spite of his weakened health, once back in the Virginia city, he found his way to visit old friends from his youth, a poetic figure always clad in black, slender, erect, the lines of his face continually fixed as if in deep, impenetrable meditation.

His schedule, arranged by Mr. White, editor of the *Messenger,* called for him to give three lectures on the nature and state of contemporary American poetry. But upon delving into his trunk on the occasion of the evening of the first event, to his utter consternation he found his notes and pages missing. Not only that, but he could not find the John Colt manuscript which he had chosen to carry with him for safekeeping and had carefully sequestered.

Momentarily he panicked, thinking of the apparitions on the train, before finding the notes stuffed into his boot, and the Colt manuscript laid out unceremoniously beneath his underwear.

The next day, while walking Broad Street, he heard a familiar voice call out to him.

"Mars Eddie!"

He turned, and the corners of his mouth broke upward in an unrestrained grin. It was his boyhood companion, the loyal slave of the Allan family, Dabney Dandridge, whose ghost stories had entranced him as a child.

His former ally hugged Poe and kissed him as if he were his own long-lost son. "I am the property of Miz Myra now," Dab explained. "She bought me after Massa Allan passed."

It was a warm Sunday afternoon. Poe's lost love of his happy youth, Sarah Elmira Royster, was now known as the Widow Mrs. Shelton. Her husband, older than she by twenty-five years, had died some years before of a heart aneurysm, leaving her at present with two grown children and a substantial estate, the deceased spouse having been in life a very successful merchant.

The Widow Shelton had matured into a handsome, pious woman, middle-aged but of substantial carriage. Informed that she had a gentleman caller, she came downstairs immediately from her chambers, dressed and ready for church.

Poe rose upon seeing her. "Oh, Myra," he exclaimed, "is it you?"

My dear Mrs. Clemm,

You will no doubt be much surprised to receive a letter from one whom you have never seen, although I feel as I were writing to

one whom I love very devotedly, and whom to know is to love . . .
Mr. Poe has been very solicitous that I should write to you [on
the occasion of our betrothal] and I do assure you it is with emotions of pleasure that I now do so. I am fully prepared to love
you, and I do sincerely hope that our spirits may be congenial.

There shall be nothing wanting on my part to make them so.

> Very sincerely yours,
> Mrs. A. Barrett Shelton
> (Miss Sarah Elmira Royster)

The widow and her poet had reached a rapid understanding. It
seemed finally that he would be delivered. As an impressionable and
ardent young man, he had gone off to Thomas Jefferson's university at
a time when their love had been very much in flower. It was his hard-
hearted stepfather, and her own wretched, overprotective parent, who
had kept his impassioned letters of youthful love from her. At the
time, neither could ever have known what these two sour, vindictive
individuals had conspired against them, and it was only now in fervent
conversation that they both came to realize fully what had happened
all those many years ago.

He had been greatly shocked upon returning home to find her
poised to marry another. Looking back, he reflected miserably, "Who
is to say this was not the beginning of the end for me? In truth I have
never recovered from this betrayal of the heart."

"Oh, Edgar," she breathed, and clasped his hand to her bosom.

Now, quite by serendipity, things looked bright for him again.
Almost with the renewed fervor of youth, he regained his stamina. He
was, after all, a man of certain fame. In Richmond he was welcome in
society and found himself looked upon favorably. The Widow Mrs.
Shelton took him to a fashionable haberdashery in downtown Richmond and bought for him a sparkling new white suit.

With the prospect of being married and living back in his once home city with no financial worries, once more feeling comfortable and whole, the poet could finally hope to achieve all that he had long sought.

"I know the winds have changed for our Eddie," Myra wrote in a second note to Mrs. Clemm. "I trust a kind of Providence will protect him now, and guide him in the way of truth, so that his feet will never again slip."

Holding each other's hands, she and Eddie whispered of him returning to Fordham to pack his belongings. She urged him to ask Muddie to come back to Richmond with him.

Their last meeting would be one marked extraordinarily by nature and the cosmos. They were standing in the portico of her home, at which point he paused and turned and lifted his hand to her in final adieu. At that very moment, as she looked upon his handsome countenance with much awe and love, a meteor appeared in the sky directly over his head before disappearing. It would be the final image she would hold of him.

ON THE WATERFRONT the following morning, he appeared at 4 a.m., visibly showing strain to his bearing and psyche. He boarded a steamer, poised to embark north for Baltimore and ultimately New York.

The trip to Gotham took forty-eight hours. Stops, one after the other, included Eppe Island, Windmill Point, Powhatan, Sandy Point, Hog Island, Day's Point, Old Point Comfort, Rappahanoc River, Smith's Point, Point Lookout, Patuxent River, Cove Point, Sharp's Island, Herring Bay, Annapolis, a second Sandy Point, and finally North Point, Baltimore.

On board there was a bar forward for the refreshment of gentlemen travelers. Poe took his cabin, installed his trunk in the hold, and before the first Sandy Point, remanded to this saloon.

He stood at the bar in his white suit facing the mirror behind the bartender. He failed to order when asked, however, merely staring off at his reflection in the silvered glass.

At Cove Point a group of five young toughs boarded the boat. They were rough, stringy men, ill dressed, who at first kept to themselves, and had an air of menace. One was a cripple, with a withered arm and leg. Another's name was overheard to be Pugsy. There was also Boffo and Ossian. They all wore soft caps. They split up and circled the deck, forward and aft.

When Poe was spotted in the barroom, the noticer, the cripple Tweeter Toohey, went limping after his fellows. They returned, three strong, Tweeter and Ossian left standing watch on deck.

One, dressed a thimblerig bully with velvet waistcoat, fancy neckerchief, gilt chains, soap-locked hair, and filigreed buttons, seemed familiar to Poe.

"From where do I know you?" he asked, the response being, with no hesitation, "The Tombs."

"And your name is?" even though he knew the answer.

"Tommy Coleman."

The poet half bowed. "I have the honor."

"You know me then, mate?" said Tommy Coleman.

There arose in Edgar Poe then, confused and paradoxically within his mind, the ideas of vast mental power, of caution, of penuriousness, of avarice, of coolness, of malice, of bloodthirstiness, of triumph, of merriment, of excessive terror, of intense, supreme despair. "Sir," he inquired of the youthful gang leader, "who among us has not, a hundred times, found himself committing a vile or silly action, for no other reason than because he knows he should not? Have we not, you and I, a perpetual inclination in the teeth of our best judgment to violate that which is Law, merely because we understand it to be such? This spirit of perverseness is the unfathomable longing of the spirit to vex itself, to offer violence to its own nature, to commit that deadly sin which would so jeopardize its own immortal soul."

The bartender eventually inquired did the gentlemen have intention of taking a drink or not?

Poe responded with a smile. "Even a failing heart demands a stimulant," looking upon Tommy pleasurably while calling for a mint rhum.

"White suits you," Tommy Coleman flattered while they awaited the spirits, surveying Poe's elegant new clothes with undisguised admiration; and Poe, for his part, Edgar Poe, staring again into the mirror, seeing his reflected image, joined with Tommy Coleman and his brethren, transfixed, mesmerized by himself, and by them who stood surrounding him, before responding:

"Yes. Yes, it does."

❧ 71 ❧

And the Fever Called Living
Is Conquered at Last

Correspondence of the *Baltimore Sun.*

BY LAST EVENING'S MAIL

DEATH OF EDGAR A. POE

We regret to learn that Edgar A. Poe, Esq., the distinguished American poet, scholar, and critic, died in this city yesterday morning, after an illness of four or five days. This announcement, coming so sudden and unexpected, will cause poignant regret among all who admire genius, and have sympathy for the frailties too often attending it. He was in the 38th of his age.

The obituary notice occupied first page in Bennett's *Herald*, first page of every paper in the city.

The high constable remained immobile on his recliner without speaking. Olga stood over him, clasping the newspaper to her bosom.

Her cheeks were stained. She had already been weeping when she entered the parlor.

She apologized. "I am so frustrated and begrieved, Papa," she said.

"As am I," taking her hand, finding it warm, dry, and firm.

Later, while drinking strong black tea and speaking of Poe dead, what must have befallen him, they are disturbed by the heavy clap of the brass door knocker at the parlor floor landing. It was Annie Lynch come calling, her eyes red, her cheeks, too, streaked by tears. She and Olga hugged in commiseration.

"Olga, I beg of you, come with me to pay a condolence call at the cottage of Mrs. Clemm. I cannot find it in myself to go alone."

Olga glanced to her father, who nodded his slow concord. "All right," she said to Annie.

Within minutes Olga was kissing and hugging her father goodbye. She inquired one last time if he was sure he would not like to accompany them to Fordham Village.

He replied he was sure, and they were gone.

Left alone, the high constable retired to the parlor. As he lowered himself back into the recliner, his thoughts returned to Poe, departed this firmament.

"Not *altogether* a fool," he conjured this man's prescience from "The Purloined Letter," "but then he's a poet, which I take to be only one remove from a fool."

The high constable's mind deferred. He dozed off into a fitful sleep, waking abruptly to a hard knock at the door.

A package messenger, a small man with a large red nose, stood shivering on Hays' stoop, awaiting the door to be answered. He turned over a parcel, damp from the drizzle that must have recently started, and departed.

What is this?

Back in the comfort of his parlor, Hays pulled away the soggy paper, finding inside John Colt's bound manuscript. A note beneath, signed "Poe," also included:

Richmond, Virginia
27 September 1849

My Dearest Sir:

I can only hope this note finds you well as I am well. Better. Best. I enclose herein the curiosity we both had occasion to scrutinize in the cottage by the river at Turtle Bay. To say these poems have caused me consternation is to understate my frame of mind. Perhaps there is something unseen hidden herein. Do you think? Even as I write this brief word of warning while waiting for the steam ferry to Baltimore and ultimately your (not mine) beloved Gotham, I feel the hard black eyes of carrion crow, the blackest bird, on my back. I ask you, what has led me here, sir? What—do I dare ask—might lead me away?

The manuscript book is as it was: fourteen poems, all in the pained and studied hand of the calligrapher.

The first:

Ligeia, there a body lies.
Go, the miserable deed done, but one ugly fear
Storms over me now, to touch this thing.
Look, nothing remains to struggle against me here,

Not in this lifeless heap.
How much more could I only wish it would spring

Full and grasp me, and strike at me, as I did it
But only a moment or two before?
I tried to lift the head, but it dropped, and slid
Fast from my grasp to its bed of gore.
What have you to do with this horrible thing?
Down—o'er grub a grave in the ground!
Grub dark with your nails! If you choose you may sing

That song so often sung. Don't start and look around!
Should I dig? How terribly slow you are!
Go and dig! The dawn in the East begins to grow!
Shan't you dig? The birds are all chirping. Bury there

So deep that body at once, and for God's sake just go!
O, all the world will be up in less than an hour,
Ram and rattle and ring along the clear road.
Strumpet, your fault. Dig for your life!
Deeper still, Dig for your deed!
Dig full speed, for what more can you do?

Cast it out upon the water? There
So close to shore. Where the tides rush and the shad tarry.
All there! Cast it out! Cast it out! Cast it out!
Zante, fairest of all flowers. Cast it out. Nevermore.
              O Nevermore!

Hays is fast to see this poem, the poem once of John Colt and his victim Samuel Adams, has changed, undergone transmogrification. Whereas when twice before he had had opportunity to scrutinize the peculiar verse, both at the Tombs and later at Turtle Bay, the poem had seemed to him to have taken itself with the Samuel Adams atrocity.

Here he found it no longer about the printer per se. No, if he was not mistaken, the subject as presently perused had been intersticed with a recognizable, if not strictly factual, rather (he no critic) shabbily executed, self-involved ode to Mary Rogers.

Why? After study, nothing else in the manuscript appeared to have changed as far as he could tell, save this one verse.

The high constable pondered the whys and wherefores for a period of time, but unable to sit still longer, he gathered up the manuscript and left his home with definite destination in mind.

Traveling first east on Lispenard, he moved at his own pace two long blocks to Centre Street and then directly south to the Tombs.

At the`gates he was admitted to seek audience with that individual who had replaced him, the superintendent of police, Mr. George Matsell, whereupon he was ushered inside, past the all-too-familiar Bummers' Cell and through the main corridor.

The day was dark and the cages, each holding one, two, or three prisoners, were in shadow. Dim lights shine, bodies slink, faces remained obscured beneath greasy caps and dented, dirty hats.

Through an open grate affording him glimpse into a cell at the end of the corridor, Old Hays observes two familiar boys slumped side by side on a cot.

He hears his name whispered, "Old Hays," before being ushered into the presence of he whom he sought.

"Superintendent," Hays spoke.

"Mr. Hays."

"Mr. Matsell, I am here in regard to the tragedy of Edgar Poe. I wonder are you in receipt of any notice arrived from Baltimore which might shed light on the circumstances of his death?"

Police superintendent Matsell shook his head with a genuine sadness, said he was much disturbed by the news of such a man passing. He was a former bookseller and held Poe in a high light. He inquired of his predecessor if this inquiry was business or idle curiosity, the response being, "Business."

Matsell said he had indeed received a number of detailed cards from that city, all of which he had full opportunity to inspect with a deep and intent interest.

The steamer on which Mr. Poe had been a passenger, he said, docked on schedule at the Baltimore wharves a few minutes before noon on September 29. Mr. Poe's trunk was evidently removed from the hold at the time of docking, and he was observed leaving via the gangplank with several young men. Opinion seems to vary among observers who these young men may have been: sports, soaplocks, swig coves, jarkmen. If they were old acquaintances or new friends also was variously speculated. Poe was said to be wearing a white suit, and seemed somewhat unsteady on his feet. The shipboard barman, when questioned by officers, said Poe had been drinking, and seemed familiar with those with whom he drank.

Reliable supporting details were as such: on the day of Mr. Poe's descent from the gangplank, Baltimore City was in the throes of an election campaign for local members of Congress and representatives to the state legislature. Because there is, as of yet, no official registration of voters in that city, if a man can hold up his hand, he can take the oath and vote. Lawless street gangs are known to round up, sandbag, and mobilize scores of potential ballot casters, keeping these coves docile with drugs and whiskey at certain dives, saloons, and two-cent coffeehouses. Sites of operation of this kind are known in the Crab Cake City as coops. Having secured their quota of these wayward individuals, the rapscallions then repeatedly deliver their charges from these crypts with the intention to vote the inebriates time and time again on the behest of whichever political party willing to pay out the highest dole.

In all probability, Poe fell prey to such agenda.

"Perhaps the Bloody Eights, perhaps the Peelers, the Rip-Raps, the Pluckers, the Gumballs. All are named. The pick is yours, sir."

To keep him taciturn, Matsell surmised, blackguards such as these curs more than likely provided Poe with a paralyzing brew consisting of nothing less than a mixture of laudanum, lager, and brandy.

"For some hours after Mr. Poe left the coastline steamer, any verifiable trace of him ceased," continued Matsell, "before he seemed to reappear on High Street, spotted by a German washerwoman behind an old engine house, thereafter stumbling into a notorious coop called the Fourth Ward Club."

During the course of that day's vote, Matsell further stated, 140 voters were counted to be held captive there, Mr. Poe assumed among them.

Later in the afternoon a seriously disabled man who may have been Poe was seen at Cooth and Sergeant's Tavern on Lombard Street, two blocks from High. He was no longer in his white suit, but dressed in ill-fitting ragged pants with a rope belt and an ale-soaked cotton shirt and gray cloth jacket.

Not long after, an old friend and supporter of Mr. Poe's, Dr. James Snodgrass, received a note while at his dinner table in his home at number 103 High Street, signed by a print-setter who had recognized Poe.

In its entirety, the communication read:

Dear Sir, There is a gentleman, rather the worse for wear, at Ryan's Fourth Ward polls, who goes under the cognomen of Edgar A. Poe, and who appears in great distress, and he says he is acquainted with you, and I assure you he is in need of immediate assistance.

Upon receiving this alarm, Dr. Snodgrass immediately rushed to the polling location mentioned, only to be referred to another location, that of Gunner's Hall. Snodgrass gave testimony that he had not seen his old friend and associate for some time, had apparently read much in the newsprints of his deteriorating condition, and was therefore much concerned. Now, he said, he found the subject of his anxiety sitting on the floor, dressed in filthy clothes, with a decidedly stupid expression on his face.

Dr. Snodgrass related that Mr. Poe looked up at him without recognition. He said that he reminded Mr. Poe who he was, that he was a friend of long standing, to which Poe responded in a dull, somber voice, "If you are a true friend, the best thing you can do for me is put a pistol to my head and blow out my poor brains."

The dying man was transported forthwith to the facilities of the Washington Medical College. For four days he struggled in his hospital bed. At some point, as the shadow of death fell across him, he became restless and called out something unintelligible that might have been a name. The room reportedly rang with his call, and this same cry was said to echo down the hospital corridors hour after hour all that Saturday night. Whatever he was trying to say, however, remained unintelligible.

Then, before the dawn, on the morning of Sunday, October 7, 1849, at five o'clock a.m., Edgar Allan Poe rose one final time in his bed and cried out, this time distinctly, "God help my poor soul!" and that was the end of him.

Additionally, Matsell handed over to his predecessor a letter for his perusal:

To Any and All Interested Parties, Authorities, and To Whom Else It May Concern:

I am the medical doctor upon whose hands it fell to administer to Mr. Edgar Poe at the last. It was I who was with him in his dying hours. I proclaim for all to know that a slander is being committed upon this man. In many circles it is construed that Mr. Poe suffered and died under the influence of liquor, but nothing could be further from the fact. Upon his arrival at the hospital it is true Mr. Poe appeared in great physical and mental distress. I did momentarily consider that he might be suffering from *mania a potu*, delirium tremens, but upon examining the patient I discounted this diagnosis as quickly as it had come upon me. Although he had been drinking, now I could see plainly that what plagued this man was a brain fever of the most malignant and aggressive kind. Still, as a precaution I took time to inquire of the hackman who had brought the ailing Mr. Poe to our facility if he had by any chance knowledge of the patient's state. The hackman replied that his passenger had not been drunk, although there was the slight smell of liquor about Mr. Poe when he lifted him into his vehicle.

As the patient's last hour approached, I bent over him and asked if he had any word he wished communicated to his friends. The dying man raised his fading eyes, turned uneasily, and moaned, "Oh God, is there no ransom for the deathless spirit?" then turned silent. After a few moments, in a croaking voice, he continued. "He who rode the heavens and upholds the universe has His decrees written on the frontlet of every human being," he said.

Then followed guttural murmuring, growing fainter and fainter, then a tremor of the limbs, a final faint, sigh, and the spirit of Edgar Allan Poe had passed the boundary line that divides time from eternity.

Signed respectfully,

Dr. J. J. Moran

"J. J. Moran?" Hays repeated the name.

"Do you know him?" asked Matsell. The superintendent was fingering his eight-pointed copper star, his head cocked, his stern face accentuated by a growth of beard beneath the chin. He wore his police cap oddly askew. His uniform was poorly tailored, the leather belt cinched beneath his rib cage tight enough to impede what Hays saw as the comfortable inhalation and exhalation of breath.

"I do if it is the doctor J. J. Moran I have severally encountered. In the spring of 1834 the necessity came upon me to arrest a young medical student associated with the New York Hospital. In the years ensuing, this individual found his way into my custody on more than one occasion, each time for the same crime for which he was arrested the first: that of body snatching. The last occurrence he was found to have robbed the grave of a young woman, digging up her body for dissection and making a most indecent exposure of her corpse."

"And this is the same doctor who has conveniently had fortune to administer to the dying Poe and attest to it?" said Matsell.

"So it seems. Curious."

"And what, High Constable, do you make of the disparity in accounts? That one version states Poe's last words as 'God help my poor soul,' while the other claims, 'Is there no ransom for the deathless spirit?'"

"I cannot say," said Hays.

"And the fact that Dr. Moran claims that it was not alcohol poisoning as causation of death, but brain fever?"

"Some time ago, through undue experience," Hays said to Matsell, "I have learned to distrust the testimony of individuals, even medical practitioners, already proven to me to be compromised. Experience and common sense dictates in no way can I take to heart anything stated by Dr. Moran."

Hays gestured his head in the direction of the first-tier cells. "Those two apaches you detain back there. I require a word with them."

Matsell craned his thin neck, ensconced in tight collar, in the direction indicated by Hays. "Of whom do you speak, sir?"

"The two boyos in the last holding tank. Do you know who they are, Superintendent?"

"I do. Two worthless and profligate characters up on the steamer from Baltimore. Run with a gang of pap-nap-nickies known in that city as the Bloody Tubs, they. My officers spotted a whole passel of them at the time the cards came to the South Street dock. My men gave chase, but these are the only two caught. What, might I ask, do you want with them?"

"If I am not mistaken, they are Oscar and Ossian Kallenbarack, sons of Frederika Loss from Nick Moore's roadhouse in Hoboken. I am intrigued they have found their way here. I haven't seen them since they were boys, the night of their mother's death. It was Ossian who shot her. I find it curious that they should find their way here, running with a Baltimore gang of billywidgeons."

Mr. Trencher, the insipid keeper, still on the job over the span of these years, keyed the lock, happy to be of assistance once more to his old protector, the high constable.

When Hays stepped into the cell, his constable's staff held with two strong hands, he said nothing, merely staring, giving the two Kallenbarack youths the once-over, waiting.

"Do you boys know who I am?" he finally asked.

They knew. Old Hays.

Fidgeting, they eyed the high constable's ash peddler's pony.

"Do you know why I might be here?"

They denied that they did.

"Good citizens tell the truth, Oscar and Ossian Kallenbarack," he warned, slamming his staff on the stone slab floor for good effect. "I knew your mother. But I have not seen you boyos for several years. Now which of you is which?"

OLGA DID NOT RETURN home from Fordham Village until late in the afternoon of the following day. By that time the weather, profligate on the island of Manhattan, was in the process of abrupt change. Any trace of the warmth of Indian summer had fled the streets of the lower island as a cold, dismembering gale tore down the long avenues from the north.

Hays heard the familiar sound of the kitchen door opening and closing. His daughter, drained of color, stormed into the parlor in a rush, chilled and much disturbed.

"The coward!" she cried. "The poltroon!"

She stood in front of the fire, her back to the blaze, her body trembling, not necessarily from cold.

"Of whom do you speak, Olga?"

"Whosoever signs his name 'Ludwig,'" she snarled. "Have you seen this, Papa?"

She tore the *New York Herald* from her travel bag and waved it angrily in the air. "I picked it up before I boarded the railroad, and have had to live with the lies and hocum ever since."

On the front page was a defamatory obituary, signed with an obvious pseudonym. "Edgar Allan Poe is dead," this nom de plumed individual began. "He died in Baltimore the day before yesterday."

The announcement will startle many, but few will be grieved by it. He walked the streets, in madness or melancholy, with lips moving in indistinct curses, or with eyes upturned in passionate prayers for the happiness of those who at that moment were objects of his idolatry, but never for himself, for he felt, or professed to feel, that he was already damned. He seemed, except when some fitful pursuit subjected his will and engrossed his faculties, always to bear the memory of some controlling sorrow.

"Do you know who I think this Ludwig-skycer is?" Olga continued to spew with acid vehemence. "I'll tell you exactly who it is, Papa. The reek of it, the smell. It is none other than Mr. James Gordon Bennett, that is who it is. He has put the Reverend Rufus Wilmot Griswold up to the task. I would bet my life on it. Papa, Muddie told Annie and me Bennett had already been to Fordham before we arrived, seeking from Muddie exclusive exercise over Edgar's literary estate."

"To what end?" Hays asked. He was paying attention.

"He wants revenge. He blames Edgar. He thinks he has forever defamed and destroyed the good name of Fanny Osgood."

"And the Reverend Griswold? Why would he partake?"

"Jealousy, pure and simple. He means to destroy Edgar's literary reputation. He is jealous, jealous, jealous! It is nothing new. He has always been. Muddie informed me Bennett possesses papers alleging Griswold Edgar's literary executor with power of attorney. She is distraught from his visit because that unconscionable, unctuous being had the audacity to make strong, scathing attempt to bully her, and now I see her right. The two are set to destroy the lifework and literary reputation of he whom she loved so deeply and they detested equally deeply."

"Olga, I fear I have more disturbing news than literary slight and besmirchment. I have been to the Tombs yesterday, and early this morning I have had a most interesting journey by skiff to the hospital at the southern end of Blackwell's Island."

She was confused. "To what effect, Papa?" she asked.

"After you left with Annie the other day to go to Fordham, I received a package sent to me by Edgar. In the package was a manuscript of poetry and a curious note."

"What kind of note?"

"Before his death, Mr. Poe professed to being followed."

Olga veritably leaped at her father. "Followed?" she cried. "Mrs. Clemm received similar note. She thought it Eddie's paranoia. What of the manuscript?"

"That of John Colt. Poe's note to me made reference to some message hidden therein."

"Where is the manuscript?" Olga clamored, coming closer. "Is anything in evidence?"

He indicated where said manuscript occupied a place on a table by the arm of his chair.

"I have been through it any number of times. I noted something inordinate almost immediately. After his escape, if you remember, I visited Colt's cell, and there, beneath a black silk handkerchief, found a poem written in regard to the murder of Samuel Adams. The same poem I again observed in the manuscript Poe received while living at Turtle Bay. In this manuscript sent to me, however, the poem included has undergone some kind of transformation. It has been altered."

"Altered? How so?"

"It is a bastardization. The initial effort concerned itself ostensibly with the death of Samuel Adams, yet here, in this doctored manuscript, this very similar poem is embellished with curious reference to the death of a woman who might be taken for Mary Rogers. My eye is not trained to the art of the scratcher, but I thought my observation keen enough to detect alteration by a hand not the hand of the original writer."

"But why, Papa? And by whom?"

"It is why I found myself at the Blackwell's Island hospital. James Holdgate, the forger, is held there in poor state, not likely to endure, suffering from a debilitative ailment of the alimentary canal. I asked him amidst his suffering if he might not have a look at the Colt manuscript. Between yelps and howls, he said that he would not object, and although giving continuous sign of pronounced discomfort, proceeded to examine the poems and paper they were written on. He said without doubt the poem in question has not been written by the same person, nor is it on the same paper as the rest."

"Meaning you are kerrect, Papa, in assuming it has been altered by Edgar."

"This is my assumption, and it has been concurred by Holdgate when I showed him samples of Poe's handwriting which I had seen to bring with me."

"But we must assess for what reason would Edgar Poe change these rhymes?"

"In his note to me he alluded to some kind of cryptic. When I visited the Poes at Turtle Bay, Edgar was not in the cottage at first. Instead I encountered Virginia. She showed me a verse she had concocted for her husband on the occasion of Valentine's Day. Within its lines, as a kind of tribute, she disguised his name in the first letters of each phrase reading down the page. I checked the one poem in question, however, and then each and every other poem of Mr. Colt's, yet could make no sense of such system."

Olga now had the manuscript in her clutches, having grabbed it literally out of the hands of her father.

"Three years ago at Annie Lynch's salon," she said excitedly, already bent over, scrutinizing the verses, "I am sure it was on Valentine's Day as well, Edgar read a poem he called 'To Her Whose Name Is Written Below.' At first glance no name was decipherable, but I later learned the secret. If one were to designate the first letter of the first line, the second letter of the second, and so on, down the twenty lines of the poem, one was able to spell out the camouflaged name, 'Frances Sargent Osgood.' Virginia must have taken a model not unlike that as her inspiration. I have no doubt Eddie Poe is sending us a message from the beyond. It is only up to us to discern it."

"Take notice of the verse that begins, 'Ligeia, there a body lies.'"

It took no more than a few seconds before she blurted, "See here, Papa! Right here, this coded acronym! The first four lines spell out the word 'LOOK'!" Her excitement, however, immediately cooled. Her expression turned glum. "But after that, as far as I can make out, nothing," she said.

Hays moved closer to his daughter, adjusting his irksome spectacles on his face so that he might see and study as well.

"It does not follow," she lamented. "After the initial 'LOOK' it is all gibberish and gobbledygook nonsense."

Together they continued to further scan the poem.

"Olga, instead of following the bias down the page," Old Hays suddenly declared, "after that first discernible word, permit us to start again at the beginning of the next line. Do you not see the second word now? It spells: 'NO. LOOK NO.' Then back to the start again: 'FURTHER'!"

"Then 'SAMUEL'! Yes, I do see!" she exclaimed.

Ligeia, there a body lies.
*G**O**, the miserable deed done, but one ugly fear*
*St**O**rms over me now, to touch this thing.*
*Loo**K**, nothing remains to struggle against me here,*

*N**o**t in this lifeless heap.*
*H**O**w much more could I only wish it would spring*

*F**u**ll and grasp me, and strike at me, as I did it*
*B**U**t only a moment or two before?*
*I t**R**ied to lift the head, but it dropped, and slid*
*Fas**T** from my grasp to its bed of gore.*
*What **H**ave you to do with this horrible thing?*
*Down—o'**E**r grub a grave in the ground!*
*Grub da**R**k with your nails! If you choose you may sing*

That song so often sung. Don't start and look around!
*S**H**ould I dig? How terribly slow you are!*

Go And dig! The dawn in the East begins to grow!
ShaN't you dig? The birds are all chirping. Bury there

So deep that body at once, and for God's sake just go!
O, All the world will be up in less than an hour,
RaM and rattle and ring along the clear road.
StrUmpet, your fault. Dig for your life!
DeepEr still, Dig for your deed!
Dig fuLl speed, for what more can you do?

Cast it out upon the water? There
SO close to shore. Where the tides rush and the shad tarry.
AlL there! Cast it out! Cast it out! Cast it out!
ZanTe, fairest of all flowers. Cast it out. Nevermore.
        O Nevermore!

"But what does it mean, Papa? 'LOOK NO FURTHER THAN SAMUEL COLT'?"

"I cannot say, Olga. Perhaps that question need be asked of that individual mentioned by name, the Colonel, Mr. Samuel Colt himself."

THE NEXT MORNING, Old Hays found himself before dawn, lying abed, unable to sleep, composing in his mind a concise note to be expressed to Colonel Colt, eliciting his presence.

Finally he rose, and by candlelight carefully worded his request for an audience with this gentleman. He had decided not to specify why he needed to see him, but sent the message to Hartford by courier, explaining that the Colonel's presence was required urgently on a matter affecting his family and the constabulary. He excused himself in the letter, writing, because the trip to Connecticut remained long for a man of his age, in deference, might Colonel Colt make time for

Mr. Jacob Hays, at his convenience, but sooner than later, even at once, here in the city.

Word came back the next afternoon to Hays by return courier. "Assuredly," Colonel Colt would gladly come to New York to meet with the high constable. They could rendezvous at an arranged hour within a few days at the Astor House on Broadway at Chambers or anywhere of Mr. Hays' choosing.

On the day indicated, thirty minutes before the appointed hour, Balboa awaited Old Hays outside his front door on Lispenard Street to take him to the settee. On their way down Broadway, Hays reached for his meerschaum pipe, a gift from Olga, but found his stash of tobacco sadly near empty. As they were coming to the intersection where Anderson's tobacco shop is so situated, Old Hays called up to Balboa to come to rest.

He gingerly alit on the west side of that avenue, waiting some minutes for the vying streams of traffic to subsist long enough for him to ford the broad width. The statue of the knighted Raleigh stood watch outside, as always, and Hays found himself reaching out to lay hands on this gentleman's hard varnished skin.

Inside, the familiar aroma of tobacco met Hays. Behind the counter at his usual post stood Anderson. In front of him a gentleman, half bent, peered through the glass of the display case. The man rose.

"Halleck."

"High Constable."

"Good to see you."

"Good to see you, sir."

"Has something befallen you, Halleck? You appear drawn. Are you troubled?"

"You remain as perceptive as your reputation suggests, sir. It is a difficult day indeed, High Constable. Have you not heard? My employer has passed on to a better place."

"John Jacob Astor dead?"

"Yes, only this morning."

"My condolences, but it could not have been sudden. I had heard that he was ill. What has befallen him?"

Halleck smiled slightly. "Nothing untoward. The cause of death was natural. He had a good life. He lived longer than most. Still . . ."

"Surely, sir," said Hays, "I need not remind you, none of us exits this life alive. We must all be thankful for what we are given."

"Eternal life holds no temptation for you, Mr. Hays? To some, living forever holds unquestionable appeal."

"So many are the aches and pains that befall us with the march of time, so much the fatigue, I cannot, even for a minute, imagine the agony after one hundred fifty or two hundred years."

Halleck laughed, relieved. "How right you are, Mr. Hays. On his deathbed, I did inquire of Mr. Astor if there was anything in the course of his life which he might have lived to regret, expecting him to answer if only I had been more honorable in my business practices, or more considerate to my son and heir, something to that effect. But no. Do you know how he responded, High Constable? He said, and this was very nearly his last gasp: 'My only regret, my dear Halleck,' he veritably wheezed, I swear to you, 'is that I did not put all of my money into New York City real estate.'" Halleck shook his head with the audacity of it. "Can you believe it, Mr. Hays?" he said, wiping tears from his eyes. "That was this gentleman to the last."

They spoke briefly of Poe, his passing. "Sad. So sad," Halleck said. "A man of such vivid intelligence and talent."

Hays chose two socks. One a Cuban cut, another a blond full-leaf Carolina. As Anderson wrapped his purchase, the shopkeeper seemed to Hays to be peering at him in a most peculiar manner, eventually answering to Hays' inquiry that he had something "tantamount" to relate. He then proceeded to confide he had been paid clandestine visit by the ghost of Mary Rogers. The apparition, Anderson said, promising to reveal the identity of her murderer to him at a later date.

Hays said, "When the presence returns, please, sir, send immediate word to me," upon which he most quickly departed.

AT THE ASTOR HOUSE, within the confines of a private drawing room
decorated with plush red velvet and black kid leather, Colonel Colt
awaited Old Hays on a brocaded divan, situated beneath a gas sconce.

"Sir, how are you?" Colonel Colt leaped to his feet.

"I am fine, Colonel, but I just encountered that gentleman Fitz-
Greene Halleck, who shared with me some unsettling news. John
Jacob Astor is dead. Died this morning."

"Astor dead!" Colt snorted. "First Poe, now this. Well, I must say
it's about time. For how many years now have I heard that Astor was
only able to take his daily sustenance from a woman's full breast?
Mother's milk straight from the glimmer mort, all him capable of
imbibing. Ah well, not to denigrate the poor fellow and his proclivi-
ties, but who would deny, not such a bad way to go either! I must say,
Hays, all my life my temperament has been sanguine, ardent, enthusi-
astic, even rash, and for all that time I have prided myself always as a
devoted admirer of women. That being so, I must say, if it was my
decision to make, I would exit this earth just the same as old John
Jacob, plenty of money in my craw and my greedy mouth to the nip-
ple. What say you, Mr. Hays? No discernible torture there?"

"Mr. Colt—"

"Forgive me, High Constable. Before we get down to your concerns, whatever they could be, I have something especially for you that
I have had manufactured with you in mind and insist on giving.
There'll be no point in refusing this time. There is no one else to possess them, and I insist."

He heaved himself from his chair. A cherrywood case with a blue
silk lining containing a new brace of Walker repeating revolvers rested
on the sideboard. The cylinder of each gun had been scrupulously
engraved with the figure of a police constable, not unlike Hays himself, bowler hat on his head, constabulary staff in one hand, pistol in
the other, caught in the act of shooting three street ruffians in soft
caps, brandishing knives and truncheons.

"I cannot take these," Hays said.

"And why not? You don't relish them? Look at the detail, man. Even the star on the constable's chest is eight-pointed."

"The guns are things of beauty, but I have no use for them."

"You might surprise yourself, High Constable. Have mercy! What am I going to do with them if you don't take them? I beg you, it will give me pleasure if you will have them, even if only to look at and admire."

Hays took the box, holding it stiffly on his lap. "Then let's be on with it, because after our conversation I do not know your estimate will remain," he said. "I am here to inform you, Good Citizen Colt, that I have received from the late Edgar Allan Poe a package, sent to me before his death."

"And in this package?"

"A manuscript of poems reportedly written by your brother John."

"I see. I have heard nothing of this artifact."

"Be that as it may, with these pages, undoubtedly your brother's, Poe sent a note. The note said I would find something hidden within the text, camouflaged by the words. After carefully scrutinizing the verses, I did discover something."

Colt had not sat back down, but remained on his feet. He stood straight over Hays, an ominous presence, his attention unwavering.

"And what was that?" he asked.

"A ciphered message."

"Ciphered message? To what effect?"

"Once decoded it read: 'LOOK NO FURTHER THAN SAMUEL COLT.'"

Colt's brow furrowed. "What can that mean?" he asked.

"I do not know. I was hoping you would tell me. Why would Poe secret a message such as this with said implication?"

"I cannot say. I find it all highly doubtful. Poe and my brother had a complicated association."

"It is my understanding Edgar Poe made a recent trip to your manufacturing plant in Hartford, Connecticut, sir."

"Yes, he did."

"If you don't mind telling me, what was the purpose of that visit?"

"He wanted money. He said he was in pursuit of a recently divorced woman and her family had balked at the prospect of having him for a son-in-law. I can't say that I blame them. It was one of those instances where Poe asks: 'Will you marry me? If you cannot, will you lend me five dollars?'" Colt chuckled at the wit of it. "You must admit, High Constable, it is all too true."

"After he left you, he informed his aunt he felt himself being followed."

Colt's expression changed, grew more somber. Hays thought he glimpsed something he recognized, heretofore hidden deep within. "I cannot say," Colonel Colt was saying. "I know nothing about such circumstance. There are some rough characters in and around Hartford, but Poe did not present himself as a man of wealth. I gave him a few hundred dollars, but I doubt he was brandishing it around. Did some dip steal it from him?"

"No, not that."

"Then what?"

"Do not trifle with me, sir. I warn you, I shall have the truth from you. You were the one married to Caroline Henshaw, were you not? I have spoken with your family friend, the songwriter John Howard Payne, and taken time to scrutinize certain papers at the Hall of Records. The baby, carried and subsequently delivered by Miss Henshaw, was not your brother's, but your own. Is this not so? The child was christened Samuel Colt Jr., not John Colt Jr., after all. Do not deny it!"

"If it is true, I do not now, and have never denied it."

"Why did your brother not say something at his trial by way of explanation? Surely he would have received a sentence other than death if the public saw him in a different light. As it was, they saw him a cad for impregnating Miss Henshaw and not having the common decency to marry her."

"It was his choice, not mine." Hays caught a look of subtle panic pass in Colt's eyes. "What does it matter, sir?" he continued. "He said always that he loved her. He did it for himself. He did not do it for me. There was never intention of allowing my brother to face execution. The family was prepared to do whatever was necessary."

"Meaning it was you, sir, who got to my man McArdel and the Tombs' keepers. I am only surprised that you did not come after me with your bribe money, Colonel. But then you did not have to. You knew me too well. You knew the prospect of remanding James Holdgate to custody would suffice. He faced a life sentence. I spoke with this criminal only yesterday. He said you offered him enough money, and the assurance your influence would change the law. Which, in fact, it did. He was released after less than two years, although he is remanded now to the alms hospital on Blackwell's Island with another death sentence. This one he will not escape.

"Your brother was present at the death of Mary Rogers, was he not, sir? Admit it! Your careless sibling carried on an affair with that young woman, which resulted in her pregnancy, and then arranged through Mrs. Loss a young doctor to perform a premature delivery. The doctor botched his work and her death was the horrid result. I am aware now of who that doctor is and where he is, and I shall have a word with him, you can rest on that. Not only did your brother lose his love, Mr. Colt, but his agitation in so doing also led to the needless death of Samuel Adams, and the ruin of his own life. It was because of these circumstances, was it not, he thought no sacrifice too grim?"

Colt said nothing.

"Where is your brother, Colonel? Is he here in New York? Is he in Baltimore? Has he not arranged the murder of yet another, his ostensible friend Edgar Allan Poe?"

"What would you like me to say, High Constable? That I am shocked? My brother is dead."

"Stop! We both know he is not. Good citizens will tell the truth! Answer me, Citizen Colt, why would Edgar Poe ensconce your name in such poem, a verse that so closely mimics the crime against Mary Rogers, a message saying 'LOOK NO FURTHER THAN SAMUEL COLT'?"

"I cannot say."

"Come now, sir. Cannot or will not?"

"Perhaps it is as you say, Mr. Hays. The late Mr. Poe implicates me not for me to point my finger back at my brother, but because he himself is guilty."

"I would hate to learn it was not your brother but you, Colonel Colt, who felt compelled to hire a gang of cutthroats to inebriate Edgar Poe and in so doing poison him with spirits and send him on to his untimely death because he somehow threatened your brother's whereabouts."

"Mr. Poe needed no cutthroats to entice him to death's door, High Constable. We both know with full certainty Mr. Poe, God rest his soul, needed only himself."

HE COULD NOT HAVE BEEN any more fatigued than he was when he returned home that evening. The house was cold and empty. He was thoroughly cautioned, and for an instant remained undecided what to do. To the substances of terror Old Hays was sufficiently alive, but of its shadow he had no apprehension. He reminded himself the word "shadow," the sobriquet with which he had been known and so long associated, was but another word for ghost. He who in his heyday patrolled the city afoot by day and by night slumped in the recliner chair that was once the sole property of the murderer John Colt. Purposefully, he searched out on his chair-side table a copy of one of Olga's many subscription numbers, *Sartain's Union Magazine*. Quickly thumbing through the pages, he found the poem of Poe's he sought, his last, entitled "The Bells," the very rhyme he had penned so painfully with Olga that sunny afternoon not so long ago in the back garden:

> *The Bells!—hear the bells!*
> *Leaping higher, higher, higher*

Ah, the melancholy menace of their tone!
How they clang and clash and roar,
What a horror they outpour!
What a tale of terror their turbulency tells!

His eyes may have grown heavy. So heavy they closed. In any event, some hours later, through his trancelike slumber, he hears Olga enter.

She had been up again in Fordham. Upon entering the parlor, she glared venomously at the two Colt revolvers in their case on the sideboard, the blue steel oiled and shimmering, sitting atop John Colt's manuscript. She bespeaks venomously:

"These are—"

"A gift from Colonel Colt."

"I see." She picked up one, felt its enormous heft. Picked up the other. Did the same. "The Colonel must hold you in great esteem, Mr. Hays. Is this your likeness, sir?"

"By his account it is."

"Very nice, Papa. I am so happy for you to be immortalized thusly with such frill and elegance on such a canvas."

"Olga, your sarcasm is unwarranted. Frederika Loss's sons Oscar and Ossian are being held in the Tombs. Superintendent of police Matsell picked them up on unrelated charges on the wharves. They had just arrived from Baltimore."

"What has that to do with anything?"

"Much disturbing has come together in your absence. I took opportunity to have two conversations with the Kallenbarack boys, one before speaking with Colonel Colt and one after. I thought of using logic on them, as you have so often urged, but my patience wore thin and my crude instincts took over, telling me to clock each on the big toe with my staff, and I would get the answers I sought quicker and with less mental anguish."

She could not help herself and half smiled. "And did it work, Papa?"

"It did."

Olga studied her father. "How so?" she asked under steady gaze.

"Police superintendent Matsell received a letter from Baltimore from a doctor who claims to have administered to Edgar Poe during his final hours. I knew this particular physician, you see, many years ago here in New York. He was a young man then much caught up in the art of body snatching, particularly the bodies of young women. I had my suspicions, and asked the Kallenbarack brothers if this gentleman might have been the young doctor so oft mentioned in the course of my investigation who performed the premature delivery on Mary Rogers at their mother's inn."

"What did they say?"

"They said yes."

"Papa!"

"I asked under what circumstance, and they were forthcoming."

"They were? How so?"

"Upon my second visit, I persisted. I thought it John Colt, Olga, who employed the abortionist."

"John Colt?"

"I was wrong."

"Oh? Who was it then? I refuse to believe it was Edgar Poe."

"It was Samuel Colt, Olga, not John. Samuel Colt is the homicide."

"Papa!"

"He will get his, I promise you. The good citizens of this city will stand for nothing less than his public execution. Caroline Henshaw might have been packed off to Europe. It is no secret she is using the name Julia Leicester. Colonel Colt says she is in Germany, with the child, but I think her in France. He claims she has remarried in Europe, but perhaps we can induce her to return to testify against him in front of the oyer and terminer."

"Was everything staged?"

"John Colt certainly killed Samuel Adams. In response, I fear, to the emotional toll taken up by his knowledge of what had happened to Mary Rogers; the realization of callous indifference manifested by his brother. As John Colt himself admitted to me during his initial confession, a large part of the inspiration for his crime against the printer came from that fragile state in which he found himself. That he made argument that such instability came from insult to his skills and credibility as a wordsmith by Mr. Adams, I accepted at the time, but now know as fabrication or, at the least, embellishment. In actuality, with unremitting certainty, John Colt's difficulties emanated directly from that certain knowledge his own brother was at center to the death of Mary Rogers. What followed, all that transpired in court and in the Tombs and after, was by craft and design of Samuel Colt's device. The marriage between John and Caroline Henshaw, a sham. John's suicide, the same. The fire, the escape, the grave robbing, all mere device choreographed by the marionetteer to cover his tracks. I now know from family friend and confidant, the actor and composer John Howard Payne, it was Samuel Colt who, on a European expedition for his Paterson Manufacturing Company, made the acquaintance of Caroline Henshaw initially in Germany when she was just a girl, became infatuated, married her, and brought her back to New York, but never acknowledged the marriage publicly, quickly coming to believe her beneath him societally, and a deficit to his ambition. She was with child, his child, when he cast her out, and that very well may have been part of it."

"Yet his brother took up with her?"

"John Colt took it as his filial duty. Perhaps he loved Miss Henshaw. I think, perhaps, the indignation he suffered beneath his brother's thumb made him susceptible to another treated similarly by such tyrant. Alas, we might never know. John Colt is in either Texas or California. We most assuredly shall never see him again in this lifetime. Samuel Colt was introduced to Anderson's segar emporium by his brother. Quickly he became one of those enamored gentlemen who frequented that establishment all too often. He had fallen in love with Mary Rogers and pursued her with urgency, even though, at the time, she was secret companion and paramour to Edgar Poe. All was clandestine, but in short order Mary had been separated from Mr. Poe with promise from Colonel Colt of marriage to him, and, too, like

Caroline Henshaw before her, she found herself with child. Samuel could ill afford to make the same mistake twice. Without her knowledge he arranged a premature delivery at Nick Moore's Inn, enticing her there with the promise of marriage."

"She thought she was going to be married?"

"She did. It was what she had been told. According to Ossian Kallenbarack and his brother, instead Dr. Moran was brought in upon the recommendation of Mrs. Loss, who knew this physician from similar procedures on her premises. Upon learning of the nature of this betrayal, Mary Rogers was seized by an hysteria. She fought her assailants futilely, resulting in the many bruises later to be discovered on her body. Instead of the bridal veil, the unfortunate girl was drugged by ether."

Olga visibly cringed.

"She was not blessed by good fortune, and did not survive the invasive procedure to end her pregnancy," Hays continued. "Samuel Colt, trying to disguise the circumstances of her death, removed her body from the inn in the dead of night with the aid of Mrs. Loss's sons. She was trussed and thrown in the river with the hope the body would not be found, but, of course, it was."

"My God, Papa, can it be true?"

"That's not the all of it, Olga. Not only is Samuel Colt the murderer of this innocent girl, but I fear he has arranged for the murder of Edgar Poe as well."

"What? How? How can you say this? Do you feel your footing firm for such accusation?"

"Unfortunately, I do."

"But why Edgar? Why in the world would Samuel Colt find necessity in killing him? He had finally found everything that he ever wanted. He had literary fame, he would have money, he was reunited with his childhood love."

"Too late. His fate was already settled when he went to Samuel Colt with John's book of poetry, looking for funds to mollify Muddie and wrest Fanny Osgood from her husband."

"Papa, I am concerned. Worried. Have you confronted this man? This monster?"

"I have had my conversation earlier in the week, when he handed me the prize of his pistols. But I have only just come upon the consequence and solution of these offenses. I shall require solid proof, not mere speculation. Need I remind you, Olga, sadly, neither you nor I reside on the Rue Morgue, and I am no chevalier."

"Enough! I can bear no more. Papa. Was it wise to confront Samuel Colt so?" All color had left Olga's face. "There is need for me to prepare your dinner," she said, her voice toneless. She stumbled for the kitchen.

Hays called his protestation, said he was not hungry, but his daughter, through a veil of tears, insisted he needed his sustenance, must eat to protect his health. She rummaged through the victuals available in the larder.

"Papa," she spoke through cracked voice, "I am running out to the greengrocer's. I shall be right back."

She poured him a brandy before she left. Had a short one herself. "You need to keep up your strength," she said to her father, placing the brandy, it was Armagnac, what would be the last for each, on the low table atop the now few days' old copy of the reprehensible Bennett's *Herald* with the obituary signed "Ludwig."

Once she was gone he took up the glass, grateful for the sharp bite of the spirits. He glanced down at the print the last line of the Reverend Griswold's foul testimony magnified improbably through the facets of the cut-glass crystal:

After life's fitful fever, he sleeps well.

He heard the kitchen door open and close as Olga departed the house for the street. She turned left on Lispenard and made her way on the board sidewalk.

At the corner, and down the block three storefronts, there was an active greengrocery, next door to a busy haberdasher with birds, English finches, in the window that chirped incessantly, "Cheep! Cheep! Cheep!"

Olga had the thought to buy a bird, a tough rooster displayed plucked yellow and hanging by its feet in the greengrocer window, some equally yellow Long Island potatoes, an onion, orange carrots, and green celery in order to make a soup nourishing for her father.

As she entered onto the crush and ceaseless rumbling of the Broadway, five young coves, strutting abreast, crowded her off the sidewalk. Tight-faced and rough, they take no notice of her, stepping hard left onto Lispenard as she continued right, down Broadway.

One of these rowdies sports a sparkling white suit, very natty, if somewhat soiled in two or three spots at the knees and elbows and along the collar line. The second imp is debilitated by a painful-looking limp, his leg cruelly withered and dragging, his foot turned out. The third spits on the sidewalk, the sputum plentiful, blossoming brown through the gap of four missing teeth. The fourth boasts arms that dangle, fists as big as hams. The fifth is lean and sinewy, a dapple of down, in lieu of real beard, disguising his weak chin. This one would put you in mind of his late mother, Mrs. Loss, if you had known her during her lifetime. All wear battered and grimy soft caps.

Olga Hays could not have known their mission—Tommy Coleman, Tweeter Toohey, Pugsy O'Pugh, Boffo the Skinned Knuckle, Charlie Kallenbarack—although as they pass she steals one furtive glance at them, and they at her, before quickly looking away and continuing to the grocer.

COLT'S LEATHER reclining chair is supple, the angle set right. In the parlor, in front of Old Hays, the phantom warmth of grayed embers and charred black remnants of a fire, hours dead, affords him nothing. A chill seizes him, he who with pride was the city's first detective, what was known in his time as shadow, what was known as shade.

A magazine title, *Sartain's*, featuring the poetry of the late Edgar Allan Poe, lies open at his elbow.

Of the bells, bells, bells, bells—
To the moaning and the groaning of the bells.

The dead poet's final words published, his last sad song.

And the people—ah, the people—
They that dwell up in the steeple
    All alone
Too horrified to speak
They can only shriek, shriek, shriek,
        To the rolling of the bells
        To the tolling of the bells
Keeping time, time, time,

He begins to recline in the patent chair as he hears the threshold door open from outside into the kitchen and softly close.

The bells. The bells.

From the bells.

Old Hays, Jacob Hays, high constable of the great metropolis, the city of New York, reaches for the matched Colt revolvers sepulchred on the sideboard, his steadfast image etched on the oiled blue steel of each cylinder, knowing full well his daughter, his Olga, his Mary Olga, could not be returned home so soon.

Forever the bells.

Afterword

ELDORADO

Gaily bedight,
A gallant knight,
In sunshine and in shadow,
Had journeyed long,
Singing a song,
In search of Eldorado.

But he grew old—
This knight so bold—
And o'er his heart a shadow
Fell as he found
No spot of ground
That looked like Eldorado

And, as his strength
Failed him at length,
He met a pilgrim shadow—
"Shadow," said he,
"Where can it be—
This land of Eldorado?"

"Over the Mountains
  Of the Moon,
Down the Valley of the Shadow,
  Ride, boldly ride,"
  The shade replied,—
"If you seek for Eldorado!"

          —E.A.P.
        New York City
        April 29, 1849

Author's Note
and
Acknowledgments

Many years ago—it seems like forever—I started this book the very next day after finishing my first novel, *Kill the Poor*, probably because I had the work ethic of Anthony Trollope on the mind.

Here we are some seventeen years later (eighteen if you include holidays) and I'm finally finished.

I want to thank, need to thank, Karen Rinaldi for countless conversations, manifestations, maturations, and invitations, Lara Webb Carrigan for editorial assistance and focus, and my agent, Kim Witherspoon, for tireless reading and savvy suggestion. My gratitude to Tony Bourdain, David Friedman, Catherine Texier, early readers all, and Jeffrey Danneman, for his eager help with start-up research.

To my editor and publisher at Canongate, Jamie Byng, to Jill Bialosky at Norton, I also say thank you. As well to Jessica Craig at Canongate for her enthusiasm and encouragement, and Rose Marie Morse at Morse Partners. Also to David Miller, Yelena Gitlin, Adele McCarthy-Beauvais, and Evan Carver, my gratitude.

Poe himself was often accused of palming off, and I, too, took this as my easy master. Great amounts of Poe's dialogue in *The Blackest Bird* are taken, sometimes word for word, from his stories, essays, and poetry.

Also stitched in are bits pilfered from Whitman, Dickens, Melville, Longfellow, Irving, and Twain, among others. I thought of these appropriations as homage and a puzzle.

Certain poems attributed to one writer are actually the work of another. Fanny Osgood's poem to Poe, not hers but the work of "the Seeress of Providence," Sarah Helen Whitman. The poems attributed to John Colt are not, as far as I know, his. The Samuel Adams murder poem can be found in Warden Charles Sutton's *The New York Tombs: Its Secrets and Its Mysteries*. Other bits of doggerel given over by me to Colt are culled from Edward Van Every's *Sins of New York*.

The version of "The Raven" included here is actually a blending of two early drafts. I have taken liberties with other of Poe's work, substituting, for example, the name "Virginia" for "Lenore."

History is story, and *The Blackest Bird* is a work of fiction. On occasion I have made certain changes in place and time and character, sometimes painfully, to accommodate the narrative.

There is neither record nor evidence that James Gordon Bennett and Rufus Griswold ever worked in concert against Poe.

The dedication of *The Blackest Bird,* attributed by me to Poe, is not actually his, but used as one of three introductory quotations to his collected poetry edition, *Al Aaraaf, Tamerlane, and Minor Poems* (Baltimore: Hatch and Dunning, 1829), plucked by the poet from "A Song of Sack" in *The Works of John Cleveland* (1687); its attribution, according to Poe scholar and compiler Thomas Ollive Mabbott, is doubted.

It was not Olga Hays who administered to the stricken Sissy Poe and the Poe family at the last, but Miss Marie Louise Shew.

Edward Coleman led the Forty Thieves, but Tommy Coleman is from my imagination.

Samuel Colt died in 1862 from syphilis, what was then called, according to George Washington Matsell, "the Venus curse." There is no proof that Colonel Colt was ever involved in the murder of Mary Rogers, or even that he ever knew her.

I am indebted to the staffs of the New York Public Library, the New-York Historical Society, and the Museum of the City of New York.

Special thanks to Marvin Taylor at the Fales Library of New York University.

My research began all those many years ago at the wonderful New York antiquarian bookstore New York Bound, with the purchase of a now completely dissolute 1928 edition of Herbert Asbury's *Gangs of New York*, and continued through any number of purchases and acquisitions. The books I went back to time and again in constructing this novel and resurrecting Poe and his contemporaries include:

Israfel: The Life and Times of Edgar Allan Poe by Hervey Allen

Edgar A. Poe by Kenneth Silverman

Plumes in the Dust: The Love Affair of Edgar Allan Poe and Fanny Osgood, Poe the Detective: The Curious Circumstances Behind "The Mystery of Marie Rogêt," and *Midnight Dreary: The Mysterious Death of Edgar Allan Poe,* all by John Evangelist Walsh

The Brief Career of Eliza Poe by Geddeth Smith

The Importance of Trifles by Avram Davidson

Sins of New York: As Exposed by the Police Gazette by Edward Van Every

The New York Tombs: Its Secrets and Its Mysteries by Charles Sutton

The Mysterious Death of Mary Rogers: Sex and Culture in Nineteenth-Century New York by Amy Gilman Srebnick

A History of the Colt Revolver by Charles T. Haven and Frank A. Belden

Froth & Scum: Truth, Beauty, Goodness, and the Ax Murder in America's First Mass Medium by Andie Tucher

The Encyclopedia of New York City by Kenneth T. Jackson

Gotham: A History of New York City to 1898 by Edwin G. Burrows and Mike Wallace

Valentine's Manual of the City of New York, edited by David Thomas Valentine

The Secret Language of Crime: The Rogue's Lexicon, compiled by New York City chief of police George W. Matsell

I have made use of any number of Poe anthologies, by far the most thorough being Thomas Ollive Mabbott's three-volume *Complete Works* collocation, published by the University of Illinois Press.

Lastly, the libel lawsuit and judgment found in favor of Poe against James Gordon Bennett in the novel was, in reality, awarded against Hiram Fuller and Augustus W. Clason Jr. and the *New York Evening Mirror,* and filed under different circumstances than those described.